THE
SCANDAL
PLAN

or: How to Win
the Presidency
by Cheating
on Your Wife

a novel

THE SCANDAL PLAN

BILL FOLMAN

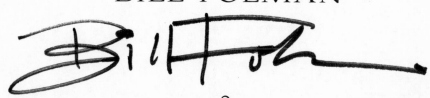

WILLIAM MORROW

An Imprint of HarperCollins *Publishers*

HarperCollins books may be purchased for educational, business, or sales promotional use. For information please write: Special Markets Department, HarperCollins Publishers, 10 East 53rd Street, New York, NY 10022.

FIRST EDITION

Designed by Chris Welch

Library of Congress Cataloging-in-Publication Data

Folman, Bill.
    The scandal plan : or: how to win the presidency by cheating on your wife / Bill Folman. — 1st ed.
      p. cm.
  ISBN 978-0-06-144765-5
    1. Presidential candidates—Fiction.   2. Political campaigns—Fiction.   3. Sex scandals—Fiction.   4. Political satire.   I. Title.

  PS3606.O46S33   2008
  813'.6—dc22
                                             2007034297

08 09 10 11 12 WBC/RRD 10 9 8 7 6 5 4 3 2 1

FOR MY PARENTS

AUTHOR'S NOTE

This story is a work of fiction.

Names, characters, places, and incidents are the product of the author's imagination, or they are used fictitiously and irresponsibly.

Any specific knowledge about the inner workings of Washington, D.C., politics acquired through the reading of this story should be considered:

(a) accidental
(b) completely untrustworthy
(c) entirely the fault of the reader.

Having been duly cautioned, please enjoy what follows.

THE
SCANDAL
PLAN

PROLOGUE

From the heavens came an idea. Hurtling toward Earth like a meteor, it took a sharp turn at the surface of the Atlantic Ocean and whizzed across the sea like Superman on a computer-generated joyride. Faster and faster, it approached the American coastline but avoided the seemingly inevitable impact, taking a hard right up the Intracoastal followed by a soft left up the Potomac. Racing down the narrowing river, it bobbed under bridges and back up again, taking one last turn, making a beeline for all things architecturally significant.

Left at Jefferson. Right at Washington. Through the Mall and then swerving into the buildings on the side. Through a congressional office, where an important secretary was sending an important message to her cousin, relaying an important feeling about a stupid little misunderstanding, it traveled down through several floors to the basement.

Here, twittery men in masks and rubber gloves slashed open the morning mail. The men did not hear the idea as it whizzed past, nor did they see it. Like all ideas, this one lacked a comprehendible physical form. It didn't *look* like anything (except perhaps air), and the faint humming noise it produced was rendered inaudible by the speed at which it traveled. Therefore, as the idea raced in and out of the building, no one whose path it crossed—not the secretary, not the men in the basement, and not the congresswoman it narrowly avoided in the lobby—was any the wiser.

The idea burst out of the building, escaping back into the humid D.C. air. It looped around the dome of the Capitol, as if trying to get its bearings. Like a slingshot, it fired its way downtown on Pennsylvania, taking a left at Freedom Plaza past the White House and its myriad of security checkpoints and then bobbing and weaving its way northwest, through side streets and steel buildings. If the idea slowed down at all, it happened just once and only for a split second, as it floated through a girls' locker room at George Washington University. But then, faster! Faster!

The path was now due north. The idea sailed higher in the sky, skimming the rooftops of apartment buildings and offices, crossing major thoroughfares with names like "New Hampshire" and "Massachusetts," until the neighborhood took a turn for the richer.

At 11:07 A.M., the idea burst through the second story of the Campman home at 2427 Kalorama Road. It whizzed through the study, through the wood-paneled wall, and into the bathroom, where it finally struck Mr. Thomas Campman in the back of the head as he sat on the john.

"Ach!"

He clutched the point of entry.

His eyes widened.

A new roll of toilet paper fell from his hands and unwound on the tile floor.

Thomas Campman knew a good idea when it hit him, and this one was a doozy.

Part
1

THE PLAN

SANDWICHES AND THE
OVERACHIEVER

Ben Phillips was the youngest person in America to vote for Adlai Stevenson. He was one year old. According to Phillips family legend, baby Ben was carried into the voting booth in the arms of his mother, Gloria, a dyed-in-the-wool Republican. Gloria liked Ike, but her young son seemed to have Democratic blood flowing through his veins, and he was the quicker of the two. As Gloria rifled through her purse in seach of her reading glasses, Ben reached out his chubby little arms, pulled the horizontal lever for Stevenson, and then—in a feat of superhuman infant strength—pulled the central handle, officially registering the vote. It would later be said that Ben Phillips started his career in politics that morning at the plucky age of one.

Now, at age fifty-three, if Ben's own presidential bid happened to be on the verge of catastrophic failure, he could hardly blame his troubles on a lack of preparation. He could blame bad strategy, foolish mistakes, a fickle media, and even bad luck, but not preparation. Ben had been training to be president all his life: from that first day with his mother in the voting booth to the fourth grade, when he memorized the capitals of every nation on the planet, from the years spent in student politics to his brief stay in Vietnam, from Oxford to Harvard Law to the Oklahoma state government to the U.S. Senate. Ben Phillips was ready. And he was due.

"FOR THE LAST time, I'm not answering any questions about sandwiches."

Senator Benjamin Phillips was starting to hope he'd never see another sandwich again, starting to regret every sandwich he'd ever eaten, starting to actually hate the things, to actually despise the notion of any item of food served between two items of carbohydrate. To his credit, he decided it would be best not to share this newfound hatred with anyone but his wife. Ben Phillips knew that "sandwich-hating" could be construed as un-American, and this was the last thing he needed right now. With yesterday's AP poll showing him 20 points behind the president and with less than three months before the election, Ben knew he could afford no more missteps.

Keep smiling. Stand straight. Be confident.

It had been his eighth-grade debate team mantra, and it continued to serve him well. Senator Benjamin Phillips, the Democrat from Oklahoma, called on his vertebrae to reengage, and they did. The muscles and bones reasserted themselves, and the senator found himself once again clothed in the portrait-perfect posture that had become his trademark through three decades in politics. Ben surveyed the journalists packed on the steps of the University City Courthouse in St. Louis and forced a smile. It was one of those "times are tough but we're gonna pull through it" smiles, weary but confident, the smile of a leader.

For that brief moment, standing on the podium with his spine at attention, the late afternoon sun picking out the orange highlights in his graying head of hair, Ben Phillips looked every bit the man he'd spent his life becoming: the passionate uncompromising statesman who'd nearly swept the Democratic primary only months before. For those fortunate enough to have been studying the senator at the exact moment the forces of time and nature conspired to present him in this most appealing light, the image served as a reminder that the struggling politician was still a force to be reckoned with. It was the image of a man who was down, but not out.

If only it had lasted more than a second. . . .

"Yes, Harry?" Ben said, pointing to Harry Maxwell of the *New York Tribune*.

"This question's not about sandwiches, Senator," Maxwell began, and Ben was halfway toward a sigh of relief when the reporter continued: "It's about the political fallout from the Sandwich-Gate Scandal."

The Sandwich-Gate Scandal? Ben could hardly believe his ears. Since when was this nonsense being called a scandal—never mind a scandal worthy of a "Gate"? It was all too stupid for words.

The whole mess started eight days ago in Nashville, when Ben enthusiastically declared that barbecued pulled pork on a bun was his "favorite sandwich," the same appellation he'd unknowingly given five months earlier to a mouth-watering pastrami on rye in New York City. A Republican Oppo researcher picked up on Ben's inconsistent culinary statements and passed them on to a right-wing blogger friend. Before you could say "please butter my toast," it was the lead story on the six o'clock news.

How can the senator have two favorite sandwiches? Small-but-inquiring minds wanted to know. The whole thing turned into a mini–civil war over the next few days, with Ben's northeastern Jewish supporters (representing the pastrami) pitted against his Southern Baptist supporters (representing the pork), both sides passionately arguing the merits of their respective sandwiches on the Sunday talk shows, and Ben in the middle, struggling to bring everyone together like a lunchtime Lincoln.

He had blundered big-time, and he only made things worse for himself by trying to have it both ways, claiming that while pulled pork was his favorite *hot* sandwich, pastrami was his favorite *cold* one. Yes, yes, of course he knew that pastrami was *traditionally* served hot, but he happened to prefer his cold—which was true, but sounded like a terrible lie—and no one let him get away with it. The Republicans, who had accused him of waffling, now accused him of pandering, and they started muttering the phrase "character issues" at every opportunity.

That was what really got Ben mad.

To be attacked on character, on integrity, on those very qualities he prized most in himself—that was the pinnacle of unfairness. He marveled at how the president, with his reckless Budweiser-soaked past, his bait-and-switch campaigning and dishonest governance, could so easily escape moral scrutiny. Meanwhile Ben, who'd been a model citizen from Cub Scouts to Congress, who'd always kept his nose clean even when it would've been smart and easy to do otherwise, was suddenly in ethical hot water over a matter of deli meat. And now Harry Maxwell of the bloody *Tribune* was calling it the "Sandwich-Gate Scandal." . . .

"That's a nice try, Harry, but I'm gonna stop you right there," Ben said, trying to sound diplomatic and not frustrated. "I'm afraid you folks are asking all the wrong questions. You *should* be asking me how I'm going to fix our economy. You *should* be asking me how I'm going to address our trade deficit, our sullied international reputation, our growing health-care problem. You should be asking how I'm going to fix the mess our president has caused with his misguided execution of Operation Freedom Fox. These are the questions I'm here to answer. These are the problems I'm here to solve."

"But Senator Phillips! How can anyone actually prefer their pastrami cold?"

They were relentless.

"Senator, to what do you attribute your conflicting statements on—"

"Some people say this minor gaffe is indicative of a greater problem with—"

"Would you prefer your pastrami open-faced or closed?"

Ben's pulse was rising.

"Do you really want to know?" he shot back.

The throng quieted for a moment, and Ben made a snap decision. "I prefer cold pastrami with two pieces of bread," he said. "Hot pastrami could be open-faced, but then, as I've stated before, would still rate second—for me—to barbecue in the 'hot sandwich' category."

No turning back now. He would answer every question they threw at him. Did he like cheese on his sandwich? What kind of cheese? Bread toasted or untoasted? He would exhaust them. He would put this whole ridiculous thing to rest, once and for all.

Slowly, Ben realized his new strategy wasn't working. He was letting the reporters lead him to a level of detail that bordered on the absurd, and the deeper he went, the more questions they seemed to have. What a stupid rookie mistake! He was completely off message now and sounding like a fool. Ben knew he needed to escape.

But he couldn't. He was in free fall. Ben imagined himself in the back of the crowd, staring up at this strange stiff man on the podium. He could see himself slowly fading but was helpless to stop the stream of words issuing forth from his mouth. As a bead of sweat ran down his spine, Ben's mind flashed back to William Howard Taft High School, back to the student council elections of thirty-five years ago, the only political race he'd ever lost. He was absorbed by a long dormant feeling of desperation, and it terrified him.

He took his next question from the *Texas Inquirer* and managed, with great effort, to relate a question about pumpernickel to the current Middle East crisis. He would get back on track if it killed him.

"I have a plan to fix Operation Freedom Fox," Ben said, "a plan to get us out of the mess we're in, and I'd like to share it with you today—"

After a clumsy segue into Middle East politics Ben was hoping to transition into military matters, but the reporters would have none of it. Forty hands shot up before he could even finish his sentence. Forty voices shouted, "Senator Phillips! Senator Phillips!"

Ben allowed disappointment to register on his face, and for a moment, he appeared to slouch.

"Yes. Last question."

From the back edge of the press horde, a fresh-faced young man stepped forward. He couldn't have been more than sixteen or seventeen years old, with brown hair parted neatly to the side, large bright blue eyes, and a clear complexion. He looked like the sort of kid one might find modeling winter wear on the back pages of the Macy's circular, and he wore his innocence like a badge on his chest. When he started speaking in his earnest midpubescent tones, the crowd grew unusually quiet.

"Senator Phillips," he said, "Peter Williams, *TeenVibe* magazine. Your poll numbers indicate that most Americans still see you as just another Washington insider. You've been accused of being dull and long-winded, and some would charge that your campaign troubles are due largely to the public's inability to relate to you . . . simply *as a fellow human being*. What would you say to those people?"

The question hung in the air for a moment. The senator swallowed hard. His mouth was dry. His usually reliable spine felt unsteady, and he felt a sharp sudden pain somewhere in his abdomen.

THE MEN IN SUITS WHO NO LONGER WEAR SUITS

Y ou seen this video, Shelly?"
    "Is Campman here?"
    "Not yet."
"He's late. Have you seen it?"
"Why am I not surprised? Seen what?"
"Another nail in the coffin."
"Don't say that!"
"What video?"
"It's all over the Web. Everyone's linking to it."
"Turn up the Re-Mix. I'm sure he'll show it."
"Everyone else is."
The young Derek Kiley unmuted the TV, and the voice of news anchor Taz McDonald blasted the eardrums of all four advisors.

TAZ McDONALD: IN ST. LOUIS, MORE STUTTERING FROM PRESIDENTIAL CANDIDATE BEN PHILLIPS! TALKIN' 'BOUT IT NEXT ON NEWS RE-MIX!

[LOUD RECORD SCRATCH]
[LOUD RECORD SCRATCH]
Taz McDonald: I'M TAZ—

"For God's sake, Kiley! Turn it down," bellowed Ralph Sorn, who frequently bellowed. Kiley fiddled with the remote.

Taz McDonald: Whether we're talking sandwiches or stump speeches, the Phillips campaign continues to struggle. Latest AP poll finds him trailing the president by as much as twenty points. In certain parts of the country he has been polling dangerously close to the independent and self-proclaimed socialist candidate, Lenny Reese Buchwald, and in Texas he is polling a solid fourth place, a few percentage points behind a day-old burrito and a horse named "Shemp."

Mayweather was incredulous. "Since when can they joke like that on the news?"

"What's with this video?" asked Greenblatt.

Kiley responded: "Some kid with too much time on his hands edited together clips of Ben talking about sandwiches. He set it to the 'Blue Danube Waltz.'"

"You're naïve if you think it was just some kid," said Sorn. "That was a professional hit—"

"Shhh! They're playing it."

Four pairs of eyes found their way to the screen. On a grainy video, Ben Phillips spoke as Johann Strauss's violins took flight beneath him.

[CU Sen. Phillips.]
Senator Phillips: If there's one thing I believe in, it's . . .
[edit.]
Senator Phillips: . . . pork . . .
[edit.]

SENATOR PHILLIPS: . . . pork . . . pork . . .
[edit.]
SENATOR PHILLIPS: . . . pork . . . pork . . .
[edit.]
SENATOR PHILLIPS: . . . but I'm particularly fond of . . .
[edit.]
SENATOR PHILLIPS: . . . young man's . . .
[edit.]
SENATOR PHILLIPS: . . . buns . . .
[edit.]
SENATOR PHILLIPS: . . . buns . . . buns . . .
[edit.]
SENATOR PHILLIPS: . . . buns . . . buns . . .

Greenblatt, the senior member of the team, buried his face in his hands.

"Damn. That's brilliant," said Sorn. "Dennis Fazo, my hat's off to you."

Mayweather grimaced. "It kills me that we're still getting caught up in all this stuff," he said.

The fourth member of the team, young Kiley, said nothing, but he nodded empathetically, hoping to convey his own winsome brand of disappointment to the other three if they happened to look his way. None of them did.

It was 9:30 P.M. in Kansas City. The four advisors to Senator Ben Phillips stared impotently at the TV set. For Derek Kiley, this scene could not have been more different from what he'd always imagined as a student, when he fantasized about being in the brain trust of a national campaign. His cinematic daydreams had always included men in suits in smoky back rooms, voices bouncing off cathedral-like walls, high key lighting, frenzied arguments, and a Charlie Parker score.

Tonight's gathering contained none of these elements. The Marriott hotel room in which they sat was tastefully appointed, but low-ceilinged.

The lighting was flat and uninspired, the walls absorbed sound like a sponge, the air was conditioned beyond recognition, and the soundtrack was ironic Strauss. With the exception of Shelly Greenblatt, no one was wearing a suit, no one dared light a cigarette, and—the big difference— no one was moving a muscle. Some of the greatest political minds in America, and they were sitting like zombies: stumped, stupefied, and sedentary.

Finally, Shelly Greenblatt walked to the TV and hit the power button.

"Enough of this garbage."

There was a collective sigh of relief, the sound of four minds suddenly liberated from digital interference and set free to pursue independent thought.

Shelly Greenblatt was sixty-six years old, and every year was showing. His baldness and deep forehead wrinkles had long since passed the point of deniability, and as he stood, hunched over with his elbows resting on a Marriott hotel chair, he had the look of a large man who had collapsed in on himself. His ancient khaki suit had started to fray ever so slightly around the edges, and where the shoulders met the arms, it looked as if the suit were fighting a losing battle to contain Greenblatt's newly soft and sloping frame. It was a testament to Shelly Greenblatt's supreme exhaustion that even his suits looked tired.

"I don't understand it," he finally managed, "we've got a Rhodes scholar, a Vietnam veteran, a three-term senator from a red state, most popular in Oklahoma history. . . ."

Ozzie Mayweather had heard this before. He was thirty-nine years old, but felt like he was pushing sixty. He was a black man but starting to look pale. It had been that kind of campaign for all of them. Perhaps if Mayweather had managed to perform a halfway decent bowel movement in the last forty-eight hours, he could have summoned the necessary fortitude to interrupt Shelly's all-too-familiar ramblings. But of course he had not, and so he did not. Instead, the pale and constipated Ozzie Mayweather let Shelly continue, in the hopes that somewhere in the repetition, the old man would find an answer.

Ralph Sorn was uncharacteristically quiet as well. An elephantine fellow with oxygen to spare, the former news mogul from New York never seemed to run out of opinions, but at the moment, he sat silently. Sorn had been brought aboard for his skills as hatchet man and media manipulator extraordinaire, but with this campaign it seemed he'd met his match. Sorn listened quietly to Shelly Greenblatt, and—as was often the case when Sorn listened—he tried to formulate his next line.

". . . leader of two Senate subcommittees on foreign affairs," continued Greenblatt, "coauthor of the East-Middle African peace treaty, coauthor of the Renew School Initiative, speaks six languages, speaks *English* beautifully, an *eloquent* man, a *brilliant* man, charming. . . ."

"Looks good in a tie," Ralph Sorn chimed in, reasonably satisfied with his contribution.

For his part, Mayweather picked up the cue: "Looks good in a sweater," he countered.

"Looks good in a swimsuit," added Kiley, the young one, just a beat too late.

Greenblatt continued unfazed: "A man who has the most practical forward-thinking economic agenda in a time of economic strife. Dammit, a *likable* man, a *family* man. Loves his kids, loves his mother . . ."

"Loves his pets," added Kiley.

"Loves his *country!*" said Greenblatt with a finality that silenced the room. "But more amazing than all this put together"—and here Shelly Greenblatt paused for dramatic effect—"*the first honest man in politics since Abraham Lincoln.*"

There was respectful quiet for a moment.

"But none of that helps us a damn, Shelly," said Mayweather. "We've been over this. They're not listening to us. They're not listening to Ben. For crying out loud, we'd probably be polling higher with that schmuck Muddville—"

All ears perked up at the mention of Warren Muddville's name.

"—may he rest in peace . . . at the top of the ticket."

Before Shelly Greenblatt could respond, Ralph Sorn leaned forward in his chair abruptly, about to speak. When most men lean forward in a chair, it is hardly a newsworthy event and certainly no reason to halt conversation, but Ralph Sorn's girth was such that a northward shifting of weight constituted a minor spectacle, and the resulting groan of the chair was tantamount to a skinnier man banging a gavel. The floor was his. Not that he needed permission to take it.

"Tell you what, boys," said Sorn, "I think we know what the problem is. The kid reporter said it, the asshole on TV said it, Campman's said it, I think it's time *we* said it: *Our man's not human!*"

"There is some truth there," said Mayweather.

"Of course, it's true! Joe and Joanne American don't speak six languages. They didn't finish top of their class at Harvard. They haven't traveled to East-Middle Africa and—"

"Okay, but we know this," said Mayweather, "where does it *get* us? People want a candidate they can relate to. Great! But what does that mean *practically?*"

"What it means . . ."

". . . it means we show the senator with his sleeves rolled up, hanging out with kindergartners, talking to little old ladies. We show him relaxing at home with his family, throwing a football around, right? We've done these things, Ralph! And it's August!"

"So, we do more!" Sorn bellowed.

"But the problem isn't quantity," said Greenblatt, "the problem is no one's paying attention!"

Suddenly, a door slammed.

The four advisors held their breath.

"Perhaps, gentlemen," said a new voice, "the reason people aren't paying attention, is that we haven't given them anything interesting to watch."

"Jesus Christ, Campman."

The room exhaled.

The man by the door spoke again.

"Boys, next time you're running a presidential campaign, try and remember to close your door all the way. Call me a crusty-old Nixonite if you will, but a touch of paranoia never hurt."

And with that, Thomas Campman had entered the room.

The surprising thing about his entrance, at least in Shelly Greenblatt's view, was that Campman had stood for several moments in the doorway without being noticed. Under normal circumstances, it was difficult not to notice Tom Campman.

It wasn't that he was markedly taller or shorter or skinnier or fatter than the average man. He was handsome enough and looked well for his age (sixty-three), but this was more a matter of genetic good fortune than commendable upkeep. For Shelly Greenblatt, whose attempts at physical fitness never yielded any visible benefits, Campman's effortlessly sleek figure was frustrating. Still, Greenblatt took pleasure in noticing that Campman's five-foot-ten frame was finally starting to stretch a bit in the middle, that his rounded facial features seemed just a bit more round than they once were. His neatly parted hair was thinning, too, and his light brown color was losing ground to the advancing forces of gray. If anything about Campman caught the eye, it would be his clothes, which were more formal than standard Democratic issue, more stylish than Republican threads, and far superior to Shelly Greenblatt's wardrobe on all counts. Campman always wore a dark suit, always with a sharp colorful tie and nary a wrinkle in the ensemble. Still, his personal costuming and good looks were not the things that made important men rise to their feet whenever he entered a room.

There is a certain rare type of charisma that can be appreciated with all five senses, a certain forcefulness of presence that draws people into one's orbit like flies around a picnic table—and Campman had it. It was an energy he both owned and exuded, like a vapor or an electric charge, and when he entered a room, it beckoned arm hair northward and made the place just the tiniest bit colder, like the nip in the air before a storm. As much as Shelly Greenblatt would have liked to deny the existence of such powers, as much as he would have liked to pretend that Thomas Campman was a mere mortal (and a significantly flawed one at that), he couldn't. Thomas Campman was a force of nature, and Shelly knew it.

"Good trip?" asked Derek Kiley politely.

"Yes, Derek, thank you," Campman replied. "Well, no, actually it was crap, but that doesn't matter. What matters is I have a plan."

"It's about damn time!" said Sorn sarcastically. "We're all just yanking each other's knobs here."

"Ralph, *please*," said Shelly Greenblatt.

Derek Kiley shifted in his chair, causing a Sorn-like groaning noise much louder than he'd anticipated. The young speechwriter began to think he was always being noticed at the wrong times, but he tried to ignore this thought and listen to what "Campman the Champion" was about to impart.

Mayweather had stopped pacing. Sorn was reclining. Greenblatt looked uncomfortable. But then Greenblatt always looked uncomfortable.

Thomas Campman smiled at the four men. He waited for his moment and then waited one moment after that. Then he began.

WHY

Greenblatt was clearly perplexed, but it was Mayweather who spoke first.

"Once again, please: Why would we create a scandal *for our own candidate?*"

Campman smiled. "To sin is human," he said. "Therefore, if we want to bring out Ben's humanity, we make him a sinner. We give him the one flaw that will make him a perfect man. And because *we're* giving it, because *we're inventing it . . .* it can be the truly perfect flaw."

"The perfect flaw?" repeated Mayweather.

"Exactly. Not so big it ruins his chances, but big enough to bring him down a peg, big enough to let him show some emotion, big enough for people to get a glimpse of the real Ben Phillips, of 'Ben Phillips, *the man.*' That's why we do it."

The room was so quiet you could hear the traffic outside. The air-conditioner hummed softly. Ralph Sorn broke the silence.

"You're a fucking psychopath, Campman," he said, smiling, "but I like where you're going with this."

The others stared at him in shock. Ralph would be the easy sell. Campman knew that going in. Everyone else would be harder.

"It's a *crazy* idea," said Greenblatt, shaking his head as if to confirm Campman's thought.

"Very crazy," echoed young Kiley.

Thomas Campman didn't miss a beat.

"It's only crazy because it's new, because it's never been tried before, but that doesn't mean it won't work. Your mind just needs time to get used to the idea."

Campman could see the doubt in their eyes, but he knew they could be swayed. They had to be. He just needed to sell it right.

"Look, boys," he said, "we've been over this before. It's like Ralph was saying: Your average American doesn't speak six languages, he didn't attend an Ivy League school, and he hasn't traveled to East-Middle Africa. That's not the stuff he thinks about when he goes to the voting booth.

"He's not thinking *résumé*, he's thinking, 'I want a president who's gonna look out for my interests.' And who's gonna look out for *his* interests? *Someone like him!* Everybody—and I mean everyone, whether they admit it or not (and Shelly you do it, too!)—is looking for a candidate who is like them. And what is everyone like?"

Campman was in preacher mode now.

"What does *everyone* have in common? Sin. Everybody lies. Everybody cheats. Everybody steals. Everybody has sex. Sometimes . . . irresponsibly. Never *criminally*. I'm not suggesting we make our man a criminal. But just think . . . about what a perfectly contained middleweight sin could do to our senator's numbers."

"Bring them down, probably," said Mayweather. "Historically speaking, I don't think there's ever been a scandal that *helped* a candidate's poll numbers."

"In the short term, of course not. There'll be an initial dip, I'll grant that. But think big picture. We're trying to create an image. No! Harder. We're trying to *change* an image."

Shelly Greenblatt didn't like what he was hearing. The senior advisor patted the remaining tufts of hair on the far reaches of his scalp, as if to make sure they were still present and accounted for. He shifted his weight, preparing to speak, but realized Mayweather was going to beat him to it and thought that was just fine. Ozzie Mayweather was a steady hand, and Greenblatt knew he could be counted on for a solid rebuttal.

"I'd still worry the numbers would be against us," said Mayweather.

"Amen," echoed Greenblatt.

Campman pounced.

"The numbers *are* against us, boys. We're losing something ugly. And Ozzie, if you're talking historical precedent, you're right, there is none. *Because no one's been able to isolate the one variable that we're counting on.* After a dip, there's a rebound. Am I right? At this stage of the game, in a presidential race, it's inevitable. You can only be low for so long, and then you start to come up again—at least a little bit. And that's something no pollster's ever studied: *the rebound!* They don't study it because it's always attributed to something else. Oh, the guy was caught in an illegal real-estate scam and everyone hated him, but then he had a good debate performance or the economy picked up or *something else happened* to bring his numbers up from where they were—but no one *ever* causally associates the bounce with the initial indiscretion."

"That's because, frankly, the two are not related," said Greenblatt sternly.

"Maybe," said Campman, "in our case they will be. Our man is too perfect. We make him less perfect. More human. More like you and me. More like every movie hero you ever watched growing up: John Wayne, Cary Grant, Humphrey Bogart. These guys weren't Goody Two-shoes. They were men with dark mysterious pasts, sinners like us! Fuckups! And we relate to that. But the reason we look up to them is not just 'cuz they're similar, but because, unlike us, they conquer their past and they go above and beyond to do extraordinary things. It's simple storytelling, gentlemen: the underdog, the comeback. Nobody was ever a hero who didn't overcome some huge personal challenge. All I'm saying is: Let's give Ben that challenge. Let's give him the chance to become that flawed hero we can all love. We do that . . . and people will listen."

Silence.

"Wow . . . wow . . . it's a brilliant idea," said Ralph Sorn in disbelief, the complete convert.

"Okay, wait," said Mayweather slowly, trying to work it all out. "Oh, man. This is not—on the one hand, it's not *totally* absurd. I see where you're coming from. But on the other hand . . . Isn't this just gonna shift focus away from the issues? I mean, the issues are where we're strong."

"It's not like anyone's focused on the issues now," said Sorn.

"That's true," said Mayweather, "but even so . . ."

"Look," Campman continued. "Will it distract? Of course. For a while. But only long enough to get people's attention. Remember, we dictate the agenda when the camera's focused on us. If we do this, that means the media is going to be forced to—"

"This is ridiculous," said Shelly Greenblatt, who had heard just about all he was willing to hear.

"Why?" asked Campman calmly, "because it's something no one's tried before?"

"No," said Greenblatt incredulously, "because it *is* ridiculous! It just is! I mean, have you thought about the risks? The *monumental* risks? Surely you must realize this can destroy all our chances!"

Campman didn't flinch.

"How?" he asked.

"How?!" answered Greenblatt. "If you get caught, of course!"

Campman mulled this over.

"Hmmm. No, I don't think that will happen, Shelly."

"You don't think that will happen?!"

"Look, Shelly, I understand why you're nervous. You think it's a risky plan. But I don't think it needs to be. See, I don't think any plan is risky just by nature. A plan is nothing but a series of steps. It's these steps that may or may not carry with them a certain degree of risk. A plan may seem risky in summary, but if each step is individually without risk, the plan as a whole may not be as risky as it first seems. The proof is in the details, and that's what I want to discuss. I don't want to do anything that will put us at risk. I'm not crazy, Shelly. But let's talk steps. Let's see if we can make this work. If it seems too risky, we abandon the plan, that's fine. But, dammit, let's not give up before we try."

"Yes! Let's try, you sons of bitches!" yelled Sorn.

Mayweather shrugged. "I guess there's nothing wrong with talking," he said, to which Greenblatt found himself suddenly lacking a rebuttal.

Campman smiled.

"Okay," he said. "Gentlemen, I want you to ask yourselves what you actually know about scandals. Surely, they're nothing new; the damn things have plagued politicians for centuries. But what makes one scandal different from another?"

No one responded.

"I'll tell you what I know. I know a political scandal can be the most damaging force imaginable. I know it can destroy a man's career. But not always. I know Ulysses S. Grant had one of the most corrupt administrations in history and he was elected to a second term in a landslide. I know Iran-Contra was a matter of treason and Reagan wasn't even touched by it. I know men who have become bigger, more powerful, and more influential *after* the scandal that was supposed to have killed their career. And what does all that mean? It means scandals are far too complex and far too variable to be written off as inherently detrimental.

"What makes scandals dangerous is their unpredictability. They are unpredictable, because they're like war. Someone starts a scandal, someone suffers for it, someone tries to expose, someone tries to conceal. There are two opposing sides doing battle with high stakes, and *that* is why it's unpredictable.

"But . . . what if both sides were controlled by the same person?

What if the party trying to expose and the party trying to conceal were actually one and the same? Wouldn't that party have absolute power to control the unfolding of the event? Wouldn't that eliminate the very risk, the very unpredictability, which normally makes such a venture so dangerous?

"If we create the scandal, we can make it perfect. We can make our response perfect. We can goad our opposition into making mistakes by luring them with the most tantalizing bait imaginable. Once they smell scandal, they'll be like a fox in a chicken coop, stupid with hunger, putty in our hands. But best of all: We give our man a challenge—*a battle!*—an honest-to-goodness test of his mettle that he can pass with flying colors. We create the war. We create the hero. And all this because we pull the strings."

"And the risk?" said Greenblatt.

"Is negligible. Because we'll cover our tracks. And . . . because it is the last thing anyone will expect us to do."

At this point, an uncontrollable smile spread across Campman's face.

"After all"—he chuckled—"who in their right mind would create a scandal for their own candidate?"

He was the only one laughing. The other men had not a breath among them. The room was quiet. Once again, Ralph Sorn broke the silence.

"What about Ben?" he asked.

"There's no way the senator would agree to this," said Greenblatt with authority.

"He'll agree," said Campman, "*if* we put up a united front and let me speak for all of us."

It wasn't the most sensitive way to put it, but then Campman never worried too much about those things. Thomas Campman won arguments because he talked straight—or perhaps more accurately, because he gave the *appearance* of talking straight. And he'd raised a good point: Convincing the senator would not be possible if the advisors disagreed among themselves. More specifically, it'd be impossible if Shelly Greenblatt—the senator's longtime political confidant—resisted.

For a few moments, the room mulled.

Then Mayweather started giggling to himself. It was a funny sort of laugh: a high-pitched, breathless staccato. In the seven months they'd worked together, Greenblatt had never heard his typically reserved African-American colleague laugh in such a way, and it made him uneasy.

"I can't believe we're gonna do this," Ozzie Mayweather tittered.

Greenblatt's face turned red with betrayal at this sudden shift.

"Who says we're gonna do this?!" he cried defensively. "I thought we were just talking here!"

"I hate to tell you, Shelly, but I'm in," said Sorn. "I say, if we can do it, we should do it."

"I'm . . . well . . . I'm definitely interested in hearing more," said Mayweather.

"Oh, God," said Shelly Greenblatt, his face now fire truck red. He turned. "You've been quiet, Derek. What do *you* think?"

It was an act of desperation, looking to the youngest member of the brain trust for backup, but Greenblatt was feeling scared and suddenly alone. Derek Kiley, the skinny thirty-two-year-old speechwriter, shifted uncomfortably in his chair.

"Well," he said, "it just . . . um . . . well . . . it seems kind of . . ."

"What?!" prodded Sorn. "What?!"

"Well . . . *wrong.* I mean, I don't want to sound naïve, but isn't this whole campaign supposed to be based on honesty? Isn't that like . . . *our thing?*"

For a split second, Shelly's spirits were lifted by Kiley's simple but powerful rebuttal. Campman did not appear similarly moved.

"*Derek!*" he bellowed in a tone Derek Kiley was rapidly trying to diagnose as either congratulatory or threatening. Before Kiley could make a ruling, Campman leaned in and spoke softly to him, "Would it help if I told you the Lord is on our side with this one . . . in, like, *a really big way?*"

Kiley could feel Campman's breath on the side of his face and could smell in it the dueling aromas of garlic and peppermint, with the peppermint finishing a close and unfortunate second. It was hot breath coming from a fiery place, and it forced Kiley to momentarily ponder Campman's innards.

What was all this talk about the Lord being on our side? Shelly Greenblatt wondered. *Was that a joke?* Campman certainly didn't look like he was joking. His brown eyes were studying Derek Kiley intently, and the young speechwriter seemed paralyzed by fear. Greenblatt observed that for the first time, the young man was hopelessly out of his league.

After a quick moment of scrutiny, Campman released Kiley from his gaze and stood up disappointed, having reached a conclusion:

"No, no, no," he said sadly, "I guess that's not gonna make a big difference with you, is it? Hmmm . . ."

Campman refocused.

"Look, Derek, we've played this game honestly for months. *Relatively* honestly. And if we keep it up, we are going to lose in . . . an epic way. Historic. And then the bad guys will be in power for another four years, and this country goes down the shitter. *We are soldiers for the good guy here, Derek!* And if we have to incur some wounds . . . if we have to suffer . . . what? *A guilty conscience?!* For *saving this damn country?!! NO! . . . I . . . DON'T . . . THINK SO!*"

Ooh, he was good. The devil incarnate, thought Shelly Greenblatt. The Washington veteran hated to admit that Campman's logic was seductive, but darned if it hadn't stirred even his own imagination. Greenblatt became slowly aware of the rhythm of his breathing and noticed how it seemed to be in sync with the respiration of his fellow advisors in the increasingly stuffy hotel room. He decided for a moment to surrender his thoughts to the open-minded contemplation of Campman's crazy idea, something he'd avoided up until that point.

The plan couldn't *actually* work, could it?

No. No, of course not. The more he thought about it, the more uneasy it made him. Never mind the details, never mind the individual steps, the plan by its very nature was too absurd, too bizarre, way too risky, and—yes, let's not forget—completely immoral. Greenblatt sighed.

"I'm not crazy about this idea," he finally said.

Campman responded quickly and without equivocation.

"You'll get used to it, Shelly," he said with a smile, "and no, we can't wait, if that's what you're about to wonder. You know we can't wait. The conventions are over, the bounces have bounced, and it's almost September. We move now."

PETER WILLIAMS, TEEN REPORTER

Ms. James was the first woman over forty to give Peter Williams a hard-on, and for Peter, this was the news story of the day. What made it newsworthy was not so much the hard-on itself—for indeed, the sixteen-year-old's erections were often inspired by the most mundane of stimuli—but rather that Ms. James had been the first woman of his parents' generation whom Peter had found to be . . . well . . . physically desirable.

She was tall—in heels, taller than Peter—and when she first opened the front door of her home to let the young reporter inside, her stature surprised him.

"You must be Peter," she said in a warm alto from on high.

He noticed her smile first, then her long dirty blond hair, and finally her eyes. Her irises were pale blue and perfect, like jewelry. For a moment, the typically unflappable Peter Williams was speechless. Then, quickly, he wasn't.

"Yes indeed, Ms. James. Peter Williams. *TeenVibe* magazine. Nice to meet you."

As Ms. James led him into the house, Peter noticed that she walked differently than other women. She walked smoother, with more confidence, with more style, and in a way that reminded Peter of his sister's cat Nancy (although he would certainly stop short of labeling Ms. James "catlike"). Peter struggled to find the perfect word to describe this unusual quality of movement he perceived in both her walk and gestures. For the life of him, he couldn't think of the right one. He was searching for the word *grace*.

Ms. James made Peter nervous—so nervous, in fact, that he messed up. Early in their interview, the young reporter skipped over one of his favorite questions entirely. He had meant to ask: "Do you feel your political opinions are usually in sync with those of your fellow Americans?"

Instead, he skipped to the next question, a follow-up to the first, which he approached awkwardly.

"Ms. James, as an average American—" he began.

But she cut him off.

"Peter, my dear, you should never refer to a girl as average. That's not polite. You should also know by now that there are no such things as 'average Americans.' We are all, every one of us, *extraordinary*."

She paused before adding, "Except the idiots, of course."

And that was the moment Peter first became aware of the extent of his arousal.

His interview with Ms. James was, for him, the most noteworthy event in an otherwise slow news day, and Peter would later write about it in great detail in his personal journal. He did not, however, feel it appropriate subject matter for his widely read blog and would instead devote that night's entry to his usual musings on the sad state of the Phillips campaign and the travails of life on the road.

"It matters not," he would write, "whether a reporter is facing the perils of a Vietnamese jungle or the perils of a bad night's sleep on a sofa-bed in Dubuque. As journalists, it is our responsibility to meet every challenge with confidence, determination, and goodwill."

Peter Williams typically ended his blog entries with this sort of motivational sentence, because he thought it important to be a positive role model for his fellow teens, particularly those interested in journalism. Lord knows there were enough negative role models out there. Peter felt that all celebrities and subcelebrities—and even sub-sub-sub-sub-celebrities (which he privately considered himself to be)—had a responsibility to understand the role they played in shaping the lives of young Americans.

Peter Williams had no delusions of grandeur. He was not big-time yet, and he knew it. But he was off to a pretty good start.

TeenVibe magazine had a readership of over two million, and that didn't include their online site. Most nonsubscription copies of *Teen-Vibe* magazine were sold at supermarket checkout counters to the pleading children of frazzled mothers and the occasional middle-aged male of dubious intent. *TeenVibe*'s glossy covers were graced by teen-pop sensations like Mickey Solara or Kimberly Bowes, and its insides were filled with articles that tended to fall into one of three categories:

1. Stories about puberty, dating, and sex
2. Stories about hot teen celebrities
3. Stories about the puberty, dating, and sex of hot teen celebrities.

There was also the occasional story about "success at school," "getting along with your parents," "fun fashions," and "keeping it real."

There was a news section as well—news *page*, to be more specific. The "News for All Yous" page was nestled in between "Dear Ramona" and "Horoscopically Speaking." Peter was the "News for All Yous" political correspondent. It was a position he had held for the last three years, although this was his first year traveling outside the greater D.C. area.

This current trip was his longest yet at three weeks and counting. He'd been as far west as Reno, as far south as Miami, and as far north as Minneapolis.

Ms. James lived in the middle of the country: Mustang, Oklahoma. Mustang was a suburb of Oklahoma City, where Peter would later spend the night. It would be his thirty-seventh town in twenty-one days.

"Sounds like you're covering a lot of ground," said Ms. James, sipping a cup of coffee. She even drank coffee differently than most women, cradling the bottom of the mug in her left hand while delicately tilting the handle with her right.

"That's a reporter's job, ma'am," Peter replied, trying to sound professional.

"Yes, I suppose it is."

Ms. James smiled to herself.

"But tell me, Peter, where do you spend the night in all these strange places?"

She was asking more questions than Peter was used to, but he tried not to let that bother him. Each interview was different. He was confident they'd get back to discussing the real questions—*his* questions—soon enough.

Peter explained to Ms. James that, because *TeenVibe* magazine lacked the budget to finance his travels, he was forced to purchase an unlimited Green Sparrow bus ticket each month and rely on Teen Buddies for housing.

"*Teen Buddies?*" she repeated, her smile widening. "And what exactly is a Teen Buddy?"

"Someone on the *TeenVibe* Buddy Program," Peter replied. "It's a feature of *TeenVibe*'s online site, designed to bring teens together from across the country and to encourage travel also. It's pretty cool, actually. Let's say I want to go to Cleveland. I just send an e-hosting request to any Buddy who lives in the Cleveland area, and I ask him to host me. We both get parental consent, the terms of the hosting are laid out online, we both click 'confirm,' and then—there you go!—you've got someplace to stay."

Peter was talking much more than he was used to, but then, certain questions were difficult to answer briefly. In fact, he couldn't help but continue.

"Of course, you're supposed to host other people roughly the same amount of times you've been hosted yourself. So while I'm on the road, my mom is basically running a bed-and-breakfast back home in Bethesda—which is not technically the way you're supposed to do it, because it's supposed to be teens hosting teens—but my mom's real cool about the whole thing, and I don't think any of the guests have minded."

Peter instantly regretted this last bit of explanation. He was running at the mouth, and he'd just told Ms. James far more than she needed to know. Peter Williams prided himself on maintaining a professional demeanor at all times, being of the opinion that most of his fellow journalists were altogether too chatty and familiar in their reporting. But here he was now, chattering away to Ms. James like a high school girl on Red Bull! *What was wrong with him?*

As for the *TeenVibe* Buddy Program, this would be a short-lived experiment, swiftly terminated by *TeenVibe* executives in March of the following year when it was confirmed that sexual predators had been posing as Teen Buddies in order to lure unsuspecting youngsters into their homes. While it is hard to say exactly when these offenses first began, it should be noted that throughout Peter Williams's many months of using the *TeenVibe* Buddy Program, no such unpleasantness had befallen him. While many of his hosting situations were less than ideal, none were completely detestable, none were dangerous, and many were actually pleasant.

"But enough about the Buddy Program," said Peter. "Let's get back to the interview, shall we?"

Ms. James was the sixty-seventh person to be interviewed by Peter Williams for his "State of the Voters" investigation. His goal was to talk with 250 "average" Americans in the hopes of getting to the bottom of what he believed to be a growing sense of detachment between the American people and the government representing them. In the wake of the terrorist attacks in Orlando, Anaheim, New Jersey, and Fort Lauderdale and the ensuing drama of Operation Freedom Fox, Peter felt most Americans were tuning out. It was as if they didn't want to hear any more bad news. The people looked to their leaders now for reassurance more than anything else, the way a young child looks to a parent, and Peter felt this was unhealthy. He believed too many important issues were getting lost in the mix.

By the time Peter Williams had finished interviewing his first twenty citizens, he realized his assumptions about America's political malaise had been simplistic at best. Yes, there were passive, apathetic Americans, but there were also active, engaged ones. There were frightened Americans, fearless Americans, and confused Americans. There were those who viewed President Struck as America's favorite son, those who felt he could do no wrong, and those who hated him with a passion that bordered on fanaticism. Peter realized he would need to interview many more of his fellow countrymen if he was to have any hope of figuring the whole thing out.

He had been trying to coordinate his interviews with his political travels, so that he could cover the presidential election and conduct interviews in his spare time. To find the average Americans for his study, Peter had developed his own highly complex system. He subdivided the American voting populace into twenty-nine groups represented by such titles as Agriculture, Unemployed Homemakers, Entertainment & the Arts, Academics & Media, and Retirees over Seventy-five. He assigned these groups ratios, subdivided by geographic location, subdivided by ethnicity, subdivided by gender, and then subdivided again by even more specific criteria. From this, Peter created a precise target demographic breakdown. He would speak to one balding tax attorney from Kansas, two African-American autoworkers from Michigan, and one out-of-work handicapped driving instructor from New Mexico.

Of all these, however, Peter would most clearly remember Ms. James, the unmarried, middle-aged, female pharmaceutical employee from Oklahoma.

Peter spent most of the James interview with his legs crossed, an unusual and uncomfortable position for him, but one he hoped would conceal the meddlesome swelling beneath his khakis. By the thirty-minute mark, Peter began to wonder if he'd ever be able to un-cross his legs again, such was the mystifying duration of his boner.

Ms. James had her legs crossed as well, although she came by the position far more naturally than Peter. She wore dark slacks that looked striking against the burgundy fabric of her chair, and as she flexed her toes, her high-heeled sandals flirted with the idea of sepa-rating from her foot—although they never did. Her tan collared shirt was cuffed expertly just below the elbows, leaving her wrists shock-ingly naked as they bent this way and that, tilting her mug of coffee up toward her purple lips. Peter couldn't help but marvel how per-fectly at ease the fashionably dressed Ms. James seemed, sitting in the middle of her artsy hodgepodge of a living room.

After the first five minutes of fractured questions and small talk, the interview proceeded smoothly. If Ms. James was not always brief in her answers, she was at least concise. She did not waste words. She struck Peter as smart, opinionated, and more than a little bit cynical.

For Peter, the most memorable part of the interview was her re-sponse to the question: "How do you feel about the politicians who represent you?"

A Nebraska farmer had said, "The good ones are just like I am, only smarter."

A female coffee house owner in Phoenix had made the point that "I know they speak for me, but they have no idea who I am."

And then there was the Dallas shoe salesman who said, "They're just like Hollywood actors, except they make more mistakes."

When it was her turn, Ms. James looked Peter square in the face and said, "*Fornicators.* They're all a bunch of fornicators."

Peter wasn't used to adults talking this way around him, and it took him a moment to figure out what to say next. He decided to tact-fully point out that, since *TeenVibe* was a magazine for teens and language restrictions were in place, it might help if she could provide him with a response that was more . . . "quotable."

Ms. James stared at him, a smile spreading across her face. Finally, she spoke. "You . . . are . . . *adorable,*" she said with a frightening intensity.

In his efforts to remain composed, Peter promptly dropped his pen to the floor, and while it may not have been necessary for him to get down on all fours to retrieve it, this was the course of action he chose. Once the errant object was located, his sixteen-year-old body sprang back to its former seated position with alarming speed, and Peter, pen in hand, lightly asked, "Can I quote you on that?"

Peter Williams didn't make jokes often, and when he did, the results usually confirmed his suspicion that joke telling was not his strong point. In this instance, the striking forty-nine-year-old did not take his question as a joke. She looked him right in the eyes and said, "Yes, Peter."

Calling on the same fortitude that once served Cronkite and Murrow in their darkest hours, Peter swallowed the cantaloupe-size lump in his throat and managed to continue with the remainder of the interview.

That night, as Peter Williams tried to fall asleep on the bedroom floor of his Oklahoma City Teen Buddy, his mind kept racing back to Ms. James—and with his mind, his body followed. Just thinking about her made his muscles tense and his stomach queasy. Needless to say, the sense memory filtered down to his nether regions as well, and Peter soon realized that if he was ever going to get any sleep, he would have to think of something else pronto.

He first pictured his girlfriend, Mary, back in Bethesda, for whom his thoughts were (he mused curiously) slightly less impure. But only slightly. This was not helping the problem.

Peter thought now about traveling, about America, about the Boulder Dam. He thought about the Washington Monument, the Empire State Building, rolling hills and mountains, voluptuous landscapes, priapic skyscrapers, and all the curves and sinews of the country. He thought of the protrusions, the gorges, and the intersections of the two. He thought of valleys, peninsulas, tunnels, and trains. Ins and outs. He thought of Old Faithful.

Finally, he thought of his work, and at long last his thoughts were cleansed. For Peter, his reporting was still the most important element of his life, and he would be thinking of politics when he fell asleep. The next morning, he would travel to St. Louis, Missouri, where Senator Ben Phillips was scheduled to give another press conference. Peter had a question he hoped to ask the candidate.

WHAT

Wh" hat sort of scandal should it be?"

The question hung in the air like dust.

"I'm open to suggestions," said Campman, "Shelly, what do you think?"

Shelly Greenblatt was thinking a lot. He was thinking that Campman was trying to empower him, to solicit his ideas for the purpose of tying them up with his own, thus making the ideas indistinguishable and Greenblatt complicit. For Shelly Greenblatt, knowing the nature of this manipulation made it strangely more tolerable.

He cleared his throat.

"Well, ah . . . I suppose the obvious one is a sex scandal of some sort."

"Of course," said Campman, "sin of the flesh. The classic. Also the cliché. Been done to death. And I'm not ruling it out by any means, Shelly. We can always come back to it. But first, I want us to think outside the box. Let's give our boy a sin that no one's thought of before. An original. A sin we can all be proud of!"

Campman smiled and surveyed the room. "Anyone?"

Eyes and torsos shifted in hotel chairs.

"C'mon people, give me a sin!"

Young Derek Kiley leaned forward hesitantly and spoke, "He could . . . steal something,"

"There we go! Thank you, Mr. Kiley!" said Campman with a smile. "Of course, I'd probably have to say no to that one. A bit too Dick Nixon. No one likes a thief."

"Although," said Mayweather, "he could be a Robin Hood–type thief. Everyone liked Robin Hood."

"So he steals from the rich and gives to the poor?" asked Sorn.

"Something like that."

"So, he'd waltz right into . . . say, Chase Manhattan, rob the place, and then use the money to buy gifts for poor kids, kinda like Santa Claus, right? That's a *great* idea, Mayweather." Sorn was mock applauding. "Maybe a bit hard to write off as a youthful indiscretion, but hey!"

"Look," said Shelly Greenblatt sternly, "we can't even *think* of doing this if you're talking about a big production. . . ."

"I wasn't serious, Greenblatt!"

"Still. My point is there's no way it could possibly work—I mean, if you're inventing something—it needs to be small. A small secret that can be discovered."

Campman smiled mischievously at Greenblatt's involvement. He decided to arbitrate.

"That's a good point, Shelly. Let's move beyond thievery, for now. Okay, boys?"

The room agreed.

"Let's give him a drinking problem," suggested Sorn, "a drug problem."

"That's not bad," said Mayweather, "but on the other hand, President Struck had substance abuse problems. It's not original."

"Well, worse than that," added Campman, "they cancel each other out. You'd just have two guys with substance abuse problems, and, of the two, Struck is still the guy most people would rather hang out and have a beer with."

"Which—of course—he can't have anymore," said Mayweather.

"Right. On top of which, we'd be the second one to come out with the confession."

"We'd look like we were only doing drugs because Struck did them."

"Exactly."

"Which is no reason to do drugs."

"Amen!"

"Okay!" said Sorn. "I get the idea. No substance abuse. How about domestic abuse?"

"Too O. J. Simpson."

"Child abuse?"

"Too . . . Homer Simpson."

"I really think we might want to steer clear of abuse altogether," offered young Kiley.

"Shut up, Kiley," snapped Sorn.

"Well, what else is there?" asked Mayweather.

This brought on another long pause. Finally the brave Ralph Sorn offered another suggestion. "Cross-dressing?" he said with a smile.

The tension broke for a moment.

"That's a great idea," joked Kiley, looking in Campman's direction, "a little something to win over those bread-and-butter states."

"Okay, Kiley, well *you* think of something!" barked Sorn, who had been barking at Kiley for a number of years now, ever since the up-and-coming speechwriter was an up-and-coming intern working under his watch at the Democratic Union of America (or the DUA, as it was commonly known).

Forced once again into the spotlight, the reluctant Derek Kiley bit his lip. "What about pornography?" he asked.

"Are you thinking porn *star*, porn *director*, or purveyor of porn?" asked Shelly Greenblatt.

"Depends," said Mayweather. "Is our man *equipped*?"

"Kiley, that is the worst idea in the history of Western civilization," said Sorn, locking in on his favorite target.

"Really? Worse than child abuse?"

"All right," said Campman, "does anyone have anything else? Anything?"

Another long pause.

"There's always rape and murder," said Sorn.

Greenblatt coughed. "I'm not fond of the whole rape and murder thing."

"Shelly's right," said Campman. "Murder and rape are *really* cliché."

"Um—and *drastic!*" said Kiley.

"I hate to say it, boys," began Campman, "but I think we need to go with Shelly's idea. I say sex scandal."

And there it was. While surely not a surprise, the realization still managed to hit Shelly Greenblatt like a heavyweight's glove. Tom Campman's conversation had come full circle exactly as intended, and suddenly, inevitably, it had become "Shelly's idea." *Just perfect.*

"*My* idea—" Shelly started but was quickly cut off.

"When you think about it," said Mayweather, "if we want a sin people can relate to, that *is* the most common one. Well, that and drinking."

"Don't forget pornography," said Sorn, grinning wickedly at Kiley. "But seriously, you're right. The more I think about it, we should definitely go sex scandal. Extramarital all the way! Good thinking, Greenblatt."

Shelly Greenblatt could feel himself overheating. He was short of breath. The proceedings had acquired a sense of inevitability that now held Shelly in its grasp, paralyzed. *What was preventing him from speaking up? Why couldn't he say something to stop this craziness?* The questions flew through his mind, but he couldn't answer them for fear of what his answers might reveal.

Across the room, Thomas Campman was confident. He wasn't looking at Greenblatt but could only assume the man was smoldering, and for the moment that was okay. Let him smolder, thought Campman. What else is he going to do? Greenblatt certainly didn't have any alternate strategies, none that hadn't been tried a dozen times already, and Campman knew it. He decided to ignore Shelly Greenblatt altogether for the moment and focus on the other three men instead. It was time to go in for the kill.

"Now, here's how I see it," he said, beginning his pitch, "if we're planting an affair, it should be something far in the past, but not *too* far in the past: history but not *ancient* history. And it should be something Melissa knows about. You know, like he cheated on her during a dark period but he felt terrible about it, begged for forgiveness. Hard times. They worked through it. You know, 'making the marriage work'! *That's* the sort of stuff couples can relate to. And we'll make the girl a known entity, someone from his past. Former girlfriend he stayed close with. We just gotta find the girl, but Kiley'll help with that."

"Uh—what?"

Young Derek Kiley had been so transfixed by Campman's weaving of the plan that he was startled to find himself a part of it. Indeed, he wasn't sure he wanted to be part of this plan. Much like Shelly Greenblatt, Kiley didn't like it.

"You gotta come with me to my hotel," said Campman.

"You're not here?" asked Mayweather.

"No. Advance didn't know I was coming tonight, so the damn place is full. I'm at the Hyatt."

"Uh, what do you mean when you say I'm gonna help find the girl?" asked Kiley.

"No secretaries, Derek. No assistants. No interns. No spouses. Just us in this room." Campman was talking to everyone now, and he was deadly serious. He knew he was speaking to men of power, men who (with the exception of Kiley) were used to delegating authority to their subordinates, men who would be less than thrilled at the prospect of a new mission without administrative support, but Campman felt this one condition was unnegotiable.

He did not expect himself to suffer for lack of such support, as he'd never been one to rely on assistants. Although he did employ a young man named Wyatt in just such a role, he delegated sparingly to him and had, for some time now, felt much closer to his personal driver than his support staff (as for Hector, the trusty driver, Campman had no worries about keeping him in the dark, as theirs was a relationship of transit not substance and the man spoke poor English besides). No, Thomas Campman would not suffer for lack of help, but looking around the room, he knew Greenblatt, Mayweather, and Sorn might. So for their benefit, he repeated himself.

"No assistants, no subordinates, no one," he said, "This is not up for discussion. And if you're wondering whether this means more travel time for all of you, it does. If we want to keep this under wraps and still communicate, we need to stay together geographically and keep this circle small. We tell Ben and Melissa obviously. The five of us know. *But that is it*. Understood?"

"Are you excluding Charlie in this?" asked Sorn, referring to Ben Phillips's personal assistant.

"Bet your ass, I am," said Campman.

"What about the general?" asked Mayweather.

"Screw the general. It'll be better if he's surprised. No, boys, it is *just us*, and no one breathes a word or looks at anyone cockeyed. Nothing like this has ever been attempted, and nothing like this will succeed if there is the slightest mistake."

Shelly was the only one to speak.

"I'm not crazy about this idea," was all he could manage.

"You'll get used to it, Shelly," said Campman. With that, he put his hands in his pockets and walked to the door, turning around at the last second to issue one final proclamation:

"Remember: Nothing is written. No e-mails. No phone calls. I don't want to see one piece of paper with anything incriminating on it. Do you understand?"

Nods all around.

"Okay, Derek, let's go."

"Why are we going? What's at your hotel?" asked Kiley.

Campman grinned.

"The one piece of paper with something incriminating on it. It's for you."

FAST HANDS

With the suit on, Hector Elizondo felt he was one fine-looking son of a bitch. The Mexican driver was only five foot two, but the shoes gave him an extra inch. The jacket did all the right things to his solid frame, containing the stomach and enhancing the shoulders, and while the thick head of black hair, the beard, and the mustache were not directly affected by the suit, they still benefited from the air of respectability and panache the suit gave off. It added up to an attractive final product.

"You must sweat like a rodent in heat," Brinita had said. "I can't believe he expects you to wear that in the summer." She made fun of the suit, but Hector knew she secretly liked it. He also knew that, despite her complaints, his wife was proud of his latest job. She'll be even prouder once the real money starts coming in, thought Hector.

"And those gloves! Who does he think you are, a circus performer?"

The gloves were Hector's idea. The boss had asked only that he wear a suit, but when Hector saw the gloves, he fell in love instantly. They were made of a very thin white leather with a soft fabric inside.

They reminded Hector of magician's gloves, and that made them all the more desirable. For his part, the boss was a good sport about it.

"What the heck! If you're gonna be my driver, why not go the whole nine yards? Let's get them."

Hector's hands were his best features. He felt it was only appropriate that they be treated in a grander fashion than his other body parts. It wasn't just their physical appearance that pleased him (although by all accounts they were attractive hands). It was that Hector's hands seemed to possess all the qualities Hector-the-person lacked. The hands were large while Hector was small, the hands were quick while Hector was slow, and the hands were precise—they seemed to actually possess a fierce intelligence—while Hector, with his constant language troubles, frequently gave the opposite impression (at least, to those who spoke English).

Hector Elizondo (who was in no way related to the famous actor of the same name) first became aware of the exquisiteness of his hands at a young age. As a child on the island of San Gomez, Hector became fascinated with magic. He taught himself a number of tricks, usually centered on the disappearance of a small rock or lizard. They were all sleight of hand gags, and Hector became quite adept at performing them. In the days before the San Gomez Cinema, young Hector Elizondo was the best show in town, and at the age of ten, his friends anointed him "Nosrapo," short for "fast hands."

For a brief period of his adolescence, Hector parlayed his sleight of hand skills into a moneymaking venture as San Gomez's first legitimate pickpocket. This was a short-lived occupation, however, one that ended abruptly when Hector's father caught him in the handbag of his ninety-one-year-old great-aunt and made him sleep outside in a rainstorm to reconsider the value of this continued career path.

As a teenager, Hector's "fast hands" proved quite valuable with the young ladies of San Gomez. It was said he could remove a brassiere with such subtlety and stealth that the unsuspecting *chica* would have no clue as to the extent of her nudity until Hector was well into the handling of her proverbial "produce" (an area where the young horny Mexican displayed less subtlety and—as more than one girl would agree—no stealth whatsoever).

This was before he met Sabrina Fortuna, of course. He started dating the fiery girl when he was fifteen, and while her effect on his life was initially tumultuous, it was ultimately domesticating. Indeed, the years since their marriage had seen Hector's hands serving much more adult purposes. They had tugged on a fishing line, they had buried two parents, and they had cradled three newborn baby girls. They were hands that had steered a boat that took the family to America. That was three years ago. And now these famous hands were behind the wheel of an automobile. Now they bore a tremendous responsibility.

The boss had an air of danger about him tonight; at least that's what Hector thought. Whether it was danger specifically or just some feeling that resembled danger, Hector couldn't tell, but he recognized it instantly, and it reminded him of the snowy night they first met.

From the Marriott hotel entrance, the boss walked briskly toward the car, which was not unusual. He always walked briskly. Hector opened the door with a smile. This was not unusual for him.

"Hector, take us to the Hyatt."

"Eeeeh-yessirboss."

He had the young one with him, the man whose name Hector had forgotten. The two seemed to have important business between them, but they weren't talking. Not yet.

Once the doors were closed, Hector settled himself into the front seat and tried not to look suspicious. He shifted the Lincoln Town Car into gear and placed his white-gloved hands on the wheel. They were off.

While nothing was said in the first few moments, Hector had a good feeling about this ride. The boss had company. There was potential here. Hector reached his right hand into the bag on the passenger seat and with the greatest of stealth, withdrew a small tape recorder. He brought it to the edge of the bag where he could clearly make out the buttons and the indicator light.

The tape recorder had been purchased one week ago at a Radio Shack in Youngstown, Ohio. The overly attentive salesman had tried to sell Hector something called a digital voice recorder, but Hector had opted for the low-tech (and low-priced) cassette recorder instead. If one wants to be a successful double agent, he had thought, one must work with technology one can count on. No fancy digital devices would be purchased by Hector Elizondo.

"I don't need to tell you how vital it is for you to move quickly on this."

The boss was speaking. And it sounded important. With his eyes never straying from the road in front of him, Hector dispatched his white gloved hand in the direction of the record button, and he pressed it.

"Of course, of course," said the young one.

When Hector felt the moment was right, he glanced down at the blinking red indicator light. Red light means record. He was recording.

"Now, we've contacted all of them before, you understand, but that was just preliminary stuff, standard operating procedure. Skeleton-check, you might call it."

Hector couldn't believe his luck. Whatever the boss was saying sounded very serious, and the tape recorder was catching it all. Hector had to exert great effort to avoid the appearance of a smile, and that effort distracted him from the obvious red traffic light in front of him.

As the black Town Car rocketed through the intersection to a chorus of honking horns, the boss's companion let out a quiet yelp and said, "Hey, watch out!"

"Eeeeh-yellowlight," said Hector.

The boss just chuckled.

"Don't worry about Hector. He's a master."

After a few moments, the boss continued. "Remember, you have to be very careful not to give the wrong impression. Let me be the one to do the heavy lifting."

"Right. Right. Now, if the women—"

"No need to be specific. We can discuss it at the hotel. I'm just say-ing, remember to leave the heavy lifting to me."

If Hector had put his mind to it, he probably could have attempted a crude translation, but was that really necessary? He could tell just from the tone that these were important words. It was a valuable con-versation for someone, someone who wasn't him, but someone who might, in fact, be willing to pay him a great deal of money to hear it. That was all he needed to know.

The Hyatt was rapidly approaching on the right-hand side. Crap, thought Hector. The ride had been too quick. Would the boss notice if he circled around the block once or twice?

"Here we are."

He would. Hector pulled into the hotel entrance. He stopped the car and helped the passengers out.

"Hector, please stick around for a little while. Mr. Kiley's going to need a ride back."

"EeeehWait?"

"Yes, wait. Good night, Hector."

"Yessireeeboss. Goodnightyboss."

Hector bowed slightly at the waist as the two men walked off through the hotel lobby and soon disappeared into its warm lights and golden trimmings. It had been a short ride and a short conversa-tion, but Hector was pretty sure he had something.

Hector turned. He nodded to the tall, clean-shaven valet who stood beside the Town Car and smiled. It was always good to smile. The valet nodded back with a look of understanding, but his face re-mained stern. Did he know something? Hector would have to be careful. He reparked the car and waited until the valet was out of sight before looking down at his hidden tape recorder.

The red light was still blinking, but on closer inspection, Hector noticed the tape heads weren't moving. This was strange. Could the tape have ended already? It didn't seem possible. It had been such a short ride. Hector began playing with the buttons on the front of the recorder, and suddenly the tape heads engaged. The indicator light that had previously flashed was now lit solidly red. Hector looked to see what he had pressed. The button read REC/PAUSE. Hector sighed deeply. It hadn't been recording after all.

GOD, SPOUSE, COUNTRY

Political mastermind Thomas Campman had to stop his prayer in the middle once the fat lady got on the elevator. This pissed him off. He first tried to continue under his breath, ignoring her, but he could tell from the way she altered her breathing pattern that she was probably going to make a big deal about it. So he stopped all together. It's amazing how difficult it is for some people just to mind their own damn business, he thought grumpily.

Once Kiley had left with the list, Campman relieved himself in the bathroom of his Hyatt hotel suite and then started his prayer.

"Oh, Lord my God, Jesus, and all spirits inhabiting this world and others . . ."

It was the way he had begun every prayer for the last fifty years, and it had been carefully thought out to include any and all deities that might possibly exist. Tom Campman knew the importance of covering his ass.

The prayer had continued out the door of his suite, down the hall-way, and onto the elevator. Campman was a firm believer in multitasking, and whether that task was an important cell phone call or an urgent message to the heavens, there was no reason it couldn't co-exist with other activities in his cluttered world of lunches, airplanes, and elevators.

Would God mind that He/She/It/They were being addressed from a treadmill or a taxi? Of course not. He/She/It/They were well aware, thought Campman, that free time was at a premium, and He/She/It/They would be thankful that Campman managed to find a moment in his busy schedule to fit Him/Her/It/Them in.

This was what really annoyed Campman about people who sub-scribed to organized religion. Their priorities were all off. They'd spend hours every week reciting the same mindless mantras, offer-ing forth the same meaningless prose to the Almighty, but never giving a damn about the words they were actually saying.

In his early adolescence, Campman grew disenchanted with the inherited Catholic dogma of his parents and decided to form his own more-personal religious philosophy, rejecting ritual and embracing the sometimes sticky relationship between logic and faith. In doing so, he found himself tackling the same great mysteries that had chal-lenged scientists and theologians for centuries, a weighty task for a twelve-year-old boy from Missouri. The key to his approach—at age twelve and age sixty-three—was to try to put himself in the Al-mighty's shoes, to understand what it was that motivated a deity.

"If I were God, would I want people telling me twenty-four hours a day how great I was? Of course not. Who needs to hear 'You are mightier than mighty! You are more merciful than mercy itself! You are more succulent than any deity that ever did suck!'? Hell no. I'd have gotten sick and tired of that garbage in the days of the first temple! Just talk to me like an intelligent human being!"

Campman wasn't a fan of pomp and circumstance. His feelings on the subject had been best articulated by a Jewish comedian he'd seen a number of years ago: "If I were God and you started praying to me while you were getting a blow job, I'd be flattered. That you should think of me in your time of pleasure . . . how wonderful!"

For Campman, it didn't matter whether you got the ancient words right. What mattered was that you were talking in the first place.

Campman would have to finish his heavenly dialogue over dinner. Elayne had not arrived yet, and his stomach was grumbling. When the elevator doors opened, he let the fat woman exit first and then walked swiftly past her into the lobby, the threads of his fine suit making a swishing noise as they caught wind.

He dined at the restaurant next door. It was one of those "attic on the walls" type places, where the owner had been so enamored of the clutter in his attic that he chose to share it with his diners, welding every last piece of detritus to the walls above their tables. An ancient bobsled, a basketball trophy, a sewing machine, a popcorn popper, and a dusty old Barbie's Dream House (that either Barbie or Ken should have clearly burned to the ground decades ago) all hung proudly on the artificially aged wood.

It was 11:00 P.M., so Campman had his choice of seating. He went with a booth in the back of the restaurant, and once there, ordered the Caesar salad with southern grilled chicken and the coconut-battered fried shrimp appetizer. He sat for a moment, staring at the grain of the heavily lacquered wood table.

"Sin . . . Will . . . Make . . . Him . . . Human." That's what the voice had said. It was so clear. Never, in Campman's many conversations with the heavens, had he ever received so concrete a response. That the voice was heavenly, he never questioned. That it was telling him the truth, leading him in the right direction, this he did not question, either. He didn't question anything about his revelation at the time.

But now, twelve hours later, he worried.

"Oh, Lord my God, Jesus, and all spirits inhabiting this world and others," he began under his breath. "Thank you again for your divine message. I was searching for the answer to a problem, and—boy oh boy—you may have really come through. Surprised me. I admit. Surprised me. Not surprised you could do it, of course. Just that I know you and I haven't been real 'buds' of late. I know you're still hung up on a certain . . ."

He coughed.

"Oh, hell, I'm not gonna go over that again. It's not like anyone was hurt. Okay, someone was hurt, but that wasn't my fault. We had no idea he was gonna—Besides, as I've said before, you can't tell me he didn't have it coming. Look at the gains! Look at the benefits! When the means are so *slightly* problematic, how can you *possibly* claim the ends don't justify them?"

"You had the coconut shrimp and Caesar, right?"

"Um, yeah," said Campman. He'd been interrupted midmumble so many times that he was no longer embarrassed, just inconvenienced.

The waiter left, and Campman continued, now chewing on a shrimp.

"So, now I'm not sure what to think. Guess you could say I'm suspicious. You put me through the ringer on that whole other situation and now give me advice like this? I mean, talk about your 'ends justifies the means' suggestions, you know? I mean, it's a damn *cynical* suggestion! Now, I don't judge. I agree. I like it. It makes sense. It's brilliant, in fact. *But I'm suspicious*...'cause does this mean you agree with me now? Have you finally come to the conclusion that I was right, and you were wrong? Frankly, if that's the case, I say 'Bravo, it's about time.' And that's not claiming moral know-it-all-ship here. I'm just talking common sense...and maybe...you agree. Maybe this new idea is proof. But if it's not..."

Campman could feel himself starting to sweat. His water glass was empty.

"...I don't know what to think when you start giving me ideas like this," he said, his low voice shaking, "I like to imagine you're helping me to help the good guy, but the more real this thing gets...."

He trailed off again. In Campman's mind existed two very different thoughts. The first was about the shrimp. It was juicy, tasty, sweet, and altogether more pleasing than he'd expected. The other thought was not food related. The other thought was one he'd first encountered in the elevator. It was a thought that made him uncomfortable: *What if God was trying to trick him?*

He took a deep breath. "I'm going with you on this one," he said, "but, I'd love some confirmation. Now, I know you gave me the big sign, and that should be enough, but if there's any way. . . ."

Campman surveyed the room.

"I'm gonna count to thirty. If the waiter comes to the table with my check before I'm done counting, then I'll know you spoke truly to me this morning. Okay. Here goes."

"One . . . two . . . three . . . four . . . five . . . six . . . seven . . . eight . . ."

The dark-haired waitress was talking to the couple across the way, but Campman's waiter was nowhere in sight.

". . . nine . . . ten . . . eleven . . . twelve . . . thirteen . . . fourteen . . . fifteen . . ."

Campman began to get nervous.

". . . sixteen . . . seventeen . . . eighteen . . ."

There he was! Campman's waiter had emerged from the kitchen, and he was coming closer. Closer. Eye contact! The waiter was definitely heading to Campman's table.

". . . twenty-two . . . twenty-three . . . twenty-four . . ."

"Hi there," said the waiter as he reached behind his back to reveal . . .

A water pitcher.

Damn, thought Campman. He had no idea what this meant. But perhaps . . .

"Can I get a check?"

"Yeah just a minute."

He finished filling Campman's glass and then shuffled back to the kitchen.

Hmm.

The waiter had come. Without a check. He had walked to the table. But no check. Not a direct yes. Not a direct no. The Almighty didn't want to give Campman confirmation, at least not now. He would just have to trust the original message.

"I'M NOT REALLY photogenic tonight."

"That's okay!" said Elayne. She snapped another close-up of her husband and then kissed him on the cheek. "I'm just so excited to be here!"

Her good humor was infectious. As much as he'd been looking forward to an evening of anxiety, Elayne seemed determined to make all things better.

Elayne. Lovely Elayne. Elayne whose wrinkles only reinforced the features of that beautiful dynamic girl he'd met at Columbia University thirty-five years ago. No, thought Campman, the lines on her face did not detract from her beauty. They just served as evidence that she was once there and she was now here. It seemed amazing to him that the delicate skin and bones of his wife had managed to travel with him through the time and space of so many years and end up exactly where he was, in that same Kansas City hotel room on this same evening in August. He knew at that moment, as he had been reminded so many times before: it was Elayne who made *him* human.

"When do I meet Ben Phillips?" she asked, snapping away.

"Okay, you're gonna have to stop or I'll be forced to trade that thing in for a wide-screen TV."

She ignored him, clutching the Canon ProDigi 3000 digital camera he had gotten her for her birthday.

"You could at least not use the flash. Are you trying to blind me?"

World-famous photographer Elayne Cohen-Campman lowered the camera from her face.

"Aw. But you looked so cute," she said. "Well, grumpy cute."

"How many grumpy cute pictures does a woman need?"

"I can delete the ones I don't want. That's the whole point of digital, baby."

"When did you get in?"

"Half hour ago. Were you with Senator Phillips?"

Campman sat down on the bed.

"Senator Phillips spoke at an early town meeting and called it an uncharacteristically early night before I even got in. I was just having dinner."

"How thoroughly unexciting."

Elayne put her camera away and fell onto the bed beside him with a curious look on her face.

"Tom, are you sure this is okay? I mean, are you sure they're not gonna mind my coming right in the middle of things?"

"I told you it's fine. Everyone knows. Everyone's fine with it."

"'Cause you know, I would've been here since the beginning of the campaign if I could've. It's just that I had Bombay to finish, and I figure it's better to catch the end of it than none at all."

"I know that, and the others understand. . . ."

"They know I'd have been here for the whole thing if I could."

"Of course."

"And everyone knows?"

"Yes."

"And they're okay with it?"

"I told you they are."

"And Senator Phillips?"

"The senator likes your work. He's looking forward to meeting you."

"Oh, good. Did he say that?"

"Yes."

"Really? Or are *you* just saying that?"

"You want it in writing?"

"Yes, do you mind?" She smiled. "I'm sorry, I'm just a little excited that's all. I've never met a presidential candidate."

"You've met a *president*."

"Okay, smarty-pants. Look, I'm just excited, okay."

Tom Campman stared at his beautiful wife lying prone beside him. A wicked grin spread across his face.

"You know, I've actually been doing this my whole life," he said, "I'm surprised it's taken you so long to join me on the road."

"No, you're not," she chuckled and sprang back to her feet with catlike ease.

Campman wasn't really surprised. He knew Elayne would never have joined him when he was working for the Republicans. It was only since the switch that she'd started to show interest in his work. She'd been a hippie liberal when they met, and not much had changed in thirty-five years. He had been surprised, in fact, at her enthusiasm toward Ben Phillips, who was something of a centrist Democrat. But then, Ben wasn't your typical politician. When Campman landed the top spot on Ben Phillips's campaign, Elayne had been even more excited than he was. He could see that excitement now.

"They moh aywann unnnnrestreh ahssiss."

Elayne was brushing her teeth.

"You'll have unrestricted access, darling, of course. Within reason."

"Whudyoooo meeeeen wih hin reeeen?"

"If the senator takes a shower, you'll have to wait outside the door till he's done."

She smiled at him through her toothpaste suds.

Elayne would be traveling with the campaign for the last few months, taking pictures for her own personal project and acting as a sort of second unit campaign photographer. It would be a new experience for Campman, having her always at his side, and now that she had finally arrived, he was starting to have second thoughts.

As Elayne busied herself in the bathroom, preparing for bed, Campman lay down. Face pressed against the sheets, he once again embraced the melancholy and anxiety he'd flirted with in the hour before Elayne's arrival. He worried about his wife cramping his style. He worried about the new plan he'd have to keep secret from her.

Tom had never told his wife about any of his dirty tricks before, but this secret would be much harder to hide, with Elayne a member of the traveling circus. And what of that? How would his free-spirit wife fit in with his straightlaced political colleagues? Campman knew it was always dangerous to mix characters from different spheres of life. The results were unpredictable.

YOUNG ADULTS IN THIS MILLENNIUM

Golly," said Peter, "that's quite a thing to say."

And it was. He didn't know how to respond. He hoped Mary would say something else, but she just sipped her vanilla milk shake and looked at him with her wide eager brown eyes. She was the most beautiful almost-seventeen-year-old in the entire world.

"It's a really cool thing to say."

Mary knew she shouldn't press him for a response. Boys didn't expect girls to make declarations of love, and they couldn't be counted on to act appropriately. All of her reading on the subject had been consistent on this point. She was taking a risk.

"Golly."

Mary had high hopes for Peter's response. He wasn't like other boys. He'd been different for as long as she'd known him. In the second grade, when James Wilnicky knocked over the block castle she had been constructing, Peter had built her a six-foot replica of St. Basil's Cathedral to cheer her up (complete with papier-mâché onion domes). That was just the sort of guy he was. Although she'd never admit it, Mary Templeton had fallen for Peter Williams in the second grade.

"I'm not really sure what to . . . um . . ."

Peter's right hand had been resting on his plate in a pool of ketchup, and when he brought it to his face, his dimpled cheeks became coated with tomato red.

"Oh!"

They both chuckled nervously. Mary took a napkin, leaned over, and wiped the ketchup off his face. Then she kissed his cheek.

He instinctively pecked her back, before she could return to her side of the table. Then he said bravely . . .

"Mary, I really like you a lot. I mean, really a lot. Just lots. You're . . . cool."

Mary took another sip of her milk shake, hoping the sip would disguise her obvious disappointment (which it did, but then Peter was never very perceptive about these things). For his part, the young reporter was silent, the echo of his previous eloquence still lingering in his ears.

"Peter," she said seriously, "would you say that you feel the same way I feel?"

"About many topics."

"I mean about how I feel about you."

"You mean how you . . ."

"Yes."

"And do I . . ."

"Mmm hmm."

"That's what I thought."

Peter adopted an intense look of concentration. He wanted her to know how hard this was for him. Ironically, the effort he had to expend in order to produce this intense facial expression made it more difficult for him to concentrate on what he was actually going to say.

"Mary, the life of a reporter is a hard one."

It seemed like a good way to start.

"Mary, I'm just not sure if I do or not."

That wasn't what he'd planned on saying next. He'd wanted to work up to his conclusion, not lead with it. But the truth was out. He simply wasn't sure.

"What do you mean?" his girlfriend asked.

"You see," said Peter, "when a reporter is on assignment, there is a certain stress; the mind is . . ."

He was making odd motions with his fingers in the direction of his brain. Mary wasn't sure what they meant. Was he telling her he was going crazy?

"Mary, I am the first political reporter in the *history* of *TeenVibe* magazine. You have no idea what sort of pressure that is."

"I understand. It's a big responsibility."

"Exactly! And right now, I'm just so wrapped up in the election, in my work, in trying to get a break. And I think I'm on to something here, with my interviews. I'm getting to the heart of America's political malaise. I mean, I'm not there yet, but I'm getting closer. And once I get there . . . once I file that really big story . . . then . . ."

"Then what?"

"Well, I don't know. But until that happens, I can't see straight. I just think that once I'm there—maybe then I'll know whether I love"—he felt the word on his lips—"you or not. But I hope you understand, for now, I'm just not sure."

There. He'd said it. And across the table, beautiful Mary was still smiling at him.

Of course she was smiling. Though it was difficult to have a boyfriend who was always on the road (particularly in the eleventh grade), Mary loved that Peter was passionate about his work. He sparkled when he talked about it. He was sparkling now. And *he cared*. That was so clear. He *wanted* to say he loved her, and she knew it.

Mary began to feel guilty thinking about her own selfish needs. For a moment, she considered letting things stand as they were, but she had come to this conversation with an agenda, and she wasn't going to give up without a fight. Perhaps Peter just didn't understand what was at stake.

"Well," she said, "I'm a little sad that you're not sure, Peter Williams."

"I'm sad, too."

"Because I feel that *as young adults in this millennium*"—it was a line she had rehearsed, but had not planned on approaching this way—"*I believe you and I are ready to start expressing ourselves romantically, in a more profound and meaningful way.*"

Peter swallowed hard.

"Are you—"

Peter put his hand down on the prongs of his fork, and his utensil flew off the table. It hit a nearby waitress in the hip and bounced to the floor.

"Ow! Say, you dropped your fork," said the woman, a surly look on her face. "I'll get you another."

"Uh, thanks."

Peter cleared his throat, waited for her to walk off, and leaned in toward his girlfriend. He spoke softly now.

"Are you speaking of sexual intercourse?"

He had debated between the phrase "making love" and "sex" but decided to say "sexual intercourse" instead, which immediately struck him as too clinical.

Mary's face grew flushed.

"No, I'm not talking about sexual intercourse."

Uh-oh. Peter was confused.

"Making love?" he ventured.

She shook her head.

Now he was really confused.

"Fellatio?"

He was shooting in the dark.

Mary laughed faintly, clearly uncomfortable. These were words neither of them had said aloud to each other, and it was shocking to hear them uttered. Still, she was secretly pleased to know that these things were on his mind as well.

"Poetry? Artwork? Affectionate similes?"

Peter feared he'd overshot the mark and was backtracking like crazy. Mary knew she had to bail him out. She spoke calmly.

"Sexual intercourse between two consenting young adults is a symbol of mutual love between them. I *might* be speaking of these things, *if* we were two young adults who shared a mutual love. As our love is not mutual . . ."

"Well, it *might* be mutual," he said, "I'm just not sure. I mean it very well could be mutual."

But Mary knew that a girl had only one shot at her first time, and she couldn't afford to take any chances.

"As we can't be *certain* that our love is mutual, we really can't be talking about such things."

Peter looked disappointed for a moment but then smiled his beautiful shy smile, and Mary began to melt. Peter Wiliams was the most beautiful boy she'd ever seen. Mary felt terrible but at the same time proud for holding her ground. Hopefully, she wouldn't have to hold it much longer.

"I understand," Peter said.

And that was the end of the conversation.

Once the check was paid, Mary drove Peter home. Before he left the car, Peter attempted to give his girlfriend what he hoped would be a very special kiss, a romantic reassuring kiss of the sort a boyfriend generally gives to his best girl before leaving town (yet again).

Their tongues intertwined in a familiar way. They had been practicing this for almost a year. The kiss was going so well that midway through it, Peter recognized the opportunity for a make-out session and altered his strategy. Instead of a romantic, reassuring, good-bye kiss, he would now attempt a romantic, reassuring, good-bye make-out session. His hands grasped her waist and then wove themselves up across her perfect little breasts, then back down, seeking the separation between her shirt and skin. But here he was denied, and the symphony of lips and tongues came to a rest shortly after. Mary didn't seem to be in the mood tonight, and Peter regretted his deviation from the original strategy.

They kissed one last time, and he opened the car door. Good-byes were exchanged and also good wishes, and as Peter ran off toward the front door, he could hear Mary shouting after him, "I hope you get your big story!"

So do I, thought Peter, so do I.

THE BILLY MACK SHOW

Putting on makeup in front of a room full of people was always a strange thing. Senator Ben Phillips wondered if he'd ever get to the point where it felt normal. Probably not, he decided. As Shelly Greenblatt and Thomas Campman peppered him with last-minute questions and his makeup man powdered him with last-minute powder, as his assistant Charlie fixed him a glass of apple juice, Campman's wife photographed him, and his own wife smiled at him, Ben realized that this predebate ritual was something very few Americans would ever experience. There was a feeling in the air that history was about to be made, and the effect was dizzying.

"Remember not to let him out-smile you," said Shelly, who was pacing. "Struck is gonna be smiling and smirking. You can't always look serious in response. Smirk back sometimes."

"Shelly, I'm not gonna smirk at the president."

"Well just don't let him out-smile you by too great a margin."

"I know. I know."

"You're gonna do fine," said Campman.

"Ben, you'll be wonderful," said Melissa, always the supportive spouse. "You'll finally have a chance to square off on the issues, and that's exactly what we want. I'll say it again: I really don't see how he has a chance."

Melissa Phillips was wearing her green dress, the one that drew attention to the blazing green of her eyes. Her brunette hair fell down in waves, stopping at her shoulders but brushing the gold necklace that matched her conservative emerald earrings just a little too well. With her red lips and warm subtle smile, she looked every bit the first lady, sitting in that leather dressing room chair. What gave her away was the overeagerness of her posture, the tension in her shoulders, and the tapping of her foot, all signs conspiring to betray her as the nervous girlfriend of a boxer, minutes before the big fight.

Melissa Phillips was a part-time member of the campaign, flying back and forth from D.C., where she continued to teach English at Georgetown University. She only had one summer class and was set for a light course load in the fall, but she refused to give up teaching altogether while her husband campaigned. He respected her for that. Ben had even grown to enjoy her constant coming and going from the campaign trail. As much as he knew it exhausted her, he couldn't deny that it energized him, these repeated farewells and rendezvous across the country. Seeing his beautiful wife after an absence of forty-eight hours was always a thrill for him, and this evening was no exception. He was, in fact, particularly excited to have her on set for tonight's televised debate on *The Billy Mack Show*.

President Struck's handlers had weaseled their way down to two debates for the campaign season, and tonight's tête-à-tête wasn't even a traditionally structured debate, but rather a casual seated double interview with America's most-watched TV interviewer, the grand softballer himself: Billy Mack.

The importance of the evening could not be overstated, particularly for Senator Ben Phillips. After months of sliding in the polls, *The Billy Mack Show* represented a crucial opportunity to turn around the momentum of the campaign, something that millions of dollars in advertising and a skillfully orchestrated Democratic convention had thus far failed to do. Ben Phillips knew he was running out of chances.

The dressing room was quiet now. Everything that needed to be said had been said numerous times. In this calm before the storm, as the makeup artist worked to define his eyes, the senator allowed his mind to wander.

He thought about Campman's crazy idea. It had been four days since his top advisors approached him with their plan to create a sex scandal. Ben thought they were joking at first but was surprised to find they actually considered this to be a viable strategy. He was even more surprised to find his old friend Shelly Greenblatt was one of the folks behind it all. After the meeting, he had pulled Shelly aside.

"Shel, do you really think this is a good idea?"

Ben knew that Shelly Greenblatt couldn't lie believably. Whenever the slightest fib was attempted, Shelly's body would have a violent physiological response. His skin would turn red, his throat would close up, and he would get short of breath. This made him a terrible choice to run for office but a great choice for an advisor, and Ben trusted him completely. For any politician who finds himself surrounded by "yes men" (and most do at one time or another), a savvy friend who is willing to give it to you straight is your most valuable asset. At the moment, Shelly's face was reddish but far from its peak hue. He would be telling the truth.

Shelly sighed. "I think it's probably *not* a good idea, Ben. But we are running out of options here. I just don't know what to tell you. Unless you can work some magic in that debate. . . . But then, I'm sure you will. You have to."

Ben found Shelly's grave tone troubling. He wondered: had his campaign really sunk this low? Was his situation so dire that they would actually entertain such a ridiculous idea?

Ben couldn't let himself believe it. He decided to stall, telling his advisors he wouldn't discuss any drastic measures for another week. "Let's see if the numbers pick up after the Billy Mack debate," he'd said.

Ben knew he was the more skilled debater, and his senatorial record was much less vulnerable to attack than the president's record
(which was riddled with broken promises, inconsistencies, and poor
judgment). Still, despite his confidence about the debate itself, Ben
was deeply troubled by the bigger picture. He knew that for whatever
reason, the public wasn't listening to him. And he knew he was losing. Badly.

Losing was unfamiliar to Ben Phillips. Since his college years, he
had won every contest he'd ever entered. From captain of the track
team to state representative to congressman, Ben had been a winner
for so long he'd almost forgotten what it was like to come in second.
The last time it happened was thirty-five years ago, when Luke Travis
defeated him in the race for student council president of William
Howard Taft High School.

Luke Travis was the star running back for the Taft Tigers, and if this
fact alone was not enough to cement his top dog social status, he also
drove a Ford Thunderbird and had blond hair, a winning smile, and as
unnerdy a GPA as any jock could hope for. He wasn't smart and had no
student council experience, but Luke was hands down the coolest guy
in school. It took only a friendly wager from his football buddies to
convince him to run for student council president, and once he threw
his hat in the ring, he was instantly the leading contender.

At seventeen years old, Ben Phillips was not considered such a
cool guy, but he was clearly the most qualified candidate. He'd served
on the student council since his freshman year, had the highest
grade point average in the school, and had founded more extracur-
ricular clubs than any student in the school's forty-year history (these
included the Foreign Policy Club, the Student Volunteer Club, the
Future Democrats of America Club, the Etiquette Club, and the Juggling Club). He'd spent his first three years in student government
exploring the ins and outs of Taft High School politics, befriending
teachers and learning from the mistakes and successes of the older
student politicians. By senior year, no one was more prepared to assume the role of president than he.

In the end, it was the "coolness gap" that led to Ben's defeat. Too many guys were friends with Luke Travis and too many girls had crushes on him for Ben to have ever stood a chance. The blond running back won the race with 60 percent of the vote, leaving young Ben baffled and heartbroken. That Luke Travis would prove to be an ineffective and ultimately forgettable student council president provided Ben with little consolation and only reinforced his belief that a terrible injustice had been committed.

All this thinking of Luke Travis soon provoked thoughts of Ben's other teenage nemesis: Randy Denholme. Randy was a second-rate bully from Ben's hometown of Century, Oklahoma, a wedgie and noogie specialist, who'd plagued Ben since well before the onset of puberty. In the eighth grade, Randy committed his greatest atrocity when he anointed young Ben Phillips with the uninspired nickname: "Butt Fill-Up."

"Hey, Butt Fill-Up!" he would taunt. "Do you want your butt filled up? I bet you want your butt filled up with dick!"

The nickname made Ben seethe with hatred, but there was nothing he could do about it. Protesting only made things worse. Randy was larger, tougher, and more popular, and Ben was hard-pressed to alter this bully/victim dynamic.

The nickname probably wouldn't have bothered Ben so much if only it hadn't been so moronic. "Ben" didn't sound anything like "Butt." It was without question the dumbest nickname in the world!

But it stuck. That's what really drove him crazy. Once again, it was the injustice of the situation that most enraged Ben, the injustice that such an unfair ill-constructed nickname would be co-opted by his peers. This injustice was what Ben remembered most clearly.

The majority of his classmates stopped addressing him as Butt Fill-Up after a few months, and by the time of the Luke Travis election several years later, the only one who still remembered the nickname was Randy Denholme himself (who still used it from time to time). In high school, as Randy's star faded and Ben's began to rise, the former bully was no longer a threat to Ben's physical or mental well-being, but the scars inflicted in those early years would take a long time to heal.

Ben knew that verbal abuse and heartache were all part of being an adolescent, and even as a teenager he could appreciate the normalcy of his troubles. He knew that kids were cruel and stupid because kids have always been cruel and stupid, and he was reassured by the inevitability of maturation. He looked forward to entering the adult world, where his talents would be valued: the adult world, where he knew he would thrive.

Now at age fifty-three, Ben Phillips was running for president of the United States. He was master of the adult world, a place where the Randy Denholmes and Luke Travises finished second to him, a place where intellect mattered, a place where justice reigned supreme.

Or did it?

"Would you get the senator to the stage, please?"

"Ben, they're ready."

It was time. And where were his thoughts? Why couldn't he stay focused? Why did his mind keep racing back to *high school* of all things?

Keep smiling. Stand straight. Be confident.

Ben Phillips reengaged command over his skeletal-muscular system. He stood up from his chair and walked toward the soundstage.

GREGORY XAVIER STRUCK never had a problem fitting in. As a young man, he liked football, beer, and bragging. He liked girls and always tinged his female interactions with a touch of condescension—never enough to qualify as chauvinism, but enough to make it clear who was in charge. Struck was a guy's guy and spent time with other guy's guys.

"Guess you could say that makes me a *guy's guy's guy*," he said once in college, before adding quickly, "but always for the ladies, if you'll excuse the double-negative."

When his smart-ass friend Michaelson pointed out the lack of any negative—double or single—in his previous statement, Struck did his best to conceal his embarrassment.

"If anything," Michaelson added, "you're talking about a triple-positive. Quadruple if you want to count that bit about the ladies."

Struck smiled coyly and went on the offensive.

"I'm sorry, Michaelson. But I don't recall asking a *gal's gal* for her opinion."

This elicited a chuckle from all present fraternity brothers, but Struck knew he'd just suffered a small defeat.

As the fourth Struck to be attending Harvard, and armed with a less conspicuous set of book smarts than his predecessors or his peers, Struck always held the vague suspicion that some of his cohorts found him to be studying beyond his intellectual station. Struck was always bothered by this suspicion because he considered himself every bit as smart as the sharpest of his colleagues.

It all had to do with how you defined *smarts*. Struck would often find himself tripped up in the intricacies of language, waging a war on the wrong side of outdated grammatical laws. Words themselves could be his most frustrating enemies, sauntering about clumsily, obscuring the path between him and the elucidation of an idea.

But his ideas were sound. And it was the idea that mattered. Most people, Struck thought, tended to focus on all the wrong things. They got so caught up in details that they didn't see the big picture. Struck was the opposite. He hated details but was brilliant at the big picture. Hell, he was *master* of the damn thing. The vision of Gregory Xavier Struck was so spot on, in fact, that he could even see the big picture . . . of the big picture itself!

"How'd'ya like *that* double positive, Michaelson?"

HE'D GOTTEN BETTER. No doubt, he'd gotten better. That's why Fazo was confident. Everyone underestimated the president. That had been key to their victory four years ago, and it would be key to their victory tonight.

Through the tragedies in Orlando, Anaheim, New Jersey, and Fort Lauderdale and the early stages of Operation Freedom Fox, Struck's oratory skills had quietly improved, and much to the astonishment of the president's critics, he had begun to look and act downright . . . *presidential*. Chief executive was now a role he could wear comfortably. It suited him.

"Are we ready, Dennis?"

Political guru Dennis Fazo smiled at his charming protégé. Of all the politicians he'd worked with over the years, Struck was his finest work, and Fazo couldn't help but feel a bit of paternal pride about his boy's accomplishments.

"Your public awaits, Mister President."

The president smiled at his first lady, Daisy Struck, and she smiled back.

He winked.

"Let's get him."

The presidential entourage set off through a maze of hallways toward the soundstage. Like a mini Tour de France, they were lined with interns and assistants, all eager to get a glimpse of the president, to shout a greeting, to shake a hand. Greg Struck was in his element.

"Howdy." "Oh, thank you." "You have a lovely studio here." "From Chapel Hill, really? Always nice to meet a Tar Heel." "You're too kind." "Hi there."

As they turned the final corner, Dennis Fazo spotted the competing entourage, led by his former colleague Thomas Campman, who seemed thinner than when they'd last met. Leaner. Hungrier. More desperate. Campman was down, but not out. Fazo knew better than to underestimate his former partner in crime. Still, for the moment, it was nice to have the upper hand.

"Tom, what are you doing here?"

Campman smiled.

"Just figuring out how much longer before we actually start campaigning, Dennis. It's only fair to give the weaker player a head start."

"And what a generous head start it's been. Good evening, Senator."

The hands were shaken, the greetings exchanged, the ribs elbowed.

The senator seemed less rigid than his recent TV appearances might have suggested. But then, the cameras were not on. He'd stiffen up for sure once those cameras started rolling. Even his temporary and comparative fluidity could not disguise the fact that Phillips was ill at ease. Something wasn't right.

Yes, thought Fazo, there was definitely something off balance about Senator Ben Phillips, and while he couldn't tell exactly what that thing was, he sensed weakness. He smelled blood. He looked over at the president, who smiled back at him. Yep. Struck smelled it, too. His political instincts had only sharpened in the four years since his last campaign. He'd gotten a lot better.

DEBATE, TAKE 1

Well, apparently the senator doesn't think the American people know how to spend their own money. And that's a shame. It's a shame he doesn't trust *America*. And you know what, Billy? I do. I trust America with my life. The American people are the finest people in the world, and it's a shame the senator doesn't think so. Because I do. I trust . . . America."

America. He said the word as if he'd just invented it and wanted a prize for his efforts. Ben Phillips envied the president's shamelessness. As much as Ben prided himself on upholding higher rhetorical standards than his opponent, he realized the limitations of such standards. He had to pitch to a smaller strike zone.

But he was ready to pitch. Fiscal responsibility had become a strong Democratic topic, and Ben was eager to take this one on. If only the oily and aged Billy Mack could ask him a decent question.

"What do you say to that, Senator? We've heard you don't trust America. Is that true?"

"Billy, it is not true. I trust America with all my heart. But that's not the issue. You have to understand, we have a twenty-trillion-dollar debt. That's *twenty trillion dollars of debt,* and it's been created entirely by this administration. Now that's not gonna just disappear. And if the president thinks he can get votes by simply giving away all the government's money, promising tax cuts he can't afford—"

"Do you hear that, everybody? I'm sorry to interrupt, Billy, but I want everyone to hear what the senator just said: 'the government's money.' The *government's* money. Now, I want everyone at home to listen, because I think this is an important point. This is where the senator and I find ourselves in 'disagreement.' Because frankly, I think that money belongs to the people. To hardworking *Americans.* If the senator really cared for those Americans, he'd agree with me."

"Senator, do you care for the American people?"

What sort of question was that? Ben Phillips took a deep breath through his nose.

"Of course I do. But more than that, Billy, I *trust* them. I trust the American people to know the difference between an empty promise, and a realistic one. I trust them to know that a government cannot function without revenue, and that they cannot depend on all the services the government provides—on the military, on Medicare, on public education—they can't depend on these things if they are not willing to fund them. That's why giving huge tax breaks to the wealthiest Americans when we are in a time of crisis is flat-out irresponsible."

"Mr. President, a response."

Struck was shaking his head.

"Billy, I'm not going to pretend to understand the Washington jargon I just heard from Senator Phillips. I'm not. And you know why?"

Here, Struck smiled widely.

"Because I don't speak that *language.* Because, when I talk . . . and I don't know, maybe it's because I'm from the South"—he chuckled—"but, when I talk . . . it's the *truth.* In plain, simple *American.* Look, let's be honest here. You can use a lot of *words* to try and make a point. You can use *words* to say things like 'I think Americans are foolish,' or, 'I don't like America,' or, 'I want the terrorists to win,' and maybe that's what the senator is trying to say tonight. Maybe he's not. I'm not really sure, because I—Billy, I don't understand that Washington *doublespeak*.

"But I do know this: If the senator wants to come clean, if he wants to tell us why he hates America, then I say 'Go right ahead.' Now, I have a lot of things I want to say to your viewers tonight, but *I will yield the floor to him*. Because he's the candidate for the greatest office in the world, and if he has something awful to say then I think, by God, the American people should hear it. Tell it to us straight, Senator."

Ben Phillips couldn't believe his ears.

Suddenly it hit him. For the first time in almost forty years, he was being called Butt Fill-Up. And by the president! On national TV! The feelings were so similar that Ben couldn't believe it had taken him this long to make the connection. The injustice! The stupidity! Just like in high school, he felt a burning, indignant rage, and just like high school, he knew he had to suppress it at all costs. *He had to be presidential.*

"So, Senator Phillips, do you want to tell us about any anti-American feelings?"

Keep smiling. Sit straight. Be confident.

"Billy, this is ridiculous. I have no anti-American feelings. The very suggestion is preposterous."

Struck butted in. "Are you saying you're going back on your word?"

"Those are *your* words, Mister President, not mine. *I have no word to go back on!*"

Ben could imagine Campman grimacing. That was a sound bite for sure.

"So, Senator," said Billy, "for the record, you claim you are not anti-America?"

"No. What sort of question is that? Billy, I love my country with all my heart and all my . . ."

What was he saying?

He was defending himself against an imaginary charge. It was a rookie mistake of the worst kind—*another one!*—and he'd walked right into it. Now he was in a tailspin and couldn't seem to get out. Once more Ben Phillips took leave of his body. This time, he imagined himself at home, watching the debate on TV. He could see the strange stiff senator talking on the other side of the screen, but he was powerless to control what he was saying.

PETER WILLIAMS WISHED he had been watching the debate from a TV, rather than a live Web feed on his laptop, but at the moment, the young reporter had no choice. Curled up inside a sleeping bag in the home of a New Jersey Teen Buddy (whose parents observed an unnaturally early curfew), Peter watched Senator Phillips on his laptop screen and marveled at the sudden downward turn the conversation had taken. In his online journal, Peter would later write about the sad state of the Phillips campaign, and the poor moderating skills of Billy Mack.

Inside the studio, Ben's faltering could be seen in the tensed muscles and sweaty pores of his entourage, who watched on the dressing room TV. Melissa Phillips was gritting her teeth. Shelly Greenblatt had turned a bright shade of red. Ben's assistant Charlie was shaking his head back and forth. Sondra Reddi, the head of Phillips's New York office, was slowly plucking hairs from her arm.

Elayne Cohen-Campman was not watching the actual debate and therefore thought it to be going better than it was. Her lens was focused on the Phillips handlers watching the show, and she couldn't understand why they all seemed so dour. Ben wasn't doing that poorly, was he? Why did they all look like someone had just died? Elayne snapped away. As the seconds passed, she began to focus the camera on her husband, who watched the proceedings with a blank expression.

Tom Campman was trying very hard not to think about the

president's advisor Dennis Fazo but was thinking about him anyway. He kept imagining Fazo's stupid insidious smile. He felt it chasing him, taunting him. It made him sick. Campman knew he had to banish the former colleague from his thoughts, he had to focus again on his own man in the interview chair, his brilliant struggling senator. Campman sent a silent prayer up to the heavens: Please, God, just contain it. Don't let him mess it up too bad. We can still bounce back. Just please contain it. Please.

But the senator was still talking, and he wasn't at his best.

"I shouldn't need to defend myself," he blustered, "against allegations that seem to have been made up on the spot. Now, as I said, I was *hoping* we could talk about the state of the economy, but the president seems to prefer playing word games."

"Well, that's interesting," said Billy Mack, "because the president has accused *you* of doublespeak and now you're accusing the president of playing word games."

"*But he's the one that's doing it!*" the senator protested.

And as the words left his mouth, Ben Phillips felt as low as Ben Phillips had ever felt in his fifty-three years on the earth. He knew this evening would haunt him for the rest of his life. And he knew he was going to lose the election in a big, terrible, embarrassing way.

A RADIANT MESS

Where the hell was she? It was three o'clock. This was getting ridiculous. Maybe she forgot. Maybe she was blowing him off. Maybe she'd been kidnapped by aliens—or worse, Republicans. Perhaps by Republican aliens. Could such things exist? An interesting question. Maybe *she* didn't really exist.

No. That was stupid. Derek Kiley had taken this line of thought too far. Besides, he'd *talked* to Sharon Balis, hadn't he? That meant she *had* to exist. She just wasn't *existing* where she was supposed to be existing. *Where the hell was she?*

The front door of the Horse Sense Tavern in West Memphis, Arkansas, swung open and a tall woman in her forties with a long broad face walked in. She had one of those reverse hourglass figures—thin delicate arms and a Sumo waist—and a manner of walking that Derek Kiley would best describe as a "purposeful waddle." She waddled toward his table.

Could this be her? Kiley hoped not. After eleven interviews in four days, Sharon Balis was their last chance. And this certainly wouldn't work if she was homely.

The tall woman walked past him. It wasn't her. That was good. But this only brought Kiley back to his original problem: Sharon Balis had still not arrived.

He picked at the remains of his turkey sandwich for the two-hundredth time. He felt resentful again, right on cue. Having left all the phone messages he could politely leave in the two hours since they were supposed to have met, Derek Kiley found himself cycling through the same emotions and mundane activities in a continuous loop, trying to distract himself from the helplessness of his situation and the epic nature of his boredom.

He was a *speechwriter*. That was what was so absurd about the whole thing. Over the course of the last four years, young Derek Kiley had become one of the most sought-after speechwriters in the Democratic Party, and had joined the Phillips campaign with hopes of authoring the next "Ask not what your country can do for you." At this point, Kiley realized he'd be lucky if he managed an "I am not a crook." Since he joined the campaign, his serious contributions had been disappointingly few, and he'd been increasingly put upon of late to do what he liked to call "odd jobs." But nothing like this. This was the ultimate. Hunting down the senator's ex-girlfriends was nowhere in his job description.

Kiley blamed it on Ralph Sorn. Eight years earlier, Kiley had been an intern for Sorn at the DUA, and the dynamics of their relationship were cemented during that time. Although eight years and many accomplishments separated then from now, Sorn still treated Kiley like the intern.

And he encouraged the others to do the same. Mayweather and Campman had met Kiley for the first time under Sorn's watch, and Kiley was convinced that exposure to Sorn's condescension had influenced their treatment of him. There's no way Campman would have given him this task if it hadn't been for the contagious "let Derek do it" mind-set perpetuated by Ralph Sorn.

Six days ago, in that Kansas City hotel, Campman gave Kiley his marching orders and handed him the only document that could possibly be interpreted as "incriminating."

"Back in the beginning," he'd said, "we asked Ben to tell us about every girl he ever slept with, ever dated, ever played spin the bottle with, ever so much as held hands with."

Campman handed him a single sheet of paper.

"It's a short list."

Twelve names. Addresses. Phone numbers. A few e-mail addresses. Kiley thought the list to be more of a "dangerous resource" than an "incriminating document" (the Republicans and many in the press surely had their own version of this list), but he didn't quibble over Campman's previous linguistic choice. From this list sprang the next four days of his life. Kiley's assignment was to track down every non-platonic female in the history of Ben Phillips and to determine whether any had the potential to be the "it" girl for this election year.

The door to the Horse Sense Tavern swung open, and the next eligible female walked in. She was short, red-haired . . . and about eighty years old. Kiley smiled to himself. As flustered as he was, he had to laugh at his split-second consideration of this octogenarian. "Senator Slept with Grandma!" Now *that* would be a story! Derek Kiley still had a smile on his face when the door opened again, just a moment later.

When Sharon Balis finally entered the Horse Sense Tavern 124 minutes late, she didn't see the eighty-year-old woman pausing in the entryway and nearly knocked her over.

"Oh, my God, I'm sorry. I'm a worthless klutz, I don't know why I let myself out of the house. Are you okay?"

"You should be careful," the woman crowed at her.

"I know! I know I do. I'm so sorry," said Sharon Balis.

At this point she looked up, and her eyes met Kiley's. There was a sparkle of recognition.

Sharon Balis was a radiant mess. That was Kiley's first thought. Definitely beautiful. No doubt about that. She had long dark brown hair, a nice figure, and large childlike eyes that demanded affection and made you instantly want to provide for their owner. Kiley read Sharon as the sort of woman who drew men to her with a charming neediness that eventually drove those same men away. He wasn't completely wrong.

"Are you Mr. Kilbourne?"

"Yes, please sit down," Kiley replied.

"I'm so sorry I'm late. I can't believe no one's shot me yet. I mean, you probably want to shoot me, right?"

Kiley thought it was an odd thing to say, but he smiled and responded, "No, no, that's fine."

Sharon leaned in and half-whispered, "It's my son!"

"I'm sorry?"

"He crashed his car."

"My god."

"Yeah, terrible. Terrible."

Kiley shifted into conciliatory mode.

"I'm so sorry."

"Well, yeah . . ."

"Wow."

"Yeah, the insurance finally came through last week, and Chester told him we'd go shopping for a new car today, but I wasn't aware he'd said that. . . ."

"I'm sorry?"

"Chester's my boyfriend."

"I mean the accident."

"Oh, that was last month. But the thing is, my maternal services had been *promised* for today without my consent, and this caused a whole big stink, and Chester was being a major jerk, because, of course—*of course!*—there's no way he could have possibly just *forgotten to tell me*. No, of course it was my fault, and that—ha!—that caused a little discussion, you know?" She sighed. "Then he started chasing me and blah, blah, blah . . . it was almost an hour before I could sneak back into the garage and get the car and . . . well . . ."

She seemed to be searching for an end to her story in Kiley's befuddled face.

"I'm very sorry I'm late, Mr. Kilbourne. You have my humblest, humblest apologies."

So, she had some domestic issues. Discouraging, thought Kiley, but not a deal breaker, at least not yet.

"No problem," he said. "I'm just glad that you're here and that we can talk."

"Well, you know, anything for Ben." She laughed nervously.

Kiley took a breath and then launched into his spiel.

"As I said on the phone, the reason I wanted to speak with you is that we've become concerned about certain actions taken recently by Dennis Fazo and the president's reelection people."

This wasn't a lie. Phillips's advisors were *always* concerned about "certain actions" taken by Fazo and the Republicans. Kiley had given this speech eleven times already, and it had been carefully crafted to lead the interviewee but never directly deceive her.

"Opposition research. Naturally, they're looking for dirt, and they've been thorough about it. They've questioned Senator Phillips's former employers, girlfriends, acquaintances, probably barbers and dentists for all I know. As you can imagine, these are sneaky guys, and they're out for blood. So in order for us to protect the senator, we need to stay one step ahead. We can't afford to have them find something out before we do."

"How can I help?" Sharon asked.

"For now . . . just answering questions."

First Kiley asked about the past. Sharon had dated Ben Phillips in college at Oklahoma State. She was a sophomore, he was a junior. She fell in love, he never quite did. Ben was the one to call it quits. Was he ever inconsiderate? No, never. Did he ever cheat? No, never. Did he ever do anything wrong? Anything at all? No, never. Not Ben. He was the perfect gentleman.

Dammit, thought Kiley. Sharon's answers were maddeningly typical.

The senator was a Goody Two-shoes of the worst kind. He was sensitive, caring, thoughtful, and respectful. What's worse, any girl who went out with him more than a few times usually fell in love with him. When asked about their past relationship, most of these former girlfriends would sigh and say something winsome like, "Ah, Ben..." The senator never put sex ahead of friendship, never betrayed anyone's trust, and seemed to be the most skilled breaker-upper in the history of Western dating. None of his past flames held any grudge. How wonderful. How amazing. How terribly boring. The diary of a monk couldn't have been less sordid. There were no past iniquities to mine. Any scandal would have to be created from scratch. But how? And with who?

And what of this Sharon Balis? The more she spoke, the more grounded and intelligent she seemed, but Kiley couldn't shake his initial impression that there was something unstable about her. Could he be imagining it?

"Have you been contacted by anyone in the Republican Party?"

"I've been contacted by a couple reporters, but no one political, I don't think."

"Are you sure? Can you be sure they were all just reporters?"

"I don't know. No. I mean, there weren't *that* many, but whenever I was contacted, I'd just say, 'Yes, I dated Ben in college, but that's in the past and it's nobody's business.' So, who knows? There were no long conversations, if you get what I'm saying. Why? Do you think they were *undercover agents*?"

She said the last bit with a playful lilt in her voice.

"I don't know," said Kiley, "but for everyone's safety, we want to make sure the senator's old friends are not taken advantage of. Now what would you say if you were contacted by one of the president's people?"

"What do *you* think I'd say? I'm not gonna do something that's gonna hurt Ben."

"Okay, okay. Good. I just have to ask," said Kiley. "Now what if you were contacted by someone who asked you to do something to *help* Ben?"

"Who?"

"Someone you didn't know."

Sharon bit her tongue. "Mmm. Well obviously, I'm not going to trust a reporter or anyone who's on the president's side, so I'm assuming you're talking about someone claiming to be a Democrat."

"Okay."

"Well, what am I being asked to do?"

"What do you think they might ask you?"

Kiley realized from the look Sharon shot at him, that he couldn't get away with being so evasive. She was smart. All these women had been smart. The senator liked smart.

"Okay. It could be anything. Let's say they asked you to lie about your past with the senator, to twist the truth somehow."

"In a way that would *help* him . . . ?"

"Yeah."

"I'm not really sure how that would work."

"We're just speaking hypothetically here."

Sharon looked him in the eye and smiled. Kiley felt suddenly drawn to her.

"Look, Mr. Kilbourne, there are too many variables up in the air here. Obviously, I'd have to be careful who to trust, I'd have to think that whatever I was doing would actually be helping Ben . . . if you're asking would I let some Dennis Fazo goon trick me into screwing up Ben's campaign, the answer is no . . . *but* . . . if you're asking me whether I'd take action to help Ben . . . if I was sure I wasn't being tricked. . . ."

"Yes?"

A mischievous look spread across her face for half a second.

"Mr. Kilbourne, I know it's probably not what you want to hear, but I might do it. If I knew I was helping Ben, I'd lie, sure. I would . . . well . . . I might do a lot of things, I guess. *If* they'd help Ben.

"But don't worry. I'm not a sucker. And I'd never do anything to screw up your campaign. Besides, I don't think any of these scenarios are very realistic, do you?"

"I just need to ask. You understand."

Kiley did his best to exude nonchalance as he finished up the interview, but inside he was churning with a great mixture of excitement and fear. He realized he'd found someone with the potential to take this thing forward, and forward it would go for better or worse. He hadn't liked the idea to begin with, but now he was complicit as could be. *He* had been the one to the find her. *He* had done it. Derek Kiley. And no one else.

Certainly there were many questions still to be answered. Whether Sharon was exactly what Campman wanted remained to be seen, and whether the senator himself would even agree to the plan was highly doubtful. But that afternoon, as Derek Kiley left the Horse Sense Tavern, he was sure about one thing: Sharon Balis had been worth the wait.

GETTING HOME

On top of it all, the plane was delayed. There was a thunderstorm in New York City the night of the infamous Billy Mack debate, and the Phillips entourage found itself grounded at JFK for two hours. The senator spent much of his time chatting up airport employees and waiters at the Carmel O'Flanagan's pub, where the campaign staff ate a late dinner.

Elayne Cohen-Campman was amazed at the senator's rapport with the airport workers. They were a mixed bunch (Republicans, Democrats, and Independents), but Ben Phillips seemed to make more than a few converts during his stay, answering questions from all comers. He honestly cared about these people, whether they supported him or not, and it showed. Elayne found it hard to believe this was the same man who couldn't connect with the larger electorate, the same man who'd just been made a fool of on national TV. If only the rest of the country could see him as she saw him tonight at the airport, they'd surely feel as she did. Elayne gripped her Canon ProDigi 3000 tightly and snapped away.

By the time the group was up in the air, everyone was so tired that the discussions on postdebate spin and the next two days in Washington were shorter than they might have been otherwise. The Democratic talking points were predictable. The Phillips team accused the president of using school-yard tactics to evade the issues, and proclaimed Ben Phillips the clear victor both on actual policy debate and on style. But everyone knew it was a tough sell. The pundits and the online polls were already declaring *The Billy Mack Show* a major Struck victory.

Campman was tempted to force the senator's hand on the scandal idea that very night but decided to hold off. Ben was tired. The wounds would still be fresh tomorrow, and the senator's mind, hopefully, more open.

HECTOR ELIZONDO HAD been waiting at Reagan National Airport for two and a half hours, and had to pee badly. Security was tight at Reagan, so he couldn't leave the car unattended, and he didn't have time to drive elsewhere and come back. He knew the boss's plane was delayed but didn't know for how long. By 1:00 A.M., the pressure on Hector's bladder was intense, and by 1:23 A.M., he was starting to consider drastic measures.

When Hector finally caught sight of the boss at 1:46 A.M., his relief at the prospect of imminent urinary discharge was tremendous. The boss had his wife with him, and one other man, the fat one.

"Ralph lives on California Street, so we'll be giving him a ride."

Campman didn't want to make a habit of carpooling with Sorn, but it was late, and he did live in the same neighborhood. Just this once, he thought.

For his part, Hector wasn't thrilled at the prospect of making an additional stop, either, but he knew it would only be a matter of a few minutes. He could make it.

The fat one would be sitting in front, which meant Hector had to clear his possessions off the seat. He scurried around to the opposite door and quickly rearranged the space. As he moved, he was aware of the liquids shifting within his body. He wedged the bag with the tape recorder in between his seat and the driver's-side door. There'd be no time to double-check the placement of the recorder within the bag.

As the Lincoln's engine awoke from slumber, the horns of Shirley Bassey's "Goldfinger" announced their presence on the eight-speaker stereo system.

When Hector first decided to become a double agent, he had visited the gift shop of the World Spy Museum on F Street and purchased their best-selling recording, *Tunes to Spy 2*. It was a collection of classic spy themes from movies and contained no less than five James Bond title songs. Hector took an immediate liking to the CD, and it had been in constant rotation on the Lincoln's stereo ever since. At first Hector only played it when he was alone, to put himself in the mood, but Campman seemed to enjoy the music the one time he heard it, so Hector deemed it safe to play, regardless of his boss's presence. Hector even took some guilty pleasure in the idea of playing spy music for the very person he was spying on.

The fat one seemed to like "Goldfinger."

"Haven't heard this in a while."

The fat one smiled at Hector, but Hector didn't notice because he was too busy experiencing a sharp pain in his bladder. Oh, crap, he thought. Hector had never felt a sharp pain in his bladder before, and he was pretty sure it was bad news. His foot crashed down on the accelerator, and the car sped off into the gloomy Washington night.

"Sanskrit is good. Have you tried them before?"

The boss was continuing a conversation he'd started before he got in the car. *This could be big.* Hector knew he'd have to focus despite his pain. His left gloved hand snaked its way into the bag at his side. Fortunately, the recorder was within easy reach.

"Yeah, they're okay. Actually, what they do really well is sea bass."

"Is that the one they serve with the couscous and that cranberry thing?"

"I think it's pomegranate."

They were talking fast now. Hector pressed record.

The Lincoln Town Car merged onto the Washington Memorial Parkway, and Hector slammed on the brakes. They were sitting in bumper-to-bumper traffic.

"What the hell is this?" asked the fat one. "You're not allowed to have traffic at two in the morning."

"It's construction," said the boss.

Hector began to sweat. He could deal with the flight delay. He could deal with making an extra stop. But construction! This was too much. He was tempted to loosen his belt but wasn't sure if that would help or hurt. He bit his lip and kept his white gloves on the wheel.

". . . but the best ever was in New York. My gay son's boyfriend is a chef—my son is gay, you know. It can be tough but we accept it and support him. . . ."

Elayne Cohen-Campman was resting her head on her husband's shoulder, falling in and out of consciousness, but she smiled to herself as she heard Ralph Sorn. She knew there was no better way to showcase your liberal credentials than to brag about your homosexual offspring.

". . . anyhow, his boyfriend, Freddie, is a chef at this place on Forty-sixth called Gastron, and he made us this lamb: butterfly cut, and he cooked it in about fifty cloves of garlic, enough to make your head spin. . . ."

The tires squealed. Hector Elizondo had swerved into the breakdown lane and was now driving very fast. The legality of this maneuver would have been questionable on a good day, but now it was downright criminal. He had no choice. The liquid-filled Mexican kept his eyes glued to the road in front of him. As he drove, he could tell he was recording some conversation of consequence but found himself unable to focus on the meaning of the words being said. Normally, he might have been able to pick out a few words here or there, but now his attention was focused on one thing at the expense of all others: He had to get to a bathroom.

Campman marveled at Hector's driving. He was a maniac, but he was skilled. Amid nighttime construction, going seventy miles an hour in the breakdown lane, the Lincoln zoomed past a police car, and, unbelievably, the policeman did not given chase. Perhaps he'd been looking away at just the right second. That wouldn't have surprised Campman. Hector's timing was impeccable.

The construction soon passed and Hector rocketed across the Theodore Roosevelt Bridge at ninety-two miles per hour, just as conversation shifted to crème brûlée.

Six minutes and thirty-five seconds later, his heart pounding, his face pale, his bladder about to explode, Hector pulled up in front of Ralph Sorn's town house on California Street. After the first drop-off, conversation ceased, and only three minutes later, Campman and his sleepy wife were dropped off at 2427 Kalorama Road.

"Good night, Hector."

"EeeeGoodnightyboss!"

He'd made it. Almost. After dropping off the boss, Hector double parked in front of a twenty-four-hour McDonald's, grabbed his bag, and ran inside.

It was a truly glorious urination. Birds perched themselves on Hector Elizondo's shoulder. Angels threw handfuls of rose petals from above. A choir sang. Trumpets sounded. Bells tolled.

It wasn't until five minutes later, when Hector left the bathroom and bought himself a burger, that he was able to reach inside his bag and remove the tape recorder. The red light was solidly lit. The tape heads were engaged. He pressed stop. Hector smiled. He had been recording. *He got it.*

CONVINCING

I t's August, Ben."

"I know. I know."

It was full court press once more. In the senator's living room, Shelly Greenblatt sat on one end of the sofa, Ralph Sorn on the other. Ozzie Mayweather sat on the ottoman, Derek Kiley sat on the chair near the TV, and Thomas Campman was standing. Melissa was in Georgetown, ten miles away. Ben Phillips was alone, and he was outnumbered.

"So who would be my alleged accomplice?" he asked.

Ben decided to consider this proposal the same way he'd consider a new piece of legislation. He'd take it apart, see how it worked, see *if* it worked, and then weigh the potential benefits and losses. He fully expected the proposal to crumble under close scrutiny.

"Remember Sharon Balis?" asked Campman.

"Sharon Balis?" Of course he did. "We dated in college. You talked to Sharon?" Ben was suddenly embarrassed.

Campman nodded. "She doesn't know anything yet. But from our conversation with her, from our understanding about her feelings toward you, we feel confident she can be persuaded to go along."

Derek Kiley felt dirty, hearing Campman talk about his conversation with Sharon Balis. A morally deviant plan is made up of many steps that may be individually quite innocent. Like words in a sentence, it is the connection that gives them meaning. However Kiley may have rationalized the innocence of his information-gathering trip as a solitary action, in the context of Campman's larger plan, it seemed much dirtier. Kiley swallowed hard as Campman continued.

"Here's the story, Ben. You and Sharon stayed friends, but gradually as the years went by, you lost touch. Then you ran into each other again, sixteen years ago in Oklahoma City. You talked. You had lunch. And at this time, as it just so happens, you were going through a rough spot with Melissa. This was the most painful time in your life. You were living with Melissa in the same house—for the kids, of course—but for all intents and purposes you were separated. You were *both* having doubts about your marriage. Both of you considered leaving, getting a divorce, seeking a new mate. You were both depressed, but no one knew about it, *because you were responsible.* And you knew the importance of keeping up appearances. For the kids' sake! You didn't tell anyone about this horrible anguish you were feeling—except for Sharon Balis. With Sharon you spoke of your marital problems and she counseled you, as a friend (and everyone needs a friend in times like those). What you didn't realize—what you were *too distraught* to realize—was that Sharon Balis was falling in love with you. And then one day, things went too far. . . ."

Campman laid it all out. Beat by beat. The history of the affair, Ben's confession, the painful late-night discussions with Melissa, the way the couple worked through it, and the way their marriage grew stronger as a result. Campman talked about how the information would be leaked to the press, how the story would break, and how the campaign would react.

Thomas Campman was a master storyteller. He covered every angle, examined every nuance, and left no scenario unexplored.

Derek Kiley was entranced. Even Shelly Greenblatt started to feel a twinge of hope penetrate his well-worn anxiety as he listened to Campman weave his story. Mayweather and Sorn, now both staunch converts to the plan, sat still and nodded their heads from time to time. After a while, Mayweather realized it was the longest he'd been in a room with Ralph Sorn and not heard the New Yorker speak.

For his part, Senator Ben Phillips kept a straight face and took it all in. Whenever he seemed about to ask a question, Campman would anticipate and address the concern before he had a chance to voice it.

As Ben's logistical challenges were disposed of one by one, the candidate found himself gravitating to emotional and spiritual objections, but soon even these were faltering under the weight of new doubts. Ben thought of his wife. He thought of his children, Jim and Stacy. Surely, *there* was good reason to pause! How could any father willingly subject his children to a scandal of this sort? How irresponsible!

Or was it? The kids were, after all, fully grown. While they had been brought up knowing the difference between right and wrong, like most political children they were hardly naïve. They'd matured into worldly, hard-nosed adults, not ones to be shaken by a little scandal—or even a medium-size scandal for that matter. And furthermore, were they told about Campman's crazy plan (not that they would be, of course, but still—), there was a high probability they'd actually be in favor of the thing (or at least *more* in favor than he). Wasn't Stacy the one who always accused him of being too nice? Too straightlaced? Too boring? And wasn't Jim always begging him for God's sake to just play dirty? Yes, bless his heart, thought Ben, Jim would probably love the stupid idea.

The senator did not mention these thoughts to Campman; he didn't need to. For whatever reason, his objections were resolving themselves within his brain, as if the damn things were secretly conspiring to meet Thomas Campman halfway.

As for Campman, he pressed on, bringing his whirlwind argument to a close.

"In the end, you come across as the guy with integrity," he said, "because you didn't hide anything your average American wouldn't have hid anyways, and you came clean as soon as it was brought up. It's far enough in the past, it won't blemish your recent record. There's really nothing you have now that you would lose."

"Except my soul," said Senator Ben Phillips.

Campman knelt down in front of him.

"Ben, you're a politician," he said, "you can get it back. Get elected and you can govern like the pope if you want. But get elected."

"Don't be stupid, Ben. Get elected," offered Sorn. Mayweather checked his watch. It had been twenty-two minutes since Sorn last spoke. Impressive.

"Look," said Campman, "the Lord's on your side here, Ben, and I mean in a 'big way,' if that makes a difference. Trust me. What do you lose? Nothing. What do you gain? *What do you gain?*"

Campman counted on his fingers.

"People see your intimate relationship with your wife. They see you as a guy who has struggled to defeat the most common problem an American man can face. They see you defending your privacy, defending your marriage, in short, being a man."

He paused now.

"Ben, they're gonna love you."

Campman was staring Ben straight in the eye, and Ben was staring right back.

To his amazement, Ben heard the little voice in the back of his head urging him on. That old reliable voice, that unfailing moral bungee cord, always snapping him back from one ethical compromise or another, was now, *unbelievably,* on Campman's side.

Do it, Ben! it said. *Do it, and you'll win!*

For whatever reason, he actually thought the plan could work.

Ben recognized the classic nature of the choice before him: Stick to your principles and lose, or bend them a bit and . . . well . . . perhaps win. Faced with a lifetime of similar choices, Ben had always taken the high road, and he'd never regretted it. But this election was different. At every occasion he had tried to do the right thing, and at every occasion it had cost him. To think, the press was still talking about his alleged "character issues"!

The little voice in Ben's head was insistent. It wanted to go forward. It only needed the proper rationalization. He found it.

Could America afford for him to bend his principles just this once? Yes. Yes, it could. The republic would still stand. But . . .

Could America afford another four years of Gregory Struck as president?

Hell, no.

Ben blinked.

"I'd need to convince Melissa first."

Campman smiled.

"Of course. Of course. And if you need any help . . ."

Ben shook his head. "I need to be the one."

"Of course."

Mayweather, Sorn, and Campman were all trying to hold back smiles. They didn't want to overreact to this tentative yes, for fear of startling the senator. It was like convincing a small child to dive into a swimming pool. Be gentle. No sudden moves.

But, of course, Campman couldn't resist putting in his extra two cents, wrapping up the argument in a way he knew would have an effect.

"You'll be amazed how many levels this works on, Ben. You think it won't help you with women voters, but I think it will. You'll get mystique. You'll be desirable. Sexy. Why, any man who could so easily get a Sharon Balis to fall for him . . . just think about it." And then one final pause. "It'll make you cool, Ben."

A million new voices inside the senator's head were suddenly screaming no. Yellow caution flags were being waved. Somewhere on his shoulder, a little cartoon angel shook its head disapprovingly. Ben Phillips ignored them all. And for one brief moment, for a man who'd been feeling a lot like Butt Fill-Up lately, the idea of being "cool" didn't sound half bad.

CONVINCING MELISSA HAD not been as hard as Ben thought it would. But then, he'd really given her the works. All day he'd played the "I'm secretly despondent about something" card, only to reveal the source of his angst later in the evening when they were about to go to bed. By the time Ben finished spilling his guts, she didn't know what hit her.

What was he so upset about?

He was upset because of what he'd have to ask her to do.

What could be so bad? Didn't he know she'd do anything for him?

But this was something terrible. Truly terrible.

It couldn't be that bad, could it?

He cried. He actually cried. And to his credit, while his presentation may have been over the top, it was not fraudulent. Ben simply took real emotions he was feeling and allowed them to fly freely until they achieved the desired effect. It was a method politicians had been using for centuries. Not lying. Not acting. Just . . . amplifying. The whole thing was cathartic in a way.

And when it was over, to his disbelief, Melissa said yes.

OUR INTEREST

The full ramifications of her talk with Ben did not hit Melissa Phillips until the next day, when she was in the middle of giving a speech. She'd been thinking about last night nonstop, thinking about "Campman's plan," but until this point her thinking had been limited to certain aspects of the plan and not others. Now suddenly these others were confronting her in all their ugliness.

The troubling thoughts first crept into her brain during that bit about "shared international responsibility," and by the time she'd hit the point about "the economic burden on our grandkids," she knew the meddlesome things were not going away anytime soon. Melissa found it particularly hard to focus through the last third of her speech, and she worried that the senior citizens of the Lavender Bark Center for Mature Living might notice her lack of composure. More unsettling thoughts, each one more perplexing than the one preceding it, bounced about inside her head through the question-and-answer period, but again, to her credit, she managed to remain on point. In fact, her only slipup came in the mingling aftermath of the

function, during which time Melissa was pretty sure she'd told a befuddled group of seniors that there was, in her opinion, "too much
deviant sex in nursing homes."

She had to get Ben on the phone. They needed to talk. But what
would she say to him? Her first impulse was to say she couldn't go
through with it. But could she? Was she giving him an absolute no?
She could say she was having second thoughts; that was true. But
had she even been permitted to have *first* thoughts? She realized now
that she hadn't, and she wondered: *Can one have second thoughts if
one hasn't thought about something a first time?*

Melissa had never seen Ben so upset as he was the previous night.
That was why she hadn't probed too deeply, why she'd said yes so
swiftly. Ben was the love of her life, and he was in pain. She needed
to fix that pain. As she looked into his watery gray eyes, she wanted
nothing more than to save him. She'd make any sacrifice, fight any
foe, bear any burden, and do it gladly if only it would help the man
she loved.

But what a thing to ask of your wife! She'd found the idea ridiculous when Ben first mentioned it, but she'd taken great pains to justify it to herself for his sake. Now Melissa's justifications seemed
transparent, and the more she mulled it over, the more she began to
consider something she'd not considered for some time: *her interests.*

For as long as she could recall, *his* interest and *her* interest were
not separate things. It had always been *"our* interest." If something
was good for one, it was invariably good for the other. This wasn't to
say husband and wife didn't make sacrifices, but these were never
unreasonable and were always undertaken willingly. Melissa's teaching meant Ben had to sacrifice a full-time campaign partner. His
campaigning meant she had to sacrifice . . . well, quite a lot. But
these were happy sacrifices, because they were both working for a
cause they believed in. Getting to the White House was in their mutual interest.

But, this is a real sacrifice, thought Melissa. And it affected *her* interests very differently than *his.* He was the one who would be having

the imaginary affair. She'd be the wife who was cheated on. They were hardly equivalent roles. Hers brought with it a whole series of presumptions that made her uncomfortable: presumptions about her status in the marriage, about her aptitude as a wife, her talents as a lover. Just thinking about it made her queasy. It wasn't a role any proud wife and mother would want to play.

What really bothered Melissa was how easily she'd been convinced to play it. She'd been willing to compromise her honesty, her marriage, and her reputation without so much as a second thought.

A second thought. Yes, that was it. *She was having second thoughts.* Her first thought (which she now remembered) was that the scandal idea was in their mutual interest. That was why she'd said yes. Her second thought, however, which she experienced at the Lavender Bark Center for Mature Living, was that, while this scandal idea might, in some obtuse way, be in *Ben's* interest, it was most definitely not in *hers.* This second thought made her wonder how many times she'd mistaken "*his*" for "*ours.*"

Melissa needed to be alone. She marveled at how difficult being alone had become. Even in the limousine, driving back to Arlington, she wasn't alone. There was her assistant, her driver, and her Secret Service agent. Three people too many, she thought.

Melissa began to feel claustrophobic, and with each passing moment, that feeling built on itself. Her head pounded. She became angry. She realized the feelings she'd been having that morning were more than just second thoughts. She truly *hated* Campman's idea. It was ugly, it was dishonest, and it was bound to get them all in trouble. It was, in every conceivable way, dreadful, and she had to stop it.

The limousine had scarcely driven half a mile when Melissa asked the driver to pull over. He seemed surprised by her request but obeyed, and within moments they were on the side of the road. Melissa Phillips opened her door, stepped out of the car, and walked briskly to the adjacent woods, her brown hair floating upward in the unexpected breeze. The forest crunched with every step of her tan leather pumps, and she felt instantly invigorated by the fresh air. She walked and did not look back.

Fifty paces from the car, experiencing some approximation of privacy, she pulled out her cell phone and pressed the number one.

THE MEETING WITH the Democratic brass had just ended, and the buffet was being attacked. At any other time, Senator Ben Phillips might not have answered his phone. He'd turned it on only moments before it started to ring.

"Hey Mel, how did it go?"

As he listened, the senator's face changed, and Thomas Campman noticed immediately. There was a problem; he could tell. And it didn't surprise him. Everything had been going too damn smoothly anyhow.

"What do you mean?" Ben asked the caller.

Campman was used to problems. They were an expected and necessary phenomenon. They kept you honest. In fact, Campman was of the opinion that any plan that came together too effortlessly in the early stages was probably headed for trouble down the road. If you had no problems, it probably meant you were blind to some obvious detail that was going to screw you later.

Yes, it had all been going too smoothly. In the last twenty-four hours, Campman had flown to Memphis and back, he'd met with Sharon Balis, and he'd convinced her to play a part in his little scandal plan. Campman liked her. She was pretty, she was smart, and not quite as flaky as Kiley had warned. She quickly understood what was at stake and became quite enthusiastic (almost *too* enthusiastic) when Campman laid out the plan for her. She wanted very much to be of use. He was confident she would work nicely.

"Could you hold on one sec?" Ben said into the phone.

He eyed Campman and got up from his seat stiffly. Campman rose as well. Ben started for the exit and Campman followed, weaving his way through the crowded room like a fish in charcoal pinstripes. The two men escaped out the door and into the hallway. They were followed by two Secret Service agents.

"Look, Mel, I've had second thoughts, too. Of course, I have. I mean, I've agonized, and I . . . but the thing is . . ."

"Would you gentlemen mind giving us some space?" asked Campman. The two Secret Service men nodded and walked in opposite directions down the empty hallway.

". . . and sometimes you need to do things you may not feel comfortable with at the time, but they ultimately serve a higher . . ."

Campman rubbed his teeth with the tip of his tongue. What had he been expecting anyway? Ben, Melissa, and Sharon all signing on within thirty-six hours of each other? It was too good to be true, and Campman knew it. But he also knew Melissa could be brought into line. He was aware that most people took her for the independent political spouse, but he felt confident she was really the old-fashioned type at heart. She'd stand by her man. No doubt about it.

"She doesn't want to do it," said Ben, his hand over the phone.

"Tell her it's too late."

"Look, honey, in any case, Tom says it's too late."

"The wheels are already in motion."

"It's just, the wheels are already in motion on this thing . . . well, I'm not lying to you. I'm just telling you what Tom told me . . . What? Yeah, he's right here."

The handoff was made, and Campman took over the call.

"Melissa, what can I do for you?"

She sounded out of breath, clearly more agitated than he'd ever heard her, but—typical Melissa—she remained logical and straight to the point. *Why couldn't they call this thing off? If it hadn't happened yet, what was the big deal?*

"You're right," said Campman, "it's not impossible. Inconvenient, but that's no problem. If you say no, we kill it, that's fine. But first, let's just be sure we're doing that for the right reasons."

Ah, here it comes! Ben knew if anyone could convince Melissa other than himself it would be Campman. The well-groomed advisor licked his lips, as if to confirm Ben's thought.

"I'm actually happy to be able to talk to you about this," he continued. "Now, you're probably worried how *you're* gonna end up looking, right? . . . Well, it's a concern, and that's totally understandable. I mean, no one wants to be the"—Campman spoke quietly, conscious of the hallway's echo—"the *spurned wife.* Am I correct?"

Watching from the sidelines, Ben Phillips looked like someone who desperately wanted to fidget, but whose fidgeting skills had been beaten out of him long ago. He could only listen, look, and learn.

"Well, the whole point is: *This thing is gonna work,*" said Campman. "We wouldn't do it otherwise. And when it works, you're gonna come off better than anyone."

Ben was nodding.

"Of course you are! Are you kidding me?"

Campman felt a vibration on his thigh. It was his cell phone. He would ignore the call, of course, but he wondered who it was. Should he check the number?

"Just think about it—" he continued.

"Ben!" said a booming voice.

The doors of the conference room had burst open, and Tony Watson, the leader of the DUA, was extending his rather large hand.

"Could you hold on, Melissa?"

"Ben, we're gonna take off," said Watson. "What time are you guys heading out today?"

While Ben answered Tony Watson, Campman looked at his government issue Verizon 2900 SuperG Secure cell phone. The incoming number was an 870. Somewhere in Arkansas. Campman knew his area codes. He also had a bad feeling.

"So long, Tony, you'll have to excuse me." Campman indicated his cell phone juggling and answered his own device.

"Hello."

"Is this Tom?"

He recognized the voice immediately.

"Yes, is this . . . ?"

"Sharon Balis," the woman answered.

Shit, thought Campman, taking great pains to maintain his smile.

"Could you hold one moment please?" he said.

Tony Watson finished up his good-bye: "Have a good trip, gentlemen. We're gonna turn this thing around, I just know it."

"So long, Tony."

"Take care, Tony."

Campman quickly returned to Ben's phone.

"Melissa, I'm sorry. Hang on just another minute."

He waited as Tony and his entourage walked off down the main hallway. Slowly. Slowly. Slowly. Just a few more seconds and they would be gone.

Campman reached for his own phone.

"You're not supposed to call this number except in an emergency. I'm gonna have to call you back."

"You can't call me back," said Sharon, "I have to go. Besides I'm on a public phone."

"Well, you're just gonna have to hold a minute."

"That's fine, but—"

Phone switch.

"Sorry about that, Melissa. Look, you come out of this looking better than anyone. By talking about your past problems . . ."

Senator Ben Phillips's eyes darted up and down the hallway. Tony Watson's crew had long since hit the stairs, and the two Secret Service men were out of earshot. The coast was clear.

". . . you come out as a survivor, a champion. You've faced a hardship and overcome it. It makes you a hero!"

Melissa didn't refute his main point but did call him on his exaggeration. She wasn't about to become a hero because of this.

"Are you kidding?" said Campman. "The whole point is that you were *both* having trouble. It wasn't just Ben. You considered straying, too, but you stood by your man! You become a role model for the resilient woman who kept her family together, who took a weak thing and made it stronger! Don't tell me you're not the hero here."

His phone was vibrating again, same Arkansas number.

"Melissa, I need to give you to Ben for a sec."

Phone switch.

"Hey, Mel," said Ben.

"Yeah?" said Campman on his phone.

"My time ran out so I had to call again," said Sharon.

Ben nodded, listening to Melissa on his cell.

On Campman's cell, Sharon Balis was upset: "Look, I can't do the plan," she said.

"*What?* Why not?"

"He makes a good point though," said Ben.

"I'm in a tough spot with Chester," said Sharon.

"Chester?"

"My boyfriend. Look, I'm sorry, I really want to help, but now is just the wrong time."

"Of course, it's changing history," said Ben calmly, "but the whole point is that it's for the better."

"Chester and I are going through some serious issues, and this whole scandal thing would just mess everything up."

Campman was tense. He had nothing. Well, maybe . . .

"Leave him," he said. "Break up today. We start the plan tomorrow."

"I can't just do that."

"Well, what *can* you do? How can we make this work?"

"It's not *gonna* work right now. I'm sorry. I've given this a lot of thought."

Ben looked up.

"Tom, she wants to talk to you."

"I can't! I have to—"

Ben was frustrated with the phone back and forth. Whoever Campman was talking to could surely wait. He grabbed Campman's phone and said, "I'm sorry. Mr. Campman's simply going to have to call you back."

"*No, no, no!*" said Campman grabbing it back. "No, I can talk now, just a sec. . . ."

He mouthed to Ben, "*It's Sharon!*"

"Sharon?"

"Shhh!" Campman said, covering Ben's phone. "Here, take this for a sec."

The two men switched phones.

"Melissa! I'm sorry. It's just not a good time to talk. Can we call you back in a minute or two?"

Meanwhile, Ben held Campman's phone tentatively and slowly put it to his ear. "Sharon?"

Campman pulled the phone down from the candidate's ear and mouthed ferociously: "Do NOT talk to her!"

"No, no, that's good, Melissa. And I understand . . . and we've already thought of that. Yes. I hope Ben told you we have every angle covered. Remember, we'd have no reason to do any of this if we didn't think it would make you look good!"

Campman kept listening on the Melissa phone but grabbed the Sharon phone and spoke to her, his tone of voice reversing itself once again:

"I really don't understand the problem. You gave us your word—"

"I'm not leaving Chester. And as long as I'm with him, this is not going to work. I'm sorry, but I have to go."

She hung up. Sharon Balis had cut off communication, and that was that. Campman couldn't believe it. His insides were burning with rage, but he knew he couldn't let it show. He kept the phone to his ear. "One moment," he said to the dial tone and switched over to Melissa.

"Melissa, I agree absolutely," he said, "and you have to trust me that we are not going to go about this in a haphazard manner. Everything is planned out, everything will be done in a way you'll be comfortable with . . . well, *relatively* comfortable with . . . Yes, I understand . . . none of us *wants* to do this, but I hate to say: it might be just the thing we need. I mean, it could make the difference. . . . Yes, I truly believe so. . . . Yeah? . . . Okay, good . . . Now, I need to give you back to Ben. We have a plane to catch. But we'll be talking a lot about this. Hopefully not on the phone anymore, but just in person, okay? . . . And you have a safe trip, too."

As Ben Phillips took the phone back from Campman, he witnessed his advisor making one last phone switch.

"Yes, okay," said Campman into his own cell phone. "Yes, you win, Sharon. That's fine, as long as it doesn't deviate from the main plan. . . . I'm sorry? . . . well, good! I'm glad that's not a problem. Let's not argue about the little stuff from here on out, okay? All right, and remember, now that we've solved this tiny issue . . . phone silence. No more calls. Okay? . . . Okay, you take care as well. Good luck."

TAMPA BAY ABLUTIONS

O
h, Lord my God, Jesus, and all spirits inhabiting this world and others, thank you for my family, my health, and all your plentiful gifts. . . . And if you'll excuse my bluntness, I'd like to know what's going on. If you're just putting challenges in my path, then fine, I'll figure something out, I'll overcome them, BUT . . . if you're trying to send me some other message by having Balis turn into a flake . . . Look, I'll ask you again: *Is this a trick?* Do you actually want me to go through with this plan or are you just yanking my chain?"

From the balcony of his Tampa hotel, Campman could see two lanes of traffic illuminated by the streetlights. A convertible passed. Then a compact. It was a busy stretch of road even at this late hour. Campman licked his lips.

"Okay," he mumbled. It was his standard volume for prayer, louder than a whisper, but just barely. "If an SUV passes my line of vision on the count of five, I'll know you're not trying to trick me, I'll know this challenge is nothing more than a challenge—and I'll overcome it. If there's no SUV . . . all bets are off."

He paused for a moment, as if waiting for the Almighty to respond, then began his count.

"One."

A van passed.

"Two."

Nothing.

"Three."

A compact. A sedan. A minivan.

"Four."

A large sedan. A midsize sedan.

"FIVE!"

What the hell was that? Something passed, but it wasn't an SUV, at least not like any he'd seen before. But then it wasn't your typical station wagon, either. It was something in between.

"Damn hybrids."

Campman pursed his lips.

"Okay, I'm sorry, I get it," he said, although he wasn't sure he did.

"It's a faith thing, isn't it?" He was guessing now but continued his line of reasoning, gradually warming to it.

"You want me to have faith. You don't want me to question you. You don't want me thinking you're trying to trick me. Well, okay, I'll say it: *I'm sure you wouldn't deliberately try to trick me. . . .* Even if you *were* still pissed. . . . You'd just punish me directly. Because you're straightforward. . . ."

But that wasn't right.

"Straightforward . . . except that you're totally fucking obtuse, what with your 'working in mysterious ways' and all. . . . But clearly you *have* been punishing me. Because look where we are. . . ."

He was going in circles, and sarcasm wasn't helping. Campman's body tensed and then relaxed in defeat.

"Oh, shit. Shit. Shit. Shit. . . . *How do we do this without a girl?*"

———

INSIDE THE HOTEL room, Elayne Cohen-Campman was brushing her teeth and staring at herself in the bathroom mirror. Elayne had always been captivated by her image and as a child could spend hours examining her every nook and cranny in front of her mother's looking glass. It wasn't vanity, or at least she hoped it wasn't. She was just mesmerized by seeing her form as other people saw it. The human body always held great mystery for Elayne, and she thought it only natural to scrutinize the specimen she was most familiar with. She would move her joints so she could watch the muscles flexing beneath her skin, she'd examine the landscape of her pores until she was intimately familiar with each cell, and she'd look so long and so hard at her body that after a while, she could swear it was possible to see straight through the external physical structure and into her soul itself, the very center of her being. From there, she would draw conclusions about her mental state, she would diagnose ills, and prescribe treatments. Mirror time was Elayne's preferred mode of self-analysis.

On this night, Elayne saw excitement in the quivering divot above her lip, and she smiled, making the divot momentarily disappear. It had been over a week since she'd joined up with the campaign, and her initial giddiness had scarcely waned. She'd spent most of the last six months in Bombay, photographing the making of a new Bolly-wood epic by famed director Raja Pungati, and while her time abroad was thrilling and enlightening (Pungati's musical epic, a cheery re-working of Bergman's *The Seventh Seal* set in ancient times, featured a cast of Bollywood's finest actors and was filmed in numerous lo-cales throughout Maharashtra, Gujarat, and West Bengal), Elayne was happy to be back in the United States, working on a project of national and worldwide significance.

Elayne was particularly excited to be photographing Senator Ben Phillips. He'd always been a favorite politician of hers, and she found him to be visually striking to boot. Now, most people wouldn't have given the senator's Midwestern good looks a second thought, but Elayne found something mysterious and elusive in his high cheek-bones and cloudy gray eyes. She had yet to see a picture that com-pletely captured the man.

This is not to say that any one picture could completely capture the essence of any one person. Elayne felt every picture was like a piece of a puzzle, each piece telling some truth about its subject. The bet-ter pictures told the bigger truths. And while no picture could tell the whole truth, she believed the rarest of pictures could come close. These rarest of pictures Elayne would describe as "Big T" photos. They told one really big truth.

For all his press, Elayne had never seen a Big T photograph of Senator Phillips. She wanted very much to take one.

Elayne spit and then continued to brush. She was the model of oral hygiene.

Looking closer at her face, Elayne read concern in the lines of her lower forehead, and it made her think of the previous morning. Tom was meeting Greenblatt, Kiley, Mayweather, and Sorn at the sena-tor's house. He had not asked her to join them, but she had invited herself. She reasoned that although the troops may have been sta-tioned in D.C. for the day, this was still clearly a campaign meeting. Didn't that mean she should have access? Besides, it would give her the chance to see the senator's Arlington home. Tom reluctantly agreed. Once in Arlington, however, he told her the men needed to speak in private, and Elayne had to content herself with touring the rest of the grounds on her own, taking pictures of such fascinating subjects as the senator's bedroom and the senator's garbage dis-posal.

She knew none of this was a big deal, but Elayne couldn't help be-ing put off by the men's secrecy. She hadn't realized there were going to be meetings she wouldn't be allowed to attend. She had, after all, been promised total access.

While that morning's exclusion was an isolated event, it wasn't the first time Elayne had felt an air of secrecy among the men of the inner circle. Maybe she was just imagining things, but her gut told her otherwise. She knew she couldn't let it worry her, but she resolved to stay vigilant, lest she find herself locked out of more meetings.

She spit in the sink, examined her teeth one last time, and left the bathroom.

Tom was on the balcony, probably mumbling away, thinking she didn't know. She opened the sliding glass door and exited into the heavy Florida air. She approached her husband from behind and wrapped her arms around his waist.

"So, are you going to tell me what the big secret was with yesterday's meeting?"

Campman tilted his head back on her shoulder.

"At the senator's house?"

"Mmm hmm."

"Just some stuff the senator is sensitive about, things he'd like to remain private. No big deal, really."

"So, you're not going to tell me?" teased Elayne.

"The man could be president, you know? You don't want to betray the president's trust."

Elayne kissed the base of her husband's neck and wondered what mysterious secrets Senator Ben Phillips might be keeping. Wouldn't it be something, she wondered, if these secrets were the very key to understanding what made Ben Phillips tick?

"Are you gonna come to bed?"

"In a little bit."

Elayne stepped away from her husband and took a good look at him. His eyes were focused on the road below, but he seemed to be far away. His face was cold. Elayne opened the sliding glass door, went back inside, and crawled into bed.

Campman stayed outside for ten more minutes. He needed time to calm his nerves before returning indoors. His mind had been racing, and it was only now starting to slow down.

He hadn't told the others about Sharon Balis dropping out. He didn't want to break the news until he'd figured out a follow-up strategy. He'd placed several tactical calls that evening, none of which had yielded any fruit, and he was still waiting to hear back from Eddie Dulces in California. After Eddie, Campman's well was dry. Even the Almighty seemed reluctant to give advice this evening.

In the end, he determined that no lightning bolt of inspiration was going to hit him as he waited on that Tampa balcony. He would think more clearly in the morning once he'd had a good night's sleep.

Campman probably would have fallen asleep quickly, too, if it hadn't been for the phone call. When his bedside phone rang, Campman first thought it was Eddie Dulces returning his message. Eddie lived in Los Angeles and kept late hours even by Pacific standards.

But this was not Eddie Dulces. It was a male voice Campman did not recognize. The caller said only one sentence, but that sentence was enough to make sleep impossible for Thomas Campman:

"I know about Muddville!"

THE MOLE FROM MEXICO

From the earliest days of their courtship, Elian Ramon Elizondo, or "Elly" as he was called, had taken Inez to sea with him. He said he could not bear to be without her for even the smallest amount of time, and this was true. Often, late at night when the other men were asleep, Elly and his bride would sneak up to the deck of the fishing ship and make love under the stars. These would always be Elly's fondest memories.

There was another reason Elly took Inez with him, and this he did not share with anyone: She was too beautiful.

The island of San Gomez was located twenty miles off the Yucatan peninsula, and while the isle itself had a reputation for astounding physical beauty, its female inhabitants did not. To put it bluntly, most of San Gomez's females were scarcely more feminine than the men, and amid such a dowdy gene pool, the exquisiteness of Inez Elizondo stood out. Elly never left Inez alone because he didn't trust the men of the island to control themselves around her. He was wise to have such doubts.

Even so, as Inez reached the advanced stages of pregnancy, Elly realized it was best to leave her behind in the care of her mother. After a while, everyone seemed comfortable with this arrangement, which was why it was surprising when Elly suddenly chose to take his wife to sea well into her eighth month. Inez herself was surprised, but she did not disobey her husband, despite her mother's protests.

"What sort of man puts a pregnant woman on a boat?!" she'd said.

The excursion was a long one, and Inez began to feel sick as soon as the boat left harbor. But Elly kept on sailing well into the night. Even when the seas got choppy and the rain started to fall, he kept going. During the second night, on stormy seas, Inez's condition worsened, and at 10:30 P.M., her water broke. Elly was with her the whole time, telling her to hold on, but never once did he give the order to turn around. He just stroked her hair and said calmly, "Just wait. Just wait."

By 12:30 A.M., as the lights of the U.S. Coast Guard swept across the fishing boat, Inez started feeling her first contractions. From that point on she remembered very little. Inez had a vague memory of Elly holding her shivering body in his arms on the deck of the ship, of rain pouring down on her, of men speaking English in loud voices over megaphones, and of Elly yelling, "This woman is in labor! Do you want to kill her? Do you want her blood on your hands?!"

After that, it was all black. The next thing Inez remembered was waking up in the medical ward of the U.S. Navy base on Key West with Elly at her side. Ten hours later, she was handed a tiny newborn with jet-black hair and a United States birth certificate and told to reboard the fishing boat. They were going home.

In the years that followed, Hector's mother never mentioned the dramatic ocean adventure to her husband. She never asked Elly whether he had planned to take her to Florida, whether he chose to leave in stormy weather to induce her pregnancy, or what he'd actually said to the men aboard the boat who stopped them in American waters. But she told her version of the story to Hector many times, and as the young boy grew up, it became clear to him that from the very beginning, his father had plans for him to be a U.S. citizen.

Hector only questioned him about it once. He was fifteen at the time and was walking home from the San Gomez market alone with his father. When he broached the question that had been on his young lips for a decade, his father stopped short. He turned and looked his son straight in the eye.

"*Sometimes, a man needs to take chances to give his family a better life,*" he said.

And that was all.

He tousled Hector's dark hair and continued walking.

It was the only time Hector ever spoke with his father about the events of his birth, and the conversation was scarcely more than one sentence long on either side. But it was satisfying all the same, perhaps the most satisfying conversation of Hector's life.

And he never forgot it.

WERE IT NOT for his father, Hector might have never met Carmelina, and he might have never needed to learn English.

It would take more than three and a half decades for Hector to return to the country of his birth, and when he arrived with wife and daughters in tow, only one year after his mother's death, it was a moment of quiet drama, much less harrowing than his first visit. The family settled in Miami, in a cramped apartment amid the projects of East Little Havana. Here he met Carmelina.

Carmelina Jacinto Maria Bella Josanna St. Ronda was an ancient woman with fierce eyes and cavernous wrinkles who lived four doors down from the Elizondo family, and she offered to teach Hector English in exchange for some minimal manual labor. Carmelina was an eccentric woman who had thirteen brown cats, two red parakeets, a smoking problem, and a speech impediment. Her problem was that she always seemed to be caught on the vowel *e*. She would greet

Hector every day with, "Hectoreeeeeh! Eh-HowAreYooo—eh Today-eeeeeeeeh?"

If Carmelina had spoken Spanish to Hector, he might have quickly figured out that her proclivity toward the letter *e* existed regardless of language, but as she insisted on speaking only English whenever he was around, Hector naturally assumed her *e*-centric dialect to be correct pronunciation. The damage of this misapprehension cannot be overstated. Also damaging to Hector's future in the English-speaking world was the fact that Carmelina died from a bizarre smoking-related accident only a few months after he'd begun lessons. As Hector did not have the money to seek English instruction elsewhere, his learning curve swiftly plateaued.

This is not to say Hector couldn't have improved his speech on his own through study and observation. He just chose not to do so. This did not sit well with his wife, Sabrina, who, after four years in the United States, had become the most proficient English-speaking adult in the Elizondo household, thanks to her keen observation, tireless study, and admirable self-discipline.

"How long do we have to be in this country before you start talking like an American?" she would chide him. "You still sound like that wretch Carmelina for crying out loud! No! Not even as good as her!"

And perhaps she was right. The problem was, Hector had no patience for language. It bored him. And once his English studies were cut short and he began work as a taxi driver, he found there were very few situations where his linguistic shortcomings actually proved a hindrance. Brinita was the one who interacted with grocers, pharmacists, doctors, teachers, bankers, and the like. Hector just had to drive a cab and converse with family and friends, all of whom spoke Spanish. The cabdriver's nomenclature wasn't difficult to absorb, what with its reliance on numbers, addresses, and speed-based verbiage such as *rush, late,* and *hurry.* These sorts of words came quickly to him: Numbers came quickly, geography came quickly, swearing

came quickly. It was the other stuff that was difficult. Once Hector
mastered the limited taxi driver's vocabulary, his interest in the English language swiftly faded. And the more he tried to listen to the
nongeographical, non-speed-based, non-number-based conversations
that took place in the back of his cab, the more he tried to understand
these wordy, elaborate, and usually pointless discussions, the more
he became convinced that native English speakers had—on the
whole—appallingly little to say.

So, he stopped listening. And the less he tried to understand the
words themselves, the more Hector realized how unnecessary these
words were. Sure, his limited English would cause trouble from time
to time, but it also became a secret source of pride for him. He decided he was—in his own way—*enlightened.* He was living proof of
the irrelevance of the English language, and if there was perhaps an
irony in Hector's unabashed fondness for America, for his ever-
renewable subscription to the American dream and his perpetual
fascination with American culture and cinema, if there was an irony
in the coexistence of all this with his disdain for the country's primary language (not to mention many of its speakers) . . . well, let's
just say this irony was not something that kept Hector lying awake at
night. Like most men, Hector was far more concerned with paying
the rent and caring for his family than pursuing an unironic existence.

In the end, perhaps Brinita was right. Maybe he was a bit lazy.
Maybe his self-righteous criticism of the language was merely a
product of his own frustrations with it. If English was something he
took to as easily as magic tricks or driving, perhaps he would love it
just the same. But for whatever reason, this was not the case. For
whatever reason, the moment he tried to focus on the learning and
discerning of new English words, they all seemed to resolve into a
meaningless mumble inside his ear.

And so it came to pass that after four years in the United States,
possessing a severely limited vocabulary, an impatience with the English language, a lovely but nagging wife, three rapidly growing

daughters, one quick-witted pair of oversize hands, a legitimate U.S. birth certificate from 1964, a gift for driving a Lincoln Town Car as if it were a Maserati, and an inherited speech impediment from an emphysematic zoologically preoccupied crone acquired in the dawn of the new century, Hector Elizondo (formerly "Nosrapo" or "he of the fast hands" from the island of San Gomez, Mexico) came to work for the presidential campaign of Oklahoma Senator Ben Phillips as the personal driver to one Mr. Thomas Campman.

THE RECEPTIONIST DIDN'T seem to understand him. Hector couldn't quite tell why. He thought he was being perfectly clear. He started at the beginning.

"Eeeeeeeeemyname eees eh JuanGomez."

"Juan Gomez."

"Yes!" Hector said, nodding his head.

"Eeeeh I want-ey to speak-eeeeeeh-DeneeseVaso."

"You want to speak . . . to Denise?"

"DeneeseVaso."

"Dennis Fazo."

"YesYes. Eeeeh-Very-Eeeemportant!"

"Okay. One moment please, Mr. Gomez. Why don't you have a seat?"

Hector looked her in the eyes.

"Um, won't you please have a seat?" she repeated, motioning to her left.

Hector walked over to the burgundy leather behemoth of a couch and sat down. His eyes scanned the high ceilings of the National Republican Association's third-floor lobby. Where the wall met the ceiling, there was some sort of sculpted border depicting bald eagles and stars and branches. The floor was marble, and there were patriotic oil paintings hanging from the walls, framed in gold. It was all very dramatic and official. This was surely the right place.

When he first decided to become a double agent less than two months ago, Hector assumed that once he had information about the Democrats, the Republicans would be eager to purchase that information from him. What he hadn't figured out exactly was how to get in touch with the Republicans once he had information to sell.

His limited reading on the subject of presidential politics led him to the conclusion that Dennis Fazo was the man he needed to find. Fazo, by his understanding, was the man in charge of the president's re-election campaign and therefore the one who would be most willing to pay for information about the Democrats. But how to reach him?

Hector tried the Yellow Pages. After failing to find Fazo's name anywhere in the book, Hector decided to look for Republican organizations. This is how he came to visit the national headquarters of the Young Republicans of America earlier that morning. Here he managed to have three dizzying conversations with three different young men, none of whom seemed to understand the reason for his visit, and all of whom seemed utterly confused by his presence. The first young man was at least polite, which is more than could be said for the other two, who were both condescending and snippy. Hector was no expert at spotting racism, but he was fairly sure he was being treated poorly because of the way he looked. He seriously doubted whether either of the young men had ever seen a person with a complexion darker than skim milk before, and from the way they gawked at him, he half expected them to chase him out of the building with torches in their hands. No such thing happened, thankfully, but before long the third young man (the rudest of the bunch) did ask him to leave. Such was Hector's disdain for these Young Republicans that on his way out, he made sure to steal one of the message buttons from their gift shop. He didn't have a chance to read it until after he'd left the building, but once outside, he examined it fully. It was a yellow pin with the following message in large red bold type: NO WELFARE FOR ME, THANKS. I HAVE A JOB.

He was wearing the pin now as he sat on the burgundy couch. The receptionist had one ear to the phone as she spoke to him.

"Mr. Gomez, I just spoke with Mr. Fazo's office and they don't seem to be expecting you. Is there something I can do for you?"

It didn't seem like she was going to let him through. He would have to explain. Hector dismounted the mighty sofa and walked back to her desk. He pulled out his tape recorder.

"Eeeeh I wanttooey speak-eeeeeeh-DeneeseVaso."

"I understand that, but—"

"I yehhhyam Spayeeee-to-eeeeh-TómasCampmon."

"I'm sorry?"

"EeehSpy. Spayeeee."

"You're a spy?"

"*Sí. Sí.* Yes. Eeeeh-TómasCampmon."

"Thomas Campman."

"Yes."

She was getting it! Hector held his tape recorder to her face and pressed play. Ralph Sorn's voice came through the recorder's small speakers and the tinny sound reverberated through the large atrium.

"New York. My gay son's boyfriend is a chef—my son is gay, you know—"

Hector pressed stop. He'd just give her a taste. From the look on her face, it seemed a taste was more than she wanted to hear. The receptionist looked uncomfortable.

"Okay! Um, if you wouldn't mind just sitting down for, uh, one more moment, Mr. Gomez, I'll see what I can do for you, okay?"

Hector obeyed.

The woman picked up her phone.

"Hi, Gerry? This Mr. Gomez who wants to see Dennis Fazo. . . . I think you might want to come down here and meet this guy. . . . I just think you should come down here."

About five minutes later, a well-groomed gentleman in his late thirties walked into the lobby and approached the receptionist's desk. His hair was slicked back, and Hector noticed he had several rings on his fingers (more than was normal for a man, thought Hector). The newcomer whispered back and forth with the receptionist, who pointed to Hector. The two of them talked at her desk a while longer before the man turned and walked in Hector's direction. As he approached, his face lit up with a million-dollar smile.

"Mr. Gomez!" He extended his arm. "My name is Gerry McDowell, I'm the assistant to the undersecretary of affairs here at the NRA. So nice to meet you."

Hector stood, shook, and smiled in turn.

"Why don't you follow me, and you and I can have a talk?"

Hector followed Gerry McDowell down the hall and up the large marble staircase to the fourth floor. Here they walked through a series of corridors and cubicles before entering a rather inconspicuous conference room. Now that they were away from the gilded reception area, the office struck Hector as not too dissimilar from the other offices he'd been to. Hector's experience with office buildings was fairly limited and acquired almost exclusively in the last six months. Before February, there'd been very little reason for Hector to set foot in an office. Once he'd had the opportunity to see a few of them, however, he was struck by how similar they all seemed. The office of the National Republican Association was no exception.

Still, he felt his heart beating faster as he walked down the hall with Gerry McDowell. It reminded him of the excitement he felt when he visited his first "office"-type office, back in February. It had been the evening of the big snowstorm, the evening he'd first met the boss.

Hector did not accept the job as Tom Campman's driver with the intention of becoming a double agent. That idea came later. At first, he saw the job merely as an opportunity to improve on his cabdriver's wages, working for an employer he genuinely respected. The boss was friendly, but he took no bullshit. He knew how to get what he wanted and never broke a sweat doing it. Hector liked that about him. But what really impressed Hector was the sense of power and adventure the boss seemed to carry with him. Whatever this thing was, this strange energy, Hector found it intoxicating, and it made *him* feel all the more powerful and adventurous simply by virtue of his proximity to its source. In fact, one might wonder whether Hector would've ever had the gumption to spy on his boss were it not for the contact high the boss provided.

Hector had been fascinated by the idea of espionage since he was introduced to it as a boy on the big screen; growing up, Sean Connery's Bond had been his hero of choice. But unlike other boys who related to Bond primarily as a man of action or a seducer of women, Hector most admired Bond for his stealth, for his ability to deceive. Perhaps it was this notion of deception that most fascinated young Hector. He was, after all, a young magician, and what was a magic trick if not deception in its most artful form?

Hector couldn't remember exactly when the first seeds were planted in his mind, but the idea of becoming a double agent took a long time to develop. It was just a romantic thought at first, turned into a plan of action only through the collaborative efforts of time, greed, imagination, and necessity. It took a while for Hector to realize just how important a person Thomas Campman was, and it took even longer than that for him to notice how many potentially significant conversations he was overhearing in the course of his travels with the political mastermind. And then finally, somehow, at some point (the exact date of which Hector had since forgotten), a lightbulb clicked on in his mind: *There was money to be made off the boss.*

Once the light clicked on, Hector did his best to click it off again. After all, why would he want to exploit the very man who'd been so kind to him? Why would he want to put himself at risk just for a few extra bucks? It didn't make sense. And so for a little while longer still, Hector Elizondo tried to put all thoughts of double agentry aside. He tried to forget.

But he couldn't. Once the light had been clicked on, it refused to go off, and as much as Hector tried to suppress his thoughts of political espionage, the darn things kept fizzing to the surface. When he was with the boss, they spoke to him, whispering in his ear like little devils, and when he was alone they didn't even bother to whisper. They hollered.

In June, there was trouble at home. His eldest daughter, Maribel, was punched in the face on the school bus, and suddenly she needed braces. Only days later, and just as suddenly, the Elizondo family refrigerator broke, and then to complete this karmic trilogy, the family cat Keanu became deathly ill. A few thousand dollars and one feline thyroidectomy later, the family finances were in perilous shape. The Elizondos needed cash.

Hector kept coming back to espionage, and the more he thought about it, the more the idea started to excite him. He allowed himself to wonder what it would actually be like to be a double agent. He imagined the sort of money he could make. Once necessity deemed these fantasies acceptable, Hector indulged them whenever he could, and pretty soon, they were all he thought about. By the middle of this summer he'd started making plans.

Now here he was, walking with Gerry McDowell down the hallway of the National Republican Association, his insides burning with excitement. He caught his reflection in a passing pane of glass and for a moment was surprised by the short well-dressed Mexican who looked back at him. He'd half expected to see James Bond.

The conference room looked exactly like the two other conference rooms Hector had seen in the last year, except bigger. He sat down at the large table, and Gerry McDowell sat down next to him.

"So, why don't you tell me why you've come to the NRA today," he asked.

"I yehhhyam Spayeeee-to-eeeeh-TómasCampmon."

"You're a spy?"

Hector nodded.

"You spy for Tom Campman? Tom Campman, the Democrat?"

"*Sí.*" Hector nodded.

"You spy *for* him? Or you spy *on* him?"

"*Sí.*"

Gerry McDowell grinned to himself. "Hmmm. Are you a Democrat or a Republican?"

"Spayeee."

"Okay, I see."

"I yehhhyamRepublican."

"You're a Republican?"

Hector nodded. He'd never given much thought to political affiliation. If he were forced to choose between the two parties, he might have supported the Democrats because that was the party his wife preferred, but someone like Hector could not afford to have political convictions, at least not strong ones. The Republicans were the party he could get money from, so a Republican he was.

"And you're a spy?"

Hector took out his tape recorder. He pressed PLAY, but Gerry objected immediately.

"No, don't! I don't want to hear your recording."

Hector was puzzled.

"Eeeee-I-workeeeeh-buyTómasCampmon."

"You work for Tom Campman, yes."

Hector indicated the tape recorder again, and Gerry flinched.

"Eeeeh-ToooRecord."

"You recorded . . ."

Hector decided to spell it out.

"*I*-eeeeh-giveh *yooo*-eh-*TopSeeecret*. AndeeeeeeYoooGiveh-*Meeee* . . ."

Hector made the international symbol for money.

"Two thousand dollars," he said, in flawless English.

Gerry smiled nervously.

"Mr. Gomez, if you'll excuse me for one moment."

Gerry cleared his throat twice, got up from his chair, and left the room.

He was gone for some time. After a while, Hector got bored and started to explore the conference room. He walked over to the windows, huge modern things shut off from the world by vertical blinds, which were closed. Hector parted the blinds so he could see outside. The view was breathtaking. He could see straight out to the Capitol, now aglow in the orange light of late afternoon.

"Hello, Mr. Gomez. Sorry it's taken me so long."

Hector turned around and took several vertical blinds with him. Gerry McDowell was standing with another man, a bit older.

"Okayboss," Hector said.

Several vertical blinds fell to the floor, making a loud clattering noise.

The older man spoke.

"Mr. Gomez, my name is Dustin Brollers. Nice to meet you."

Another hand. Another shake. All three were seated. The older one continued.

"Mr. Gomez, Mr. McDowell has informed me that you are a 'spy,' and you wish to sell us information about our Democratic rivals. I would just like to say for the record that the National Republican Association and the Republican Party at large does not participate in such information-gathering activities. When the president is re-elected in November, it will be because he campaigned on issues important to America, not because of insider information or dirty politics. We play a clean game here at the NRA, and I just want to be clear on that, for the record. If you're interested in getting money for whatever information you have, I suggest you peddle your wares someplace else. We don't do that sort of thing here at the NRA."

Dustin Brollers had spoken in a clear dispassionate voice, as if he wasn't addressing Hector specifically, but rather some larger assembly of listeners. Hector didn't understand every word, but he got the gist. They weren't buying.

"So," said Brollers, standing, "I hope you understand our position. I wish you all the best with your future endeavors, and I hope we can count on your vote in November. Don't forget, the president has always been a friend to the Latino American. Isn't it only fair to be a friend to him?"

With that Brollers exited the room, leaving Hector alone with Gerry McDowell. Gerry produced a piece of paper and a pen.

"I do hope you understand our position, Mr. Gomez. If you wouldn't mind just filling this out before you leave. For our records, of course."

He smiled. Hector looked down at the sheet of paper. It had spaces for contact information and requested a signature at the bottom of a large block of text. Hector filled out the contact information as the fictitious Mr. Gomez might, and wrote his proper address and phone number. He was wary when it came to the signature. Hector Elizondo was too smart to sign something he didn't understand. But Gerry was staring at him. Hector decided to draw a dramatic and meaningless squiggle on the signature line, and once that was done, he handed the page back.

As Hector walked out into the warm Washington evening, a passing bird took a crap on his shoe, adding insult to injury. Exhausted and disheartened, Hector lowered himself down onto the cold cement stairs and sat there for a few moments with his head in his hands. Any passerby who wasn't distracted by his or her cell phone might have found it an unusual sight: a short Latino man in a black suit and gloves, crouching on the stairs of the National Republican Association headquarters, wearing a NO WELFARE FOR ME, THANKS. I HAVE A JOB button on his chest, and bird crap on his shoe. Fortunately for Hector, no such person was anywhere in the vicinity, and he was permitted to wallow for a few moments in relative privacy, the public privacy of an ignored man.

KENNEDY AT REAGAN

It had been a grueling day for Hector. After driving the boss to Arlington and then the airport, after frustrating encounters with the Young Republicans and the NRA, and then one more late-night run to the airport (this time to pick up the boss after his short trip to Memphis), Hector was dog tired. He was also depressed. He couldn't very well be a double agent if only one side would hire him.

Hector worried that he wouldn't be able to sell his tape in Washington. The campaign left for Florida the next day, and they wouldn't be back in town for at least three weeks. Could he find any Republicans to sell it to on the road? And if not, would the tape still be valuable in three weeks?

Hector was scarcely home five minutes when the phone rang. The voice on the other end was one he didn't recognize. It was soft and high pitched, almost feminine, but definitely a man.

"Mr. Gomez?"

"Sí."

"Meet me at Reagan National Airport. American Airlines. Arrival gate. Thirty minutes. I'll be in a blue BMW."

———

HECTOR WAS GOOD at following airport instructions. But he didn't quite understand the phrase "Blooobeeh-em double you." Which is why he sat parked in the American Airlines arrival gate behind a blue BMW for about five minutes without thinking to approach the vehicle.

The airport security was not so shy, and after about three minutes, they began pestering the BMW to move. Another officer approached Hector's car with the same request.

"Sir, you can't sit here. We need to keep the traffic moving."

Hector smiled, nodded his head, and flashed the international "wait just a sec" sign.

"Yesboss-eeeeee-Yes."

At this point, the BMW backed up alongside the Lincoln Town Car.

A man wearing a baseball hat and sunglasses stared right at Hector. He mouthed the name: "Gomez?"

"*Lo siento?* eeeee-Sorryboss?"

He mouthed again: "Are you Gomez?"

Hector put his hand to his ear.

"NoHeeeeeer!"

The man in the BMW seemed frustrated. He rolled down his window and shouted in a high-pitched voice: "Mr. Gomez!"

"*Sí!*"

He motioned for Hector to follow him, and then pulled out.

HECTOR FOLLOWED THE BMW south into Alexandria, where it finally pulled over into the empty parking lot of a Subway sandwich shop. Hector got out of his car and approached the BMW. Its passenger was not moving. The strange man stared ahead, a blank face behind those impenetrable sunglasses.

Hector opened the passenger door.

"Good evening, Mr. Gomez." The strange man did not turn.

"Good-Eeeeh-veh-ning."

The strange man wore dark pants and a light blue polo shirt. His brown hair grew neatly from under his Washington Nationals baseball cap, and his slender chin was conspicuously clean-shaven for a 1:00 A.M. meeting.

"I'm told you have an item you'd like to sell."

He'd spoken quickly, and Hector didn't understand much of what he'd said except the word *you*. He decided to pull out the tape recorder.

The man seemed pleased.

"May I?"

Hector handed him the tape recorder, and he pressed PLAY. Sorn's voice was first.

"enough to make your head spin."

There was the sound of tires squealing.

"Should I be scared for my life?" Sorn again. Campman spoke next.

"No. Just take it as it comes. I wouldn't worry yet. So, it's called Gastron?"

Just as a hint of recognition seemed to be forming around the mouth of the strange man, Hector grabbed the tape recorder and pressed STOP. He had given a preview, but he wouldn't give away the whole show. Not for free.

"Two thousand dollars."

"So that was Campman? And who was the other guy? It almost sounded like Ralph Sorn."

"Eeeeh-yessir boss—Eh-TómasCampmon."

The strange man eyed him for a moment, then reached into his pocket and pulled out a wad of bills.

"One thousand."

"Two thousand dollars."

"One thousand."

"Two thousand dollars."

"Seven hundred."

Hector was quiet. This wasn't the way haggling was supposed to go.

The strange man started the engine. He put the wad of bills in Hector's pocket.

"Seven hundred for now. I don't know if there's anything useful on that tape. If it's not bullshit, you'll get the other three hundred."

He grabbed the recorder, took out the tape, and pocketed it. He then handed the recorder back to Hector along with a small cell phone.

Hector smiled and chuckled quietly to himself, even though he had little reason to do so. This caught the strange man off guard, but he continued warily with his instructions, showing Hector the new phone.

"If you get something else, call me. One. Send."

He pressed the number one followed by the send button, and suddenly another cell phone started to ring elsewhere in the car. The man pointed to a phone attached to his belt. It was flashing.

"My name is Kennedy. I am an independent contractor. I work alone, but I have powerful friends, so if you try to fuck me, I'm gonna know about it. They're gonna know about it. You're gonna suffer. This phone line is untraceable, so save yourself the effort and don't even try. If this is a sting operation, that's a *bad idea for you*; rest assured, you will find yourself *severely fucked*. I am connected to no one and everyone. I am simply transacting a deal with you on a one-to-one basis and *that is all*. There is no conspiracy, no higher-ups, and no one else involved. Any insinuation to the contrary is both erroneous and unwise, and that's the way we're going to proceed from this point onward, *if*—in fact—we proceed at all. Do you understand?"

Hector looked him straight in the sunglasses.

"Eeh, no."

The strange man looked back blankly.

"What did you—Is there a specific part you didn't understand?"

Hector did not answer.

The strange man seemed flustered. He spoke again, this time with more gesticulation.

"Look, my name is Kennedy, okay? I am an independent contractor.

I work alone, but . . . I have powerful friends, so if you try to fuck me . . . I'm gonna know about it . . . They're gonna know about it . . . You're gonna suffer. This phone line is untraceable, so save yourself the effort . . . don't even try. If this is a *sting operation* . . . that's a *bad idea for you*; rest assured, you will be severely fucked."

He sighed and picked up speed.

"I am connected to no one and everyone. I'm transacting a deal with you on a one-to-one basis, that's it. There's no conspiracy, no higher-ups, no one else is involved, and any insinuation to the contrary is erroneous and unwise, and that's the way we proceed from this point onward, if in fact we proceed at all. Do you understand?"

Hector took a moment, and then a smile spread across his face.

"Yes. *Sí. Kennedy!*"

TINA JAMES

Her name was Tina James. She was Eddie Dulces's girl, and the two of them went way back. She was Eddie's first good lay. Not his first lay, mind you, but his first good one: his first time with an uninhibited girl who liked the dirty stuff and knew that sex wasn't some paint-by-numbers exercise you learned about from the diagrams on the inside of a condom box. Sex was something exhilarating, something that thrills and tears and breaks and screams. That's what Tina James thought, and that's the type of sex she introduced to Eddie Dulces.

To say she was the one to point him down the path to sin would be to give her too much credit (and also too little). That Eddie would go on to become Hollywood's most notorious producer of sleaze and sleaze-based programming was not Tina's doing in the slightest. That was all Eddie. If Tina advanced his career in any way, it was by giving him confidence at a crucial point in his development.

The two met in high school in Oklahoma City, although they were never close friends. But high school was where he saw her onstage, and that's how he knew she could act. That's how he knew she could've been the next Julie Christie if she'd wanted to be. She was that good. Tina never pursued it, of course, and in the end, her theatrical résumé would consist of two high school plays and nothing else. But Eddie had seen both plays and knew she was brilliant. He was the only one who knew.

They met again in California—he was attending USC and she, UCLA—and it was on the West Coast where they became friends and eventually lovers. They fell for each other in a big way, but their actual courtship was brief, barely three months, about the time it took for them to realize they were a self-destructive couple. Still, they remained friends and never lost contact, even though she moved back to Oklahoma and he remained in Los Angeles.

It was always a secret relationship, and they liked it that way. In college they each had their own friends and would meet alone in the city or at one of their apartments in private. Eddie had roommates at the time, but there were too many women coming and going through that apartment for Tina to have made herself memorable. Tina's roommate Polly was the only one who really knew about the relationship, and she died in a motorcycle accident two years after graduation. In the decades that followed, Eddie and Tina would correspond and occasionally meet, but it was always a one-on-one event; no spouses or significant others allowed. This secrecy would end up being crucial. If there had been any way of connecting Tina and Eddie, the plan wouldn't have worked.

For Eddie, this sort of relationship was typical. It was important for him to have a lot of friends, but from his early days in TV, working on the groundbreaking info-tainment show *Nightly Shocker*, it became equally important for many of these friends to remain secret. As he grew to become an icon of sleaze and exploitation, many of his closest friends could not afford to be publicly linked with the infamous Eddie Dulces. Thomas Campman was one such friend.

For Tina, discretion was more a habit than a necessity, secrecy more a naughty indulgence than a standard prerequisite. But she practiced both in the case of Eddie Dulces.

From the start it is important to stress that Tina James was not a whore. She never was. She was just a brilliant, confident, and lonely woman who happened to love sex. She wasn't promiscuous, either. She was very choosy in her partners (sometimes too choosy) and very discreet once they were chosen. Again, had she been any different, the plan simply wouldn't have worked.

Tina James never intended to return to Oklahoma once she left, but after medical school her mother became sick with ovarian cancer. When the opportunity arose to do her residency at Midwest Regional, Tina took it, and when the hospital offered her a position as an anesthesiologist, she took that, too. A year later, when her mother finally passed away, Tina found herself with a good job in the one place she'd promised herself she wouldn't end up. And she probably would have moved, too, if she hadn't had the questionable fortune to fall in love with a bright young cardiologist named Henry Sawyer.

Henry was the perfect man except for one tiny flaw: He didn't want to get married. More specifically, he didn't want to marry Tina. This last part she learned about the hard way, as Henry ended their seven-year courtship to shack up with and quickly wed a young resident. Devastated by the breakup, Tina was finally ready to leave Oklahoma for good, except now it was her father's turn to get sick. His ailment was Alzheimer's, and his death (for he was dead long before he physically passed away) took six and a half painful years to reach its completion.

Tina James was now forty-nine, single, bitter, depressed, and still living in Oklahoma. A spurious malpractice suit three years earlier had stripped her of her medical license and forced her to take a job with a large pharmaceutical company, a job she had quickly grown to despise. As for her love life, she'd had several boyfriends and a few more lovers since Henry Sawyer, but none recently, and her few friends were becoming increasingly worried about her mental state.

"You've got to get the hell out of Oklahoma!" Eddie Dulces had told her when they last spoke. "It doesn't matter where you go, but you need to get the hell out of there!"

He knew there wasn't anything wrong with Tina physically or mentally. She'd just had a string of shitty luck. She was someone far too smart, far too dynamic for the life she had led.

Tina knew it, too. And she was ready for something different. She didn't know what, exactly, and that was the scary thing. But she knew it was time for some movement in her life. Both parents were dead. Her big job and big love were behind her. To put it plainly: She had nothing more to lose.

So when Tom Campman spoke with Eddie Dulces on that fateful day in late August and said, "I need a woman who's beautiful, smart, and willing. And it would really help if she'd spent some time in Oklahoma," Eddie didn't even have to think.

"I've got the absolute perfect girl for you, or I've got no one."

"THE GREAT THING about creating a scandal from scratch, is that you have no contradictory evidence. A girl you don't know is better than a girl you did know, because no one knows you ever knew her!"

After the effort expended on Sharon Balis, selling Tina James was a snap. The senator actually preferred the idea of Tina, because he didn't feel like he was imposing on the shared history of someone he'd actually been intimate with. Melissa and the other advisors agreed. Only Shelly Greenblatt made a stink, insisting the Sharon Balis failure was an omen that the plan itself was too dangerous. He was quickly overruled.

The senator, having made the initially difficult decision to proceed, did not want to consider the matter again and gave word that things would go forward as planned. It didn't take long to double-check facts and get personal histories straight, and it looked as if everything would start without much delay. There was only one sticking point.

"She wants to meet you."

"To meet me?"

"Yes."

"That sounds dangerous, don't you think? I'm really not comfortable with that."

"It's her one condition."

The senator shook his head. "How would we do it?"

The campaign was spending the night in Jackson, Mississippi, but very little sleep would be had by anyone. In the end, a car would be purchased for the occasion. Trains, planes, and taxis involved other people. Car rental agencies would keep track of mileage and require identification. Campman insisted that nothing be traceable.

Naturally, Derek Kiley would be the one dispatched to purchase the car. He was given $6,000 in cash and told to be as inconspicuous as possible. That afternoon, while the senator attended a rally at Belhaven College, Kiley donned a pair of sunglasses and went shopping. For the small shred of anonymity the sunglasses provided, they proved to be an annoyance when it came to inspecting the used vehicles, particularly on such a dark overcast day. In fact, Kiley might not have purchased the lime-green Honda Civic that he did, had he a chance to view it under more impartial conditions.

At 11:45 P.M., Senator Ben Phillips slipped unnoticed out the kitchen entrance of the Jackson Grand Hotel, where Kiley's lime-green Civic was waiting. It had been a trick working his way past the Secret Service man who guarded his hotel room door, but Ben had managed it with a mixture of stealth, charm, and good old-fashioned bribery. Now, he could feel the heavy nighttime air against his skin, and he saw the small car only fifteen feet away. He walked briskly to it. Campman was in the passenger seat, so Ben got into the back, and they were off.

"Lie down on the seat. Make yourself invisible," Campman ordered. Then after a moment, "Can you believe this ridiculous car Kiley picked for us?"

"I had very little to choose from. We needed something that would get us to Texas and back without breaking down."

"And there's nothing more inconspicuous than Life Savers green, is there?"

Kiley fumed. It wasn't his job to buy cars—never mind playing getaway driver.

Ben Phillips was all business.

"Tom, let's go over the story again."

"Okay. Okay."

They had not even cleared downtown Jackson.

"We met in Oklahoma in the summer of 1972. I was about to head to law school, she'd just finished up her first year of college out west."

"You met . . ."

"We met in the supermarket. I happened to be picking up some groceries for my mama. . . ."

BY THE TIME the green Civic crossed the border into Louisiana, Kiley was fairly certain they were not being followed, and he breathed a bit easier. The story of Ben Phillips and Tina James's romance had been completed, and Campman was cross-examining the senator.

"Why don't any of your friends remember you dating Miss James?"

"Well, the first time, when we met, we were only together for a couple weeks. Right after that, she headed back west and I started dating Ellen Millsworth. Ellen was the real headline that summer."

"But your friends . . ."

"There weren't many who were around during those couple of weeks if I recall. That's one of the reasons we were able to spend so much time together. I know I mentioned her to Scotty, I remember we had a long talk about her. . . ."

"Scotty? Scotty Roland, your friend who had the stroke?"

"Yeah, Scotty's not with us anymore, unfortunately, God bless him. I mentioned her to Scotty. And I think I must've also mentioned her to a few of the other guys, to Bill and Tad and Jay. I don't know if they remember or not, but I'm sure I must've told them. But then, as I said, Ellen Millsworth was right after that, and I was real crazy about Ellen, so . . . she was the main topic of conversation that summer."

SHELLY'S SHOULDER

S helly Greenblatt was clipping his toenails when he heard a knock on the hotel room door.

"Shelly?" called a female voice.

"Just a minute."

Greenblatt stood up and walked to the door. It was 12:15 A.M., and this unexpected solicitor, whoever she was, had quickened his lethargic pulse. Happy to be distracted from his thoughts, he put his eye to the keyhole, curious to know the identity of his caller. The fish-eyed face of Melissa Phillips stared back at him from the other side.

"I woke you, didn't I?" was the first thing she said upon entering. Before he had a chance to respond, she spoke again: "You look tired. I woke you."

"Not at all, Melissa. I was just getting ready for bed."

This wasn't exactly true. Shelly Greenblatt had no intention of going to bed before 2:00 A.M. at the earliest. He knew it wouldn't do him any good if he tried. He'd just lie there, staring at his alarm clock, listening to the faint sounds of his own digestive system, waiting in vain for sleep to overtake him. This had been going on for so many weeks that Shelly no longer even bothered getting under the covers now until his drowsiness had reached such extremes as to make imminent collapse inevitable. There was no point in fighting a losing battle.

"I'm so sorry, Shel. I shouldn't be bothering you this late, I know. You're tired, and . . ."

Yes, he looked tired. He *was* tired. He was damn tired.

"That's okay."

"I'm sorry, but I had to talk to somebody. I feel like I'm going crazy here. I've been sitting in my room thinking and stewing and thinking some more, and it's just not healthy."

Shelly felt touched by her words. Here, finally, was someone going through the same emotions as he! But surely, he corrected himself, Melissa must be having an even worse time of it.

"Oh, Melissa."

Shelly had been doing his own stewing when Melissa knocked a few moments earlier. He'd been thinking about Thomas Campman and his obnoxious wife, the pretentious no-talent photographer Elayne Cohen-Campman, who'd used her marital connections and questionable artistic reputation to insinuate herself into the campaign's inner circle. While Shelly Greenblatt had yet to spend a significant amount of time with Mrs. Cohen-Campman, he felt he didn't need to. He instantly disliked her. If the woman's choice of mate wasn't enough of a reason to warrant his disapproval, Shelly had had the misfortune of seeing her photography on two different occasions, and he was not impressed. For all its praise, he found her piece on the Bisanthian children to be amateurish at best, and *The Tongueless Women of Botú* . . . well, that was downright exploitive.

Now Elayne Cohen-Campman had the sort of access most reporters could only dream of, and the whole thing made Shelly suspicious. Why did Campman want her so close? What was his ulterior motive? Surely, he had one; Thomas Campman always did. *But what was it?*

Shelly thought if only he could anticipate Campman's next move, he might be better prepared to counter it.

But he had nothing: no clue, no strategy, and no hope for improvement. Shelly's nail-clipping brainstorm session had long since devolved into just the sort of self-torturous self-pitying stewing Melissa Phillips was surely experiencing on the floor above, and he realized he needed to talk every bit as much as she did.

"Where's Ben?" he asked her.

"Oh, you know," she said, making a beeline for the armchair, "they've gone off to see . . . *her*."

"To see *who*?"

"Oh, you know, Shel."

But he didn't know. Neither Ben nor Campman had told Shelly about that night's dangerous road trip, and it was now Melissa's job to bring him up to speed. By the time she'd finished, Shelly was furious; he didn't like being left in the dark. But at the same time, he understood. The others had probably assumed Shelly would have tried to stop them if he'd known, and they were right. *Traveling in the dead of night to introduce the candidate to the very woman he must not be seen with? Actively, publicly, and undeniably involving the candidate in the planning of his own scandal? Making the candidate complicit in a potentially provable way?* They were asking for trouble, and Shelly didn't like the sound of it one bit. Apparently, neither did Melissa.

"Why are we doing this, Shel? I mean, are we crazy?"

"We're crazy."

"I should have just said no. This is my fault. I should have killed it when I had the chance."

"Don't be ridiculous, Mel. It's *my* job to look out for your interests. I should have put up a bigger stink, I should have had more tricks up my sleeve, I should have just . . . I don't know."

Melissa crossed to where he sat on the bed and hugged him.

"Oh, Shel," she said, her eyes watering, "just promise me you won't go over to the dark side."

He promised.

"We have to look out for each other, Shel. We may be the only two sane people left."

"What about Ben?" he asked, a spark of hope still present. "Couldn't we just talk to him together? He trusts the two of us more than . . ."

Melissa shook her head and smiled slightly.

"When his mind is made up . . ."

"Hmm."

They both smiled.

"He's not that easily swayed," she said, "no matter what the Republicans would have you believe. And besides, we have nothing new to offer. What's our counterstrategy?"

"I know," said Shelly.

The two of them sat quietly for a moment. Melissa looked at the floor. Shelly looked at Melissa. She was wearing green again, definitely her best color, and it made him notice the matching emerald glint of her iris, reflected in the light from the night table. *There's just something about a beautiful woman when she's sad*, Shelly mused, and his mind flew to thoughts of chivalrous protection. Why couldn't he make things better for her?

Finally, Shelly made a tentative offer. It was the one thing that had remained unsaid, and he feared this might be his only chance to say it.

"You could just . . . refuse to do it."

Melissa's eyes quickly filled with tears, and Shelly at once regretted having made the suggestion.

"You know I want to," she said.

He reached out, and she fell into his arms once more. He let her cry into his T-shirt.

As she held him, Shelly thought about Ben and Campman's risky cross-country drive and tried to imagine where they might be right now; he thought of the great distance that separated them. Shelly also thought of his own diminished role in the campaign, and he wondered: *Was he now nothing more than a shoulder to cry on?*

Perhaps this last thought should have deepened Shelly's depression, but to his surprise, it had the opposite effect. While he was by no means cured of his malaise, he observed that it had become more bearable in the minutes since Melissa's entrance. For the first time in a long while, in Melissa Phillips's teary embrace, Shelly Greenblatt felt useful.

TINA JAMES, IN THE FLESH

Five miles to Monroe, Louisiana.

Ben Phillips had contemplated trying to sleep but knew he wouldn't be able. He was too nervous about meeting Tina James.

"I don't have any pictures to show you," Campman had said, "but she's the right age, and take my word for it, she's one good-looking broad."

Sitting in the backseat, Ben tried to assemble the "good-looking" Tina James part by part in his mind. She surely had a good-looking mouth (full lips) . . . a good-looking nose . . . good-looking eyes (perhaps blue—or, no, let's say hazel) . . . and her hair (of course!)—what did her hair look like? . . . Maybe a light brown . . .

Once the image of his anonymously good-looking Tina James prototype was fixed in his mind, Ben couldn't help but notice she was a dead ringer for Campman's wife, Elayne.

Oops, he thought guiltily.

But the guilt quickly dissipated. Campman had certainly screwed around with his personal life. What was wrong with a little Freudian revenge fantasy?

After a few moments of free thinking, Ben returned to his senses. He knew Tina James was not going to look like Elayne Cohen-Campman. She'd be a different person altogether, and there was no way for him to know any more about her until they met face-to-face.

It's just like a blind date, he thought. How odd. How often does one get to meet a former lover for the first time? A part of him was excited. The other parts were suddenly sick and terrified. For whatever reason, he thought of his month in Vietnam.

THEY MET AT an EZFill gas station off of I–20 in Kilgore, Texas. The last twenty minutes of driving had been particularly harrowing for Kiley and Campman, who had not wanted to make any unnecessary gas stops and were secretly praying (each in their own way) that the fumes of gasoline in the Honda's tank would be enough to carry them to Kilgore. They were.

As they approached the EZFill, Ben Phillips once again laid his head on the backseat, ducking out of sight so that no security camera could take note of his presence. Campman noticed a blue Oldsmobile waiting in the shadows at the edge of the parking lot. Just as planned. Once the Honda had refueled, Kiley pulled up next to the blue Oldsmobile. Campman saw a female silhouette in the driver's-side window. He nodded to her. She nodded back.

The Honda made a left out of the gas station and drove away from the highway.

"Is she following us?"

There was no reply. Then . . .

"Yes. Yes, she is."

They drove past some shopping centers and through a residential district. The buildings began to thin out. Soon there was nothing but darkness. Then, just a series of what appeared to be streetlights.

"Pull over here."

"Where are we?"

"It's a small airport, I think."

"Perfect."

The lights of a distant car drew closer and then slowed. The blue Oldsmobile drove past them and then backed up, coming to rest twenty feet in front of the Honda.

The three men exited the car and stood awkwardly beside it, bodies stiff and necks extended in anticipation, waiting for some sign of movement from the blue Oldsmobile.

Finally, a door opened and a pair of denim-covered female legs hit the ground. The rest of Tina James soon followed, and suddenly she was walking toward them. She was tall, perhaps five foot nine, and had long wavy hair that made her approaching silhouette resemble something out of an episode of *Charlie's Angels*. Indeed her T-shirt and tight jeans advertised a figure most women thirty years her junior would have envied.

As she walked into the light, her features became visible. First her nose, then her eyes, then her lips. And, yes, they were all good-looking parts. Eddie Dulces had told Campman she was beautiful, and now Campman could see he'd not been misinformed. But it was more than just that.

"Good evening," she said in a breathy alto.

About this time, a strange thing happened. All three grown men experienced simultaneous and spontaneous erections. From the looks on their faces, one might have thought they'd all just wet themselves. They were dumbstruck. Each of them secretly hoped one of the others would be the first to speak, but none of them had the slightest idea what to say. Tina James had always had this effect on men. To her credit, she pretended to be ignorant of it.

"So which one of you is my ex-boyfriend?"

The three awkward men hovering near the lime green Honda Civic said nothing, their collective IQs having taken a severe tumble in the last thirty seconds. What did she mean?

Tina James broke the silence again, laughing.

"I'm kidding, of course. Obviously, I know who you all are. Except you."

Trying hard to exude confidence, Kiley ambled forward with his arm outstretched.

"I'm Derek Kiley. Speechwriter and, uh, chauffeur for the night."

"Nice to meet you, Derek. Mr. Campman . . ."

"Very nice to finally meet you."

"And Ben Phillips . . . wow."

"Wow" was exactly what Ben Phillips was thinking. He'd certainly met women more attractive than Tina James, women who were younger, women with more exceptional features, but never had he been in the presence of a woman who simply oozed sex the way Tina James did. That her sexiness was unintentional made it all the more alluring. Nothing about her was designed to titillate, but everything did all the same. Sex evaporated off her skin, it sweated out her pores, it escaped her lungs in hot breath. Right then and there, Ben decided that Tina James was the sexiest woman he had ever met, and he suddenly felt much more single than he actually was.

"You look like a girl I once dated, name was Tina James."

It was a stupid corny thing to say, but Ben couldn't take it back. Tina just smiled.

"I get that all the time."

He looks just like on TV, thought Tina. He was a powerful presence, but not quite as self-possessed as she'd expected. He was more human, more real.

"I want to thank you for doing this," he said.

"Well, I've been bored. So, I figure what the heck?"

"No, really. Thank you."

"Okay."

Tina was struck with sadness. Here before her was a great man, perhaps the first great man she'd ever met. Was there any reason they couldn't have been lovers in real life? Was there any reason she couldn't be a first lady? Why were there no great men in Tina James's life?

"We don't have much time," said Campman. "Tina, I don't know if you have any specific agenda, but I want to make sure neither one of you has questions about this little history we've created."

They went over details. The first time they met. The second time. Names. Landmarks. Objects. Geography. All three men were impressed with Tina. She was sharp and meticulous, an actress researching her role with gusto. As the minutes passed, the collective confidence grew.

Soon it was time to go.

"Not yet," said Tina, "first, we take a walk."

"We really should be getting back," said Kiley.

Tina motioned for the senator to join her.

"Just don't be long," said Campman.

Tina extended her hand, and Ben Phillips took it.

AS THEY WALKED into the darkness, Ben felt aware of the ever so subtle limp of his right leg, the sole reminder of the injury that sent him home from Vietnam after only one month. Most people didn't notice it. He wondered if Tina James did.

The two didn't talk. Ben decided since this was Tina's idea, he'd let her call the shots. She didn't seem to want to talk about anything, so he didn't speak. They just walked.

A crazy idea ran through Ben's mind. What if she was trying to kill him? What if she was an assassin hired by Campman and Kiley? What a perfectly untraceable murder this would be.

Too ridiculous, he thought, but kept his guard up.

She looked at him, flashing her large blue eyes—they were definitely pale blue—and a smile. And then away. Still, she said nothing.

Eventually, Ben's curiosity got the better of him.

"Is there anything you want to discuss?"

At this, she stopped. Her face was quite serious, and Ben searched her eyes in vain for a clue as to what was to come.

Then she grabbed him.

She grabbed his face in her hands and swallowed him whole. It had been a long time since Ben had been kissed with such force. He wondered if he ever had.

Her hands went to work, down his body, grabbing his rear, pressing him up against her until their bodies were as close as clothing would allow. In his shock, it did not occur to Ben to resist.

So this is what it feels like, he thought, loving every second and suddenly wondering whether he'd been missing out on kisses like this for his entire life. He felt strangely free from guilt. The whole encounter was out of his control, wasn't it, and part of a larger script, one his wife had already signed off on. By the time Ben's superego reengaged a few moments later, by the time it occurred to him to object, the spasm of intimacy was already coming to an end. Tina slowed down and kissed him delicately once, twice, and then once more.

When it was over, all Ben could do was stare at her, befuddled. He said something that sounded like "huh." Tina just smiled, grabbed his hand, and started to walk back. Ben awkwardly adjusted himself and tried to keep up.

"REMEMBER NOT TO seem too eager for publicity. If you give an exclusive interview, be sure it's with someone good. Get your message out there, but don't accept every offer. You have to remain credible."

Tina just nodded her head.

"Don't worry."

"We're gonna get back late if we don't leave now," said Kiley, impatiently.

"Okay, okay."

Campman and Kiley shook Tina James's hand, and Ben followed suit. He knew it would be inappropriate to give Tina the standard Ben Phillips political handshake, so instead he just held her hand in his for a few moments, as if he were going to kiss it (which he didn't do). This felt awkward, but Tina showed no awkwardness in response.

"This has been really helpful for me. Thank you."

Ben wanted to say "my pleasure" but thought it unwise. He just nodded.

BACK AT THE NRA

T he question we need to ask ourselves," said Wendy Relsh, "is: Are we being set up?"

Dustin Brollers nodded but did not reply.

"I want to hear it again."

They'd listened to the tape twice already, but Brollers did not hesitate to press PLAY a third time. He didn't know what to make of it, either.

The audio quality was poor. The muffled sounds of a car motor crackled off the small speakers in the National Republican Association's dark multimedia studio. The song "Goldfinger" was playing in the background, sometimes drowning out the voices, particularly during the brassy chorus. One of the voices sounded like Tom Campman, and the other more talkative voice was probably Ralph Sorn, or someone doing a darn good Ralph Sorn impersonation.

Wendy Relsh, the vice chairperson of the NRA, reclined rigidly in her leather-backed chair, her bony hands grasping at the edges of the armrests as if afraid she might fall off. She was a lean and business-like woman, and her eyes sparked with concentration. She was listening as hard as she could.

Finally the gray-haired Dustin Brollers spoke. "I don't think it's metaphoric at all," he said, "I think they're just talking about food."

"Perhaps," said Relsh, "but doesn't that seem . . . a little too simple?"

"Hmmm." Brollers scrunched his forehead. "It was definitely recorded in a car."

"Someone *wants us to believe* it was recorded in a car," Relsh corrected him. "That's what we need to figure out. What do they want us to think?"

"It seems to me, this is a bargaining chip. He's letting us know he has access."

"Assuming he's legit. Which, of course, he *wants* us to assume. But he can't count on it. Don't we have to assume that he must assume we're too smart to make that assumption?"

"Which one?"

"The middle one."

"Okay."

"Say he's not legit and he knows we're not gonna trust him. If he thinks we're not gonna find him credible, then what's his motivation?"

"Good point."

"To have us solve a riddle?" she said. "How about this: What does the song mean?"

" 'Goldfinger.' "

"Think of the odds: *that specific song* being played over *that specific conversation* in *that specific car* . . . Does that add up to you? Does that sound like something that *just happened*?"

Brollers grimaced again. "As I told you, Wendy, it's unusual."

"I think what we need to ask is: Who . . . is Goldfinger?"

Brollers did not respond.

"*He's the man with the Midas touch.* Is Goldfinger the name of the person pulling the strings behind Gomez? Is Gomez telling us that *he's* Goldfinger? Who's Goldfinger?"

"You think there's a man behind Gomez?" Brollers asked.

"Or a woman," said Relsh. "Maybe. Could be Campman. Could be anyone. Could be no one."

"It seems too unusual to be a Democratic trap," said Brollers. "Even for Campman, this is weird."

"Particularly this," Wendy Relsh said, listening intently. "The conversation stops, Sorn appears to get out, and we have this long silence."

"This is why I think it's a real recording. Why else would you have that silence? Then the car stops. Then the weird foreign swearing—Spanish, I think. And then . . . then I don't know what?! Then we're suddenly in a bathroom, and there's that *unending* urination. . . ."

"Why have urination?" asked Relsh. "Why put that on the tape?"

"I don't know. I don't know!"

"Assuming it *is* urination."

"What else could it be? That was piss. No doubt about it." Brollers sighed, then continued: "It drives you crazy, doesn't it? Even if the tape is real, why would he include the urination bit? If the point is to show he has access, then why not just cut off the tape after the conversation ends?"

"Unless . . ."

"Unless he forgot. Unless he's just an idiot!"

"No," said Wendy, her eyes suddenly catching the glare of the overhead lamp, "no, that's just too perfect. It's too ingenious. He *wants* us to think he's an amateur. He wants us to believe he's just some independent nobody trying to make a buck."

"You know what Kendrick thinks. He thinks it's an act. He said when they met, Gomez seemed to be wiser than he let on. It was as if he'd play dumb whenever he didn't like what he was hearing, pretend he didn't understand English. *He understood all right.* Kendrick thinks he's one smart son of a bitch."

"Of course he is!" said Relsh, standing. "But what does he want us to think? Would he want us to think he's stupid? Why?"

Now there was a fierceness about her that Brollers had not seen before.

"Unless! . . . Unless he knows we won't buy into the clueless foreigner bit, unless he wants us to read into the recording. What if the urination is a commentary on the rest of the tape, a big joke on us, the same way the song is?"

Brollers shrugged. "If that's the case, we're still no closer to understanding what Gomez's motivation is."

"Gomez. Gomez. Gomez!"

"He's the key."

"We need to know his story. We're just clutching at straws until we do."

Wendy Relsh leaned back in her chair again, and Dustin Brollers exhaled deeply. They were right back where they started, and one more round of listening to the tape would not make a difference.

Just then, Ray Mulligan knocked on the door and stuck his head in.

"Sorry to butt in. You guys need to turn on the TV *right now*."

Dustin Brollers switched on the set nearest to him, and within moments, the puzzling Mexican was banished from his thoughts.

They were watching NewsNet. A stunning woman with dirty blond hair was holding a press conference in front of a suburban home.

Below her face was a caption that read:

TINA JAMES

Below the name were these words:

CLAIMS TO BE SENATOR PHILLIPS'S EX-LOVER

Below that caption was the banner headline with these words:

DOW DROPS 2 POINTS, NASDAQ DROPS 1 POINT

Below that banner headline was this banner advertisement:

POP SENSATION KIMBERLY BOWES ON THE *BILLY MACK SHOW—*
TONIGHT AT 10 P.M.

Below that banner advertisement was this scrolling headline:

EARTHQUAKE IN ZAIRE—750 CONFIRMED DEAD, HUNDREDS MISSING

It was the first caption that most interested the Republicans.

THE SCANDAL

GETTING HONEST

A fter our brief courtship in 1972, the senator and I did not keep in contact. We did not meet again until we ran into each other by chance in Oklahoma City in July of 1984. This was not long after Ben had been elected lieutenant governor, and I was working in anesthesiology at Midwest Regional Hospital. The hospital was where we bumped into each other, and when we did, Ben asked me out to lunch, and I accepted."

Tina James was reading off a prepared statement she held in her hands, but there was an unmistakable genuineness to her words. She spoke slowly and deliberately.

"This began a new phase of our relationship. We both had busy schedules but tried to have lunch whenever we could, and over the course of a few months, we became quite close. Mostly, we would talk about our jobs and our significant others; I was in a serious relationship with a fellow doctor at the time, and Ben, of course, was married. Ben talked a lot about his wife. It was clear they were going through some tough times and he was unhappy. I tried to be as much of a comfort as I could.

"However, it became increasingly difficult for me to hide my own feelings. Ben Phillips is a warm . . . and magnetic human being, and before long . . . *I fell in love with him.*"

She said it unapologetically. A 1960s Motown diva would have envied her conviction.

"One night, after having a few drinks, I told him how I felt. He was staying in a hotel at this point—he and his wife were considering an official separation—and we returned to his hotel and we made love . . . and that was . . ."

Here she seemed almost to venture off script, and it would have been easy for the viewer to imagine the subtle northward bend of a smile in her purple lips.

". . . well, it was wonderful, actually. It was very special."

She took a deep breath while many in the country held theirs.

"But the next morning, Ben was a wreck. He told me it had all been a terrible mistake, and that it wasn't me, but just that he loved his wife and felt sick he'd been unfaithful to her and he had to go back to Melissa and beg her forgiveness. At the time I was heartbroken, but, um, I understood. After all, she was his wife. And I know he felt strongly . . ."

Was she going to cry?

She was taking a moment.

". . . I mean, if you'd seen his face . . ."

Her voice had lifted just the right amount. She was close to tears, but America wouldn't see them.

". . . well, I understood why—I just—I was very sad."

It was every woman's story. Across the country, women were crying tears of empathy for Tina James while at the same time their husbands found themselves strangely aroused by the whole spectacle.

"I've been going back and forth . . . whether I should come forward about this. And it is after much painful deliberation that I've decided to do so."

She regained control. She was strong now.

"It has been particularly hard for me to hear Senator Phillips and his wife talk about their perfect marriage and his commitment to her. It seems hypocritical. Wrong. Because there was a time when Ben Phillips and I had our moment together, and by not making mention of that, it's as if it never happened.

"I know it *did* happen, and as a result, I feel I have a historical responsibility to tell the truth. While I will surely not benefit from this confession, I will at least have the comfort of knowing I have served history and my country by setting the record straight about Senator Ben Phillips. I recently heard President Struck speak about how we need to get honest as a nation. When I heard those words, I thought to myself, Well ... I guess that means me ... I guess it's time to come clean."

THE GENERAL

W hat's the score, Ben? Did you do it?"
It was the general.
"Well, Joe, I—"

"So, you *did*. I'm at the airport. I'll be there in four hours."

He arrived in three.

General Joseph Demerol did not mince words. It was something Ben had always liked about him and was one of the reasons he'd chosen him as a running mate.

Throughout the general's forty years in the armed forces, he built a reputation for being fiercely intelligent, fiercely punctual, and fiercely brief. His most infamous Pentagon meeting, held in 1988 to discuss the progress of a covert operation in Colombia, consisted of one word: "Faster." It was said Demerol accomplished more in a single day than most four-star generals did in a month (and more in a month than most officers did in their entire careers).

For many years, there had been a joke about Demerol that went something like this:

QUESTION: How long does it take the general to bring his wife to orgasm?

ANSWER: Thirty seconds faster each time, if she knows what's good for her.

The general had written three books in the three years since he left the army, and had been a regular commentator on several news-flavored television programs. Two years ago on the *Billy Mack Show*, he became the first person with serious military credentials to question the viability of Operation Freedom Fox and the president's justification for an extended war. The infamous clip went something like this:

GENERAL DEMEROL: Just because it's convenient to believe something is true doesn't make that thing true.

BILLY MACK: Are you saying there's no reason for us to be at war? Are you saying the president is misleading us? Are you saying, General, that because there's no international precedent for our unilateral actions, no international support, no actual threat, no exit strategy, and sharp criticism from the very allies who have traditionally expressed the same values as us in these matters, are you saying because of all this, in your opinion, it was unwise for the United States to have gotten involved when and how it did?

GENERAL DEMEROL: Yes.

His provocative comments caused quite a stir among Democrats, and there was some talk of a Joseph Demerol presidential campaign, which never quite materialized. Still, the general remained in the public eye throughout the primaries, making appearances on all the major news programs and criticizing the president at every turn. When Ben Phillips wrapped up the party's nomination in the early spring and was looking for a running mate, he found himself attracted to the general's independent thinking, straight talking, and acute political instincts. Together they made a strong ticket. At least that was the thinking at the time.

THE TROOPS RALLIED in Des Moines that night. Melissa canceled her class and flew out hours after the story broke. Ozzie Mayweather, who was stationed in the Washington office at the time, flew out with her. They arrived at 7:00 P.M. The general, who had been campaigning in Detroit, arrived at 1:00 A.M., three hours after speaking with the senator.

The tricky part was the kids. There was no easy way around that one. Stacy Phillips, the twenty-six-year-old med student, was in class at Case Western when the story broke, and she was reached in time. Jim Phillips, the twenty-two-year-old, was not. Jim was interning at an advertising firm in New York City and had just seen the news break over the Web when he got a phone call from his father.

"What the hell's going on? This isn't true, is it?"

If ever Ben Phillips regretted his decision, it was during the hour he first spoke with his kids. Sure, they seemed to take it okay, there were no tears or hysterics, but they'd been dealt a major blow, the impact of which Ben could only imagine, listening to the unsteadiness in his children's voices. As he absorbed their emotions through the phone line, they seemed to him suddenly like little kids again, and he was reminded of the power he'd once possessed when Jim and Stacy were still young enough to be surprised by something their mother or father did. They were now not just surprised but also shocked, and it was the sort of shock Ben Phillips had been unprepared to deliver.

On the other end of the line, Jim and Stacy each found themselves holding back tears for what they thought was their parents' sake and then wondering why those tears were there at all. Both parents spoke separately to both kids, but they tried to present a united front. Stacy thought it odd that while she felt sorry for the whole family, she also felt proud. She was proud of her parents for dealing so discreetly with this past trauma, proud they'd managed to shield her and her brother from the ancient skeletons that must have once haunted their relationship. It was an odd sort of pride, but undeniable, and in the hours to come it would serve as her silver lining and consolation.

Unlike his sister, Jim's feelings of sympathy were mixed with anger, not pride. He didn't like to be the last to know and was angry with his father for creating a situation in which he could learn about a family secret over the Internet.

"This is absolutely inexcusable!" he'd said on the phone, and his father had agreed with him.

The family felt it was time to come together, and Jim and Stacy flew out that evening. They arrived in Des Moines at 9:00 and 10:00 P.M., respectively.

Ben was met by a screaming mass of reporters that night at Theodore Roosevelt High School, where he was scheduled to speak in front of the Des Moines Teachers' Union. He walked through the press gauntlet without comment, all smiles as usual. Tonight, he would take questions only from the teachers. This, he hoped, would delay the possibility of having to address the Tina James accusations for one night, as the teachers had been asked to submit their questions in writing the previous day. Predictably, the topic managed to come up anyhow, but it was not until late in the evening, at which time a lanky male science teacher chose to depart from his scripted text and asked the senator—as polite as could be—if he wouldn't mind commenting on "the Tina James press conference."

"Look, all that's personal stuff," Ben told the man. "There'll be a press conference tomorrow about that. I'll tell you everything you want to know. But I'm not gonna talk about it now, because that's not what you folks came here for. You came here tonight to find out how we're going to take back America, and *that's* what I want to talk about!"

There was thunderous applause.

When Ben had finished speaking and shaking hands, he returned to the hotel where the others were waiting, and the family was re-united at last.

"ARE YOU OKAY?" the general asked.

"I'll be okay, Joe. I'm glad you're here."

It was 1:30 A.M. and the meeting had officially broken up for the night. The general pulled Ben aside.

"If you want to talk . . ."

"Yeah."

"This shit's terrible. Sometimes you need to talk."

"I'm okay, Joe."

"I'm here. One on one. Say the word."

"Thanks, Joe."

"You got these . . . guys around you. *I'm* a real person. I've been married forty-three years. Know what I mean?"

"Yes, Joe, I—"

"I'm old but not ancient. We can shoot the shit. No politics."

"Well . . ."

"Sometimes you need to unload. Anytime. Understand?"

"Yes."

"Don't be shy."

"I appreciate that, Joe."

The general wasn't satisfied. He pointed to his midsection.

"Punch."

"I'm sorry?"

"If you want to," he said, "letting you know you can."

"I'm not gonna hit you, Joe."

"Sometimes you need to unload. Know what I mean?"

"Of course."

"I'm here. Anytime. Talk." He made a punching motion. "What-ever."

"Thanks, Joe."

"I'm room five twenty. So you know. Understand?"

"I'm gonna be okay, Joe."

The general looked him up and down, and then made his determination:

"Of course you are," he said with a firm hand to the shoulder, and then, "Five twenty. Remember."

"Good night, Joe."

"Good night, Chief."

A LITTLE BIT OF JESUS

Step one had gone off without a hitch. The girl was brilliant. Every pause, every blink, every syllable, it was all pitch-perfect. She didn't come across as some anonymous tramp; she was a sharp, warm-blooded American woman. Heck, thought Campman, Tina James could probably run for president if she wanted to. First impressions were the most important, and Miss James had done herself proud.

In Campman's mind, the hardest part was over: the time between confession and response. He knew it was important for the campaign not to respond too quickly or too smoothly, lest it appear as if they'd seen the scandal coming, but in this age of instantaneous political reaction, keeping lips tight when the pressure is on could be a difficult thing to do. The natural response would be to defend yourself the second a blow is struck.

Campman wanted to drag out the suspense. He'd originally wanted to hold a press conference thirty-six hours after the story broke, but Shelly Greenblatt managed to talk the senator down to twenty-four hours instead.

Twenty-four hours was still pretty good, Campman thought. It gave the impression of preparedness without looking too calculating. No one could accuse the campaign of dragging its feet on the issue, but it did allow for a modicum of suspense. Perhaps Greenblatt was right on this one. The campaign remained quiet during those first twenty-four hours, offering muted denials, but nothing official from any of the power players. The suddenly changing travel plans of the members of the Phillips family and the general would, of course, be leaked to the media and raise expectations for a major revelation at the eventual press conference.

The masterstroke had been getting them all in front of the cameras together. From the side of the press podium, Campman held back a smile as he watched the entourage take the stage. Ben had Melissa at his side, and they were flanked by Jim, Stacy, Mayweather, and the general. The whole family was rallying behind the injured father. Were Ben bleeding, the photo op could not have been more humanizing.

But that wasn't all. Surrounded by family, facing a rabid press corps, Ben Phillips didn't look merely human. *Something was different*, and at the other end of the room, looking through the lens of her Canon ProDigi 3000 camera, Elayne Cohen-Campman felt it, too. As the senator opened his mouth to speak, both Campmans reached the same conclusion at exactly the same time. It was Thomas Campman who named it, quietly under his breath:

"Dammit, he looks presidential!"

[CU Nick Flynn. Round face, brown hair, impeccably groomed, high voice.]

NICK FLYNN: Once again our top story this hour, Democratic presidential candidate Ben Phillips admitting . . . he . . . had . . . an affair . . . with Oklahoma pharmaceutical employee Tina James twenty years ago. Flanked by his wife, Melissa, his two children, and running mate General Joseph Demerol, the Oklahoma senator took responsibility for his past actions today at an emotional press conference in Des Moines, Iowa.

[Roll tape of press conference. Ben Phillips speaking, holds hands with wife at podium, looks somber.]

SENATOR PHILLIPS: Our marriage was going through some tough times. We were separated. We were both considering divorce. We both considered straying from our vows. And I was the weaker party. I was unfaithful to my wife with Miss James, and it was the worst thing I've ever done.

[edit.]

SENATOR PHILLIPS: . . . I begged for forgiveness. . . . They say you don't know what you've got until you lose it. Well, I almost lost the most remarkable woman in the world. And I've thanked the Lord every day since that she found it within her heart to forgive me.

[edit.]

SENATOR PHILLIPS: You don't rebuild trust overnight. But like many other couples, we worked on it. And over the course of the last twenty years, our marriage has grown stronger than I ever could have imagined.

[Senator Phillips shares smile with his wife.]

NICK FLYNN (VO): When the senator was questioned about the secrecy of this extramarital affair, his wife, Melissa Phillips, answered for him, declaring, "It was nobody's business but ours."

[edit.]

MELISSA PHILLIPS: What goes on in a marriage . . . it's between a wife and her husband. We never told our children, Stacy and Jim, and it's not that we were hiding it from them. They were little kids when it happened. We didn't think they needed to know. If I forgive Ben, and I do, why is it anyone's business but our own?

[edit.]

[CU Nick Flynn. Upper right-hand box CU Amy Soocher. Beautiful. Stern. Lower right-hand box CU Donald Thomas. Short. Small eyes.]

NICK FLYNN: We have with us Amy Soocher from the randy right and Donald Thomas from the loopy left. Amy, what's your take?

AMY SOOCHER: Melissa Phillips asks whose business it is? I'll tell you whose business it is, Nick: It's the American people's business. This guy is running for the presidency of the United States of America. He can't even be faithful to his own wife and he expects us to trust him with the presidency? No way, Nick. He is un-Christian, un-American, and liberal as the day is long. He needs to be removed from the race, removed from his job in the Senate, and put in prison for lying to the American people.

NICK FLYNN: Donald?

DONALD THOMAS: Nick, this is absolutely absurd. The senator admitted his mistake immediately—

AMY SOOCHER: Immediately?! He waited twenty years!

DONALD THOMAS: Let me finish. The allegations came out, he immediately fessed up, he talked emotionally and honestly about rebuilding his family. He said—and I'll quote him because I think this was his best line: "It took compassion, it took patience, and it took a little bit of Jesus, too." Nick, that's gonna play well. I thought it was a very classy press conference.

NICK FLYNN: We have to go to break. I'll give you each one more word. Donald!

DONALD THOMAS: Classy.

NICK FLYNN: And Amy!

AMY SOOCHER: JailBaitLiberalLyingTraitor.

NICK FLYNN: When we come back, we'll talk about fallout from the senator's confession, and answer the following question: Does the number of TVs in your home affect your pet's chance of getting pregnant? Find out after the break.

FIG, BRIE, AND CRUMBLY CRACKERS

Peter Williams couldn't believe his eyes.

What about his ears?

They only confirmed what the eyes reported.

It could still be a coincidence, couldn't it?

The quickening of his pulse, the sweat under his arms, and the tingling sensation in his nether regions provided the final conclusive proof. It was indeed Ms. James, no doubt about it.

Yes, there on national TV, the very woman Peter had interviewed *less than a month ago* was claiming she'd had an affair with Senator Ben Phillips.

Peter wasted no time. He referenced his interview database, found Tina James's number, and dialed. No answer. He tried her alternate phone number and got a machine. He left a message. He tried the first number again. Still nothing.

He went back through his transcript of the James interview several times. Had she given anything away? Were there any clues? The best Peter could come up with was her line about politicians. She had referred to them as "a bunch of fornicators." Peter supposed that line now had new meaning. Politicians were indeed people who fornicated. They fornicated Ms. James. At least one politician did. Peter wondered if there were others. Did Ms. James make a habit of fornicating politicians?

Now that would be a story, thought Peter Williams. He quickly realized, however, that even though Tina James fornicating with a boatload of politicians might, in fact, be a hot story, it probably wouldn't be a story *TeenVibe*'s editors would be all too eager to publish.

In the end, it would be Tina James who would contact Peter the following day. He picked up the phone and knew instantly who it was.

"Is this Peter?"

"Yes, this is he."

"The reporter?"

"Yes, ma'am, Peter Williams of *TeenVibe* magazine."

"This is Tina James. Remember me?"

"Of course, Miss James."

"Tina."

"Tina, of course. I'm so glad you called. I wanted to know if we could sit down for another interview."

She was allowed one interview, wasn't she? Why not with Peter Williams?

"Can you make it for dinner?" she asked.

Peter paused for a moment.

"I'll find a way."

He hung up the phone, his heart racing. He paused for less than a second before entering the number three into his speed dial and pressing send. When his editor answered the phone, Peter made his pitch: This was an *exclusive interview with the candidate's former mistress*. He needed immediate transportation assistance, and he needed bigger guns. A lone journalist with a digital voice recorder would not be enough for this assignment. It was too important.

After some considerable wrangling on the part of Peter and his boss, a deal was worked out with a local cable station. They would lend camera equipment for the interview and would share ownership of the video once edited. In return, they would promise not to release the video version of the interview until after *TeenVibe*'s printed version hit the streets (at which time, *TeenVibe* would also post the video on its website).

The magazine paid for Peter to fly from Des Moines to Oklahoma City, and he arrived at 5:24 P.M. that day. He was met at the airport by Dave, the cameraman from WXLG 30, and the two of them piled into his green Dodge van for the short trip to the suburb of Mustang, where Tina James lived. Dave was a tall wiry fellow with a weathered face that Peter romantically assumed to be the hard-earned product of a cameraman's life in the field. He struck Peter as a real pro, his silence telling the tale of a thousand journalistic adventures, and the young reporter was embarrassed that Dave's first impression of him would always be of the cell phone call he received upon first entering the van.

It was his mom.

Dana Williams insisted that her son Peter call home at the beginning and end of every bus or plane ride. This frequent phone contact helped calm her nerves and allowed her to feel she was exercising a modicum of motherly influence on her independent-minded teenage son. On this particular occasion, she called Peter because he'd been delinquent in his postlanding communication and she naturally feared the worst: a bungled takeoff, a midair collision, or at the very least a minor hijacking.

Peter usually didn't mind these sorts of calls, but on this particular occasion it reddened his face. The call reinforced his status as a rookie reporter, the kid who still needed to call Mommy.

"Yes, I understand, Mom. I'll talk with you soon . . . okay, tonight. I'll talk with you later tonight."

To his credit, Dave just smiled and refrained from any comments once Peter hung up the phone. He looked straight ahead and kept driving. In fact, he said very little for the duration of the ride. Peter prodded him with some small talk, but Dave's answers were always short and simple. They did not invite follow-up questions. After a while, Peter gave up trying to engage his cohort and turned his attention back to the list of questions he'd formulated on the plane ride over, questions he would be asking Tina James within the next couple of hours.

By the time he looked up from his page of notebook paper, he found himself on a familiar-looking street. He spotted Tina James's house several blocks away, surrounded by TV vans. Like barnacles clinging to a ship's hull, they formed a solid mass around the periphery of the James property.

Once the van had parked, Peter helped Dave lug equipment through the gauntlet of loitering reporters and up the path to the front door. Several journalists looked strangely at the duo, undoubtedly thinking, What are those guys doing? Don't they know the rules?

The paparazzi barely had time to ready their cameras when Tina James opened the door and let the boy reporter and cameraman into her home.

It was Peter's second visit to Tina James's home, and as he entered the family room where the interview would take place, the objects in the room became familiar; the oil paintings of colorful seaside towns, the antique lamps sitting on modern end tables, the gold leather couch and the red fabric chairs.

Peter's knowledge of interior decorating was admittedly limited, but he felt certain he was not looking at a typical Oklahoma family room. He was struck once again by how the contents of the large space didn't seem to match, at least not in a conventional sense, and it surprised him that he liked this. He'd always assumed that "matching" was the most important rule of decorating—it was the *only* rule he knew—but here was a room that did not seem to match at all, and yet somehow it worked. There was a vibrancy to the decorating scheme that pulled everything together and made the disparate items work in harmony. Looking around, Peter decided the room was full of life and hope, and at the same time, sadness, as if the house itself was a shrine to fanciful promises still waiting to be fulfilled.

Tina James matched her home. She looked even more beautiful than when they'd first met, wearing a top that Peter (whose understanding of women's fashion was even more limited than his scant knowledge of interior decorating) could best describe as "vaguely Japanese." Her tight pants were black, her earrings silver. Peter felt the ensemble made her look both exotic and completely American. And stunning. She was stunning.

"I thought we'd do it in here," said Tina James, who had a way of sounding postcoitally careless and businesslike at the same time.

"That would be great," Peter squeaked.

Yep. It had happened. Once more, after less than a minute in the presence of Tina James, Peter found himself to be—as his friend Wayne Keesman would say—"a certified boner-owner." Peter had blanched when he first heard the phrase but slowly warmed to it, the way one gradually surrenders to an infectious song that refuses to leave one's brain. Peter had always wondered, though, about the word *certified*. Was there indeed a certification process for boner-owning? And if so, what was it? Who was doing the certifying? For half a second, Peter allowed himself to imagine Tina James in that role.

"Would you like some fig and Brie?"

Peter was waiting in one of the interview chairs as Dave set up the two cameras. Tina James was in the kitchen. She walked out with a platter, on which she had meticulously arranged two dozen oval crackers topped with melted Brie cheese and a large purplish blotch Peter could only assume was fig.

"Eat."

He did. The combination was sweet, hot, and messy, and Peter had to struggle to avoid spilling cracker crumbs and Brie on his lap. From nowhere Tina produced two glasses of white wine and offered one to Peter.

"I don't think I need to card you, do I?"

"Um, no thank you, Miss James. I brought water."

Peter reached down for his ever-ready water bottle and drew it up dramatically above his head to take a sip. Perhaps he squeezed too hard or perhaps the cap wasn't on tightly, but when Peter squeezed, the squirter fired off and hit him in the face along with a heavy stream of water, which ran down his clothes.

"Oh, my!" said Tina.

"No problem!" said Peter, leaping to his feet as if the answers to his troubles lay only an arm's length away.

"Let me get you a paper towel," said Tina. And she was off.

How could he have been so stupid! This was highly unprofessional. Peter looked around for a quick solution but found none.

Tina James returned from the kitchen with a handful of paper towels.

"Here, why don't you sit down."

He did.

She started dabbing Peter's face, then Peter's shirt, then going lower down on his shirt, and then lower and—

Where was she headed?

"No! That's okay!"

Peter had worn his tight white briefs for the occasion, but even those marvels of constrictive engineering could not adequately disguise what Peter feared the aggressive dabbing of Tina James would soon reveal.

"Peter."

Tina put her finger to his lips.

"Calm down, honey. Did you bring a change of clothes?"

She was on her knees in front of him with her arms resting on his legs, talking as plain as could be. Had he imagined something flirtatious in her tone earlier? If he had, it certainly wasn't there now. Crouched before him, Peter found her position sexually charged, but her face gave no indication of anything out of the ordinary. Perhaps this was just how adults acted around other adults. Perhaps it was all in Peter's head.

He made every effort to look in her eyes (as she was looking in his) and to avoid the dark area of shadow separating the mass of her two breasts. He tried not to notice how soft and real her skin looked, all tan and freckled. He was amazed how comfortable she was kneeling before him, flashing her cleavage. Peter envied her nonchalance.

"These are the only clothes I brought in," he said.

And he usually *did* bring a change of clothes! Peter always traveled with a backpack containing a miniature first aid kit, extra batteries, extra pens, a calculator, a compass, and a change of clothes. "Just in case" was his motto. But today he'd been so distracted he forgot to pack the change of clothes, and the suitcase with the rest of his belongings was in the van, on the other side of the press gauntlet.

The one time I forget . . . !

Peter made a mental note that, as a reporter, there is never any substitute for proper preparation.

"Hmmm." Tina was thinking.

Where was Dave through all this? Fiddling with sound equipment only a few feet away—but totally oblivious. For a news cameraman, thought Peter, Dave's reflexes were not very sharp.

"How big are you?"

"Sorry?"

"Are you a thirty? Thirty-two? Stand up, let me take a look at you. I have a few things, but I'm not sure if there are any your size."

Peter could not stand up now. Not with Tina sitting on her knees in front of him watching. Not unless he wanted his boner-owning to be certified. That would be a disaster. He had to come up with something quick.

"Do you have . . . maybe . . . a hair dryer?"

Tina smiled and stood.

"Come with me, gorgeous."

PETER HAD INTENDED to dry himself, but there seemed no way around the issue. There he was, standing in Tina James's bathroom with a raging (and very obvious) hard-on, and she was pointing a hair dryer at his pants. This was not how he'd envisioned his big interview. Not only was it embarrassing, not only was it awkward, not only was it completely unprofessional . . . but it was also very hot. Painfully hot.

"I'm not sure you're supposed to do this while you're still wearing the clothes," he said.

"Is it uncomfortable? Do you want to take them off?" she asked innocently.

"It's not that bad," he said quickly.

Not that bad?! His skin was being scorched! What was he saying? She could be causing permanent damage—and to a very sensitive portion of his anatomy no less!

"Maybe if you could switch it to low . . ."

"Sure," she said, "it just might take longer."

The hair dryer was switched from high to low, and Peter took a deep breath. He was still in pain, but his immediate fears of third-degree genital burns were lessened slightly.

"So tell me about yourself, Peter."

What was this?

"Tell *you* about *me*?"

"Yeah. Where are you from again?"

"Um . . . from Bethesda. Maryland."

"Really? Is that where you go to school?"

"Ow!"

"What?"

"Nothing. I mean, yes it is."

"Hmm. I've never been to Maryland."

Peter didn't quite know what to say to this, so he just nodded.

"Do you have a girlfriend back in Bethesda, Peter?"

"Um . . . yes."

"What's her name?"

"Mary."

"Peter and Mary. That's cute . . . very biblical. . . . Do you make love with her?"

"Sorry?" he said, shocked, and then quickly countered, "Wait, aren't *I* supposed to be the one asking *you* the questions?"

"It's not your turn yet," she said, smiling, looking him right in the eye. "Besides, fair is fair."

"Valid point." He didn't know what else to say.

"Do I make you uncomfortable, Peter?"

She was pointing the hair dryer directly at his crotch.

"Uncomfortable?"

"Nervous."

"Nervous? No! No, of course not. Miss James, I am a professional reporter. If my nerves were rattled by every woman who served me fig and Brie, I wouldn't stand much of a chance in this business, would I?"

"No, I suppose not."

"Nervous," he chuckled. "Ow! Nervous like a warrior maybe!" Peter instantly regretted his choice of metaphor.

"Yes. Yes, just like." Tina James grinned.

She was still pointing the hair dryer at his crotch. It had to be dry by now. His shirt remained conspicuously wet. Peter wasn't sure if he should say something, but just then, as if reading his mind, she stood up and pointed the hair dryer at his shirt.

Thank God! he thought, breathing a sigh of relief.

Peter's greater pelvic region tingled in pain as his nervous system scrambled to assess the damage. It took him a moment to realize Tina James's face was now at eye level, and she was studying him.

"God, you are the most beautiful young man and you don't even know it, do you?" she said, almost to herself. "That's positively . . . oh, what am I thinking?" She chuckled, shook her head, and became quiet, as if slipping into a very urgent thought.

"It's good that we were able to do this on such short notice," said Peter, changing the subject, confidence and comfort now returning to his body.

"Yes."

"And you know," he added hopefully, "I think I'm almost dry."

At this Tina James turned off the hair dryer and looked at him, not saying a word. Peter didn't know what to make of her facial expression but decided he'd wait for her to speak. She clearly had something on her mind.

"Okay, I'll tell you something," she finally said, "but you have to promise me it's off the record."

What was this? Peter instantly forgot about the pain in his crotch.

"Of course. I promise."

"I need your word as a journalist, that nothing in this bathroom goes on record."

Now this was exciting. Peter imagined how Woodward and Bernstein must have felt when they first caught wind of that whole Watergate mess. He was about to enter the realm of the big boys, and his heart was racing.

He began to think perhaps his water spill hadn't been such a bad thing after all. It had enabled him to establish a level of comfort with his interviewee, a level of comfort that now allowed her to open up to him. Whatever came next was going to be big, he could tell.

"Miss James, you have my word as a journalist and a United States citizen."

Tina James chuckled again. She put the hair dryer on the counter and turned to face Peter, suddenly quite serious. She was a few inches taller than he, but she looked him right in the eyes. He could smell her Chardonnay breath. She put one hand on his neck, the other hand on his rear end, and kissed him mightily.

ISSUE NO. 242

No. 242 was the bestselling issue in the history of *Teen-Vibe* magazine. The cover featured pop sensation Mickey Solara, grinning wickedly through his bleached blond curls. There was a photo spread of Mr. Solara on page forty, and a pull-out poster featuring the twenty-something teen-idol and his newly gym-worthy body parading around a zoo in a wife beater and bandanna. The lead article of issue no. 242 read "Be a Better Kisser: What You Need to Know to Give the Perfect Kiss," and it featured several sections: fifteen pointers on kissing, eighteen testimonials about best and worst kiss experiences, and a quiz designed to determine whether you were a Kissing Casanova or a Make-Out Moron. Other high profile articles in issue no. 242 included: "Hottest TV Couple," "What's with All This Hair?!," "Astrology Lowdown," and a glowing review of the new Lana Lane album, *Rock Your Equilibrium*.

But most people who purchased *TeenVibe* magazine on September 3 did so for the article on page seventy-two: "A Sinner's Story: The Exclusive Interview with Tina James."

In the article, political correspondent Peter Williams went one-on-

one with Ms. James in her Oklahoma home and asked some tough questions about her personal history, her affair with presidential candidate Ben Phillips, and what drove her to come forward with her story.

A lesser reporter might have focused almost exclusively on James's interaction with the senator, hoping to dig up as much dirt as possible, but Peter Williams was not such a reporter. While he did ask many questions on the obvious topic (and managed to come out with the most detailed version of events to make it into the public record), he also probed deeply into her past, trying to understand what drew Ms. James to the senator in the first place and then what motivated her to tell the world about it.

The interview told the story of a forgotten woman, a woman trapped by circumstance and forced into the background of other people's lives, a woman whom love had passed over time and again, who'd reached a half a century on earth with nothing to show for it.

Did she truly believe her confession was a public service?

Yes she did, but she told Williams it was also a form of therapy. It was a way to put the episode to rest once and for all.

Was there no ego involved? Not even the slightest bit?

Perhaps a little, she admitted, but that was not the main reason for her coming forward. Her confession was more about reclaiming a part of her personal history that had been previously denied her. The affair, however brief, was meaningful to Tina James, and to have her partner pretending like it never happened robbed her of that memory. Through confession, Ms. James managed to regain ownership of her sexual past.

Peter Williams wrote an editorial preceding his interview that placed James's confession in the context of several other high-profile mistresses throughout history. "I believe," he wrote, "that while Ms. James's confession may have been triggered by a need for validation similar to those of the other women, to suggest her motivations were purely selfish would be to unfairly simplify the issue. In every respect, from her fierce intelligence to her history of charitable and selfless acts, Ms. James forces us to reexamine our assumptions about what it means to be a politician's mistress and ultimately challenges the notion that a 'mistress' is any different from the rest of us."

With the introduction, the interview was four pages long. It was a stellar piece of reporting.

The public bought the magazine faster than it could be printed. Historically, *TeenVibe*'s sales tended to fluctuate within certain reliable parameters. The publication had a teenage audience that was dependable and rarely surprising. While certain savvy adults in the political establishment were known to purchase the magazine for Peter Williams's reporting, this was a small niche that rarely affected overall sales. Adults buying the magazine for themselves (and not for their kids) accounted for 1.35 percent of *TeenVibe*'s normal readership, but with issue no. 242, 64 percent of the readers were over the age of eighteen. Readership had nearly tripled.

Mary Templeton was on the escalator at the Montgomery Mall when she first glanced at the cover of the new *TeenVibe* magazine. Mary was surprised to see the new issue released a day early but was even more surprised to see that an elderly gentleman was reading it. She looked over the man's shoulder, where the magazine was open to a kissing quiz ("Are You a Kissing Casanova or a Make-Out Moron?"). Not wanting to trouble the old man, Mary ran quickly to the nearest magazine shop, where two issues remained. Her face lit up when she saw Peter's story, and she'd barely started to read it when her phone rang.

"Hey."

"Hey."

It was Peter.

"I'm reading your article! I'm so proud of you!" said Mary.

"The title was *their* idea," said Peter.

"But, Peter, this is huge! You've really made it. Four pages!"

"It's a start."

"Aww."

"Thanks."

"So, where are you? Are you back?"

"Not yet."

"Well, am I going to see you tomorrow? There's school, you know. It's kind of starting again, in case you forgot."

"Yeah," said Peter, "I'm not gonna be back full-time for a little bit."

Mary didn't like the sound of this.

"What do you mean?"

She held her breath for a response. It took a while to come.

"Actually," he said, "I've been promoted."

THE REAL NEWS

R uh—Remix . . . Ruh—Remix . . . Ruh—Re—Re—Re—
Re—Re—Re—"

[record scratch.]

[record scratch.]

[quick edit. quick edit. quick edit. quick edit. quick edit.]

"Oh, I think he should drop out of the race."

[edit.]

"It was an affront to God, and then he lied . . . it's a double affront."

[edit.]

". . . no, I think it's refreshing to see a politician so open and honest about this sort of thing. I do!"

[edit.]

"Ben Phillips should be strangled with his own intestines and his balls should be roasted over an open flame in the fiery pit of hell."

"You don't like him."

"No, I don't."

[edit.]

"If his wife's already forgiven him, and it's twenty years ago, I don't
    see what the big deal is. It doesn't bother me."
[edit.]

"Well, I think it raises serious character issues. If a man can cheat on
    his wife, what makes us think he's not gonna cheat on us?"
[edit.]

"Oh! His poor wife! I feel sorry for her."
[edit.]

"That woman! What's her name? Tina James! Shame on her! Shame
    on both of them!
[edit.]

"Are you crazy, man? I'd tap that ass too if I had the chance. Damn."
[edit.]

"She's very attractive . . . if that's the sort of thing that attracts
    you."
[edit.]

"What? No, I'm serious! If you had to cheat with anyone—aside from
    Marilyn Monroe—it would definitely be Tina James! Are you
    kidding?!"
[edit.]

"She's a hussy. Plain and simple. She's a hussy and he's a charlatan.
    A liberal charlatan. I hope his wife divorces him."
[edit.]

"No, I'm just saying it's interesting the timing of it all. Why haven't
    we heard anything before? Why does she come forward now?"
[edit.]

"Definitely a Republican plot. She's a Republican. They're paying
    her."
[edit.]

"She came across as very genuine. I think she was hurt—they were
    all hurt by it. I just don't think it speaks well for Phillips."
[edit.]

"He's in TROU–BULLLLL!"
[edit.]

"I don't think he's gonna bounce back from this. I mean maybe he
　　could've bounced back before, but not after this."

[edit.]

"It's just sad. And it's the voters who suffer. Because you can't trust
　　anyone, not anymore. She was cute though."

[record scratch.]

[record scratch.]

[quick edit. quick edit. quick edit. quick edit. quick edit. quick edit.
　　quick edit. quick edit. quick edit. quick edit. quick edit. quick
　　edit. quick edit. quick edit. quick—]

PRESIDENT GREG STRUCK so enjoyed the Tina James scandal that
he allowed himself more TV time than his standard two hours. He
usually stayed away from the news channels but this week watched
them regularly. Segments that usually turned him off, like man-
on-the-street interviews and insignificant online quizzes, he now
watched with rapt attention.

　　"Why should I care who Joe Schmoe thinks is more evil, Sheik Al
Kulami or Abu Omar? What does that have to do with real news?"

　　Which is not to say that President Greg liked real news, either, but
this was a typical response from him. If there was one thing the
president hated more than real news, it was inconsequential fluff
masquerading as real news.

　　His usual derision was nowhere to be seen, however, during the
first week of the Tina James scandal. For the first few days in particular, even the most chatty mundane news programming delighted
him to no end. Some of his favorite moments included a left-versus-
right debate entitled "Is Phillips Finished?" a NewsNet online poll
entitled "Should Ben Phillips Drop Out?" and the headline from the
Chicago Messenger on the Friday after the confession, which posed
the question: "Tina James—The Nail in the Coffin?"

　　And, of course, he loved that hour-long Peter Williams interview
with Tina James. He liked her quite a bit. Hearing Ms. James's sultry

voice and watching her purple lips move through the confession one detail at a time made Struck heady with anticipation. He savored every passing word, just as he savored the thought of another four years as president, the words and years similarly inevitable now.

The president invited his advisor Dennis Fazo to watch the second late-night airing of the Tina James interview in the President's Theater in the East Wing of the White House. As they sat alone in the empty space, the two men raised glasses filled with nonalcoholic beer and toasted:

"To reelection!"

NONJUDGMENTAL

The polls went down. But only by a little. How much further could they slip? There was a 20-point gap before the Tina James story even broke. By the time Peter Williams's interview had been published, that gap had widened to 23 points.

But then it stayed put. And three days later, in a NewsNet poll conducted after Ben and Melissa Phillips's emotional prime-time interview with Rhoda Clark, the initial 3-point loss appeared to have completely evaporated.

With Tina James causing hard-ons nationwide, men found it difficult to pass judgment on the senator for his misdeeds. Every man was forced to wonder what would happen if *they* were tempted by such a woman (never mind such a woman when she was twenty years younger!). Would they have been able to resist? Women, on the other hand, were taken with the way Ben and Melissa Phillips worked as a team to rebound from their past problems, and they admired Melissa for the enviable grace and strength she showed in handling her husband's infidelity.

Vladimir Downs, a professor of Politics and Sexuality at Hampshire College who monitored nationwide sexual activity and analyzed it in the context of current political events, reported a sharp increase in nationwide sexual activity in the week immediately following the Tina James confession and would later develop a theory that directly attributed public ambivalence about the scandal to this explosion of sexuality. Professor Downs's much-maligned theory (derived from his weekly polling of hundreds of couples across America) was that Tina James's frequent and scintillating appearances on TV and other media caused an increase in national male sexual excitement, which in turn led to an increase in copulation. Since couples who have recently engaged in the act of copulation tend to be less stressed, more open-minded, and less judgmental (particularly with regard to passing judgments on the sexual indiscretions of others), they were also relatively untroubled by news of the senator's past impropriety.

On September 12, *New York Tribune* columnist Harry Maxwell wrote an editorial accusing the Republicans of overplaying their hand and thus squandering the political capital afforded by the Tina James scandal. While Struck himself was careful not to criticize the senator, the rest of his party went on a fierce offensive, labeling Phillips everything from "Sodomite" to "Satan" and all but blaming him for the disintegration of modern American morality. Maxwell claimed that when forced to choose between the insufferable anger of the Republicans and the heartfelt remorse of the Phillips family, many Americans found the senator from Oklahoma to be the more sympathetic party.

Whatever the reasons, Phillips's poll numbers seemed ultimately unaffected by the Tina James scandal. In fact, eight days after the scandal broke, an American News Corp. (ANC) poll showed him one point *ahead* of his previous numbers! The news media was uncharacteristically cautious in reporting this Phillips bounce, but privately, many in the press were scratching their heads.

In the meantime, the campaign traveled to the key battleground state of Michigan, now with one additional member of the official press corps in tow.

In the wake of his much-heralded interview with Tina James, Peter Williams had been assigned to follow the Phillips campaign exclusively. This meant he'd no longer have to finance his own travels, taking buses across the country and sleeping in the homes of Teen Buddies and their odd families. Instead he'd be traveling on the campaign's airplane, sleeping in actual hotels, and having his other expenses subsidized by *TeenVibe* magazine.

"So, Williams, they finally let you on board!"

That was Chip Rogers's welcome when Peter first boarded the plane to Detroit. Rogers was a well-respected correspondent for ANC, and like many in the campaign press corps, he'd worked alongside Peter for the last three years of the youngster's brief journalistic career. If he ever fancied himself a mentor to the young reporter, this notion was dispelled early on. There was little to teach Peter Williams that the sixteen-year-old didn't already know. In fact, Rogers was well aware that most of his peers had more lessons to learn from Peter than they had to impart. The young man's rigorous preparation, his tenacity, his energy, and his uncompromising journalistic principles were a model to all in the field, and Chip Rogers wasn't the only one who thought so. Once Peter Williams's presence on the plane became known, the rest of the reporters welcomed him with a round of applause.

"Don't know how you did it, Peter."

"Every person on this plane would've killed for that interview."

"Congratulations, buddy."

Peter just grinned.

"You can sit here if you'd like."

The invitation came from brunette bombshell Jennifer Dial.

"I'm new here, too."

And she was. Ms. Dial was a former soap opera star who had recently joined the XLGNN News team. While her journalistic credentials were as slim as her waistline, she had been hired during XLGNN's big shakeup two months prior. The onetime news leader, XLGNN had slipped to third place in the ratings as NewsNet and

ANC began attracting more viewers with their flashy formats and loudmouthed newscasters. In an effort to reverse their slide, the company did a major firing and rehiring of talent, resulting in a younger, hipper, and decidedly more attractive news team. Jennifer Dial was just one of several actresses and former models to find work at the suddenly sexy XLGNN.

Like many of her new XLGNN cohorts, Jennifer was not widely regarded by her fellow journalists. Perhaps this explained why she was sitting alone. Whatever the reason, she now seemed quite eager to share her empty seat with Peter Williams. He accepted her invitation.

"I want you to know I've been following your work for some time now. I read 'News for All Yous' every week."

"That's great," said Peter.

"Can I tell you something? I think you're the only one who really gets it. I do. Seriously" and here she lowered her voice—"I don't think any of these blowhards *gets* it, or if they *get* it, they don't *talk* about it. Not like you do."

Peter didn't know how to respond, so he let her continue.

"I'm gonna be *watching you*," she said, "know what I mean? I'm *really* looking forward to working with you."

"Thanks," said Peter.

Jennifer Dial talked a good while longer but eventually ran out of steam. She fell asleep shortly thereafter, her head on Peter's shoulder and her arm draped lazily across his lap. As he inhaled the aroma of whatever hair products Ms. Dial had used that morning, Peter's mind flew back to the subject of Tina James and the embarrassing aftermath of their kiss. It was embarrassing for *him*, anyway; Tina James hadn't seemed too fazed by the event. He couldn't help but feel it should have been the other way around. After all, thought Peter, she was the one who threw herself at me. She was the one whose advances were rebuffed.

How could Tina James have acted like nothing out of the ordinary had happened? Had what transpired between them been so insignificant? And if that was the case, why was Peter still so embarrassed by the whole thing?

Perhaps it was a matter of maturity, he thought. A young man was supposed to feel awkward around the opposite sex. That was part of adolescence. He'd read that somewhere. He was sure of it.

Gazing at the exquisite hand of Jennifer Dial, placed as it was so precariously across his lap, Peter became horny once again and thought of his girlfriend, Mary. Was he in love with her? He didn't know. His mind was too crowded for him to think straight.

Peter still clung to the hope that he would achieve brilliant clarity on the Mary issue as soon as he had his big story. That his thoughts remained foggy was even further evidence that he'd not yet found that story. Oh, sure, the Tina James interview was a major score, but it hadn't yielded any real surprises. Peter knew that to make it as a star reporter, he needed to break news. He needed to be the first one to get to the bottom of something big. Surely there were big things happening in the Phillips campaign that people didn't know about yet. He just had to find out what those things were.

But how? Peter was in the right place and it was certainly the right time. He just needed the right story.

And then, once he got it, he'd know for sure about Mary. At least he hoped he'd know for sure.

THE DETROIT RALLY

Keep smiling. Stand straight. Be confident.

It sounded like a good crowd, but then, it was always hard to tell from backstage. Ben Phillips had promised himself he'd stop trying to guess, but he always did anyway.

The general was onstage introducing him.

"Remember, this is your victory lap," said Campman. "The scandal's over. They tried to bring you down, but they failed. *They* failed. *You* won."

For the first time since the scandal erupted, Ben was feeling a little better. The initial grief and stress had subsided, and a sense of acceptance had taken hold. Yes, the lie was out there. Yes, it was a terrible thing to have done. But now the worst was over. Now he could go back to honest campaigning. He could get back to changing the country.

"It's time," said Greenblatt.

Keep smiling. Stand straight. Be confident.

Through the echo of the convention center, he heard General Demerol's booming bass:

"The next president of the United States ... Senator ... Ben ... Phillips!"

There was a roar. Yes, this was different. Ben could tell right away.

There were several stairs to not trip on and then bright blinding lights, and then Ben would be on a stage—a stage like any other— pumping his arms wildly. Another anonymous crowd was on its feet.

But wait. This was different.

Why? Perhaps the crowd was larger than usual. Perhaps they were louder. It wasn't just these things though.

Ben could see faces now, many of them, and that's where the difference lay. These were people in pain. They were hurting. For him! Was it empathy? Yes, but also love. Also respect. Also trust.

The crowd stayed on its feet and continued applauding.

"We're behind you, Ben!"

"We support you, Ben!"

"We won't let those bastards win, Ben!"

"We love you, Ben!"

Ben embraced the general and waited by the microphone for the applause to subside. It took a glorious eternity.

Finally, they were quiet.

"*I was thinking,*" said Ben slowly, "*that I'd like my country back.*"

Mad screams.

He didn't know why he said it. It just felt right. Propelled by the frenzied crowd, Ben Phillips let go of his control and let instinct guide him.

"I'd like my country back because I'm starting not to recognize it. ... Because people have been saying when I raise my voice for change ... that it's un-American ... and that ... makes ... me ... mad!"

Ben Phillips never improvised. Where was this coming from?

The audience roared with approval.

Ben's typically smooth baritone strained under the weight of his newfound passion as he continued.

"*So,*" he said, "*I think it's time to take it back.*"

The crowd exploded.

Shelly Greenblatt was red in the face.

The general smiled broadly.

Peter Williams stared blankly.

Ben's assistant Charlie whistled quietly under his breath.

Elayne Cohen-Campman felt a sudden urge to pee, while her husband, Thomas Campman, stood frozen, staring at the candidate in disbelief.

"*It's time to take back the country,*" said Ben with uncharacteristic ferocity, "*from special interests . . . from billionaires . . . from arrogance . . . and from those who tell us it's not patriotic to look at your government and say 'WE CAN DO IT BETTER!'*"

Ben felt high but totally in control. He owned the moment and reveled in the completeness and perfection of that ownership. He felt blood racing about inside him like electricity, energizing every muscle fiber and bringing life to the perfect machine of his body. He was superhuman. He could do anything.

The improvisation wouldn't continue much longer. Ben would segue back into his prepared text only moments later, but he'd deliver it as never before. After a long campaign filled with enthusiastic crowds, it seemed the audience in the Detroit Convention Center had changed Ben. They'd made him feel for the first time like a commander in a war, like a general with an army at his back. These people didn't just support his policies; they supported him as a man. They didn't just love his résumé; they loved him. They *owned* him, like family, in all his imperfection. His scandal was their scandal. His pain was their pain. His victory could be their victory.

For the first time in a long time, it all felt possible.

THE BEST WORST THING

It was official. They were on the rebound—and even sooner than Campman had predicted. A new barrage of TV advertising would get the credit, of course, but Thomas Campman knew better. People were suddenly interested in Ben Phillips—perhaps for the wrong reasons, but they were interested—and that's why the new ads had such an effect.

Granted, they were good ads. Ben had wanted to focus on a more positive message, and Campman helped him craft it. Working through Ralph Sorn's advertising master, Betty Rohan, they produced a series of ads that connected episodes from Ben Phillips's personal biography with specific elements of his "Plan for America." A commercial on health care, for example, would tell the story of Ben Phillips's mother, who died of breast cancer, and use that story to illustrate how committed the senator was to making prescription drugs afford-able for all seniors. Campman explained the ads as *the experience makes the man makes the policy.*

While vigorous attacks on the president had proved effective in Phillips's primary victory over Warren Muddville, these attacks had

grown repetitious and less effective over the course of the general campaign. Now September turned out to be the perfect time for a re-
vamped positive message. Just as Americans were asking, "Who is this
Ben Phillips guy, *really*?" their TVs told them how Ben Phillips planned
to change the country and why he was doing it the way he was.

Struck's team countered with rebuttal ads, dismissing Phillips's
ideas as gimmicks and "further evidence of the liberal obsession
with big government." The ads were more name-calling than sub-
stantive. They were designed not-too-subtly to remind people of the
senator's problems with Tina James, and rather than weaken Phillips, they furthered the perception that the Democratic candidate
was being undeservedly attacked.

And the polls went up.

On September 14, two weeks after the Tina James confession, the
senator's numbers had gone up 6 more points. They were now 13
behind.

"THAT PICTURE IS going on the cover of *Politics Weekly*. I tell you,
you two look so genuinely beautiful together."

Photographer Elayne Cohen-Campman was making it very difficult for Melissa Phillips to hate her. Elayne's tone was so warm, her
demeanor so modest, her compliments so heartfelt, she was becoming positively appealing.

Melissa had many reasons for wanting to dislike Elayne Cohen-
Campman, the most obvious being Elayne's choice of husband. The
scandal plan had revealed a side of Thomas Campman that Melissa
had not seen before, and in the course of a few short weeks, he'd
come to represent everything in her mind that was corrupt and ugly
about politics. What did it say about Elayne that she could be in love
with such a dark man?

And why had she joined the campaign so late in the game? Surely
there was no need for a second campaign photographer. Why should
she get special treatment just for being Campman's wife?

Then there were the juvenile reasons. Despite herself, Melissa also wanted to hate Elayne for her tiny waistline, for the way she threw together even her most casual outfits with the artfulness of a *Vogue* fashion editor, and for her seemingly effortless rise to the top of her profession only a few years after first picking up a camera.

But she couldn't. While there were many reasons to dislike Elayne on paper, in person she was sweet and genuine. She was one of those people who brightened every room she entered, and her genius was that she did it without drawing attention to herself, unlike her ego-maniac husband. His was the charisma of a rock star, hers the gentle fizz of champagne.

Melissa had been sitting with Ben, and she let him put his arm around her. They were in a hotel room with the throng of advisors, but it had been a quiet moment, and they were enjoying being tired together. It reminded her of how things used to be, when they were a young idealistic couple on the campaign trail.

Elayne snuck up and snapped a picture before they noticed her.

"That picture is going on the cover of *Politics Weekly*," she said. "I tell you, you two look so genuinely beautiful together."

The comment softened the couple, and they turned inward to share a smile, both happily self-conscious. Despite the insanity of what they'd just been through, they still *did* make a good couple, didn't they? Was it crazy to think it might all turn out okay?

"I think you guys are handling this real well," said Elayne, as if reading their thoughts. "Really, quite admirably. And I think it's gonna pay off. I think this whole scandal thing might end up being the best worst thing to happen to you. Adversity just brings out the best in some people."

She was crouching on the floor and wearing a thin, low-cut V-neck sweater. Melissa's eyes were drawn to her perfectly framed cleavage.

"Thank you, Elayne," she said, making a conscious effort to look upward into Elayne's warm eyes. "That's nice of you to say."

"Of course, it's none of my business," Elayne demurred. "I shouldn't have said anything."

But I'm glad you did, thought Ben as he felt his wife exhale deeply, relaxing into his embrace. Melissa had been twisted in knots ever since the Tina James confession hit the airwaves, and she needed every bit of reassurance she could get. As someone theoretically outside the plan's inner circle, Elayne's words of comfort carried more weight than his. Ben wanted to thank her for saying exactly the right thing at exactly the right time. Instead, he said, perhaps too gruffly, "That's quite all right. We don't mind."

Elayne flashed them both a broad smile as she sprang to her feet and waltzed away. When she was out of earshot, Melissa said the only thing she could think of to say:

"My God, she has perfect breasts."

Ben, who had been admiring Elayne's breasts for some time, paused just a little too long before attempting a playful response:

"Well, sure, if you like that sort of thing. . . ."

ELAYNE'S PICTURE OF Ben and Melissa's quiet moment together did not make the cover of *Politics Weekly* as she predicted. It did, however, make the front page of the *New York Tribune* and was featured prominently in no fewer than six major news magazines. It was the lead picture on NewsNet.com for a full ten hours, and the country's most popular supermarket tabloid ran a two-page spread of the picture underneath a one-inch-tall headline that read: THEY REALLY DO LOVE EACH OTHER!

Elayne Cohen-Campman had scored major points.

A MEMORABLE PHONE NUMBER

I f we let this slip through the cracks, we're stupid."

Greenblatt was speaking.

"He's right, Tom," said Sorn.

Congress was back in session, and Phillips had been in town for two days to vote on the new crime bill. The key advisors, Greenblatt, Mayweather, Kiley, and Sorn, were meeting at campaign headquarters. Campman found himself outnumbered.

"It was Danny Chervin himself, Tom. *CEO of GasCom!* Meeting privately with the president *to formulate national energy policy.* This is *exactly* what we've been saying all along: that this guy is in bed with special interests, that they're running the country. And now there's proof."

"Not proof, Shelly."

"Not yet. But you know it's true."

"They're not gonna have proof. Nothing that'll stick before the election."

"Not if we don't pounce on this bastard," said Sorn.

"Boys, it's not either/or here," said Campman. "We can still keep

the pressure on without getting our hands dirty. I can't overempha-
size how important it is that we stay above this one. We don't make
accusations unless it's fact. We don't deal with fraudulent information, with insinuation. That's *them. They're* the ones. If we pounce on
this before there's evidence, it makes us look the same as them. You
all know that. We have to let the press handle it."

"The press?" said Mayweather incredulously. "Oh, yeah, they're really pouncing on this one. Can't you tell?"

"We can't look like we're *hoping* our president is a crook. I think
the senator agrees with me on this. That's old Democratic mind-
set."

"It's commonsense tactics, Tom. We're not suggesting mudsling-
ing, but a little insinuation. . . . If they think our man's a wimp,
what's it prove if we don't attack? If we . . ."

Sorn kept speaking, but Campman tuned him out. Just then, his
cell phone buzzed in his pocket. He was happy for the reprieve.

"Excuse me, Ralph."

Campman put the phone to his ear, unaware that only seconds
later, all thoughts of GasCom, Danny Chervin, and the president of
the United States would be banished from his mind, replaced by a
sense of cold, heavy dread.

Once again, there was that same soft male voice. He had called in
Tampa. He had called in Green Bay. And now he was calling in
Washington. When Campman heard the voice, he froze.

"I know about Muddville. *And I know what you're doing now!*"

There was no use responding. The line went dead.

Campman stared at the caller ID. It was a D.C. number.

I know this number! he thought.

Nearly four decades of dirty tricks had left certain "anonymous"
public phone numbers rattling around inside Campman's brain. It
could be one of a few places. . . .

Campman raced to the window. He looked out across the street at
McPhereson Square. At the public phones.

Unbelievable. Sure enough, there was someone who'd just finished a call. A man in a gray suit, an outfit most likely purchased from *Covert Political Operatives Monthly*. And he was wearing sunglasses, too! How embarrassingly obvious!

"What is it, Tom?"

"Kiley, get over here!"

Kiley sprang to his feet and joined Campman at the window.

"See that man in the suit?"

"With the glasses?"

Campman almost asked Kiley where his car was, but he knew the answer. He had seen it parked out front. Every second counted. So he just yelled:

"Follow him! GO! GO!"

Kiley looked at Campman, confused.

"What—?"

"He's gonna hail a cab! I'll explain later! GO!!!!!!"

"Okay!"

As Kiley ran out the door toward the stairs, Campman shouted after him. *"Find out where he's going! DO NOT LOSE HIM, WHATEVER YOU DO!!!!!"*

HIS FIRST CAR CHASE

This was beyond the call of duty. No doubt about it.

But he was on the move, and there was no turning back.

As Kiley left the building, he could see the man with the sunglasses getting into a cab. He raced across the street after him, forgetting for a moment that streets have cars and cars can be dangerous when in motion.

"Watch it, dumbass!"

Kiley stutter-stepped to a chorus of honking horns and eventually found his way to the other side, where his brother-in-law's Mercedes was waiting. His wife's brother Gerry was spending two months in Europe on business and had lent them his car to drive while the young couple shopped for a new one. The Mercedes was Gerry's great masculine joy, and out of respect for his brother-in-law, Kiley had driven it as delicately as traffic would allow up until this point. Watching the yellow cab peel away down Fifteenth Street, Derek Kiley realized such genteel driving would no longer suffice.

The car was facing the right direction (*Thank goodness!*), and Kiley stepped on the gas. He was about a block behind the cab but could see it clearly. With his free hand he reached for his cell phone and called Campman.

It rang.

"Hello?"

"Who the hell am I following and why the hell am I following him?"

Campman didn't seem pleased by the question.

"I don't know. *That*'s why you're following him! Now don't let him out of your sight! I want to know who he is and who he works for! *Do not lose him!*"

Dial tone.

Way beyond the call of duty. No fucking doubt. Where was Campman's assistant, Wyatt? Why wasn't *he* the one racing down Fifteenth Street? Or what about Hector? What good was having a personal valet and a personal assistant if neither were available for car chases? Kiley was angry.

Traffic forced the cab left onto F Street.

Kiley had almost caught up but now had to wait for his turn to make the left. He wasn't going to make it. The light turned red.

Kiley stepped on the gas and screeched through the intersection, nearly sideswiping an oncoming SUV. A mixture of anger and excitement propelled him forward.

"You want to play James Bond?" said Kiley. "Let's play James fucking Bond!"

And then, "Dammit!"

Kiley slammed on the brakes. Another red light.

The lanky young speechwriter loosened his tie and pumped up the air-conditioning.

Why was he getting all the reds? Why now?

He could no longer see the cab, but every light on F Street was red. Most likely the cab had stopped. But how much farther had it traveled? Had it turned? Kiley swallowed nervously.

Green light.

The Mercedes roared. Kiley's system flooded with adrenaline. The car raced ahead, weaving through traffic, passing slower vehicles on every side. The race was on. But where was the yellow cab?

Kiley passed a yellow cab on his left but quickly realized it wasn't the one he wanted.

He spotted another yellow cab—this one more promising—turning right two blocks ahead. At least it seemed like two blocks.

Was it Eleventh Street?

He passed Eleventh.

Was it Tenth?

He turned.

He'd guessed right. The yellow cab was directly in front of him and had paused for a moment in front of Ford's Theatre.

He had caught up. Now all he had to do was follow.

The cab turned left on Pennsylvania. It went straight for about two blocks and then turned left after the Navy Memorial. It pulled off to the side.

The man was paying. He was about to get out.

Kiley had no place to stop! He drove past the cab on Seventh Street and pulled over to the side. The car behind him honked.

"Okay! I know!"

As long as he doesn't go to the Metro station, Kiley thought, we might be all right.

A few moments later, the door of the cab opened. Out stepped the man with the sunglasses. He carried a small laptop bag around his shoulder, and Kiley noticed he had a pointy chin.

Sure enough, the man closed the car door, turned, and headed straight for the Metro station. Kiley's heart sank as he saw his prize getting away. Then at the last moment, just as the man was about to enter the station, he stopped short.

For whatever reason, Kiley wondered if he'd been noticed. He considered ducking down.

The man with the sunglasses stood completely still. Then he turned to face the Mercedes and started walking forward.

"Oh, boy."

The man was getting closer.

Kiley scrunched down in his seat, his mind racing. Did this man know who he was? Did he know he was being followed? Could this man be dangerous? Could this all be a trap? Was Campman setting him up?

As the scenarios in Kiley's mind grew more and more ridiculous, he slowly became aware that the man crossing the street was not actually looking at him. He was not even looking at the Mercedes. He was looking beyond.

The man walked right past the driver's-side window of Kiley's borrowed car and onto the sidewalk. From there, he walked into the crowded Javaliscious Coffee Shop and took a place in line.

BWWWWRRRRRRRRRRRRRRRRRRRR!!!!!!!!!!

Another car was honking. Kiley was blocking traffic and needed to move. Quickly. He needed to find parking before the man ordered his coffee and left the shop.

Kiley merged back onto Seventh Street and began his search for an empty metered space. There were none to be found.

"Come on . . . come on . . . give me something, anything!"

As far as the eye could see, there were no spaces.

One block more. Still nothing.

He turned right. He circled around the block. Still nothing.

"We can do this . . . come on . . . dammit."

He hit a light, and there was no way around it. Traffic was on all sides.

Kiley realized he was freezing and turned the air-conditioning down. He was dripping with nervous sweat. He quickly reassessed his situation. What was he doing here? He was three blocks from the man he was trailing—scratch that—from the *sitting duck* he was trailing, the man who at that very moment was slowly—leisurely!—finishing his coffee and slowly—leisurely! sluggishly!—creeping away into oblivion, never to be seen again. And here *he* was, helpless, immobile, trapped, about to fail miserably, and all because *he couldn't find a parking space?!* And on top of it all, *this wasn't even his job. He was a speechwriter for God's sake!*

The light turned green. *(Thank you, Lord!)*

Still no empty spaces.

He rounded the corner onto Pennsylvania.

"Oh, please be there . . . please be there," he said, about to complete his circle. He turned right onto Seventh and slowed down with the traffic just in front of the Javaliscious Coffee Shop.

The man was still there! But he was next in line. Kiley had to park quickly. Ahead, there were no spaces to be found.

For a moment, Kiley questioned whether he should double-park but quickly decided it would be a bad idea. He'd be towed for sure. Kiley's old Volkswagen had been towed in D.C. once, and it never drove the same afterward. He couldn't take that chance with Gerry's prized Mercedes.

"Crap! Crap! Crap!"

There was nothing. He was getting too far away. He had to circle back.

Were there any parking garages nearby? Kiley racked his brain. He knew of a hotel a few blocks away. But that would take too long. If only he'd gone there first . . .

"Dammit!"

Another red light.

Kiley imagined the man with the sunglasses ordering coffee. Please, oh please, thought Kiley, make it a frozen hazelnut cappuccino smoothie with whipped cream and extra flavor syrups! Please make your order as needlessly complicated and labor-intensive as possible! Please order a bagel and ask for it toasted! Please try your drink and complain they put too much milk in it! Please, oh please!

Green light. Should he go an extra block?

No time. He'd double back the same way as before.

"Oh, God! . . . come on! . . . Something! Something!"

He banged his hands against the wheel. Why was he having such terrible luck?

He turned the corner back onto Pennsylvania with a sick feeling in the pit of his stomach. Then the turn back onto Seventh Street.

He stopped in front of Javaliscious. Again.

BWWWWRRRRRRRRRRRRRRRRRRR!!!!!!!!!!

"Fuck you!" yelled Kiley, startled out of his wits.

The man wasn't there. He was no longer in the coffee shop.

Kiley looked around frantically.

There he was! Crossing the street toward the Metro station, coffee in hand.

BWWWWWRRRRRRRRRRRRRRRRRRRRR!!!!!!!!!!

"Dammit!"

Kiley kept driving.

"I need to pull over now. I should do it. Crap! I should double-park. No, I can't. I have to. He's getting away. Dammit! Damndamn-damndamndamn!"

He could still catch up if he found a space now. Whatever train the man was waiting for probably wouldn't arrive immediately. He'd have a few minutes to find him and get on the same train. He just needed to find a space. Right. Now.

Kiley turned left onto a less crowded street.

Nothing, nothing, and more nothing, but at least he was going fast. Kiley raced toward the next intersection and, in a last-minute decision, turned right when he should have turned left.

"What am I doing?!"

He was traveling even farther away from the Metro station.

Kiley imagined the man wearing the sunglasses getting on his train and waving to him, like in that Gene Hackman movie. Or was it Hitchcock?

"Oh, God."

Derek Kiley was definitely not in a Hitchcock movie. People in Hitchcock movies never had trouble finding parking. People in Hitchcock movies never hit red lights. People in Hitchcock movies didn't drive their brother-in-law's Mercedes!

Grim acceptance started to creep over him.

Dripping with sweat, Kiley circled around the block a few more times, but after about twenty minutes, he realized that even if he could find parking, his chance of locating the man in the sunglasses had long since past. *He'd lost him.*

ELAYNE COHEN HYPHEN CAMPMAN

Elayne Cohen-Campman prided herself on being one of the earlier women to hyphenate. Not that being first mattered. But it did, in a way. Elayne liked to see the look on other people's faces when she introduced herself as Mrs. Cohen-Campman. That simple hyphenation told people everything they needed to know about the nature of her marital vows. She stood beside her husband, proud to carry his name, but she was also an independent woman, an individual; and she liked it that way.

In college, Elayne was an outspoken feminist and ardent liberal. After graduate school, everyone was shocked when she started dating the unapologetically Nixon-loving Tom Campman. Even after they married, few of her friends could understand what she saw in the man who once publicly derided JFK as "that dead pansy from Bahhston."

What Elayne saw was her intellectual equal, a dashing man with a devilish wit, a man with a passion for righting the world's wrongs, and, yes, a good and moral man as well. Elayne would never know of all Tom's dirty political tricks (and perhaps this was for the best), but she knew enough to realize he didn't always play fair. He *did* play with the country's best interests in mind, however, and that was something most people just didn't understand about Thomas Campman. Whether Tom and Elayne always agreed on what the country's best interests were was beside the point. She knew that, regardless of his methods, his motivations were pure, and that was one of the reasons she could love him as strongly as she did.

As the years went by, the differences in Tom's and Elayne's ideologies grew less distinct. She became more cynical, Tom, more open-minded. When Tom switched to the Democratic Party in the late 1990s, the couple found themselves espousing similar political beliefs for the first time in over thirty years. These ideological shifts were due in large part to external forces, of course, but neither Tom nor Elayne could completely deny the other's influence. Consciously or not, they were meeting in the middle.

In Elayne's mind, that was a part of being married. Each person becomes the other to a certain degree. And now, after thirty-four years of marriage, Elayne was proud to admit that a large part of her was Tom Campman.

But she kept her name. That was important.

Their daughter, Debbie, also adopted the name Cohen-Campman when she rediscovered her Jewish roots and began training to become a rabbi. The only problem was that Debbie had been engaged for six months to a young man she had met at Brandeis University named Joshua Kepplebaum, and she was planning on keeping both her names.

"*Deborah Cohen-Campman-Kepplebaum?* That's a limerick, not a name! Add 'and Schwartz' to the end, and you've got a damn law firm!"

Her father's expression of concern was well intentioned but, like much of his advice, was not received as such.

"Well, Dad," said Debbie, holding back tears, "I guess you just can't handle two forward-thinking women in your house."

"Let's hope your daughter doesn't make it three! If she follows suit, she'll need a table of contents to read her own name!"

At this Debbie stormed off, and Campman, who had great respect for most of his daughter's life decisions, felt guilty.

Elayne often marveled how the magical communication skills of Tom Campman could evaporate in the presence of their only daughter, but she knew her husband meant well. Tom tried hard to be a good father and succeeded—in her estimation—about 70 percent of the time. Many men with more natural fathering talents have done far worse, she thought.

When Debbie was born, Elayne decided to become a stay-at-home mom. She satisfied creative urges by working in her home studio, producing abstract oil paintings and three-dimensional sculptures made from found objects. When Debbie went off to college seven years ago, Elayne's world opened up. She began to travel and let photography become her main form of expression. She bumped out her home studio and created a darkroom.

Elayne's photos of the starving and limbless children of Bisanthia first won her international acclaim and put her on the map as a serious artist. More projects followed, including: the Starving Children of Coal Country, the Limbless Families of the Tellusia Swamps, the Tongueless Women of Botú, and the Rhythmless Amateur Dancers of Hackensack, New Jersey. This last piece marked a shift for Elayne toward more "performance-based" subject matter. In the last year and a half, she'd explored New York's alternative theater scene, the Young Debaters of America competition, and most recently, Bollywood.

In creating a niche for herself in the art world, Elayne felt she'd finally achieved balance in her life. She was an independent and successful artist, a warm and supportive mother to a fiercely intelligent daughter, and a loving wife to a world-renowned political mastermind. She had done it. Career. Family. All of it.

Then what was missing?

Had it all become too easy? One hour into the flight to Phoenix,

Elayne started to ponder the possibility that she'd grown bored in her marriage. It was a wild thought, one without much initial evidence to support it. Indeed, there was a great deal of evidence to the contrary, and if Elayne were to have been purely analytical, weighing the scant evidence of marital boredom against the formidable evidence of marital satisfaction, she would have dismissed the notion outright as being both ridiculous and temporary. But she didn't. She couldn't. For whatever reason, the troublesome thought lingered in her mind. Now why was that?

She'd recognized for some time that she was a person who thrived on conflict; the conflict of being an independent woman in a man's world, the conflict of being a mother who works, the conflict of being a Democrat married to a Republican, these were the daily challenges that sustained her, that provoked her, that made her better for their existence, and while she welcomed the resolution of these struggles, she also mourned their absence. As much as she enjoyed sharing Tom's political world, as energized as she was by their mutual cause, a certain type of excitement was missing. Perhaps she didn't like agreeing so much.

But she did love the campaign. It was all the excitement of a war except without the danger: long hours, constant travel, camaraderie, patriotism, teamwork, and a common goal of—yes, that's right—saving the world. Elayne was inspired by the people she met in all these different American towns and cities, all these ordinary people, so engaged by the political process.

And then there was Ben, the man behind it all. He was the great mystery. To be fair, if Elayne had a rose-colored view of the Democratic candidate, it probably had a lot to do with good timing *and her own presuppositions*. Before Elayne even joined the campaign, Ben Phillips could do little wrong in her eyes. Once she began traveling with the candidate, he did no wrong at all—at least not while she was watching.

When Ben Phillips was heckled during a speech in Boise, Elayne didn't see it. She'd just been stung by a bee and was seeking medical attention. When Ben tripped getting off the campaign bus in Green Bay, Elayne was too far back to get a good view. When he sputtered in response to an immigration question in Mobile, Elayne was distracted, taking pictures of the other reporters. In short, if ever Ben faltered, Elayne was invariably unaware. When he was brilliant, though, she caught him every time. So it could be said, the sun always seemed to hit Ben brightest from wherever Elayne Cohen-Campman was standing.

The Tina James scandal had only made him more intriguing to her. What other secrets was he hiding? She wondered what motivated a man like Ben Phillips to strive for such a high office. Elayne imagined that behind the perfect posture and likable grin, there were dark forces at work. Ben Phillips struck her as a man who battled daily with the fiercest of demons and every day emerged victorious. Perhaps these demons were psychological, created from past events, or perhaps they were just . . . ideas. Yes, ideas! Elayne found this theory particularly romantic.

For all her speculation, Elayne still remained in the dark about Ben Phillips's supposed *true nature,* that mysterious otherness she was so sure he kept hidden. She wanted desperately to know more. Whatever percolated under the surface, whether it was dark and scary or soft and sacred, Elayne wanted to glimpse it. She wanted to know who he really was, to see him not as a god but as a man. Only time would tell whether she'd get that chance. She had yet to take a "Big T" photograph. The photo of Ben and Melissa together was close, but not quite there. She knew there was more to capture of Ben Phillips.

"IS THERE A reason you're riding back here with us?"

"Oh, just a change, I was gonna take pictures, but then . . . I guess I got distracted. Tired, I guess. Just zoning out."

There was something about Peter Williams that made her feel the need to explain herself.

"They didn't kick you out. . . ."

"Oh, no. They let me hang around."

"You're Thomas Campman's wife."

"Guilty as charged. Yeah, you've got me. That's my 'in.' They know I'm partisan anyway—I mean, I'm with the campaign. I take photos, but I'm not press. I'm sorry, I think I just woke up. I apologize if I'm not making sense."

"That's okay."

"You're the kid reporter."

"Peter Williams."

"Nice to meet you, Peter Williams. My name is Elayne. Elayne *Cohen-Campman*."

At that moment, the plane dipped violently and unexpectedly to the north.

SOME MORE RECORDING

You couldn't find parking?!"

The boss was repeating himself. He'd been yelling at the young one for some time now, taking breaks to pace quietly across the longitude of the plane's shallow carpeting, but returning to the same exclamation over and over again in a grisly nagging fashion that reminded Hector uncannily of his wife.

Brinita had a tendency to latch onto a grievance and declaim it ad nauseam until the perpetrator of the misdeed (usually Hector) suffered a degree of guilt and shame roughly equivalent to the original transgression plus interest. In Brinita's peculiar brand of justice, there were no checks and balances, no appeals, and, at times it seemed, no logic. Hector would often find himself suffering retribution for a crime he had no memory of.

On one such occasion, Brinita had dreamed Hector was cavorting on a beach with Kimmy and Libby, the Dude Beer girls. Needless to say, despite Hector's distaste for Dude Beer, his relative unfamiliarity with its tantalizing TV spokeswomen, and his complete innocence with regards to Brinita's charges of sandy sun-soaked infidelity, Hector spent the next eleven nights snoring fetally on the couch. Hell hath no fury like a woman dreaming of scorn. In the years since the dream, Hector's wife would speak occasionally of his "torrid affair with the beer girls," whenever, in a wave of anger, she felt the need to leverage her credentials as put-upon wife and martyr. When something bothered Brinita you heard about it, and usually more than once.

Now, in his boss's unrelenting harassment of the young one, Hector found himself thinking of his wife.

"I can't believe it. I just can't believe we missed such an opportunity . . . over a parking space!"

The young one no longer protested. He slouched sullenly in his leather airplane recliner, unaware his silence was being recorded that very moment by a small tape player on the floor beneath him.

Hector Elizondo's eyes, nearly hidden behind the latest issue of *Star Spotter Weekly*, flitted back and forth between the young one and the boss, who seemed to be speaking more to himself than to anyone else in particular.

". . . so close to unraveling the mystery!"

Suddenly, to Hector's delight, the candidate himself chimed in.

"Tom, I don't even know what you're talking about, but you sound like a crazy man. Leave the poor kid alone and go find your wife. I think she's back there eloping with one of the reporters."

There was scattered laughter throughout the cabin, and Hector joined in, though he wasn't quite sure what he was laughing at. In truth, his excitement at Ben Phillips's participation in the conversation—and thus his recording—was reason enough. Hector only hoped the candidate wasn't too far out of the tape recorder's range, sitting as he was at the opposite end of the aircraft.

Hector had no sooner begun pondering the recording potential of his planted device than the plane took a violent and unexpected dip to the north, and that very device bounced from its hiding place and slid toward the center of the plane, finally coming to rest on a conspicuously unoccupied and centrally located stretch of carpeting about five feet from where he was sitting.

Hector swallowed hard, staring in shock at his newly exposed secret.

If only he'd had time to secure the device in advance, this might not have happened.

Naturally, he'd been afforded no such luxury. The planes were combed for bugs before takeoff, and Hector's only chance to get his tape recorder strategically hidden was to drop it on the floor as he boarded (along with his carry-on bag, to disguise the act) and then subtly kick it under a seat. Once the recorder was out of view, it would be up to chance whether or not the important people happened to sit within its narrow range.

To maximize his chances of getting a good recording that evening, Hector chose the most centrally located row of seats under which to drop his tape recorder. He hadn't expected to see it again until the end of the flight. But now suddenly . . . here it was. His bold microphone placement had backfired, and in that perilous unending moment, he found himself trapped, staring helplessly at the tape recorder sitting in the middle of the empty carpet for all to see.

Fortunately for Hector Elizondo, all eyes were not staring at the floor in that moment. That is to say, most eyes were staring at a different part of the floor, a part several feet to the west, closer to the cockpit, where the bloodred stains of a cranberry juice cocktail and the long amber legs of a flight attendant apologetically probing for AWOL ice cubes managed to grab the attention of most of the front cabin's passengers.

There had been a spill.

"I am *so* sorry," the attendant implored.

Hector seized the opportunity. Without a moment's hesitation, he tossed his copy of *Star Spotter Weekly* to the ground, and it landed on top of the tape recorder, concealing it perfectly. He jumped up with all the grace of an epileptic at a disco and—now suddenly the subject of stares—retrieved his newspaper and the device beneath it before anyone was the wiser.

"EeeeYes-Scyoose-meee."

Hector returned to his seat, and with a masterful sleight of hand disposed of the tape recorder in the one place where no one would possibly notice it: down the front of his pants. Eager to appear innocent, Hector immediately unfurled his newspaper, as if to say, "See! I have nothing to hide!" And if a poll had been taken of those watching in that very moment, most spectators probably would have agreed Hector overplayed his nonchalance, although no one would have guessed to what end.

As the flight continued, however, more than one fellow passenger would quietly notice an unusual bulge in the front of the Mexican's slacks. Ozzie Mayweather was one such passenger. He probably wouldn't have even noticed the bulge were Hector not slouched in his chair like a sleep-deprived teenager and were he not curiously rocking his pelvis back and forth to the rhythm of conversation, like a masochistic tennis fan with a scrotal death wish. Misinterpreting Hector's attempts to operate his hidden tape recorder like a boom mike and convinced he was seeing Hector's sexual side for the first time—something he had never seen before, something he had never wanted to see in the first place, something he had always assumed (for the sake of his own peaceful night slumbers) was nonexistent, and something he prayed he'd never have to see again—Ozzie Mayweather began to feel sick.

Still, when he vomited some ten minutes later in the candidate's first-class commode, Mayweather found himself hard-pressed to isolate the primary source of his nausea. Was it the highly dubious beef stroganoff consumed earlier that afternoon, residual guilt over his complicity in Campman and Greenblatt's fake scandal, the rocky flight itself, or the unwelcome eroticism of Campman's Yucatecan valet? Most likely, he thought, it was a combination of the four.

CLASS

And what is it about Nora's story that we find so compelling today?"

"It's her independence. The fact that she doesn't need a man."

"Okay, but I think we can do better than that. Can we be more specific?"

The students of ENG 340b, "Theater as Literature," stared glassy-eyed at their professor, Melissa Phillips. It was too early for this sort of give-and-take: 8:47 A.M., to be precise. She should've known better.

Finally, a recently roused sweatshirted sophomore responded.

"Is it that she's strong?"

"Well, she is strong, but . . ."

"She makes a choice."

"Ah!"

If it were possible for Melissa's groggy students to relax any further, they did, relieved that their professor had found the answer she desired.

"She does make a choice, doesn't she? That's a big deal, don't you think? I mean, I know we all take for granted the idea of a woman's subservience in those days, but I think for us to fully appreciate what's going on here, for us to take it out of the academic and make it tangible, we need to really put ourselves in that mind-set. Can we do that?"

They could do that. Melissa knew she could summon their imaginations at this hour, even if she and Mr. Ibsen couldn't count on their enthusiasm.

"Ladies, can you imagine what it'd be like for you a hundred years ago? You wouldn't be in this room, obviously."

"We'd be at home."

"You'd be prisoners. Prisoners of . . . ?"

"Our husbands."

"Yes. And worse: you'd be prisoners of your husband's *choices*! Can you imagine that? Just think for a moment how much your lives are guided by the choices you make. *Your choices* determine . . . everything! Every single thing that happens to you in your life relates *directly* to the *choices you make*."

She paused for dramatic effect or some other reason she chose not to share.

"Now take that away. What's it like now? What's it like now that your entire life is dictated by choices *your husband* controls? If your husband makes stupid choices, then guess what? Those are *your* choices, too! Those are *your* stupid choices!"

Her eyes indicted the whole room. They were paying attention now.

"But I know what you're thinking: 'I'll choose a husband whose opinions I'll respect, we'll make those decisions together, I'll give him my two cents, he'll heed my advice.' . . . Wrong. Wrong. Wrong. Wrong! That's modern feminist fairy-tale bullshit! Not in Norway! Not in 1881! Your husband chooses you! He steers the boat! And if he points you toward an iceberg, guess what, honey?! You go down with the ship! And that's the way it was! *That's the way it was!* Not like . . ."

Melissa paused. She regained her composure and finished the sentence.

"Not like today."

The room was silent.

In the back row, a junior by the name of Darrell sent a text message to the cell phone of his friend sitting across the room. It read:

MS PHILLIPS KICKS MY ASS

RESTROOM, PART 1

Melissa Phillips was in the third-floor ladies' bathroom of Georgetown's New North building, relieving herself in a stall and adjusting her wristwatch (which seemed to be losing time), when she overheard the news as it passed from one student to another.

"Jenny!"

"Oh, my God! How *are* you?"

"I'm reeeelly good. It's so good to *see* you! So, wait—did you just *hear*?"

"No, what?"

Their voices were lower now.

"About Ben Phillips?"

"No, what about him?"

"That they found another woman he slept with."

"Oh, wow."

"There's this other woman who says they had an affair."

"So, you don't mean Tina James?"

"No, *another* one. That's what I'm saying."

"Oh, my God." And then she whispered, "You know Melissa Phillips is here today. I totally saw her before."

"Oh, my God!"

"Wait—"

The two girls were suddenly quiet, and Melissa worried her presence might be discovered. Determined not to betray herself with a labored breath, a tug of the toilet paper, or—God forbid—anything that might be interpreted as a sob, and feeling suddenly unsteady despite the low center of gravity afforded by her seat on the porcelain bowl, Melissa Phillips cautiously moved her left hand so as to brace herself against the side of the stall. In her distraction, she forgot about her watch, which she'd unfastened only moments before, and which now fell from her wrist, landing in the toilet bowl with a resounding "Plop!"

"Oh, crap!" she said—an exclamation whose unfortunate connotations became apparent to her when the bathroom girls let forth a barrage of stifled snorts and giggles from the other side of the stall. They raced out of the bathroom, eager to escape its echoic confines before their giggling overture exploded into an inevitably volcanic fortissimo. As the lavatory door swung closed and the girls' voices faded, Melissa could swear she heard one of them say:

"Oh, my God! I bet you that was *totally* her just now!"

RESTROOM, PART 2

Interestingly enough, both stories of discovery happened to involve restrooms. For Ben Phillips, it also involved a plane. He was airborne over Wickenburg, Arizona, en route to Los Angeles, when Chief Political Advisor Shelly Greenblatt received a call alerting him of a press conference that would begin only seconds later.

On the airplane's satellite TV, Ben and Shelly (along with Campman, Mayweather, Kiley, Sorn, and the rest of the entourage) watched open-mouthed as a newly tanned, dewy-eyed Sharon Balis reported to the world that she'd had an affair with the Democratic candidate some fifteen years ago.

She spoke slowly and seriously. She was an unsteady person, summoning steadiness from somewhere in her bowels, and the rich hollowness of her voice, much like a well-trained singer suffering from mild laryngitis, served to ground her and endow her supposed angst with a legitimacy and accessibility it might have otherwise lacked.

"He was the love of my life. When I saw him again after all those years, I couldn't help myself. Neither of us could really. We couldn't keep our hands off each other. He was just so real, so tender . . . so powerful. . . ."

Ben was red in the face. Since entering adulthood, he'd never felt so embarrassed. He couldn't move, couldn't speak, couldn't breathe. He sat frozen, his stillness barely concealing the fireworks inside.

Elayne Cohen-Campman gazed at him through her camera lens, the voice of Sharon Balis echoing in her ears. What was this power Ben seemed to wield over these women? What was it about him, Elayne wondered, that made every ex-girlfriend fall hopelessly in love with him? And whatever it was, would she be able to capture it?

Her reverie was broken by her husband.

"Elayne!" He didn't want pictures now.

"I can't believe it," muttered Derek Kiley.

Of course, he *could* believe it. That was the problem. He believed it all too well. This was what happened when you ignored your better judgment. This was the unique brand of karmic retribution reserved especially for cheaters.

"I'm coming forward because it's the right thing to do," said Sharon Balis, "for me, for Ben, and for the country."

Anyone who had not seen Tina James's confession probably would have found Sharon Balis to be quite convincing. For those who *had* been privy to Tina James, however (and this included much of the Western world), Sharon's performance seemed, by comparison, a little forced, much like a novice actor who conjures the surface reactions of other actors rather than exploring the genuine motivations of the character he or she is to portray. Sharon's confession didn't ring false, but it didn't exactly ring true, either.

What it did do, though, was present a problem.

"We are seriously screwed," said Mayweather.

"She's going with the same exact story!" said Sorn.

Ben didn't say a word, but all eyes were on him, waiting for a reaction. None came.

Thomas Campman immediately suspected the Almighty was to blame for the new trouble. Sharon Balis was a flake, yes, but she didn't seem the type to pull a stunt like this, at least not on her own. And who could she possibly be working with? Who could have convinced her to come forward? If Sharon was coerced, if her mind was poisoned somehow, who but the Almighty could be responsible?

But why? To what end? Campman couldn't understand that part of it. He/She/It/They had been responsible for the idea that set this whole chain of events in motion. Why would He/She/It/They sabotage that idea now? Why would He/She/It/They deliberately suggest a course of action that would lead to ruin?

Unless . . .

It was almost too troubling to consider.

What if the Almighty hadn't actually suggested anything at all?

Campman pondered the original revelation: "Sin Will Make Him Human." When the message first came to him, he'd interpreted it as a direct answer to some very direct questions he'd been asking:

"How do we win this election?"

"How do we make them listen?"

"How do we humanize our candidate?"

The response: "Sin Will Make Him Human."

Campman's interpretation of the interchange was thus as follows:

CAMPMAN: How do we do it?

HE/SHE/IT/THEM: Sin.

At the time, Campman's interpretation seemed perfectly natural. But had he been blinded by context? The words of the revelation were, after all, phrased more as a prediction or warning than as an actual suggestion. It wasn't "Sin *Would* Make Him Human," or "Sin *Could* Make Him Human," but "Sin *Will* Make Him Human." It was an incongruity Campman had too quickly overlooked.

And what did it mean to be "Human"? Again, Campman had assumed He/She/It/Them to be speaking in the same context as he, referring to all the positive connotations of humanity: genuineness, empathy, and warmth. But what if that wasn't the case? What if He/She/It/Them was making a reference to humanity's less desirable traits, such as fallibility, imprudence, and mortality? What if "humanity" was something to be avoided at all costs?

Had he unwittingly doomed the campaign?

Campman felt a chill. How could he not have thought this through? It was so unlike him! Thomas Campman prided himself on covering every angle, anticipating every move, preparing for every contingency. How could he have missed such an obvious potential miscalculation?

Of course it was still possible his initial interpretation had been correct, and this whole Sharon Balis mess was just one of a series of tests designed to challenge his faith. But how was he to know?

He needed to speak to the Almighty right away. But there was no time for that. The others would now want to talk strategy. He'd have to wing it.

Meanwhile, Ben Phillips was on fire. The candidate had gone from shock to embarrassment to anger and back again. With all three emotions present in his voice, he turned to Campman.

"Tom, I think we should talk."

It was the first time he'd spoken since Sharon Balis's press conference began, and his words brought quiet to the cabin. Inside, Ben felt a mix of cold and hot, queasiness and steadiness, humiliation and pride. He was aware of every muscle fiber that awkwardly flexed to raise him from his seat, and he hated each one. He hated everything about himself in that moment: the way he walked, the way he looked, the way he dressed, even the sound of his voice. He struck himself as ridiculous, as a caricature of the pathetic man he'd suddenly become, and he couldn't help but think back with embarrassment on the youthful idealism that initially propelled him into politics. He'd always wanted to be a champion of justice. Now justice was biting him in the ass in the most brutally ironic fashion. And while Ben felt anger toward those advisors who'd conspired to put him in this absurd situation, his self-loathing was no less for their shared responsibility.

Campman rose along with Ben, and the two men made their way to the lavatory, followed not-too-subtly by Greenblatt, Mayweather, Kiley, and Sorn. The plane's lavatory was larger than a typical coach commode but not quite roomy enough for six, and the clown car entrance of the senator and his five advisors did not go unnoticed by the others in the campaign entourage.

Even those in the press section of the plane became suspicious. The Sharon Balis news had spread quickly among them, and everyone was miffed they'd missed the scoop. The press staff was giving them nothing, and the journalists felt trapped and powerless. When they heard angry voices, loud jostling and knocking sounds coming from the executive washroom, just on the other side of the paneling that separated campaign folks from reporters, each person jumped to his or her own separate conclusion.

"Are they fighting?"

"Are they having a meeting in the bathroom?"

"Did they not know this was coming?"

"Can you hear anything?"

Meanwhile, inside the bathroom:

"How did this happen?"

"Dammit, Kiley, move over!"

"I don't know, Ben. I don't know."

"Ow! My foot!"

"I did not sign up for this! This was not the plan!"

"Let's stay quiet."

"Who is touching my ass?!"

"Oh, God! That's disgusting!"

"Did anyone talk with her?"

"I need to boil my hand."

"Why would she be doing this now?"

"Ow. Ow. Ow."

"The question is, what do we *do* about it?"

"Shut up, everyone! Just shut up!"

"Gentlemen . . ."

The advisors paused for a moment and ceded the floor to the senator. The round-robin breathing of tightly packed bodies gave the impression that the crowded bathroom had become a living, breathing
organism unto itself.

"Listen, this is not acceptable," said the man who would be president. "Tom, I was *not* the one to talk with her. I don't know how you
left things, I don't know what transpired, I don't know how this
whole ridiculous thing happened! . . . But it's unacceptable. I did not
agree to this!"

Campman's mind raced.

"Ben, I understand you're furious. I'm furious. And you're right;
this shouldn't have happened—"

Mayweather interrupted, "Campman, what did you and Kiley *say*
to this girl?"

"You don't need to yell," said Kiley, "I'm only three inches away
from you."

"Everyone quiet!" said Greenblatt.

The senator once more took command.

"You ask if I'm furious? Yes. Of course. You've taken my reputation and flushed it down the toilet"—all five wisely resisted the urge
for scatological witticism—"and dammit, Tom . . . my good name
was all I had left."

For the first time, Campman began to realize the full extent of the
devaluation of his credibility with the candidate. He sent a silent
prayer: Let me get through this meeting, and I'll fix it, I promise. I'll
fix it all!

"I should clean house," said Ben Phillips, "I should rant and rave
and make the heavens tremble . . ."

The bathroom organism held its collective breath.

". . . but that's not going to fix this problem."

Exhale.

"I'm gonna take responsibility for what happens in my own campaign," said Ben. "I'm not gonna waste time assigning blame. At
least not now. *Now,* I want ideas. . . ."

That's why this man is running for president, thought Kiley. In the course of twenty seconds, his faith in politics was restored. It wasn't the first time Ben Phillips had performed such a service for those who worked for him, and it wouldn't be the last.

As Ben continued, Kiley was reminded again of the importance of their mission. I will do whatever it takes to get this man elected, he thought. It was a feeling shared by all the men in the uncomfortable room.

"We've behaved foolishly to get ourselves to this place," said Ben. "Now, how do we get ourselves out?"

Shelly Greenblatt, the senator's blameless and loyal advisor, had been biding his time. He knew it wasn't prudent or even necessary to pounce on Campman when he was down. "Campman the Champion" and his little plan had self-destructed all on their own. Now it would be Greenblatt's turn.

"Ben, here's what I think you should do."

"Talk to me, Shelly."

And he did. Shelly Greenblatt spoke simply and calmly for about four minutes while the others listened attentively. Once he was done, they took turns commenting. This was the way Ben Phillips liked to work, hearing all sides before making a decision. He thrived on conflicting opinions, on discussion, on debate; it was the best way he knew to attack a problem.

This particular debate was muted. Sorn disagreed with Shelly's strategy, but the others seemed to accept it without much objection. Campman, for his part, did not speak at all.

Eventually Greenblatt couldn't resist prodding him for a response. Campman took a dramatic beat before answering.

"What do I think, Shelly? I don't think we have a choice. You are absolutely right. And furthermore . . . that's *exactly* what we'll do. Unless, of course, you object, Ben."

And that was that. Campman had co-opted the majority response and issued it in the form of an order. It was a crafty move, and it allowed him to remain in charge (albeit shakily) for the moment.

Greenblatt just sighed. It made him think of the first meeting about the scandal plan, when Campman had everyone run in circles to come up with the very idea he'd already decided upon. The illusion of choice can taste almost as sweet as the real thing, thought Greenblatt. Now, the illusion of power . . .

Campman's wings were singed, but he was still airborne. For now.

The strategy was set, Sorn farted, and the packed lavatory cleared with great haste. As he was leaving, Ben Phillips turned pale and put his hand to his forehead.

"Oh, good Lord, *Melissa!*"

The time was 2:46 P.M. on the East Coast. Melissa would be teaching for another forty-one minutes. Upon dismissing her class, she would walk to the second-floor bathroom. She would not talk to her husband until 3:37 P.M.

NOTES

Peter Williams
Notes for September 16, 5:45 P.M.

BP accused of 2nd affair w/Arkansas woman, Sharon Balis.

Campaign has not yet issued statement, altho press conference is scheduled for tomorrow morning.

Tonight's activities will go on as planned.

Staff seems distracted by new allegations. Mood changed.

Talked (very) briefly w/Elayne C.C. getting off plane. She referred to BP as "mysterious." What is his mystery? Noises from front of airplane arouse additional suspicion. Must learn more about this mystery w/BP, whatever it is.

Attempted conversation once again with Campman's valet Hector @hotel.

Still trying to make headway w/him. Think he could be good source. Despite best efforts, conversations have been brief & uneventful. His English is quite poor, & I think he sometimes responds w/out fully understanding what has been asked of him. Note to self—review Spanish vocab & grammar.

Back at hotel, found brassiere in backpack. C-cup. Note attached w/room #. Think it belongs to Jennifer Dial of XLGNN. Clasps of brassiere similar to Mary's but located in the front, not the back. Must study its mechanics before I return to owner. Should probably return it anonymously so as not to embarrass her.

Gained 2 pounds. Pants seem shorter. Noticed first sprouting of dark hair on chest. Penis growth seems to have slowed. Acne remains clear, but skin becoming dry. Must remember to use colder water when washing face.

Fond of complimentary hotel lotion for M use. Brand is Flora-Derma. Should remember and purchase for home use.

Note to self—be sensitive to time zone changes when making phone calls home + Mary.

Ideas for online journal entry:

- relay anecdote about noises from first-class cabin
- explore relationship between knowledge & trust as it relates to the electoral process
- investigate meaning of the word "*love*"

THE FIFTH TAPE

He calls himself Gomez, but with the Democrats, he's been going by the name *Hector Elizondo*. He seems to be working as Campman's personal valet of sorts. The relationship isn't clear, but we know he travels with the campaign, and they have a car waiting for him in each city, a black Town Car, which he uses to drive Mr. Campman around—"

"But Tom loves the bus," Dennis Fazo interrupted.

National Republican Association Vice Chairperson Wendy Relsh was prepared for this sort of cross-examination and didn't miss a beat.

"Well, yes, he travels on the campaign bus when there is a bus, sometimes in the candidate's limo, but for all other travel: on his own, with his wife, with other advisors, a few times with the candidate himself, and, of course, whenever he's in Washington. . . ."

"This guy's his chauffeur, of course," said Fazo with a smile, as if it suddenly all made sense. "Tom likes to be independent. He distrusts everyone. Even Secret Service."

"It's a bit strange, if you ask me," Wendy Relsh ventured.

"But I didn't, did I?"

"No. Right. Nobody knows much about this Hector Elizondo, but it seems he's been working for Campman since February. He started around the time of the Muddville suicide."

"Of course he did!"

Political guru Dennis Fazo rocked back in his leather armchair. He didn't expand on his cryptic exclamation, mainly because he didn't have anything else to say. But he liked to keep Wendy Relsh off her guard. She'd continue with her report in another moment, once she realized he had nothing more to add.

"Um, it seems Campman really trusts this guy," she said. "He follows almost everywhere he goes. There have been a few short trips of Campman's where he's not tagged along—he just waits for him in D.C., picks him up from the airport—but generally, the two share a very similar itinerary."

Wendy Relsh read her briefing off a plastic clipboard, sitting upright in her chair. Fazo admired her bone structure and thought about how much he would enjoy having his way with her if only things were different. Fazo had started the day in a bad mood. The previous night his wife of seven years had called him a Makeout Moron, whatever the hell that was, and he'd come to the conclusion that things between them were probably not going to improve. Just what he needed: another divorce. Fazo was in a funk.

But then his day swiftly improved. First the news of the Sharon Balis confession, then a visit from the slender and serious Wendy Relsh, and now this Hector Elizondo character. Things were looking up.

"What's his background?" Fazo asked.

"Details are sketchy here," Wendy began. "There are ninety-seven men named Hector Elizondo in the United States. Only fifty are in the proper age range, and of those, all but ten are employed in the state of Texas. Of the remaining serious contenders, there is a mechanic in New Jersey with a wife and three kids, a single real-estate agent also from New Jersey, a grocery clerk from Indiana, a televangelist-slash-singer in Miami, and . . . the guy who is our most likely candidate: a taxi driver from Hillcrest Heights, Maryland."

"And . . . ," Fazo prodded.

"And, we know he's got a wife and three daughters. He's been working in D.C. for a couple years, before that he worked in Miami for about a year, and before that . . . we have no record of him at all."

"Nothing?"

"Just a birth certificate. Born on Key West in 1964."

"And that's it?"

"That's all we could find."

"Hmm."

Fazo sat up in his chair for the first time and looked Wendy Relsh right in her eager eyes.

"There's only one thing you're forgetting to mention, Wendy."

Her eyebrows and chin drifted north in anticipation.

"*Why the hell am I only hearing about this now?* I'm curious what you were waiting for, maybe November?!"

Ahh! Now she was squirming! Fazo smiled inside.

"Well, I didn't want to bother you with something I didn't—"

"Didn't want to bother me? If you knew the guy was Campman's chauffeur, don't you think—"

"That's true, but we didn't know that at first. And as I told you before, we didn't feel we had any reliable intelligence. This is the first tape that had anything useful on it."

"Hmm."

She was so damn sexy when she was on the defensive. Fazo let her stew for a moment, and then he asked, "So, what about the other tapes?"

Wendy Relsh took a deep breath.

"Well, the second tape was a complete wash: just forty-five minutes of engine noise and the sound of someone eating crackers. Naturally, we assumed Gomez—er, Mr. Elizondo—was upset with the amount of money we gave him for the first recording, so we doubled our price. And the third tape was better, although still not exactly useful. It sounds like it was recorded at some campaign event, because you can hear Phillips giving a speech in the background while Campman and some other guy discuss the Orioles game. The fourth tape is one long discussion on the state of the music industry. It wasn't until this fifth tape that . . . well, perhaps we should just play it."

"Perhaps that's a good idea."

Dennis Fazo enjoyed making Wendy sweat, but he wasn't actually peeved. Things were going far too well for that, and now he found himself growing excited, eager to hear this potentially explosive recording.

Wendy Relsh produced a small boom box, put the audiotape inside, and pressed PLAY with her long arachnid index finger.

"The conversation starts soon," she said. "I actually cued the tape up a bit. There's a lot of foot traffic and jostling before. Sounds like the microphone was planted on the ground or something, and we're pretty sure it was recorded on an airplane."

When Thomas Campman's voice crackled through the small speakers, a smile crept across Dennis Fazo's face.

Campman sounded angry. He was berating someone for . . . what? . . . for losing someone? . . . for not finding parking? . . . for a missed opportunity?

Fascinating!

Fazo grinned and even chuckled a few times.

"Here's where we basically lose it," said Wendy Relsh. "The voices continue, but you can't really understand what they're saying. You just hear this rustling against the microphone, as if it were under a blanket or something. It's weird."

Wendy Relsh pressed STOP and waited for Fazo to say something.

"So," she said, "does this discussion make any sense to you?"

Fazo just smiled.

"How much are you paying this guy?" he asked.

"Two grand a tape."

"Well, don't increase his salary. The tape's not worth much. That I happen to find it personally amusing raises its stock somewhat, but only somewhat. Although it does make me wonder. . . ."

"What?" asked Wendy Relsh.

"I think we may be starting to get to our friend, Tom Campman."

Fazo smiled. Relsh didn't quite understand, but he continued before she could question him any further.

"Keep paying this guy," he said. "You never know what he'll bring in next. Could be useful, and *I want to hear it.*"

"I agree, sir."

"That said, we're doing just fine without Hector Elizondo. He's small fish, and we've got bigger *pescado* on our plate. With the news this afternoon of the good senator's apparent compulsion toward infidelity, our course of action is pretty clear. These guys can't stop playing defense long enough to think straight. All we need to do is throw the knockout punch, and it's just about time. Wouldn't you agree, Wendy?"

He smiled at her, and she smiled back weakly.

"Yeah," he said, "now, we go in for the kill."

CAGE MATCH INTERVIEW

[CU on news anchor BETTY HAN, Early thirties. Asian. Attractive. Intense.]

HAN: In a moment, we'll bring you our report on the terror of third-hand smoke, but first, our Weekly Washington Roundup—Cage Match Edition. Today Ben Phillips's press secretary, Ozzie Mayweather, is in the hot seat for six minutes of questioning by our select panel of reporters: Jennifer Dial, Gwendolyn Myer, Chip Rogers, and Peter Williams. Our panelists are live in Los Angeles with the campaign, and Gwendolyn Myer, we'll start with you. Show no mercy!

[INSERT—Live feed of panel discussion inside cage.]

[CU on ancient reporter GWENDOLYN MYER]

MYER: How about it, Mr. Mayweather? What's your response to these new allegations by former Phillips girlfriend Sharon Balis?

[CU on OZZIE MAYWEATHER]

MAYWEATHER: As we said in our press conference this morning, there is simply no truth to this story. The senator dated Miss Balis when the two of them were in college at Oklahoma State. The relationship ended there, and he has not seen her since. Any talk of an alleged affair that supposedly happened fifteen years ago . . . it simply didn't happen. It's a fabrication. The senator hasn't even seen Miss Balis for thirty years. He is deeply saddened she has gone public with this lie. He does not know what could possibly be motivating her, but he is . . . saddened by it. Yes?

[CU on reporter CHIP ROGERS]

ROGERS: We've heard from various sources that the senator is quote "a liar," "a lying liar," and also "someone who lies." Is there any truth to these labels, and if there is, how can we be expected to trust the senator when he claims Sharon Balis is a liar? Also, even if the labels are inappropriate, how do they affect the senator's credibility problem, if he has one? Finally, is it credible for him to be calling Sharon Balis a liar? Is it appropriate for him to be attacking her?

[CU on OZZIE MAYWEATHER]

MAYWEATHER: I don't know where you're getting all that. Ask anyone who knows him, Senator Phillips is a very honest man, and I don't think anyone's attacking anyone here. Yes?

[CU on reporter JENNIFER DIAL]

DIAL: I'd like to know if there's anything the senator finds particularly gross or disgusting about his wife—you know, anything specifically that drove him to become a . . . um . . . serial adulterer.

[CU on OZZIE MAYWEATHER]

MAYWEATHER: That's a ridiculous allegation. Once again, the senator did not have an affair with Miss Balis. Yes, Gwendolyn?

[CU on GWENDOLYN MYER]

MYER: Mister Mayweather, I'd like to know how many other women the senator has had extramarital affairs with, and if there is one that was his favorite.

[CU on OZZIE MAYWEATHER]

MAYWEATHER: Gwendolyn, the senator has committed only one transgression, and he has already talked extensively about that.

He has otherwise been completely faithful to his wife. They have a wonderful marriage. It is a strong marriage, and there is nothing more to say on the issue. Yes, Peter?

[CU on teenage reporter PETER WILLIAMS]

WILLIAMS: Thank you, Mr. Mayweather. Peter Williams, *TeenVibe* magazine. Do you think it's at all unusual that Miss Balis has come forth with a story so remarkably similar to that of Miss James? Do you believe Miss Balis to be a copycat of some sort? Are there questions about her mental health? OR do you believe the two are somehow in cahoots, that this whole series of revelations is being orchestrated by some outside entity? In short, to what do you attribute the similarities in their stories?

[CU on OZZIE MAYWEATHER]

MAYWEATHER: (pause) Well, that's a very interesting question I'm afraid I don't have the answers to. Yes, there are some similarities, no doubt about that, but your guess is as good as mine when it comes to the why and wherefore. The critical difference between them is this: Tina James was telling the truth for the most part and the senator confirmed that. Sharon Balis is simply lying.

PLEASE DON'T CALL AGAIN

Campman got the first call on his cell but chose to ignore it.

Then came the call from the campaign office. He picked up the phone, and his Washington receptionist Courtney Rosewood was on the other end.

"Hi, Tom. I have Sharon Balis on the line for you."

"Who?!"

"Sharon Balis."

"Why the hell would *she* be calling me?"

"She didn't say. Would you like me to ask?"

"No, that's okay. Gosh. I don't understand why that woman would be calling *me*. Uh . . . I don't like it. The whole thing sounds fishy. Get rid of her."

"Should I take a message?"

"No, just get rid of her. Let's pretend this didn't happen."

Campman hung up the phone.

"Who was that?" asked the senator.

They were backstage at the Hollywood Bowl, and Ben's makeup was being applied.

"Wrong number. Very strange. I'll tell you later."

There were too many people in the damn room. Campman wondered if anyone noticed him sweating, but a quick glance about revealed perspiration to be a standard culprit, awash on the shores of multiple brows in the packed dressing room.

Elayne moved in for a close-up of the candidate.

"Are you getting my good side?" asked Ben.

"They're all good," responded Elayne. "Remember, I want to get a session with you one of these days when you have some downtime."

Ben chuckled at the notion of downtime. So did several others.

"I know, I know." Elayne smiled. "But seriously less than an hour. Just casual. One with Melissa, too. Tom, do I need to schedule that with someone?"

"I'm sure we can squeeze something in," said Ben, "just keep reminding me. Remind Charlie, too."

Just then, young Derek Kiley's cell phone rang.

He answered.

"Yeah? . . . Yes, this is he."

Campman saw Kiley's face turn white and knew instantly who it was.

"Uh . . . yes he is . . . um, could you hold on one moment?"

Kiley glanced helplessly at Campman, his eyes trying desperately to communicate what his lips could not. For their part, all his lips could manage was two whispered words: "For you."

As Campman grabbed the phone, he nodded to Kiley, as if to say, I know what's going on.

Campman walked calmly and slowly to the small bathroom in the rear of the dressing room and closed the door. Once alone, all semblance of calm disappeared.

"*What the hell are you doing?!*" he whispered into the phone. "*What are you thinking, calling my office?*"

"You weren't answering your cell phone!" protested Sharon Balis on the other end of the line.

"I wasn't answering my cell phone because you shouldn't have been calling me! *Do you realize what would happen if someone knew we talked?! Why are you calling?*"

"Why are you calling me a liar?"

"Because you *are* a liar! You didn't have an affair with Ben Phillips!"

"I know! But I'm trying to help here—"

"*Help?! . . .*"

"And I don't understand how you can go on TV and call me a liar!"

"Look, we don't need your help! I don't know why you suddenly saw fit to provide us with it!"

"Hey! Hey! Hey! Do you think I *wanted* to come forward?"

"Okay, all right," Campman said, trying to calm things down. "Look . . . look, I think we should end this call."

"I told you, I couldn't do it while I was breaking up with Chester, but now that we're separated, I thought—"

"Listen," said Campman, summoning all his powers of persuasion, "if you really want to help us, you have to realize we're gonna deny this affair."

"But *why*? You didn't deny the other one."

"The other one is in the past. Besides, one affair is forgivable. Two is not."

"I disagree. If it's all in the past, it shouldn't matter how many. If anything, two affairs is *more* believable. It establishes a consistent character flaw."

"*Consistent character flaw?!* Are you crazy? This is not up for discussion."

"Why not?"

"Because we can't afford to have the senator look like a compulsive adulterer, *especially* when—in fact—he is not. You *knew* he didn't have an affair with you, and you came forward anyway. Now, it's too late to change that. Some people are going to believe you. Some will believe him. And although it's not likely"—he lied for her benefit—"there's still a chance this may help us. But that *will definitely not happen* if we confess to an affair we did not commit. Do you understand?"

There was silence on the other end of the line. After a moment, Sharon responded reluctantly, "Yeah, I guess so, but—"

"I'm hanging up now. Please don't call again."

Campman closed the flip phone and exhaled mightily. He ran his fingers through his thinning hair. He glanced at his reflection in the mirror and wondered at what point he'd become such a tired old man.

"Oh, Lord my God, Jesus, and all spirits inhabiting this world and others . . ."

He looked away from the mirror, trying his best not to focus his eyes on anything in particular, thinking it narcissistic to pray while looking at one's self. Eyes adrift, he continued his prayer.

"If you're trying to make a point, then I get it, okay? This heavenly message of yours, it *was* a warning, wasn't it? You didn't want to encourage me but to warn me . . . against my own good ideas, was that it? . . . Well, was it?"

He sighed. "I'd ask you to make your point in a more obvious way, but I'm not sure if the campaign can take it. Now I don't know what to ask you, but I do know this: Our strategy is to deny. Deny, deny, deny. From here on out we're gonna deny like crazy!"

Campman's eyes wandered back to the mirror. He didn't buy his own bravado. He saw how transparent it was.

"We are going to deny . . . *unless* . . . unless that's not the right thing for now."

The terrifying truth was that Thomas Campman didn't know what "the right thing for now" was.

"I will look for a sign," he said finally, "I will look for a sign tomorrow . . . *by air.* If that sign does not come, denial will continue to be our plan. Okay? Good. Thanks for all your generous gifts. Please bless my loved ones. Grant us peace on earth. But not till after the election. Amen."

NOT ACCORDING TO PLAN

So this was how it was going to be. Her help was without value. Her sacrifice was irrelevant.

Sharon Balis slammed down the receiver, folded her arms, and stared at the telephone, contemplating her next move. She could call back, but the results weren't bound to be any different. Was calling back her only course of action? There had to be something else. The status quo was too much to bear.

"No! No! No!"

Sharon Balis stomped her feet on the floor several times. The impact's boom reverberated through the frame of the house. Then quiet.

"ERRRRRGGGGGGHHHHH!"

She longed for an echo, but her cries were swallowed by the low ceilings and wall-to-wall carpeting.

Sharon did not mind suffering. Hell, she'd suffered before. She could play the part of the home wrecker if that would help. She'd suffer the public scorn, the humiliation, the derision. She'd do it all . . . *if it would help.*

The idea that she had done this to herself for no reason at all, that her suffering suddenly had no purpose, that she would be seen as a liar and—worse!—a fool for creating a masochistic spectacle of herself, hurting everyone and helping no one . . .

It was all too much to bear.

She marched to the liquor cabinet, occupying a corner of the room that had grown invisible in its familiarity. She was greeted by rows of ancient bottles, lined up like tired old soldiers ready to go to war, if only they could remember what side they were fighting on, bottles with long-forgotten associations, received as gifts or purchased in moments of puerile abandon (as if she'd ever have a need for Curaçao).

A drink was poured, imbibed, and poured again. The TV was turned on, and Sharon watched. It was Ben Phillips speaking live from the Hollywood Bowl.

Although the sun was still pink in the sky, Sharon Balis had settled on an agenda for the evening. She would sit on the couch, drink, and brainstorm her next move. Alan, her son, was spending the night at a friend's house, so there was no one to disturb her or be disturbed by her (as long as she remembered to unplug the suddenly active phone). Thus, the evening was set: Drink, think, sit, watch, and weep.

The weeping wasn't actually part of the original agenda, but as Sharon's mind became softened by vodka, she found herself in possession of even fewer promising ideas than she had started with—if that was possible. So she began to cry.

There had to be *something* she could do, if not for herself, then for Ben.

She would not be a martyr without a cause, of this she was determined. Furthermore, she would not let that smug bastard Thomas Campman treat her like an annoyance, not after putting herself on the line for *his* idea.

She tried to think back to the original plan, the plan she'd faithfully executed the second that abusive son of a bitch Chester was excised from her life. Sharon had been told the purpose of the scandal idea was to *humanize* Ben, to make him more like an ordinary flawed American. Had she not done that? So what if she wasn't the only woman to come forward? Was that a bad thing? Everyone knew JFK was repeatedly unfaithful, and did that hurt his popularity? No. In fact, wouldn't a pattern of infidelity ring more truthful than a one-time dalliance?

"I did the right thing." She held on to this thought for dear life, although she could feel herself being pulled down by some invisible force. She kept returning to the unfairness of the whole thing, to the spitefulness with which she was hung out to dry. There had to be something she could do to redeem herself, particularly now that she was in the national spotlight. There had to be some way to take advantage of it all—for Ben's sake, of course. But how?

The more she drank, the less sense everything made, and the more angry she felt. The more angry she felt, the more she drank. And so on.

At 10:15 P.M., a very drunk Sharon Balis placed a call to her contact (she now had many of them) at American News Corp.

"I want another press conference," she said.

Arrangements were made for the next morning, the phone was once again disconnected, and Sharon Balis fell asleep on the couch in a position too embarrassing to describe here.

THE VIRGIN MARY

He was on the West Coast, so his daily call would come later than usual. Mary Templeton's parents had gone to sleep, and Mary lay on her bed with the TV on, her hand poised only inches away from her cell phone. Her other hand played with the waistband of her flowered panties, starting to get moist with sweat on this unseasonably warm Maryland evening (in a house whose patriarch was notoriously reluctant to engage the air conditioner). The goose bumps traversing her bare legs were therefore a result of nervousness, not cold. She was nervous for the upcoming conversation, but also for the coming month, the coming year, and the coming decade. Like her boyfriend, Mary managed to balance a reasonably happy existence with a premature and overwhelming anxiety that extended to the far reaches of time and space.

Mary Templeton felt her biological clock ticking like mad, and she was only seventeen. Her two best friends, Jeanine Berry and Jennie Zatopee, had both started having sex in the last year and had both become obsessed with it. Mary could no longer bear sitting with them in honors algebra while they talked about oral sex and condoms and the dimensions of their boyfriends' penises, whose girth they would approximate using cylinders of pens, pencils, and highlighters. (They both said girth was a more critical dimension than length, which confirmed what Mary had read.) When they would ask Mary about her and Peter's sex life, she would deflect the question, claiming she had too much respect for her boyfriend to talk of such private matters. These pronouncements of moral and maturational superiority inevitably met with derision and jokes about her seemingly perpetual (and, it seemed, universally acknowledged) virginity. In whispered tones, these catty young coeds referred to her as The Virgin Mary, an obvious, uncreative nickname she was all too eager to discard.

It wasn't that Mary wanted to brag about sex. Quite the contrary, she found such crude conversations—of the sort that seemed all too prevalent at her school—to debase and trivialize what she imagined to be a most beautiful act. And she *did* respect Peter far too much to ever conceive of making public his prowess as a lover or his most intimate dimensions, if and when she became privy to such things.

But she did want to have sex for two reasons. The first (and she would confess this to be a juvenile and by itself insufficient reason) was that she wanted to join the club. Mary had always thought of herself as mature for her age: smarter, savvier, and (dare she say it) more sophisticated than her peers. It therefore maddened her to no end to observe these less mature, less worthy, and clearly less "in love" girls gain admittance to the new, thrilling world of sexuality before her. It smacked of unfairness, *injustice* even! How could these dim little girls (who wouldn't know love if it hit them upside the head) become privy to the deep dark secrets of an act so inextricably linked to the word as to be inseparable from it both linguistically and emotionally, while Mary, who was in love right up to her pretty little ears, who was in love so much her bones ached, still remained in the dark? To put it simply, she was envious and curious (and, though she would admit it to no one, not even herself, just the tiniest bit scared as well).

Mary's other reason for wanting to have sex was more noble: She loved Peter Williams just that much. She had known him for as long as she could remember, and they'd been dating for a little over a year. They had, what was in her mind, a very adult relationship, and it seemed only natural to take things to that next "adult" level. She was eager to explore the mysterious intermingling of physical and emotional sensuality that the act seemed to promise.

But first, of course, she needed to hear that he loved her. She had read far too many stories of girls who'd lost their virginity to the wrong boy only to regret it later; the magazines were littered with them. Mary had long ago promised herself not to become such a girl. If there was one thing she'd learned from such indispensable periodicals as *TeenVibe, Teen Girl,* and *Teen Home Journal,* it was that there was a right way and a wrong way to go through one's teenage years, and Mary Templeton would be darned if she didn't choose the right way. Choosing "the right way" meant getting good grades, wearing nice clothes, doing lots of extracurriculars, falling in love with the perfect boy, and, eventually, making love to him using proper contraception (and only once you were both *really* ready). Choosing "the right way" meant waiting for Peter to say he loved her, which he would do in time, she was sure. She just had to be patient.

Oh, if only he were back in Bethesda!

Mary tried to remember that a little suffering and anticipation could be healthy for a relationship. She'd read that somewhere. She wished it were easier to believe. While Peter's daily phone calls still thrilled her, Mary couldn't escape a lingering feeling that something was not right between the two of them, and this feeling troubled her.

As was her custom when she was upset, Mary turned to the Internet. The Internet, she'd discovered, was full of people with problems and people with solutions. No matter what problem she might be experiencing, Mary could be confident there was someone else on the Internet who had experienced the same thing before, someone who invariably was all too eager to offer suggestions on how others might cope with such a dilemma.

It was this Internet research that led Mary to the subject of phone sex. She had been conducting searches on the issue of "keeping your long-distance relationship alive" (as we_togetherness.com phrased it), and as she clicked from one website to another, she found the subject of phone sex kept popping up.

Now, as best as Mary could understand it, phone sex was not actual sex, but rather a sort of dirty talk over the telephone, dirty talk that might or might not be accompanied by masturbation.

The more she researched the topic, the more Mary became convinced she'd seen such dirty telephone talk in a movie once when she was younger. It had been a grown-up sort of movie, undoubtedly one her parents had rented, and she did not recall its name, nor was she familiar with the actors involved. In fact, there was very little Mary remembered about the movie except for that one scene. She'd found it quite strange at the time, and that her parents seemed so clearly uncomfortable watching it in the same room with her only served to magnify that strangeness. Midway through the questionable scene, her father launched into a coughing fit of such volume and intensity that it became hard for Mary to understand all of what the actors were saying. Still, she heard enough for it to make an impression.

What she heard was a telephone conversation between a man and a woman, each one describing in great detail what they would be feeling and what they would be doing were the other one present. The two actors were sweating, and they wore intense, almost pained, expressions on their faces. The scene made Mary tingle, although she didn't know quite how to describe what she was witnessing. Had she been more mature, she might have used words like *lust, longing, desperation,* or simply *horniness,* but these were not in her vocabulary at the time. Young Mary was also quite unaware of the significance of the actors' hands, and what exactly those hands were doing offscreen, just below the frame. Mary put together this part of the puzzle quickly now.

The more Mary read about phone sex, the more eager she was to try it. But she had some concerns. First and foremost, she wondered whether it was advisable to have phone sex if one had not had *real* sex before. This was an issue none of the websites seemed to address, and after a good deal of searching Mary contented herself with the conclusion that its lack of mention was indicative of its relative unimportance. Surely, if it was something to be wary of, she would have found a warning somewhere.

Second and perhaps more troubling was the issue of how to initiate this unique brand of intimacy. Here there was plenty of e-literature to be absorbed, and absorb it Mary did, to the best of her ability. She pored over numerous websites and parsed the overflow of advice, trying to pick and choose those suggestions that seemed most relevant to her situation.

Then she switched on the TV, got undressed, and tried turning her mind to other things.

That evening, as Mary waited for her nightly phone call, feeling her usual blend of longing, desperation, and, yes, horniness, she noticed the goose bumps on her legs and immediately diagnosed herself as nervous. She felt as if she'd been studying for a test for the last few hours, and she was all too eager to pass.

At that moment, her phone rang.

PHONE INTERCOURSE

P eter Williams fastened the cap of the Wilshire Grand Hotel complimentary hand lotion and returned to his bedroom. His laptop waited faithfully atop the tightly made queen-size bed, its psychedelic screen saver beckoning like a siren with a drug habit. Before long, Peter had clicked his way through several of his regular sites. He tried searching for the name "Sharon Balis," but the Web was already inundated with stories about the Arkansas woman, and most of these links simply reproduced stories he already knew. Peter narrowed his search to include only those pages more than forty-eight hours old. There were thousands of hits. Sharon Balis was not an uncommon name. He narrowed his search to include "Arkansas," then "Memphis," then "Oklahoma," and then . . .

Then Peter remembered Mary. It was late, and he'd forgotten to call. He grabbed his cell phone and pressed the number two (number one was to call home) followed by the send button. Peter turned his attention back to his computer as the digital delay of satellites and cell towers put his call through.

The phone rang twice. Then, the most beautiful voice in the world answered.

"Hey."

"Hey. I'm sorry I'm calling so late. As you might have guessed, it's been a crazy day."

"That's okay. I'm just glad you called."

"You're what?"

"I said I'm glad you called."

"Oh, me, too. I'm sorry, my cell reception's not great here."

"That's okay. Where are you?"

"In my hotel room. Where are you?"

"Ummm, in my room, silly."

"Oh, yeah. I guess it's late."

"Do you know *where* I am in my room?"

"Nope."

"I'm lying on my bed."

"I'm on my bed, too."

"Are you really?"

"Yes, really. Are you really?"

"I am."

This was not a bad start. Mary sensed an opportunity.

"I wish you were here right now," she purred.

"Yeah, me, too."

"Do you know what I'm wearing right now?"

It was the first big step. Peter looked up from his laptop.

"How would I know that?" he asked.

"Well, I'll tell you."

"Okay."

"I'm wearing my flowered bra and matching panties," she said softly.

Peter smiled at this then sensed an opportunity to address a question that had been on his mind for some time.

"Is that the brassiere that's made from the other kind of fabric? It's like a softer kind of . . . ?

"Satin?"

"What?"

"Satin."

"Is that it?"

"Yeah, satin's a little softer than the other fabrics."

"Hmmm. Say, while we're on the subject of brassieres, yours have hooks in the back, right? But some bras have them in the front, don't they?"

Mary didn't know quite what to make of Peter's line of questioning.

"Yeah, some do."

"Is there a reason why some have it in the back and some have it in the front? Does it have to do with the size of the breast or is one hook simply more effective at clasping than the other? Is one more mechanically sound?"

"Um, I think it's just different styles."

"Really? That's interesting. The brassiere is a very unusual garment."

"Yeah, I guess that's true," said Mary. "In any case, that's all I'm wearing, just my underwear."

"What did you say?"

"I said that's all I'm wearing, my underwear."

"Sorry?"

"I'm just—I'm just wearing my underwear. That's all."

"Really?"

"That's all."

"Wow. Are you cold?"

"What?"

"I said: Are you cold?"

"No," she said, trying to slip into her sexiest voice but feeling phony at the same time, "actually, I'm getting quite hot right now. What about you?"

A wicked smile spread across Peter's face. He put on a matching sexy voice.

"They turn up the AC way too high. I just put on my sweatshirt."

Sexy voice: "What else are you wearing?"

Sexy voice: "Socks. Pants."

"What about underneath?"

"Uh, a T-shirt."

Peter shifted his weight, accidentally pressing down on the TV remote with his thigh. The TV clicked on and Ben Phillips filled the screen. Peter's mind switched tracks instantly.

"Say, did they televise the Hollywood Bowl speech tonight? Did you see it?"

Mary sighed.

"Peter, I really don't want to talk about politics right now."

"Sorry."

TV off.

"Politics is not what's on my mind."

"Okay," said Peter, shifting once again into sexy mode, "too hot for politics, huh?"

"Yes! Exactly!"

"I know what that's like."

"Oh, yeah?"

"Yeah."

He was into it now. She could tell. Mary tingled with excitement.

"Ooh, that's good, Peter Williams. Because I don't want to talk about politics now. I want to talk about other things. I want to talk about you. I want to talk about me . . . *I want to talk about all the wonderful things we could do together.*"

That was better. Now she was really getting in the mood. She tried picturing Peter standing in front of her as she gave him instructions.

"I just want you to close your eyes and imagine you are here with me in my room . . . lying right here . . . next to me . . . on my bed . . . I'm just wearing my flowered bra . . . and panties . . . the soft satin ones you like . . . I'm feeling very hot . . . and I miss you . . . very . . . much. . . . Now . . . what would you do . . . to me . . . if you were here right now?"

"I'm sorry, I missed that whole thing. Everything after 'Peter Williams.' What did you say?"

"Oh, Peter! Are you serious?"

"I swear. You cut out for like forty-five seconds."

Mary tried to repeat herself to the best of her ability. *She had said it so well the first time!* She threw herself into an encore performance with as much passion as she could manage but knew she wasn't being as sexy or persuasive this time around. When she was through, Peter took a moment to respond.

"What was the question?"

"Oh!"

"No, I heard everything except for the last sentence! I know you're feeling very very hot and that we're imagining what it would be like if we were together, and that's"—he paused for emphasis, suddenly aware of his boner-owning—"that's *really cool.* I just didn't hear that last question."

Now Mary paused. She knew it was important to stay in the moment, to not let her frustration get the best of her.

She began softly, "I'm here in my underwear . . . and I'm so hot. Peter, I'm on fire . . . and you know how I feel . . . I miss you sooooo much . . . if you were here . . . I would wrap my arms around you as tightly as I could . . . and kiss you. . . ."

Peter closed his eyes.

"I'd kiss you so long and hard. . . . And I'm just wondering . . . what would *you* do if you were here *right now?*"

Peter Williams opened his eyes. His erection softened ever so slightly. This time, he'd heard his girlfriend loud and clear. He was being asked an important question:

What would he do if he were there right now?

He was being tested. Suddenly, it was all too clear. Peter wanted to continue the sexy banter, but now he feared a trick question. He had certainly flipped through enough "Is Your Boyfriend a Keeper?"-type quizzes to know that when a girlfriend poses a hypothetical question, it is always in the boyfriend's best interest to answer with as much sensitivity as he can possibly muster. But what was the sensitive answer?

His mind raced through the previous conversation. Had Mary's erotic tone been simply a ruse to make him let down his guard? Was she trying to trick him into admitting that he was no different from any other sex-crazed guy, that all he thought about was sex, that he wanted her as a sexual object first and a girlfriend second?

He would not fall for that trap. He would answer like a good boyfriend, the boyfriend who listens. Hadn't she said something about being hot? Perhaps . . .

"If I was with you right now," said Peter, "and if you were so hot . . . I'd try to find you a fan somewhere. I might also go down to the kitchen and get you a glass of water."

Mary's response surprised him. She almost seemed to be crying.

"Oh, Peter! Wouldn't you *at least* want to get to second base?!"

What on earth did that mean?

"Of course!" Peter protested, "but that's not *all* I want!"

"I have to go now. Good night."

And with that she hung up.

He would call back, of course, and they would talk more, but Mary seemed reluctant to go into any detail about what he'd said to trouble her so. When the call was over, Peter had the distinct feeling he'd done something wrong, although he hadn't the slightest clue what. In the end, he decided she must still be upset about his reluctance to make a full-on declaration of love, and if that was what troubled her, he knew there was nothing he could do about it.

As Peter slipped beneath the covers of his large hotel bed, he had the following thought: Women are strange creatures indeed. It might have been the least original thought ever to pass through Peter Williams's spry young synapses (competing for that title with the thoughts "I'm hungry," "I'm tired," and "I have to pee"), but it passed through them all the same, and his ability to fall asleep was hindered as a result. And so it followed that a highly unoriginal thought caused Peter Williams to have an evening of highly unoriginal insomnia.

LATE-NIGHT FLIGHT

Fine! Fine! Fine!

At 2:11 A.M., Peter Williams admitted defeat. He would not be getting any sleep, at least not anytime soon, and he finally resigned himself to this fact.

Lack of sleep was not, however, something he needed to take lying down. The young reporter slipped on a pair of cross trainers, grabbed his room key plus two dollars and change, and opened the door to his hotel room. He paused there for a moment, his eyes adjusting to the light from the deserted hallway. Peter wondered who else might be stirring in the hotel at this late hour. How many hotel workers were on call at 2:11 A.M.? He was certain the restaurants and gift shops were closed. Perhaps he would search out a vending machine. He thought he recalled seeing one near the ice machine on the other side of the fifth floor.

Peter heard someone approaching. For whatever reason, he shrank back into his room, closing the door behind him just enough to leave a tiny crack from which to peer out. After a moment, a short man in dark clothes strode purposefully past his door. Peter eased the door open again as the fast-walking man receded down the hallway. As he turned the corner, Peter caught a quick glimpse of his profile. Allowing for the possibility that his recently contracted pupils were not functioning at peak accuracy, Peter could swear he'd just seen the profile of Thomas Campman's valet, Hector.

Peter closed the door to his room and ran down the hallway. At the end of the hall he stopped, peered cautiously around the corner, and observed Hector Elizondo waiting for the elevator. Yes, it was Hector. No doubt about it. Even without his telltale suit, the bearded Mexican was unmistakable.

Here was a story indeed! The campaign manager's chauffeur on a secret late-night assignment! Peter thanked his lucky insomnia.

Once the elevator doors closed behind Hector and the floor numbers began to drop, Peter raced to the stairs and bounded down the five flights to the ground floor. He arrived only a second after the Mexican disembarked. Hector walked briskly through the lobby, and Peter followed twenty feet behind, drawing more than a few stares from the hotel employees, who were unaccustomed to seeing sixteen-year-old boys traipsing through the lobby at 2:00 A.M., particularly sixteen-year-olds dressed only in a pair of pajama pants, a T-shirt, and cross trainers. On his way out the door, Peter stopped at the concierge desk.

"Can I borrow a pen and a piece of paper?" he asked.

So forceful was Peter's request that the befuddled concierge granted it immediately and without editorial.

Wilshire Grand pen and stationery in hand, Peter proceeded out the front door and—walking past the valet stand where Hector Elizondo stood impatiently—made a beeline for an idling yellow cab.

"Good evening," said the young reporter.

The cabdriver, a Korean man in his sixties, did not respond. He seemed to be waiting for Peter to name his destination, but the young man said nothing further.

"Where you going?"

"One moment," said Peter, looking out the cab's rearview mirror.

The hotel valet pulled a black Lincoln Town Car into the carport and then got out. Hector Elizondo got in.

"See that car?" asked Peter, indicating the Lincoln. "I need you to follow that car."

The driver looked at him warily. "The black car? You want to follow?"

"Yes, please."

Peter glanced at the driver's badge, which contained a most unflattering picture and a name: Choe Song Ho. Peter considered whether it would be proper protocol to address the driver by his name, but he couldn't remember which of the Korean proper nouns was considered the first name and which the last. What a faux pas it would be to call Ho "Choe" or Choe "Ho"! In the end, Peter decided to play it safe and made no attempt at familiarity.

Hector's black car roared down Figueroa Street, and the chase was on. Within moments, they were speeding down the highway. Peter, who was unaccustomed to traveling by taxi, eyed the meter as it climbed steadily upward. He exceeded his $2.75 vending machine budget about thirty seconds into the drive and quickly started wondering how he was going to pay once the time came to do so.

"This guy's crazy!"

Choe Song Ho was referring to Hector Elizondo, who was weaving his way through the late-night traffic on the Santa Monica Freeway at a hundred miles per hour.

"Just stay with him," said Peter firmly.

The engine grew louder, and Peter noticed Choe Song Ho shoot him a disapproving glance in the rearview mirror.

Fifteen minutes later, the Lincoln exited the 405 and headed off the ramp in the direction of Los Angeles International Airport. The night sky was suddenly alive with the neon of chain hotels and restaurants. The buildings were large and bright, and before Peter knew it, they were driving into the most impressive structure of them all. They had entered the loop of the airport's terminals.

"LAX flat fee. Thirty-five dollars," said Choe Song Ho.

Peter became nervous.

"I may not be getting out yet," he said.

The black Town Car came to a stop in front of the American Airlines arrival gate at Terminal 4. The taxi pulled up about forty feet behind.

Peter's pulse raced. He felt more awake than he'd felt in a long time, maybe ever. Ironically, this hyperconsciousness reminded him in some ways of dreaming. Could he be dreaming? He was in his pajamas, it was late, and this whole chain of events was certainly more unusual than anything he'd experienced in his waking life.

But no. The cold leather seat of the taxicab confirmed the reality of the situation. He was definitely awake.

A blue Audi pulled up alongside Hector's Lincoln, and it almost looked as though Hector exchanged a hand signal with the car's driver. *Was this someone Hector knew?* Sure enough, a moment later, the Audi pulled away, and the black Lincoln followed it.

"Okay, let's keep on his tail."

Peter worried that Choe Song Ho might not have understood the expression "keep on his tail," but before he could rephrase himself, the cab pulled away from the terminal, and Peter privately chided himself for his prejudiced assumption about the man's English skills.

Before long the automotive caravan was on Century Boulevard, heading away from the airport. A couple of minutes later, the two lead cars turned left into the darkened parking lot of a Fatass Burger Restaurant.

"Don't turn!" said Peter. "Keep going."

The cab drove straight for another block, then turned right into a twenty-four-hour gas station.

"Do you need gas?" asked Peter.

"You treat?" asked Choe Song Ho.

"No, sorry."

"That's okay. I get. But meter's running."

As Choe Song Ho filled his tank, Peter strained his eyes to see what was happening across the street. He saw Hector leave the black

Lincoln and get into the Audi, but he couldn't discern anything of what was going on inside. It was a brief interaction. After only a minute, Hector exited the car, patted his back pocket, and returned to his own vehicle.

"We have to go," Peter shouted out the window.

Choe Song Ho responded, but not quickly enough. The Audi sped away. By the time the cab had started again, the Lincoln's lights were already receding into the distance.

"Is he heading back to the hotel?" asked Peter.

"Okay," said the driver, who seemed to have heard the question as "Can we go back to the hotel?"

Regardless, they seemed to be going in the same direction as Hector, and although they'd completely lost sight of him by the time they merged onto the 405, Peter was confident Hector would be heading back to the hotel. Whatever business had been transacted was now over and done with. It was time to call it a night.

They'd lost the man in the Audi. He would have been the big prize. Still, Peter knew he'd made an important discovery. Whatever Hector had been doing in that Fatass Burger parking lot was certainly suspicious. Peter just needed some context to understand exactly what it was he'd seen.

They arrived back at the Wilshire Grand just in time to glimpse Hector Elizondo striding through the front doors into the lobby. Peter's hunch had been right. Hector had gone straight back.

With the help of the hotel's valet, Peter managed to convince Choe Song Ho to wait in the carport while he returned to his room to get money. His final tab was $110, which was five dollars more than the young reporter had on hand, but the cabbie, in a show of unexpected good humor, accepted the lesser sum, causing Peter to wonder whether Choe Song Ho had perhaps enjoyed this late-night adventure after all.

His bill paid, Peter Williams returned to his room for the last time that evening. He spent forty-five minutes typing up a report of the night's events and then turned off the lights for a second attempt at slumber. This time he was successful.

IN THOSE DAYS

This third day of the Sharon Balis scandal began just as the first one had: with a press conference.

"Miss Balis, Senator Phillips has denied your alleged affair ever took place. Is he lying? Clearly, one of you isn't telling the whole truth. Who is it and why?"

It was the question on everyone's mind, the only question that really mattered.

"Yeah, it's sad that he had to deny it," she began. "I mean, it certainly happened, and it puzzles me why they would say what they did, because Ben isn't usually one to lie. But then I did wonder—and I realize it doesn't paint me in the most flattering light to say this—but a part of me wonders whether Ben even remembered our affair fully."

The reporters buzzed loudly.

"Miss Balis, you can't credibly suggest that the senator *forgot*, can you? How does one forget about something like an extramarital affair?"

"I know. It wouldn't reflect well on *me* if he forgot it that easily," she said with a halfhearted smile, "but there are two reasons. First is that I simply don't think our time together meant as much for him as it did for me, and second, as you're all probably aware, he was a drinker in those days and I don't know to what extent alcohol may have clouded his recollections."

The third bomb had been dropped.

RED, WHITE, AND BLUE MESSENGERS

Senator Phillips, do you have a drinking problem?"

"Not that I know of. Why? Should I?"

As Ben walked back away from the crowd, he pulled Campman toward him.

"Okay, Tom. What the heck's going on?"

"Sharon Balis just told America you used to be a drunk."

"That's ridiculous. I've never had a drinking problem."

"So she's lying."

"Of course she's lying!" the senator whispered, still sporting a wide public grin.

Thank goodness the charges were false, thought Campman (not that he really expected them to be true). If this claim could be refuted with solid evidence, Sharon Balis's credibility would suffer, and the senator would benefit.

Problem was, Sharon Balis now seemed intent on causing trouble. She was a loose cannon, and it petrified Campman to no end that she knew about the scandal idea. If Sharon was truly intent on causing problems, she had the power to single-handedly destroy the campaign. If she decided to come forward and claim that both scandals were frauds, then . . . it was too horrifying to think about.

Campman tried to reassure himself with the reminder that— above all else—Sharon seemed determined to *help* Ben win the election. Surely she would have to realize that any massive confession of conspiracy would be political suicide. Surely she would know not to take this thing much further.

As reassurances went, this one was decidedly weak. Still, Campman knew it was more important to reassure Ben than to reassure himself. And while the situation was dicey, it seemed their new strategy was, at least now, fairly clear. It was time to go with the idea he'd prayed about only the previous afternoon: they would continue to deny everything.

Always wary of the cameras, Campman turned to the senator with a cupped hand over his mouth.

"So she lied. That's what we tell them. *Deny, deny, deny.*"

That very moment, Campman saw the balloons.

They were red, white, and blue—not surprising colors, all things considered. He had noticed them before in front of Sacramento City Hall, but at the time, all the balloons had owners, patriotic Americans attached to them by slender strings. Now these helium beauties were emancipated, each balloon an independent contractor with the sky. And they were drifting his way.

His mind flashed back to yesterday.

"I will look for a sign tomorrow . . . by air. If that sign does not come, denial will continue to be our plan."

The tribulations of semantics had long plagued Campman's existence, but as the balloons drew nearer to him, as they honed in on their target, he felt the room for plastic interpretation grow smaller. As the first balloon and then the second one lightly brushed the remnants of his receding hairline, there was suddenly little doubt in

Campman's mind that the heavenly message he'd awaited from the air had been received.

What now?

As he was about to forfeit the senator's attention to the Sacramento public, Campman made one last request:

"Try to avoid the subject if you can, Ben—don't lay it on too thick. We'll discuss serious strategy tonight before the town hall meeting."

BOYS' CLUB

Melissa wouldn't talk on the phone, but Ben received an earful when she arrived in Sacramento.

"How could you let them do this to us?!" . . . "I should *not* have to hear about another bullshit scandal every time I turn on the television!" . . . "I really wish you'd listened to me, when I told you this was a bad idea!" . . . and so on.

She was angry, and she had every right to be.

Once she'd blown off steam, however, Melissa was compelled to agree with her husband that the only practical solution was to deny Sharon Balis's claims and hope for the best.

She sat beside him as the meeting began (the meeting before the town meeting, that is), cloaked in the quiet of a wounded animal, ready to strike at any moment.

"So let's talk about it," said Shelly Greenblatt. "How are we dealing with this whole drinking thing?"

"Elayne darling," said Thomas Campman, "would you mind leaving the room for a few minutes?"

"I'll be quiet," she responded with the smile.

Her husband shot her a room-clearing glance, and she quickly got the message. This was serious.

As the door closed behind Elayne, the senator began.

"Look, I don't know what made Sharon say what she did, but it's total bull. I've never been a drunk. I've never even been a drinker! You can ask anyone who knows me."

"I know you're not a drinking man, Ben," said Greenblatt. "Have you ever even been drunk?"

"No! Never!"

"Well then, this seems like a pretty open-and-shut case. There's no shortage of people out there who can attest to your not being a drinker. This is all just further proof that everything that comes out of that woman's mouth is total bullshit."

"I agree," said Melissa Phillips. It was the first time she'd spoken since entering the room.

"So for tonight," said Ben, "I'm just gonna say the allegations are ridiculous, and we'll work on backing that up with character witnesses over the next couple days."

"Sounds like a good plan to me," said Sorn.

"Shall we move on?"

"I think that's probably fine, Ben," said Campman, "but it does make me wonder: *Are we missing an opportunity here?*"

Campman could feel Melissa's dagger eyes on him.

"What do you mean, Tom?" asked the senator.

"I'm talking about your program to keep teens off alcohol. I'm talking about an opportunity to bring up social issues where you can speak with authority."

At this, Melissa Phillips jumped in.

"I do hope you're not about to suggest we take credit for another sin we have not committed. I *seriously* hope that is not your plan."

"Of course not," said Campman. "But you have to remember that in every lie there's a little bit of truth."

"No, no, no, no!" said Melissa sharply. "You are *not* going to do this to him again!"

She stood up and addressed the room, focusing most of her ire on Campman.

"I hope you realize you are skating on really thin ice. You're lucky he hasn't fired the whole lot of you after this bullshit. My husband is the only honest man in Washington and you've been trying to market him dishonestly! And guess what? It hasn't worked! And now you're saying you want to make the same mistake again! Well, we're not going to let you do that!"

"Melissa, please."

"Mr. Campman, your Republican employers may have preferred dishonesty and manipulation to achieve their political ends, but that's not the way we do things here! We are going to run an honest campaign, and we'll do it with you or without you."

Ben Phillips grinned. In those luckiest of marriages, the husband and wife can seem to share ownership of the same brain. The practical applications of such shared ownership are many, but chief among them is the ability to play good cop/bad cop with practiced ease. Now Melissa was doing more than playing bad cop; she was channeling her husband's emotions, speaking for him, and if her delivery was a bit over the top, Ben didn't mind at all. These were feelings he needed to get out of his system, and he was proud and pleased with his wife for doing it for him.

Campman just listened. He waited. Then, when he was sure Melissa had run out of steam, he began.

"Melissa, I agree with you," he said. "Honesty is Ben's hallmark, and we don't want to take that away. We've told one big lie already, and I promise we aren't going to tell any more. However, our actual honesty means nothing if the public doesn't buy it. And in order to convince them we are indeed on the level . . . we may have to paint with some shades of gray here."

"Not sure I like the sound of that," said Greenblatt.

"It seems like a very black-and-white situation to me," echoed Melissa.

"Let's at least let the man speak before we rip him to shreds," said Ben, coming to Campman's defense.

Melissa turned to her husband in surprise. So much for a united front. But the more she thought about it, this was typical of Ben. He was so obsessed with debate, so preoccupied with fairness, so in love with the idea of letting all sides have their say, that he could let a discussion go on much longer than it needed to. Why couldn't he be overbearing for once and act brazenly in his own self-interest? Why couldn't he just tell Campman to take a flying leap off a tall building?

"Thanks, Ben," said Thomas Campman. "Here's my question: You say you've never been drunk. Is that actually true? Haven't you been drunk, even once?"

Ben thought about it for a moment.

"No. I honestly don't think I have."

"What about in college? Even once? Surely, you drank a little bit."

"I drank alcohol once I came of age, but I never got drunk. Not even in college."

"Tom, for the last time I'll thank you to stop trying to turn my husband into an alcoholic."

He ignored her.

"But you've been buzzed."

"Well . . ."

"Alcohol has affected you, right?"

"I don't really drink to that point."

"But you have *once*, right? I mean you must have had *one time* where you drank enough that alcohol had *some* effect on you. *One time* where it altered your behavior *somewhat*! Am I right?"

The senator thought about this for a while.

"Well . . . yes, I suppose . . . well, there was a New Year's Eve party I recall, when I was in law school."

"Ben, this is ridiculous," said Melissa.

"And you got a little drunk, right?"

"Ben!"

"No. No, I didn't get drunk. But I did have more than one drink, I'm sure. And I remember feeling a slight buzz. That is to say . . . yes. Yes, I suppose I was a bit more animated that night than I usually am."

"*A bit more animated!* More talkative, less inhibited . . ."

"Well, yes, not that I'd ever call myself inhibited."

"Of course not! But there were people present who knew you, people who might have noticed your ever-so-slight change in anima-tion, people who are still alive today?"

"Yes, I suppose so. Some of my Harvard buddies . . ."

"*Aha!*"

"No! I don't like where you're going with this!" said Melissa. "Not one bit! I don't like it! You're NOT going to try and pass Ben off as a drunk!"

"Melissa . . . Melissa . . . Melissa . . . *of course not.* Look, I told you. We're not gonna say Ben's a drunk when we know he isn't one. Of course not! Of course, we're going tell everyone she's lying. We are. But there's more to it. Now just hear me out for a second. . . ."

WHEN MELISSA LEFT the room, she found Elayne Cohen-Campman sitting cross-legged on the hallway floor, flipping through pictures on the viewing screen of her Canon ProDigi 3000 camera. Had Campman's wife been in a less self-deprecating pose, Melissa might not have paused at all. She might have walked right past her.

As it was, she said the following:

"Hi. Just needed a little breather from the boys' club in there."

This made Elayne chuckle, and she flashed a smile that could melt icebergs.

"Yeah, I'm taking a break, too."

Melissa wasn't sure why, but she laughed at this. They both did.

"Say, I'm glad you're here," said Elayne, "because I wanted to make a date with you."

"Is that so?" said Melissa, who was surprised by how pleased this request made her.

"Yes, I have too many Y chromosomes in my shots, and I wanted to know if I could borrow some of your Xs."

"Okaaaay," Melissa responded, a bit confused. "I'm sorry, but . . ."

"No, *I'm* sorry. I'm not being clear. I wanted to know if I could borrow you at some point for a photo shoot. I'd love about forty-five minutes, but it could be less time than that—really whatever you're willing to give me. It would be very casual. I just want to have some time alone with you—I'm gonna try and do the same thing with Ben—just to get some candid out-of-the-limelight-type stuff."

"Is this for your . . . ?"

"Well, it's *all* for my own project, of course. But as you know, I also have some open-ended offers from several magazines that might possibly be interested. I know *American Chic* in particular has expressed interest in photos of you, although I'm sure there'd be other offers." She lowered her voice to add, "Of course, this would only be if you and I both liked them—and everything totally pending your approval."

There was something Melissa found undeniably attractive about hearing the phrase "everything totally pending your approval," but that wasn't why she agreed to the photo shoot. At least, it wasn't the only reason.

Melissa had exchanged few words with Elayne since she'd joined the campaign a little over a month ago, but she was starting to sense a quiet bond growing between them as two of the only women in the campaign's inner circle. Sometimes, when the collective male bravado was at its most unruly, Melissa would catch Elayne shooting her conspiratorial glances from across the room, and these would never fail to put a smile on her face. Melissa had begun to look forward to these moments of eye contact. She even sought them out. Now, here she was, grinning from ear to ear at Elayne's request for a photo session. What was it about Elayne that made Melissa so delighted by her attention?

Melissa remembered how she'd first misjudged Elayne, thinking her nothing more than an entitled extension of her hideous husband. She felt guilty thinking of it now. Could there be two people more different than Elayne and Tom Campman?

As Melissa Phillips officially shelved Elayne in the "Don't Judge a Book by Its Cover" section of her library of life experiences, she noticed her mind had momentarily taken a vacation from the unpleasantness in the other room. Okay, not a total vacation. The very fact that she was aware of how unaware she was meant she was never completely unaware to begin with. But still . . .

"I think I can manage some time tomorrow morning before my flight. If we start early."

"Oh, tomorrow would be great!"

"Do you need me to wear anything in particular?"

The conversation danced about for a while longer, and when it was over, Melissa headed back to her room, her mind once again returning to the dishonesty of boys' clubs and the perilous state of the world.

TOWN MEETING

So I was watching the news today," began the angular, silver-haired matron holding the microphone.

"Oh, were you?" asked Ben.

The Sacramento crowd chuckled in anticipation.

"Yes," the woman responded, "and I want to ask you, because I have grandkids and I think it's important: Senator Phillips, were you ever a drunk?"

"Was I ever 'a drunk'?" the senator echoed, a smile creeping across his face like a father who'd just been asked to talk about his summa cum laude offspring. *"No."*

This provoked a smattering of applause from the audience, but Ben's tone quickly became serious.

"No, thank God. I was lucky enough to have avoided that demon called alcoholism. Now . . . Have I enjoyed alcohol in the past? Have I been tempted by it? Have I, on occasion—maybe on a New Year's Eve, for example—have I ever drunk a little more than perhaps I should have?"

The movement of dust particles in the air could have been audible in the moment of silence following Senator Phillips's rhetorical question.

"I'm not going to say that's never happened," he finally said. "In fact, I don't know if I'd trust a man who told me it never happened to him. *I will say* it's never been a habit . . . *certainly* never been a *problem* . . . and to accuse me of being a . . ."

He shook his head derisively. In leaving the phrase incomplete, it was as if the senator found its very enunciation unworthy of the required effort. He said instead: "Well, that's just absurd. And you don't have to take my word for it. Ask anyone who knows me.

"I've never had a problem with drinking because I was lucky enough to have parents who taught me the virtues of moderation, I was lucky enough to have teachers who motivated me to be the sort of person who thought for himself, I was lucky enough to have friends who knew you didn't have to drink to be cool, and moreover . . . I was just plain lucky.

"But a lot of Americans are not so lucky. And while I'm sad the subject came up the way it did, I am glad it came up. Because alcohol is a big problem in this country, and I think it's about time we talked about it."

And he did. Painting in broad strokes with a large palette of blacks, whites, and grays, Senator Ben Phillips spoke at length about alcohol, drugs, and the education of America's children. He preached moderation, compassion, and a new set of democratic values, based not on dogma, but on empathy and common sense.

"He's brilliant!" Elayne Cohen-Campman remarked later to her husband. "I just can't believe how 'on' he was tonight. It's like the more stuff they throw at him, the better he gets. Have you noticed that?"

Campman had noticed. And he wasn't the only one. Several of the twenty-four-hour news channel pundits who reported the event made note of the believability of the senator's denial, particularly in comparison with Sharon Balis's questionably motivated accusations. Even conservative mouthpiece Larry Gallagher had this to say:

"Do I think Ben Phillips is a drunk? I don't know. I find that pretty hard to swallow. Is he a tax-and-spend Communist who's gonna leave us vulnerable to terrorists and take this country back to the *Stone Age* if he's elected? Yes. Is he a compulsive womanizer who has cheated on his wife with multiple partners? Maybe. But is he a drunk? I will say, I think *probably . . . not*. I thought he gave a good response to that question tonight, saying of course he drinks—in fact he wouldn't trust a man who said he never did (incidentally neither would I, Senator!)—but saying the accusations of him being a 'drunk' are simply not true, and I tend to believe him. I think this Balis woman is just out for attention and she's gonna say anything to put herself on the front page."

Campman was encouraged by Gallagher's comments. If Ben could get a hard-core right-winger to believe his story, convincing the rest of America might not be that difficult. As he flipped through TV stations before bed, he found the initial signs to be encouraging.

So he probably would have shared his wife's ebullience wholeheartedly had it not been for the message he received on his cell phone.

It was that same male voice speaking in that same urgent tone:

"I know about Muddville. And I know what you are doing now."

It was the fifth such message he'd received, and like its four predecessors, it chilled him to the bone. Once again, his head filled with questions. Was someone trying to blackmail him? Who? Who could know about both Muddville *and* the current trickery? And what exactly did they know anyhow? Certainly someone was trying to scare him. But why? What could they want? Who could benefit? And how?

In the wake of each call, Campman set a hundred different scenarios afloat in his mind, but all sank due to one logical hole or another. No matter how hard he tried, he couldn't come up with an explanation that fit. He felt helpless, and on top of it all, there was no one he could talk to about his troubles.

So as his wife brushed her teeth in the next room, Thomas Campman mumbled a quiet prayer. He wasn't sure if the Almighty would trouble Him/Her/It/Them-selves with such a trivial matter as a prank caller, but he figured it was worth a shot. It made sense to pray, thought Campman, if for no other reason than that the Almighty was the only other anonymous caller on Campman's phone sheet.

"Oh, Lord my God, Jesus, and all spirits inhabiting this world and others . . . I pray for the ability to find out who the hell keeps calling me, and I pray whoever it is will do me no harm. And while I don't know if you have anything to do with this whole business, I sure hope not, because I thought we were square. I didn't kill Warren. You know that. I said it was my last dirty trick, and *it would have been* if not for you . . . yes, that's right. YOU. You're the one who has me going every which way here, and frankly I don't appreciate it. Do we lie? Do we deny? I don't have a damn clue anymore—which means I operate on instinct—unless you want to start giving me some clearer signs.

"Thank you for the positive TV coverage my candidate has received tonight and for my wife and daughter and all good things in the world. Amen."

PHOTO SHOOT

Oh, God, you look beautiful. How come you never wear this sort of thing on the campaign trail?"

Melissa blushed.

"It's a little casual, don't you think?"

"Are you crazy?"

"I have two other options, if you want to take a look."

"No, this is perfect, honey. Oh, yeah!"

Elayne's effervescence was contagious.

"And my hair and makeup are okay?"

Melissa had forgotten how long it'd been since she'd had such an unabashedly "female" conversation. She remembered her daughter Stacy's wedding. God, had it been that long?

"Here are the rules, okay? I'm not like a fashion photographer. I don't believe in posing you. I just want you to exist. Just exist in the space, and I'll capture that."

"Should I pretend you're not here?"

"I don't think that's very natural, do you?"

"Well, no, I . . . guess not."

"I *am* here, aren't I?"

"Yes."

"So, that's fine. If you want to talk, we'll talk. If not, then we won't. I want you to do whatever would be natural to you in this situation. Just be . . . Melissa. And I'll capture that."

"Okay."

Melissa suddenly felt like a child learning the rules of a strange new game. She smiled mischievously.

"I'm going to sit here on the bed."

"That's great! Just . . . be."

"Okay."

She sat.

"Oh, that's so great. This is great," and then, "Oooh."

"What?"

"Oh, nothing. It's just . . . this is so good. It's just, if you could . . ."

"What?"

"Maybe just sit a little farther from the edge. I just think we'll get more light on your face that way."

"Sure, that's fine."

"Oh, that's good. That's really good."

And it was. Melissa looked radiant. Elayne had always thought her to be attractive, with her kiwi green eyes, aquiline features, and flowing chestnut hair, but it wasn't until she had Melissa's full attention, looking through the camera's viewfinder, that she appreciated just how striking the candidate's wife was. She had a charisma not unlike that of her husband, but it was less diffuse. It could only be appreciated by those in the direct line of her gaze.

Elayne snapped a picture.

"So tell me what it's like to be married to such an amazing man," she said.

"Ben?"

"You married to someone else? (Could you turn your head just a bit more?)"

Melissa giggled, and Elayne snapped.

"Well, I love Ben, of course. We're very much a team, you know."

It was her standard line from that standard conversation, the one she could engage in while doing five other tasks at once, while sleeping, while giving birth, on a cloudy day.

"How did you meet?"

"We met . . . at a party. In Boston. He was in law school at Harvard, and I was getting my masters in English and American literature at BU, and—"

"Maybe, you could lean back now?"

"Sure—well, it was one of those parties where—"

"No, just a little farther back."

"Do you want my arm to be . . . ?"

"Wherever *you* want it to be. Remember, I don't give direction. You just exist. Ooh, not there. A little higher."

"So, uh, anyway, it was one of those parties where neither of us knew anyone, but we just started up a conversation literally by the punch bowl, and we ended up talking all night long. We left the party and went out for pancakes, and then he brought me home at four in the morning. We were just talking the whole time."

"Mmmm. Should we stand up for a little while?"

"Sure, that's fine," said Melissa, standing. "Maybe over here?"

She walked gracefully to the wide windows of the hotel suite.

"You know . . . I've been learning to avoid windows these past few months. Isn't that terrible?"

"You look *so* beautiful right now," said Elayne, "I can't even tell you."

Melissa smiled.

"It's amazing the sacrifices we make," she said, "for our *men*! Ha! We've come a long way, haven't we?"

"You don't think so?"

Melissa pondered this for a while.

"Well, I suppose no one *forces* us to make sacrifices. But certain situations, certain choices tend to carry with them certain . . . undesirable responsibilities . . . that we are perhaps unaware of at first."

"You know, I admire you so much," said Elayne. And then, "No! Don't even think about that! Pretend I didn't say that."

"Okay."

"I don't want to influence you with flattery."

"Okay."

"Your *mood,* you know. I mean we can talk, but if I'm influencing your emotions, then I'm directing the situation, which I don't do."

"Oh. Okay."

"You understand. Well, of course you do (if you could just turn your—there we go!). It's such a precarious thing, this artist/subject relationship."

"Of course."

"Anyhow, what I was trying to say was—no, keep looking out— any woman who could marry a man of such . . . vision and complexity—just keep your chin up—and have the confidence to deal so gracefully—yeah, that's it, now raise your shoulder—to deal so gracefully with such . . . adversity . . . I just think it's . . . oh . . . inspiring. . . . But please! . . . Please don't listen to anything I'm saying right now."

Elayne had been drawing steadily closer to Melissa, her camera firing away the whole time. Now she put the camera down and just stared at her subject. She was exhaling deeply, almost postcoitally.

"How are we doing?" asked Melissa.

Elayne smiled.

"Luminously. And you?"

"I'm . . . actually . . . great."

"Good."

The two women looked at each other until, simultaneously, they broke into giggles.

"This is fun," said Melissa.

Elayne just nodded.

"You look so great in this natural light."

"Um, thank you."

"But you're too constricted. Too uptight."

She looked her up and down.

"Why don't we unbutton a few buttons, shall we?"

THE DRUNK VOTE

G entlemen, I'm sorry, but I've had enough. I was hired by this campaign to be a speechwriter. *That is what I have been paid to do.* And while I am more than willing to help out in areas beyond my expertise for the good of the campaign, I feel my willingness to do so has been taken advantage of. I am not an intern, I am not a porter, I am not an errand boy, and I am not a secretary. I don't do background checks, I don't purchase getaway vehicles, and I don't do car chases. *I am a speechwriter.* That is all. And I demand to be treated with respect."

Derek Kiley had his speech ready to go. He'd been practicing it for the last two weeks, polishing and tweaking it in his mind every time his superiors provoked him. But he hadn't delivered it. Not yet.

Had Kiley been questioned on the subject, he probably would've claimed he was still searching for the right moment to air his grievances, but he knew this was just an excuse. Many "right moments" had come and gone, and he'd wussed out at every one.

What about now? Kiley fumed. He'd been polishing a new draft of the senator's speech on the environment when Sorn interrupted and asked him to call Wanda in Chicago for the latest poll numbers. "Why don't you ask Julie to call?" Kiley had wanted to say. Julie was Sorn's assistant, who had fallen asleep listening to her MP3 player. Or better yet, why don't you call Wanda yourself, you lazy asshole? I'm not your damn secretary!

If only he'd launched into his prepared speech right away. But he hadn't. Could he still do it? Was it too late? Kiley grimaced. He knew he'd have to swallow his pride once more. Too much time had elapsed between offense and grievance. He'd have to wait for another opportunity. *Dammit.* Kiley's hesitation meant he'd have to take precious time out from the work he'd been hired to do so he could perform the mindless task of calling Wanda in Chicago for poll results. Stupid Wanda. Stupid Chicago.

He bit his lip and called.

What surprised him were the poll results themselves. These new numbers surprised Derek Kiley so much, in fact, that he quickly forgot his discontent at being asked to inquire about them. Suddenly he relished the role of news bearer.

"We moved up," he said.

All eyes in the airplane cabin turned his way.

"Good," replied Greenblatt. "By how much?"

For Kiley, time slowed as he noticed everyone in the cabin looking at him, anticipation in their eyes.

"Um . . . by a lot. It's a seven-point race."

"Get the fuck out," said Sorn.

"Are you serious?" asked Campman.

"That's close," said Mayweather. "That's really respectable. I mean, with the margin of error, that could put us actually . . . close."

"All right!" shouted Ben's assistant, Charlie.

The shocked cabin now burst into a delayed applause that lingered for some time. It was as if they were waking up for the first time in a new place. Team Phillips had been the underdog for so long, they had forgotten how exciting it was to be an actual contender.

The only one who wasn't surprised was Ben Phillips himself. He sat quietly, smiling and sipping his cranberry juice.

"I knew it was coming," he said eventually. "I could feel it in the crowds. I knew we were moving up."

Ben couldn't describe exactly how he knew, but he had. Was it really the crowds? Were they actually any different? Perhaps they'd been a bit more vocal lately, a bit more passionate. But then he was usually preaching to the converted. The people who attended his political rallies were not the same voters who swung the polls. Was he just imagining things?

Maybe it was the way people looked at him. Yes, that had definitely changed, but this difference was also subtle, and he had trouble characterizing it. It was almost as if people were no longer sure what to expect from him anymore. He was now a man of surprises, and as a result, he could keep people in suspense.

Yes, the people *were* listening, weren't they? They were curious. And it also seemed he was now delivering exactly what they wanted to hear. That was the other part of the equation. It wasn't just the funny looks or enthusiastic audiences. Ben's behavior had changed, too.

For all the grief of the last three weeks, Ben couldn't help but feel energized. He had a spring in his step. He was speaking with more confidence, making more jokes, and starting to improvise on the stump in ways he never would have dared before.

Perhaps it was something about rising to a challenge. Ben was, after all, being challenged on an issue where he'd always been strong: integrity. It was something he could defend with great vigor, and furthermore (and perhaps this was most important), he knew his defense would be noted. What was that old adage about bad press being better than no press at all? Yes, it was definitely better to be challenged than ignored.

But where did this leave Ben with his question of causality? Was he behaving differently because suddenly there were these new expectations, or were there new expectations *because* he was acting differently? The senator took out a pen from his pocket and scribbled the following equation on his cocktail napkin:

$$SCANDAL \rightarrow EXPECTATION \rightarrow BEHAVIOR$$
$$or$$
$$SCANDAL \rightarrow BEHAVIOR \rightarrow EXPECTATION$$

and then:

$$\nearrow EXPECTATION$$
$$SCANDAL \qquad \uparrow\downarrow$$
$$\searrow BEHAVIOR$$

Ben quickly realized his equations were insufficient. There were too many variables to be accounted for: the media, the Republican response, the differing nature of each of the scandals. At the end of a healthy session of pondering, all Ben Phillips could really say with any certainty was that things had changed over the last three weeks, and for whatever reason, he had known he was on the rebound. The why or wherefore was too complex to be boiled down—at least not by him, at least not now. But he had known. He had felt it.

More explanations came an hour later, when the complete poll results were e-mailed to Ralph Sorn's laptop. Buried in the four-page report were a number of interesting findings that had not been mentioned in the initial phone call. Particularly revealing were the respondents' answers to the following questions:

1. If he is elected, are you concerned about alcohol affecting Senator Phillips's ability to perform his duties as president?
    (a) Not at all concerned—83%
    (b) A little bit concerned—12%
    (c) Highly concerned—3%

2. Do you believe Ben Phillips _____?
    (a) Frequently abuses alcohol?—10%
    (b) Still occasionally abuses it?—42%
    (c) Never abuses it?—43%

3. Do you _____?
   (a) Frequently abuse alcohol?—7%
   (b) Occasionally abuse alcohol?—27%
   (c) Never abuse alcohol?—58%

And perhaps most interesting:

4. Of those who answered (a) & (b) to the last question, if the election were held today, who would you vote for?
   (a) Gregory Struck—43%
   (b) Ben Phillips—49%
   (c) Undecided—8%

5. Of the same group, who would you have voted for if the election
   had been held one month ago?
   (a) Gregory Struck—46%
   (b) Ben Phillips—36%
   (c) Undecided—18%

"In every lie there's a little bit of truth," said Campman, reading
the freshly printed results.

"I can't believe people think I'm a drinker," replied the senator.

"A drinker, but not a heavy drinker. *Just like them,*" corrected
Campman. "Besides, you're missing the point here, Ben."

He smiled a broad smile.

"You've got the drunk vote."

POPULAR, ATTRACTIVE, CONSISTENT

W hat if we bombed Russia?"

Silence.

"Mr. President, the cold war is over."

"So what? Why can't we bomb Russia anyway?"

"Are you serious?"

"Mac, do you ask a president if he's serious?"

"I'm sorry, Mr. President. If you want my opinion, I don't think bombing Russia is a particularly good idea at this time. We don't really have any *reason* to be bombing them, and um, in fact, we do generally consider Russia to be an ally, sir."

President Greg Struck was smiling three miles wide. He started to cackle.

His secretary of state, James MacClure, looked noticeably uncomfortable.

"Oh, boy, you make it too easy, Mac."

At this, the other occupants of the oval office—Vice President Macon Chisholm and political guru Dennis Fazo—began to chuckle. MacClure himself smiled uneasily.

"Okay, Mac. You've convinced me. Good argument. We won't bomb Russia today."

At this, the room exploded with laughter.

"See?" added Struck, "and they say I don't listen to my advisors! Congratulations, Mac, you just saved millions of lives."

"Very funny, Mr. President," said the loyal Chisholm.

And it was funny. Struck took great pride and pleasure in his little jokes, particularly when they were performed at the expense of up-tight company men like MacClure. Although he didn't speak of it often, the president saw it as a minor personal mission to bring hu-mor to the Oval Office. At times, he thought, it seemed everyone who walked through the door was a prophet of doom, foretelling misery ahead, begging and bowing and pleading, and always warning about this threat or that. It could get real bloody depressing if you didn't keep it all in perspective.

So, he joked. And the others seemed to like it. And he liked that they liked it. And he liked that they liked him. And he liked them right back. And he wondered, in his more private moments, if there had ever been a president who was more popular with his own staff.

Most likable president. Most popular president. Most attractive president (he'd concede a tie with Kennedy). Most consistent presi-dent. Strongest president (policy-wise and physically; he could bench 260 pounds). Toughest president. Most feared president. Most loved president (conceding a four-way tie with FDR, Eisenhower, and Wash-ington).

It should come as a surprise to no one that those Americans who have achieved the rank of president tend to be more competi-tive than their fellow citizens. To what extent Greg Struck was above or below this presidential average is useless conjecture, but suffice to say, like many of his predecessors, Struck spent more time than he would care to admit concerned with his place in the ranks of presidential history. Of course, he knew such rankings to be subjective, but in his proudest moments, President Greg Struck couldn't help but think that if there were a definitive listing of presidential superlatives, he would be doing (ranking-wise) pretty darn well.

"Now where were we again?" asked Struck. "Oh, yeah, you want me to sign something."

"The letter to the United Nations, Mr. President. I really do urge you to sign it."

"That's right. Look, Mac, you know I'd love to sign that, but I just can't. I have already told the American people—what was it now?— 'America can no longer rely on other countries to be friendly'?"

The vice president recited the quote verbatim. "America cannot continue to rely so heavily on other countries when conducting foreign policy. I believe foreign policy is something we should do our own way, according to our own principles. Friends may help us. The United Nations may help us. But with them or without them, we are going to do what's right and—"

"Yeah, yeah, yeah, that's it. You see, Mac, if the United Nations wants to help us, they can, but for *us* to ask *them* for assistance, it doesn't sound consistent with what I said before."

"That may be, sir, but we do need their help. And they can't begin to lend a hand if we don't try to mend some fences, if we don't give them a reason to want to—"

"That's not my job! If they valued democracy like we do, they'd be helping us out on pure principle. This conversation is closed. I'm sticking to my guns here, Mac. Dammit, I think it's about time this country had a president who stuck to his guns."

"Well spoken, Mister President," said Fazo when they were alone together again.

"I tell you, Dennis, it burns me up when people try to make me go back on something I've already said."

"I suppose this is a good time to ask you about your comment about Ben Phillips."

"What? When I said he was 'unfit to be president *or* senator *or* a voter'?"

"That's the one."

The president chuckled.

"Oh, I liked that one a lot. Is it getting me in trouble?"

"A little."

"Fucking press. What did Felipe say?"

"Phillips says you're unfit as well, but he wouldn't keep you out of a voting booth—as much as he'd like to."

"Ooh, that's good. A bit more reasonable, I suppose."

"And your response?"

"Dennis, you *know* my response. Screw him! I voiced what I said, and I'll stick with that. There's no pussyfooting around here. We want people wondering about this guy! We want people worried about his integrity, his competence, his fidelity, his sobriety, all that stuff!"

"And they *are* worrying about it. Lucky you."

"I tell you, Dennis, he's making it too easy for us. We'd face a bigger challenge if Warren Muddville were the Democratic candidate— even with the bastard six feet underground."

"I agree. I take it you're not too concerned about this morning's poll?"

"Hell no. You?"

Fazo shook his head.

"Thing is," said Struck, "we haven't even hit with our big guns yet. And look at the opportunity! He's opened up all these questions. All we have to do is exploit them."

"So, I take it you've had time to think about what we discussed this morning?"

"Yessir."

"And I will assume you approve of the plan?"

Struck nodded and smiled.

"I can't officially endorse anything, naturally, but I will say that Ben Phillips deserves whatever's coming to him. So . . . bombs away."

FLASHBACK

It was 5:40 P.M. The sun had just set, but you would've had no way of knowing it, looking at the pale gray sky. The snow was falling in big chunky flakes, and they were all over the damn place. On M Street in Georgetown, if you were bobbing in and out of shops, you might have been reminded of one of those particularly photogenic Christmas-Eve-in-the-big-city-type scenes. Problem was, the city was D.C., and it was the middle of February.

Thomas Campman shouldn't have even been there. It was the day before the Maryland primary, and he had less than an hour before he had to leave for the rally later that night.

Ah, the primary! A bit of snow may shut down the government, but last-minute primary campaigning is canceled by no one, particularly in a race as close as this one. Sure, they'd won Iowa, finished second in New Hampshire, and racked up most of the states since then, but it was still early, and anything could happen. Muddville and Phillips were neck and neck in Maryland, and every last bit of snow-covered publicity was helpful.

Campman was shopping on M Street against his better judgment, because he knew if he failed to purchase a birthday gift for his wife that evening, there'd be little chance of it arriving in Bombay in time for the blessed event. Birthdays were important to Elayne, and that meant they were important to Campman as well.

He should've just bought something over the Internet. That's what Wyatt, his assistant, had suggested. But Campman was still wary of typing his credit card number into a computer, "secure server" or not. No, he had to shop the old-fashioned way, and he had to do it quickly. Perhaps it was time pressure that drew Campman immediately to the most expensive item in the store: a Cannon ProDigi 3000 digital camera. Elayne had been talking about a digital camera for some time now, and the ProDigi 3000 was the absolute top of the line. It was more money than Campman had been thinking of spending, but it was a sure thing. A sure thing was all he had time for now.

Campman had just finished paying for the camera when his cell phone rang. It was Jeff Brigg.

Jeff Brigg was the man on the inside. He was Campman's guy, and he worked for the enemy: Warren Muddville. Jeff spoke quickly.

"Can you get someone to the office on the Hill in fifteen minutes?"

"What's going on, Jeff?"

"I've got them. I've got the Lannahan files."

Campman's hair stood on end.

"Oh, my God. And . . . ?"

"It's a smoking gun, just like you thought, but someone needs to pick them up *right now*."

Campman swallowed hard.

This was big. This was bigger than big. This was colossal. He'd had a hunch the Lannahan files existed and that they were in Muddville's possession. Now that hunch was paying off. The Lannahan files contained information with the power to sink Muddville's campaign once and for all, if handled properly. It wasn't just dirt, it was pay dirt. They could lock up the nomination right now—before Super Tuesday even!

As Jeff talked, Campman walked briskly to the door of the camera shop and exited into M Street's winter wonderland.

"Everyone's in Baltimore or at campaign headquarters," said Brigg. "The store's empty. The other guys went down the street to pick up dinner. They'll be out for a half hour at the most. The security cameras are down, so they left me behind to watch the office."

"Can't you get it out now?"

"If I leave, the doorman will see me. And it's too big for me to take out later without arousing suspicion. Can you get someone here in fifteen minutes?"

"Fifteen minutes? Shit."

There would be no time to get someone from the Phillips campaign office—no one he could trust at least. Campman would have to make the run himself. But he was in Georgetown and Jeff was on Capitol Hill. With the bad weather and rush-hour traffic, it would take a major miracle to get there in twenty minutes, never mind fifteen.

"I'll figure out something."

"Whoever comes here needs to have a backpack or briefcase that can fit these files. There's a lot here. . . ."

Campman's eyes scanned the snowy street. He spotted a sporting goods store.

"Have them call me on my cell when they get down here, okay?" said Brigg. "We need to get them past the doorman, which shouldn't be too hard."

Campman started running toward the sporting goods store, making a conscious effort not to slip on the slushy sidewalk.

"Okay, Jeff. I'll call you soon."

Cell phone off. Campman bolted across the street, running right in front of a taxicab which—propelled by the snowy road—barely stopped in time. Campman kept running.

A bell jingled as he threw open the door to the sporting goods establishment.

"Where do I find backpacks?" He seemed to be asking the whole store.

"In the back, with the camping equipment," came an answer.

He grabbed the first backpack he saw and then headed to the register. On his way, he grabbed a few books. They were probably books on camping, but who really cared? He just needed something to fill the backpack.

The register was full. Campman waited. Seconds passed.

By the time Campman reemerged from the sporting goods store and shuffled into a taxi across the street, four minutes had passed since Jeff Brigg's initial call. He'd have to get to Capitol Hill in eleven minutes.

AS SOON AS the man in the gray coat entered his taxi, Hector Elizondo knew he meant business.

"Here's the deal. I need you to get me to Independence Ave on Capitol Hill in eleven minutes. I don't care how you do it, but it better be quick. You get me there in eleven minutes I pay triple. You get me there in eleven minutes, five seconds, you get nothing. Understand?"

Although Hector Elizondo's English comprehension was less than exemplary, he was good with numbers and addresses, and the gray-coated man's message seemed to be clear: He was in a rush.

If there had been any doubt in Thomas Campman's mind as to Hector's understanding of this proposition, that doubt was swiftly erased by the roar of the taxi's engine and the spinning of its tires.

Within seconds, they were on a side street. Campman had no sooner cried, "Where the hell are you going?" than he figured out the cabbie's plan. It was a shortcut he'd never tried before, but it looked smart, and the driver seemed to know where he was going.

"This is good," said Campman, "but you might want to get back on the main roads. I don't know how well they plow back here."

The car whizzed across an embankment and found itself airborne for a quick second before landing effortlessly on a patch of ice and gliding to the end of the block.

As a rule, Campman tended to micromanage his cab rides, from stop signs to thermostats, but with Hector he'd finally met his match. Every time he started to complain about an unexpected detour, that detour would turn into a shortcut. Hector had a mastery for the D.C. streets that Campman had never seen before. Hector was intense, he had quick reflexes, and his large hands gripped the wheel with the speed and precision of an artist. Campman liked him instantly.

By looking out the windows and listening to the roar of the engine, Campman could tell Hector was driving recklessly, like a lunatic in fact. He was barreling through intersections with no regard for the consequences, taking sharp turns at dangerously high speeds, and swerving in and out of traffic like a star running back against a lazy defense. But there was something effortless about it all. Even with the snow, even with the traffic, and despite all visual and aural evidence to the contrary, Campman wondered if he had ever experienced so smooth a ride. Hector seemed to be one with the car, in total control. Campman never felt the slightest bit of danger. The Zen calm within the car's interior was such that Campman became convinced he could've balanced a full cup of coffee on his knee without spilling a drop. He had been taking cabs in the capital city for over thirty years and had never felt this way before. It was magical.

They arrived at Muddville's private office in ten minutes. It was a deceptively large green office building that was easy to miss, sandwiched as it was between two rows of typical Capitol Hill apartments. When Warren Muddville resigned from Congress the previous year, he'd rented a floor of the building to serve as his personal office while trying to gain support for a presidential bid. He'd kept the office even after the campaign opened a more spacious headquarters on Sixteenth Street, preferring to remain on the Hill where he was most at home. The Sixteenth Street headquarters would surely be a madhouse tonight, overflowing with volunteers working the phone banks, but this place was dead. At least for a few more minutes.

"Nicely done," said Campman as he paid Hector three times his normal fare. He then reached for his phone and called Jeff Brigg.

"Let me know when you're about to enter the door," said Brigg, "and I'll call the front desk to distract the doorman. If you just act like you're going to the fourth floor, he'll let you by with no problem. They have people coming and going all the time. But then get off at the third floor and I'll meet you."

"I'll call you back in one minute," Campman said. He turned to Hector.

"How'd you like to make a hundred bucks extra?"

These were words Hector understood.

"*Sí*. Eeeeyes very much-eh-sir."

Campman handed him the backpack.

"You go in. Flash a number four." Campman held up four fingers. "Get in the elevator. Go to floor number three." Now three fingers. "You'll see a man named Brigg. He'll give you a package."

Campman repeated the instructions several times to make sure Hector understood.

"Bring it down here to me, and you've got one hundred bucks."

"EeeeTwo hundred."

"One hundred fifty, and that's all you're getting."

"*Sí*," said Hector, stifling a smile. "*Sí*. Eeeeyessir."

Hector left the cab and took the car keys with him. Smart move, thought Campman. He liked this strange little Mexican.

Campman called Brigg again.

"He's coming up."

HECTOR WALKED INTO the lobby of the small office building, and he spotted a tall man on the telephone.

"Yes, you've reached the right building, but this is just the front desk," the man was saying, somewhat exasperated. He looked up at Hector.

Whenever Hector found himself in an unfamiliar situation, he'd learned it was helpful to smile, so this was what he did. He also flashed four fingers at the doorman, who half-smiled and nodded in return. Upon receiving this greeting, Hector decided he should flash three fingers next. That seemed to be the order: four, then three. Hector flashed three fingers, but the doorman didn't notice this time. He was too wrapped up in his conversation.

"No, I understand that. Well, may I ask where you are coming from?"

The elevator door opened, and Hector got in.

Four, then three. That was what Hector remembered. He pressed the number four followed by the number three. Because of the order of the pressing, Hector half-expected the elevator to stop on the fourth floor before it traveled to the third, but this was not the case. Regardless, Hector knew he needed to travel to the fourth floor first, so when the doors opened on floor three, he stood in place and did not move.

A nervous man was waiting on the third floor, and he seemed surprised Hector wasn't giving any sign of recognition. Hector just stood there, waiting for the door to close again.

"Are you Hector?" the man asked.

How did he know his name?

"You here with Campman?"

Hector didn't understand the second sentence, but it had become clear this was the man he was supposed to meet. He walked out of the elevator.

"*So* glad you're here. Let me take this."

The nervous man took the backpack and ran off to the other end of the floor.

Hector surveyed his surroundings. It was an office all right. There were desks, cubicles, computers, and doors that seemed to lead to more private office rooms, just like in the movies. Hector began to realize this was the first genuine office he'd ever been inside. Sure, he'd been to the office of the taxi company, also a couple quasi-offices in Miami for work-related reasons, and even a few of the new medical offices on San Gomez, which he'd visited with his wife and daughters. He'd been to buildings or rooms that had the title of "office" before, but none of these other so-called offices had the distinctly "office" feel so immediately recognizable to anyone who'd spent enough time watching American TV. This was an "office" office. No doubt about it.

Of course, this particular office had its own distinguishing features, the most prominent of these being a large red, white, and blue banner that read: MUDDVILLE FOR AMERICA! There were also similar posters and pictures, most of them in that patriotic trio of colors, many of them featuring the image of Warren Muddville with windblown white hair.

The nervous man returned and handed Hector the backpack. It seemed heavier now. The man pressed the down button on the elevator and smiled wearily at Hector.

"You have a good night," he said.

"Eeeeyessir."

The man pulled out his cell phone and dialed.

What he said next took Hector by surprise. As the elevator doors closed between them, the nervous man started speaking in an entirely different voice. He was using an Indian accent, although Hector couldn't place the dialect, and he spoke into his cell phone with a peculiar sort of animation.

"Hello? Oh, yes, vee goht disconnected. I yammon cell phone. I am de mahn who ees cahming tomurrow. I huv an appointmunt in yar building, and I vahnted yoo to tell me what ees the best vay. . . ."

AS HECTOR ELIZONDO drove him back to the house on Kalorama Road, Campman asked a lot of questions.

"Where are you from?"

San Gomez, Mexico.

"Are you an American citizen?"

Yes.

"Really? No bullshit?"

At this, Hector produced a Social Security card, a driver's license, a crumpled-up lease, and a birth certificate from somewhere beneath his seat. He handed the crumpled mass to Campman.

"Okay, okay, okay. So you're a citizen. You a Democrat or Republican?"

Hector wasn't sure which way to answer. The gentleman certainly looked like a Republican (or at least what Hector *imagined* a Republican might look like), but he had doubts. He went with his gut. Democrat.

"Of course you are. Have you been following the campaign?"

Hector didn't understand the question. He said yes.

"Who you for? Muddville? Slattery? Thomas? Phillips?"

Hector replied yes with confidence although he had no clue what he was being asked. Again, Campman seemed pleased, so Hector felt he must have answered correctly.

"Phillips, eh? Me too, buddy. You have a wife? Kids?"

"*Sí.*"

"Can you keep a secret?"

Something about a secret. Hector said yes again.

"Do you drink? Use drugs?"

This question he'd heard before. He answered no.

"Now tell me something, do you want to be a taxi driver for the rest of your life or do you have bigger plans?"

YOU WANT . . . . TAXI DRIVER . . . .
LIFE . . . . BIG.

Hector was out of his league. When he had passengers who talked this much, he usually just didn't listen. Now he chose to ignore the question, hoping it would pass.

"Okay, okay, fair enough," said Campman. "I'll be direct. Do you want to work for me?"

This seemed important.

"Eeeeesorry?"

"Do you want a job?"

"Ahhhh," Hector said knowingly, although he was still uncertain as to what exactly was going on. It sounded as if the man in the suit was offering him a job. As he was already up 185 bucks, Hector figured he should respond with enthusiasm. They had just stopped in front of Campman's home at 2427 Kalorama Road, and Hector turned around and smiled. Smiling, he knew, was usually a good strategy.

Campman scribbled something on a piece of paper and handed it to Hector, along with another hundred-dollar bill.

"If you're interested."

"EeeeeThankyousir. Goodeeeeeeveningsir."

Hector drove around the corner and stopped the car. He looked at the piece of paper. There was an address and a time: 9:00 A.M.

The next day, Hector began his job as private chauffeur to Thomas Campman, the manager of Ben Phillips's presidential campaign.

As for Campman, he waited eleven days before using his smoking gun. That was for Jeff Brigg. The more time that elapsed between the theft and the discovery, the harder it would be for them to connect Jeff to the crime.

For eleven days, Warren Muddville was unaware of the missing documents. Then Muddville received a phone call. It was blackmail, plain and simple. Ugly stuff.

What Campman had not predicted, what no one could have predicted, was that Warren Muddville was going to shoot himself in the brain.

Part
3

FULL CIRCLE

CLOSER TO THE ACTION

W e've got a problem."

Kennedy's voice sounded tired. His skin was pale. Hector Elizondo guessed there were dark circles hidden behind the impenetrable lenses of his sunglasses, although he had no way of confirming this. The only thing he could confirm was that Kennedy was upset tonight, and the hot Phoenix air could not be helping.

The time was 1:30 A.M. The temperature: ninety-one degrees Fahrenheit. Kennedy had the air conditioner at full blast, but the darn thing wasn't working right. His blue Audi remained unseasonably warm. Hector noticed brown hair, slick with perspiration, sprouting from the Republican operative's Arizona Diamondbacks baseball cap.

Hector was sweating, too.

"Your tapes have been shit lately," said Kennedy, his usually delicate tone giving way to a more masculine gruffness.

Hector played dumb.

"Eh-Sorry?"

"You know what I'm saying. *Your tapes. Shit.* Listen."

Kennedy pulled out a cassette tape from his pocket, which Hector instantly recognized as his own. As the pointy-chinned operative jammed the tape down the gullet of the car's stereo system, Hector felt his muscles tense, and it reminded him of the time he was caught cheating on a math test in grade school.

Hector rarely played back his own recordings all the way through. Usually he would listen only long enough to confirm that he'd recorded some scrap of audible dialogue; then, content with his product, he'd rewind the tape, sell it, and never look back. If, at times, he secretly suspected a recording to be subpar or even useless, he no longer let this trouble him. Making a good recording was, he'd discovered, a difficult and risky endeavor, and Hector was being paid for quantity, not quality. Why put his neck on the line for a superb audiotape when a mediocre one earned him the same two grand? So he'd gotten sloppy in the last few weeks. Who could blame him?

A bass-heavy version of Crosby, Stills, Nash and Young's "Teach Your Children" suddenly filled the Audi. Hector recognized the tune from a mix CD the boss's wife had given him to play on several occasions. Now it played on the Audi's eight-speaker stereo system along with the sounds of a car motor and the *dat, dat, dat* of gloved hands tapping a steering wheel. Hector remembered this recording.

Kennedy stared at him as the tape continued to play, his expression fixed.

Hector gritted his teeth, nervous at what was to come. The clicking of a turn signal crackled through the speaker system and then quickly stopped, accompanied by the appropriate automotive noises indicative of a turning vehicle. Then, nothing. Just the sounds of the car motor and the muddied chorus of Crosby, Stills, Nash and Young:

"Don't you ever ask them why . . ."

This wasn't one of his better recordings, and Hector Elizondo knew it.

Things had been going well for him this past month—perhaps too well to continue, he thought. He'd been leading the life of a double agent, getting paid a handsome salary by the boss and an even more handsome salary by Kennedy to spy on the boss.

Since their first meeting in D.C., the two had developed a reliable system for exchanging money and cassette tapes. Kennedy would follow the campaign from city to city and await Hector's call, which would be the sign for them to rendezvous at the American Airlines arrival gate of the nearest major airport. Kennedy would drive a blue car of some sort (usually an expensive one), Hector, his standard black Town Car. Once they spotted each other, Hector would follow Kennedy to some anonymous location within a few miles of the airport, usually the parking lot of a closed food establishment, someplace Kennedy had scouted earlier and knew to be free of security cameras. There Hector would give Kennedy the new tape, and Kennedy would hand Hector two thousand dollars in cash.

If this new life of political espionage was not as glamorous as Hector had imagined, he still found it surprisingly comfortable. His food and lodgings were paid for by the campaign, his professional demands were few and never unreasonable, his boss was kind and completely trusting, and—on top of it all—he was making more money than ever before in his life. He was also having fun. The election was heating up, and Hector couldn't help but be excited by the political carnival all around him. If, during the quiet moments, he still found the campaign trail to be a lonely place, this, at least, was nothing new, and he could take solace in the fact that he would be reunited with Brinita and the girls before long. The campaign was nearing its final month.

"When you come back here, you'd better be a rich man, or I'm not letting you out of the house again," his wife had said jokingly when they last spoke.

"If you don't let me out of the house," replied Hector, *"you're* the one who's gonna have to make us rich, you know."

"Then I *will* make us rich. You just better watch out. If I'm rich, I don't know how long I'll be sticking around a loser like you."

"I love you, Brinita."

"Shut up, and go make me money, you foolish man!"

She laughed warmly and hung up. Hector smiled. This was typical of their phone conversations.

"Teach your parents well . . . Their children's hell . . . will slowly go by. . . ."

Kennedy had not moved an inch since the tape had begun. He seemed to be waiting for something.

Now on the recording came a new sound, faint but unmistakable.

"Is that *snoring*?" asked Kennedy, his target finally in view. "Am I hearing *snoring* right now?"

Yes, the period of smooth sailing had definitely come to an end, thought Hector. Kennedy was incredulous.

"Did you actually sell me a tape of someone *sleeping*? Did I pay two grand for *that*?"

Hector avoided his gaze, shifting his eyes to the late-night traffic outside. Here, something new flashed through his field of vision.

His heart stopped.

Could it be . . . ?

In the window of a passing taxi Hector could swear he'd just seen the face of the kid reporter. He couldn't be sure, of course—it happened too quickly—but for a split second it seemed very real.

The kid reporter's name was Peter Williams. Hector knew that much because the young man had made a point of introducing himself several times when he first joined the campaign. In the beginning, Peter couldn't seem to leave Hector alone, constantly approaching him in the hopes of luring him into a conversation.

In the last ten days or so, Peter had abandoned this strategy, and at first Hector was relieved. He thought the young reporter had lost interest in him. He soon realized this was not the case. The kid's curiosity about Hector had not disappeared; it had changed form, metamorphosing itself from interrogation to surveillance, and—unless Hector was imagining things—it had intensified as well.

Wherever he went, Peter Williams was there. Whenever he was trying to be anonymous in a public place, whenever he was anywhere journalists and campaign folk were allowed to mix, Peter's eyes were on him, making him uneasy, shattering his disguise.

Since Hector had become aware of Peter's surveillance, he'd taken greater pains to make sure he was not followed on his nighttime airport runs. That night, he'd been especially careful. There was no way Peter Williams could have possibly known when or where he was going.

Had Hector really seen Peter Williams just now, or was he imagining things?

He had to make sure.

Without warning, Hector bolted from the car. Hot air enveloped him as he stomped across the empty strip mall parking lot.

"Where the hell are you going?" Kennedy yelled after him.

Hector could see the taxi slowing down at the end of the block, and he could see clearly into the backseat. Sure enough, it looked empty. Hector paused. At the traffic light the taxi merged with two other taxis and a pickup truck, and then accelerated as the light turned green. The cab's rear lights receded into the distance.

Hector sighed.

Had he been hallucinating? Had paranoia gotten the better of him? It was the only explanation that made sense.

Suddenly Hector wanted very much for the whole thing to be over with: the spying, the campaign, the secrecy, Peter Williams, Kennedy, the boss, the constant traveling, all of it. He wanted to be home with his wife and daughters.

No sooner had the thought entered his brain than the blue Audi made a U-turn and pulled up next to where he was standing, and Hector quickly realized that "all of it"—at least the spying part—might, in fact, be over. Kennedy was angry with him. Kennedy might fire him. Worse, he might demand his money back.

Hector started to panic. He had no more than fifty dollars in his wallet, certainly not enough to reimburse Kennedy for his shoddy recording. What would he do if Kennedy demanded his two thousand dollars back? What would he do if Kennedy became violent?

The passenger door of the Audi popped open.

"Please get in, Mr. Gomez."

Hector turned slowly.

To his surprise, Kennedy did not appear angry (although it was hard to tell behind those sunglasses). What Hector had not realized was that his sudden and dramatic departure from Kennedy's car would be interpreted by his companion as a power play. By storming off midmeeting, Hector had accidentally made a gutsy and cunning move, and it was now Kennedy who seemed concerned about controlling Hector's temper. The pointy-chinned operative knew it was unwise to upset a potential source.

"Look, all I'm saying is these recordings have gone downhill bigtime," said Kennedy, "and I'm not paying for it anymore."

Hector nodded. He sat down.

"You're not getting any more dinero unless I get something worth my while," Kennedy continued. "Now, I have no problem paying for good stuff—hell, if it's money you're worried about, don't be. You bring me something big, I'll pay you big for it. But from now on, I don't pay till I know what I'm getting, and I don't pay if what I'm getting is shit. You understand?"

Hector did not fully understand, of course, but once Kennedy repeated himself a few times, he got the gist: he needed to take more risks. He could still make money—perhaps even more money than before—but he needed to take greater risks to do so.

The period of smooth sailing had indeed come to an end.

Hector was relieved nonetheless. He was still in the game. As he returned to his black Lincoln Town Car and started back to his hotel, the thought of a second chance energized him, and a slew of new scenarios ran through his head. He thought about his typical day on the campaign trail and wondered how and when he might be able to get himself closer to the action. That was the key, wasn't it? Getting closer to the major players. But how? When? It had been a while since Hector had asked himself these questions.

In the days to follow, Hector would go to greater lengths to try to put himself in the right place at the right time, and as he stepped up his pursuits, a new realization would dawn on him: *He'd become invisible.* Hector wasn't sure exactly how or when it had happened, but somewhere over the course of the last few months, everyone in the campaign had gradually stopped paying attention to him. One month away from election, no one even gave him a second thought. He could walk into a room and out of it, and nobody would notice. They took him for granted, like a chair or a car or a bed. How wonderful!

Upon realizing the power of his newfound invisibility, Hector quickly became more aggressive. Whereas in the past he would have contented himself to wait outside with the car at this event or that, Hector would now go *inside* to seek out a bathroom, to run an imaginary errand, or to simply check on the troops and make sure everything was okay. He would exist in inconspicuous corners, on unnoticed bridge chairs, and outside thinly walled rooms, and the more he did this sort of slinking around, the more he wondered whether it was time to expand his operation beyond the scope of mere recorded surveillance.

Should he buy a camera and start taking pictures? Should he steal papers from people's briefcases? How could he make that big score he so desperately desired?

And with all this, what were the risks? For the first time, Hector started to seriously consider the possibility that he might get caught. What would happen if a major opportunity did actually present itself? What sort of risk would go with it? Would he be forced to cut and run? Was that something he was prepared to do? These new questions troubled him.

Because Hector did not know when or if a major opportunity would present itself, he had no way of planning a proper response. He wasn't even sure what sort of opportunity he was looking for exactly, but he trusted himself to know it when he saw it. Hector resolved to be vigilant. He resolved to get close to the action. He resolved to watch. He resolved to wait.

And so he did.

DAMAGE CONTROL

D id you like my press conference?"

"We agreed you wouldn't call anymore."

"I knew you wanted Ben to be 'humanized,' as you call it, to make him more like an average guy. So I thought: Why not give him a drinking problem? Besides, drinking's much more common than infidelity, at least I think so. Anyhow, do you think it'll help?"

"Why are you calling?"

"I know. You said not to call, Mr. Campman, but I wanted to make sure we were still cool."

"We are *not* cool!" Thomas Campman exploded, then quickly changed tactics. "Look, I'm sorry. I'm sorry. I was too quick to jump at you, Sharon. Lord knows, I probably should be thanking you. The drinking thing . . . it is taking this campaign to some interesting new places—I mean, who the hell knows? There's real potential for us to run with this one. Thank you. But look—for now, you need to do me a favor. Can you do me a favor?"

"What's that?"

"You need to *promise* you're not gonna come out with any more crazy stuff about Ben. Do you understand? I *implore* you. *Please* promise me this little adventure is over, promise me we've said all the surprising things we're going to say for now. Please. Please promise me that."

One week passed, and Sharon Balis kept her word. No new revelations. While the Republicans and the press continued to search for dirt in the hopes of keeping the story alive, Sharon gave them no new material with which to work. Soon Campman started to breathe easier. He thought he'd finally gotten it all under control.

Then it all blew up in his face.

LUCINDA FOX

Campman and Mayweather jumped into the back of the senator's limousine and slammed the door behind them.

"Ben, tell me everything you know about Lucinda Fox."

"Who? I don't know anything. Who is she?"

Campman exhaled deeply. He read off the screen of his Black-Berry: "According to USA Times Online, Lucinda Fox is an actress and former prostitute who claims to have been your lover from 1989 to 1991. She's going on *Billy Mack* tonight, and she's going to say you two had an on-again off-again affair for those three years, during which time you confessed to her that you were a compulsively unfaithful husband."

Ben's head fell back against his seat.

"You've got to be kidding me," said Greenblatt, who sat next to the senator.

Mayweather took over. "According to our blog watchers, there's a rumor going around that Ms. Fox is scheduled to appear with two to possibly five other women who each allege to have had sexual relations with you. This seems to be a part of something bigger.

We don't know what exactly yet, although it may have something to do with . . ." Mayweather paused and exchanged glances with Campman.

"Well . . . *wallop*," he said.

Ben looked confused.

"The word *wallop*—does it mean anything to you?"

Ben shook his head.

"It's just . . . the word *wallop* has come up a few times. It's been referenced on a few right-wing blogs. We don't know if it's the name of another woman or of a new strategy or an acronym, or if it's just what certain people would like to do to you. We're just trying to make sense of rumors here. We don't really know anything solid yet, except the bit about Lucinda Fox."

"Tom, what the hell is going on here?" asked Ben, trying to stay calm.

"Well, Senator, it seems you're quite the Don Juan."

Campman's half smile was met with an icy stare. The senator was in no mood for jokes. He gave it to him straight instead.

"Somebody's trying to fuck us, Ben. And they're playing dirty."

Ben clenched his jaw.

"This . . . is not . . . how it was supposed to go."

"You're right. You're right," said Campman. "Look, Ben—"

The senator interrupted.

"Why have I lived life the way I have, Tom?" His question took his advisors by surprise. He spoke softly now but quickly and with great intensity. "Why have I always taken the high road? Why have I never given in to temptation, not once?—and don't think I haven't been tempted, same as any man—*Why?*"

Ben's gray eyes accused all three of them.

"If this is what my reputation is coming to—why have I even bothered? I should have been screwing around and having fun like everyone else. This is not . . ." Ben took a deep breath and shook his head. "This is not how it was supposed to go."

Shelly Greenblatt put his hand on Ben's arm. "Presidential politics,

Ben. Never does." He smiled at the senator, and then allowed himself a chuckle. Ben relaxed ever so slightly.

Campman was happy that Greenblatt chose not to attack him in
this moment of weakness, that he chose to calm Ben instead. But
then, Campman didn't want Ben too calm, either. The Secret Service
men were giving the signal. Ben had a speech to give, and Campman
needed to make sure he was ready.

"Look, they are trying to fuck you, Ben," he repeated. "Struck,
Fazo, the whole bunch. They are trying. But you need to go out there
now."

Campman's eyes locked on Ben. They didn't let him go.

"Don't worry about this Lucinda Fox; we're gonna lick her good.
But just remember"—and here he raised his finger for emphasis—
"*it's all related*. Tax breaks for the rich, poor boys getting killed in the
Middle East, character assassination for you. Same bad guys. Same
bad policies. Same ethics. *They* are the problem. *You* are the solution.
Now go raise some hell."

Ben nodded quietly with the expression of a quarterback about to
run onto the field. He took a deep breath and nodded again, this time
to Mayweather, who had his hand on the door latch.

FLASHES EVERYWHERE. WILD applause. Campman and Greenblatt
stayed several feet behind the candidate as he marched forward with
the purposeful stride of a general in wartime. He paused occasionally for the requisite glad-handing but maintained his momentum
throughout, charging his every word and gesture with pure adrenaline, giving himself completely to the moment but always staying on
task, always moving forward. He breezed through the building and
barely paused before stepping onstage.

The crowd was on its feet before Ben's presenter even had time to
utter the words, "Ladies and gentlemen, the next president of the
United States, Senator Ben Phillips of Oklahoma!"

Ben saluted the crowd, and the ovation continued for a solid minute. Ben grabbed the microphone from the podium and cried, "Who here is ready to take back our country?!"

Watching from the wings, Campman smiled despite himself, and Greenblatt noticed.

"*You were trying to get him angry, weren't you?*" he said in disbelief.

Campman took a moment before responding. "Anger is an emotion that doesn't work for most politicians," he said, making no effort to disguise his strategy. "But for our boy . . . just listen. . . ."

They did. Ben was on fire. He'd already started his bit about "common sense," stealing a page from Thomas Paine and rewriting it to illustrate the failures of the Struck administration and the last twenty years of American politics.

"Just because you've been doing something wrong for as long as you can remember . . . that doesn't make it right," Ben preached. "And once you realize you're doing something wrong . . . well, then, my friends, it's time to change."

Campman searched Greenblatt's eyes as they listened together.

"It doesn't come off as anger with Ben," said Campman. "I don't know how, but somewhere in between his brain and his body that anger turns into something different, something likable. It comes out as confidence, as passion, as determination. I mean, he's become *cooler*, for God's sake! Haven't you noticed? He goes out there now and he dares you to judge him, he *dares* you to resist his charms. He's got swagger, Shelly!"

"He's got a problem, Tom," said Greenblatt coldly. "If what you told us in the car is true, he's got a real serious problem. He may lose this election in the next twenty-four hours. Now what do you propose we do about that?"

Greenblatt's words hit hard. Campman had allowed his emotions to seesaw from panic to elation, and now they fell back to earth with a thud. The news of Lucinda Fox, of those "two to five" women, of this impending "wallop" (whatever the hell that was), it had come out of left field, and for the first time, Campman had no clue how to proceed. He couldn't figure out how these new developments fit into the

Almighty's greater plan. Furthermore, he no longer knew what that plan was, and he was beginning to wonder whether he ever had.

Thomas Campman sighed and went with the honest answer.

"I don't know what to do, Shelly. I don't have a plan yet."

At this, Shelly Greenblatt softened slightly.

"We need to hit back big-time here, Tom."

"I know. You're right. We need to take these allegations and blow them up, shoot them out of the water completely. I'm just not sure yet how we do that."

Shelly took a deep breath and waited for Campman's eyes to find him. Then he spoke the words he'd been longing to speak for the last three months:

"I have an idea."

W.A.L.L.O.P.

[Fade in. The camera cuts between close-ups of the following women.]

LUCINDA FOX: Ben Phillips was my lover from 1989 to 1991.

BLOND WOMAN: He told me we had to keep our relationship a secret from his wife.

BLACK WOMAN: He started acting REAL nice with me all of a sudden, and I thought: Where is he going with this?

REDHEADED WOMAN: Senator Phillips asked me to come to his hotel room.

LUCINDA FOX: . . . told me he had a problem. He said he was compulsively unfaithful. He was a cheater. . . .

BRUNETTE WOMAN: I said, "You're cheating on your wife with me, aren't you?"

BLOND WOMAN: This man lied. And, I mean, he lied a lot.

REDHEADED WOMAN: When I saw those other women come out, I thought, Oh, my God, he did it to them, too! And I knew I had to speak out.

BLACK WOMAN: I worked for Ben Phillips in Oklahoma, and that's the God's honest truth.

[Group shot. The women sit together, arms around each other, supportive.]

LUCINDA FOX: It's good the way the women and I have been able to come together and share our experiences with others.

[Cut to medium shot of BLOND WOMAN.]

BLOND WOMAN: The idea that Ben Phillips could be president . . . it's scary for all of us.

[Cut to medium shot of BRUNETTE WOMAN.]

BRUNETTE WOMAN: I just think if a man can betray his own wife . . . what makes us think he's gonna treat our country any better?

VOICEOVER ANNOUNCER: This ad has been paid for by Women Against Lechery and Lasciviousness in the Office of President.

IN BED WITH THE PRESIDENT

Ben Phillips didn't usually have time to watch the news, but it was late and he was alone and he couldn't fall asleep. He turned the channel to ANC and found the president staring back at him from behind a podium on the White House lawn. It seemed almost an intrusion, allowing his enemy into his sleeping quarters, but Ben resisted the urge to change the channel.

"Mr. President, are you aware of the new ads alleging that Senator Phillips cheated on his wife with multiple partners?"

The president seemed to be expecting the question, and he didn't lose a beat in answering.

"I have heard about those ads, but I have no comment on them at this time."

"Mr. President, have you heard of W.A.L.L.O.P.?"

"I'm sorry?"

"They are Women Against Lechery and Lasciviousness in the Office of President. They're the organization who ran the ad. Are you familiar with them?"

"Well, that's quite a long name, but no, I'm afraid I've never heard of those folks—although, I am opposed to Lechery and Lasciviousness as a rule—not just in the White House."

He gave a wink to the camera. Typical. Ben was repulsed. He marveled that the same charm that endeared the president to much of the nation could have such a completely opposite effect on him.

"Are you aware, sir, that many of your largest donors have also contributed to W.A.L.L.O.P.?"

Good question.

"You know I don't tell people where to donate their money, Bob. That's not my business."

Damn. Evasive answer.

"If it turns out these allegations are true, Mister President, do you believe Senator Phillips is unfit for the presidency?"

Here Struck paused for a moment, choosing his words carefully. "I believe Senator Phillips is unfit for the presidency because he's in favor of bad policies. But look, I think it all comes down to a question of character. If a man does 'bad things' . . . if a man 'cheats' on his 'wife' . . . these are things that make us question . . . the 'character' of that man. Now, I don't know anything about this organization that is leveling these charges and I'm not going to comment on that. And I don't know the latest number of how many women have come forward. I don't really pay attention to that sort of—"

Here, an unmiked voice chimed in from off camera.

"What was that?" the president asked. "Is it really fifteen now? I thought it was eight." He chuckled. "Oh, boy, that's a lot. Well, I guess he has a lot of explaining to do."

Ben was about to change the channel when the program cut back to the studio and anchor Taz McDonald. ANC's new rising star, McDonald currently hosted three broadcasts for the network, each at a different speed. *News Remix* was fast and furious and some of the worst stuff on TV. *The Nightly News* had a quick pace but was slightly more tolerable. What Ben was watching now—thankfully—was *A Closer Look*, the slowest of the three programs.

"Tough words today from President Struck," said McDonald. "The president blasting Senator Phillips for his 'compulsively libidinous behavior,' and Senator Phillips responding in an even more venomous fashion today in Toledo. Check out this clip."

Ben now watched as his own image filled the screen.

"How dare the president attack my integrity! How dare he use rumor and innuendo to call me a liar, when his administration has consistently misled the American people! It is this very arrogance that has laid waste to American foreign policy and shamelessly helped the rich get richer while the poor get poorer! I say, 'Shame on you, Mr. President! Shame on you!'"

Wow, thought Ben. I look good.

Apparently the pundits agreed.

"Wally, is it me," said McDonald, "or is the senator becoming a real son of a bitch?"

ANC political analyst Wally Clap responded, "He's become more fiery, no doubt about it."

"I mean, he looked like he wanted to bite off the president's head there. What do you think of this louder, bolder, ass-kicking—and apparently ass-*chasing*—candidate?"

"Well he's more confident as well," said Clap, "but does that matter when you have fifteen women claiming to be your mistress? He needs to address these accusations more convincingly if he's gonna have even a *prayer* in November. And frankly, Taz, even if he does, he's still probably a dead man."

Ben turned the TV off. The date was October 3, and in just a few days, he'd fallen from 7 to 14 points behind the president. Historically speaking, these were insurmountable numbers for any candidate only a month away from election. Melissa was furious, and she directed most of her anger toward him. She felt this new scandal was merely payback for the one they'd unwisely started on their own, and Ben had to admit that she might have a point.

So why didn't he feel even worse?

Oh, he was depressed; make no mistake about it. But underneath all that anger, all that resentment and self-pity, there was a part of

Ben that was secretly quite pleased. In his late-night honesty, Ben managed to finally admit the reason to himself:

He had become cool.

And not just cool-*er*, as in "cooler than he was a month ago" when he was 20 points behind, but actually legitimately independently "cool"—cool as in likable, cool as in enviable, cool as in *desirable*—and he had a feeling all these women were to thank.

Ben Phillips had never been cool before. Sure, he'd been respected, admired, liked, even *loved*, but cool . . . cool was a different story.

After losing the William Howard Taft High School student council presidential race to star running back Luke Travis, Ben determined that "coolness," the one thing he did not possess, was also the one thing that could not be acquired through any calculated means. In Ben's opinion, all other desirable traits were practically attainable if one put one's mind to it. Knowledge could be acquired through study, athletic skill through practice, physical fitness through exercise, wealth through hard work and good decision making. Even a seemingly intangible trait like popularity was not that hard to break down if you really thought about it. To be popular, you had to be well liked by many people. To be well liked, you had to be warm, friendly, and treat others as you would want to be treated.

But to be cool . . . here there was no prescription, no "how to" guide. Because this was the most elusive of character traits, it became for young Ben, naturally, the most desirable. And while he knew better than to waste his time pining away for an attribute he had no practical means of attaining, this quality of coolness became something for him to envy from afar, a private guilty fantasy he would think about in his most insecure moments, a sporadically indulged, persistent "what if" whose presence in his daydreams thankfully faded with the passage of time and the onset of maturity.

Except that now, it seemed, he had it.

Was Campman right? Had the scandals given him a mystique? Bumper stickers were now being produced that read: HONK IF YOU'VE

SLEPT WITH BEN PHILLIPS. People were suddenly looking at him as if he were a Don Juan.

While Ben despised the false accusations, while he lamented the damage to his reputation, he couldn't help but enjoy some of these new looks he was getting. And *if*, at times, it made him wonder what it would be like to *be* that person everyone else saw, if he wondered what it was that fundamentally separated him from that person, if he even wondered whether he had it inside him to do the sort of things that person might do, to fornicate and philander without fear of consequences—not that he ever would—but if he wondered, every now and then, what it might be like to *be* such a person and *do* such things . . . was there anything wrong with that? He wasn't/wouldn't/couldn't ever do those things, not in a million years. But was there anything wrong with enjoying these new looks?

To be certain, there were some looks he could do without: looks of condescension, of pity, of holier-than-thou judgment. But more frequently, he was seeing looks of respect, of deference, of curiosity. Ben would catch people examining him, people he'd known for years looking at him as if for the first time. They stared and wondered: What is it about Ben Phillips that drove all those women crazy?

It was the question on everyone's mind. And while Ben was sure he had, in fact, driven none of these women crazy, while he was determined to set the record straight on that point, the question remained. Even if he cleared himself of all but the Tina James charge, the question would still exist, just in a different form: What is it about Ben Phillips that made all those women lie?

Either way, the question was still: *What is it about Ben Phillips?*

The very asking of that question was what made him cool.

Campman liked to remind Ben that in every lie, there is a bit of truth. Even if a false accusation is proved false, he said, it still leaves an aftertaste. And in those rarest of cases, if that aftertaste is not entirely unpleasant, the formerly accused can reap the benefits of both his innocence and the romantic aftertaste of this crime not quite committed. For Ben, this could be ideal. But first . . .

First he had to prove his innocence. He'd been backed into a corner by these fraudulent W.A.L.L.O.P. women, and it was time to set the record straight. Or at least straight-ish.

As he turned out the light and curled into his blanket, Ben had the following thought: If Taz McDonald thinks I'm a real son of a bitch now, I can't wait to hear what he thinks tomorrow.

AN UNMEDIATED SURPRISE

"We ... are not talking ... about the issues! ... We are not talking ... about the issues! ... We are not talking about the issues!"

Ben's voice boomed through David Lawrence Hall at the University of Pittsburgh. He was sweating but not excessively, and it was a healthy sweat, an honest sweat.

"We are not talking about health care! ... We are not talking about how some Americans can afford it ... and some can't. ... And we are not talking about how that ... is just ... plain ... wrong!"

The crowd was alive tonight. He didn't need to think. He had them. They were listening. They were hungry.

"I want to talk about my health-care plan! ... I want to talk about my foreign policy agenda! ... about my economic stimulus playbook! ... my environmental game plan! ... my education reform blueprint! ... These are the real issues!!"

For all his effort at journalistic detachment, young Peter Williams couldn't help but feel buzzed by the electricity in the auditorium.

Ben Phillips, the new and improved Ben Phillips, was speaking with a passion and conviction he had not seen before.

"I've said it before and I'll say it again, *I have a plan to fix this Operation Freedom Fox mess once and for all*! And I'm gonna tell you what it is. . . . But first . . . do you want to hear it?"

Thunderous applause. Loud. And still going. Ben just waited.

Then suddenly, unexpectedly, he changed tone.

"See . . . I don't think you do."

What was this?

No! No! More applause! Reassuring applause! *Of course we want to hear it, Ben! Of course we want to!*

"Look," he said, "I'm sure you lovely people want to hear about how we're gonna fix Operation Freedom Fox. I'm sure you want to hear about how we're going to change this country. But that's not what's on most people's minds."

The crowd was quiet. Curious. Waiting.

"Because that's not what I hear when I turn on the television. I am not hearing the media talk about these issues. I'm not hearing anyone talk about these issues."

He was taking longer pauses now, more confident pauses. He was making the listener lean in and ask, "What's next?" Elayne Cohen-Campman put her camera down and was just watching, listening, wondering. She'd heard the strategy discussions beforehand and knew where Ben was going, but she was in suspense all the same.

"All I hear about now is scandal . . . innuendo . . . false accusation. . . . And that needs to end."

There was applause, but he did not let it go too far. He interrupted.

"Now listen, I want to be frank. I've made one major mistake in my role as husband and father. I've talked about that, I've been open about that, and as far as I'm concerned, that is in the past. I can't change it, I own it, but it's in the past.

"Now, all this other stuff . . . it's rubbish, all of it: groundless, hurtful accusations with nothing to back them up. And I want to put

them to rest once and for all. . . . To that end, I plan to take a lie detector test, to prove definitively that these accusations are groundless."

The crowd applauded, although it was not the sort of confident applause that comes from a long-anticipated rallying cry. It was the applause of a large audience hearing something it was not expecting to
hear. Was this good news? Was it applause worthy? They were receiving an unmediated surprise. They had to interpret it on their own,
without help from pundits. *How unusual.*

And so the applause was solid but not explosive at first. Then it
gradually built in momentum as the Pittsburgh crowd started to process the words and come to the same conclusion independently: Ben
Phillips was making a gutsy and smart move.

"And it is my hope!" Ben added, as the noise swelled to a roar, "it is
my hope that once we get beyond this slander . . . this dirty distraction . . . it is my hope we can start talking about the important issues
once again! So, I ask: *Are you with me?!*"

AN INNOCENT MAN

The lie detector test went brilliantly. Sure, it was tricky to set up. They had to be certain Ben wouldn't face any questions about Tina James. They had to make sure the questioning would focus only on the highly deniable fifteen women (for, as new women joined W.A.L.L.O.P.'s cause, the total number of alleged mistresses had risen to fifteen), who sought to expose him. The trick was to control this one variable yet still give the impression of fairness. Above all else, the test could not be seen as an insider job. Credibility was paramount.

Shelly Greenblatt, who had first thought of the lie detector test, brought in Marty Lewis, an independent expert from West Point, formerly of the CIA, to administer the test, and he gave him detailed instructions as to the scope of the questions. They were to address Ben Phillips's specific involvement with the fifteen women and nothing else. Ben would not be allowed to see the questions before the test, but Campman and Greenblatt were permitted to review them in the half hour before the test began.

Reporters from all the major news organizations were there. The event had to be televised for anyone to believe its authenticity, but Campman went to great pains to ensure that the actual test was as boring as possible. Ben answered all questions with confidence but little inflection. His facial expression never wavered. Campman wanted to make sure that no single answer stuck out, that no single moment of interrogation became more important or more vulnerable to scrutiny than any other. He wanted the memorable TV clips to come from the pomp surrounding the polygraph test and not the test itself.

It was an intimate setup. A small room. There was a casualness to Ben's entrance and exit, his joking with reporters, and his lingering about long after the whole thing was over. It was played off as an event to be celebrated, like a long overdue promotion or the removal of a tumor, and it was a private party where only the press was invited. Once the good news was announced that Ben Phillips had passed his lie detector test with flying colors, trays of hors d'oeuvres and glasses of wine suddenly filled the room. Journalists, politicians, campaign workers, and members of the Phillips family soon found themselves raising a glass and toasting the beginning of a new campaign, a campaign that could finally be about issues.

Even Melissa seemed pleased. Several times, as she worked the room, she caught Ben's eye and smiled. Where had that smile gone, he wondered. Melissa could work her winning charm whenever required, but in the last few weeks, it had become increasingly rare for her to focus that warm knowing grin in his direction. He could summon overused words to describe this change, words like *cold* or *distant,* but these were not words he was comfortable with. These were words other men used to describe their wives. Not him. Not Mel. After nearly thirty years of marriage it was an accepted fact that they were not like other couples. Their fire did not burn out. Their love was never compromised. They, in short, worked.

But he could not deny she'd been acting differently toward him.

That her once familiar, once expected smile was now a pleasant surprise to him only confirmed this observation. Was he worried? Perhaps. But then, now was not the time to be worried.

Besides, now she was smiling. It was nice to be smiled at.

THE MEDIA ATE it up and not just the hors d'oeuvres. The front page of the *New York Tribune* proclaimed "VINDICATED!" in two-inch type, and the *USA Times* went one further with its headline "AN HONEST MAN" in two-and-a-half-inch type.

The polls skyrocketed. It was as if the country had been waiting for permission to start liking Ben Phillips, and that permission had just been granted. Ben's numbers had already climbed to historic heights among alcoholics, adulterers, drug users, and gigolos, but now suddenly the rest of America was catching up. After five weeks of watching Ben Phillips sweat it out in the spotlight, most Americans were forced to admit that, all things considered, he'd handled himself pretty well. His vindication on all but the most ancient of charges—for the Tina James scandal (now over five weeks old) certainly seemed ancient—meant people could feel okay about having secretly rooted for him all along.

Ben had suddenly been cast in the role of feisty underdog, the put-upon everyman accused of crimes he did not commit. And what of that? Surely it couldn't have been a coincidence that fifteen women came out of the woodwork to accuse him of infidelity within one month. Was there a larger conspiracy at work? Who was really behind W.A.L.L.O.P.? A right-wing think tank? A foreign power? What about someone in the president's own camp? Who was pulling the strings?

The cherry on top was the challenge issued by Ben Phillips to these fifteen alleged mistresses. In an interview after his lie detector test, he challenged any one of the women to come forward and take the same test he had. Not surprisingly, none of the W.A.L.L.O.P. women accepted his offer.

To be fair, there were many who did not buy Ben's lie detector test as proof of his marital fidelity. Many Republicans, moderates, and right-wingers alike were convinced the test was a sham and that, somehow or other, Ben Phillips had pulled a fast one on the American people.

But most of the public was willing to give him the benefit of the doubt. While the average American may be easily misled, he or she is not without common sense. There were too many reasons to believe Ben's version of events, and too many reasons to question the motivations of his accusers. His was the more believable story.

Several new polls came out within two days of the lie detector test. They all confirmed that approximately two-thirds of the country believed Ben Phillips to be telling the truth. More important, however, they showed the senator closing the gap between him and the president to within 4 points. It was now a statistical dead heat. For the first time, Ben Phillips was in the game.

MORE TITILLATION

The pictures came out in the October 18 issue of *American Chic*. As pictures go, there was nothing truly extraordinary about them. The subject was a woman in her early fifties wearing a cream-colored blouse and conservative slacks. Her dark brown hair fell down to her shoulders and was heavily backlit by a hotel window. In some of the pictures, her blouse was unbuttoned partway to reveal surprisingly abundant cleavage held in place by a simple lace brassiere. In two pictures, the outline of an erect nipple was distinctly visible, interrupting the otherwise smooth field of cotton that wrapped about the hill of her left breast. Her face was relaxed, sometimes pensive, sometimes playful, occasionally suggestive, but always effortless. The pictures weren't exactly racy, not by any current standards (certainly nothing to write home about), and while they were undoubtedly sexy . . . was that really shocking?

Yes. They were shocking, but only because they were pictures of Melissa Phillips, the wife of the Democratic presidential candidate. They were pictures taken by second-unit campaign photographer Elayne Cohen-Campman, wife of political advisor Thomas Campman, and from the moment they were published, all hell that hadn't already broken loose did so.

On the ANC evening news, correspondent Chip Rogers reported that "no potential first lady has ever posed for such blatantly suggestive pictures."

Harry Maxwell of the *New York Tribune* said the release of the pictures was a calculated move by the Phillips campaign to appeal to "the lowest common denominator of our sex-crazed culture."

The more conservative media elements went further, the clamor of their transparently feigned shock reaching operatic heights, heralding the pictures as conclusive proof of the moral groundlessness of the Phillips family.

"These are not the pictures of a first lady," said right-wing mouthpiece Jack Sternhom. "These are the pictures of a woman who is openly promising sex. Is that a *campaign* promise? I wonder."

Melissa, for her part, couldn't see what the big deal was. To her there was nothing scandalous about the photos, no body part that hadn't already been exposed by a first lady in the past (surely there was an incidental protruding nipple in *one* of Jackie O's photos). She wondered why everyone had suddenly become so puritanical.

What Melissa could not have understood was the effect of her face. Anyone the least bit familiar with pornography—hell, anyone familiar with pop culture, anyone who has ever seen a sexy picture before in his or her life—will agree it is the facial expression that makes a sexy picture truly sexy. And Melissa's expression was irresistible.

There was something about her green eyes, the subtle pout of her lips, the sleepiness in her cheeks, something about all of it put together. Hers was the look of a lover in the morning, a warm inviting gaze charged with a secret erotic promise. It was this sensuous expression that put the rest of her body into context, activating the arch of her back, insinuating itself into the curve of her neck, and forcing the viewer to consider the shapliness of her breasts. To everyone but Melissa, the pictures were undeniably sexy.

Of all the yammering to come about as a result of the picture's release, the most important sound bite came late in the day, and this was from President Struck himself.

"You don't really want me to comment on that, do you?" he asked the reporter who had broached the topic. And for a second, Gregory Struck stayed with the game plan. He actually resisted. But the temptation was too great, the target too wide, the opportunity just too damn juicy.

"Look, sex sells, doesn't it?" he said finally. "Throughout history there have always been those people . . . men . . . women . . ."—and here he gave one of his characteristic winks—"who use 'sexual *titillation*' to advance their cause. And if Senator Phillips or his lovely wife think that sort of thing is 'appropriate' in a presidential race, well that's their decision, isn't it? I'm not going to comment. It's for the 'American people' to decide what they think of that."

The president's quote was all over the nightly news, all over the Internet, and all over the morning paper. It is important to note, however, that Ben Phillips did not hear about it until late the next day. This was Campman's doing. But more on that later. . . .

Like most of America, Ben did see his wife's pictures in *American Chic*, and he was aware of the stir they were causing.

"You're not upset, are you?" she had asked him.

"No. No, of course not," he answered quickly. "I probably would've liked to have seen the pictures beforehand, but—"

"Elayne ran them by Tom and me. We didn't really think there was anything controversial about them."

No, of course not, thought Ben. He had been aware for some time now that Tom Campman possessed an unusual interpretation of "controversy," its causes and benefits.

"Well, I suppose it's a subjective thing," he said.

"You're upset, aren't you?"

"No, I'm not."

"You are."

"I'm not upset."

"You *can't* be upset, but you *are* upset," Melissa clarified. "You know you *can't* be upset because that would be monstrously hypocritical of you, because you know you lose the right to complain about other people's unintentionally embarrassing actions once you've made it your personal *mission* to embarrass yourself. But that doesn't mean you *aren't* upset."

"Okay . . . but I'm *really not upset* about them."

She just looked at him.

"*Really,*" he insisted, his eyes wide. "I like the pictures. I don't think there's anything wrong with them. They're . . . they're beautiful."

He should have stopped there, but foolishly, he continued.

"And it's absolutely ridiculous what people are saying—and I'm going to make sure they stop saying it. You know I will support you on this no matter what."

His words felt cold to him as they left his lips. It was a political pledge, not a husbandly reassurance.

Melissa looked sad.

"Yes," she said, "well obviously that's what I would expect."

And that was the end of it.

When Melissa left the room, Ben privately berated himself. The conversation hadn't gone as he would've liked. He had been telling the truth when he said he wasn't upset about the photos. He really wasn't. He really *did* think they were beautiful. But his honesty had been improperly delivered.

Ben was struck by the irony that he'd somehow become more adept at lying than truth telling. For whatever reason, his lies just sounded more convincing. Now why was that?

And had he really been telling Melissa the truth?

The more he thought about it, Ben had to concede that he was, in fact, a little upset—but not about the photos.

He was upset about Melissa, about how . . . *out of character* their relationship had become recently (he consciously avoided the word *strained*). He was upset by the way she looked at him—or didn't look at him—upset that the very same "looks" that had caused such a stir in the last thirty-six hours, those warm, sensual, knowing glances of hers, were ones to which he no longer felt privy. It made him jealous that the rest of America could experience them, but he couldn't.

It was yet another injustice that needed to be set right.

SAYING IT

Jennifer Dial was conspicuous. That was the problem. The leggy XLGNN correspondent, the soap-opera-star-turned-reporter, the statuesque brunette with the big chest and the broad smile, Ms. Dial would have drawn attention to herself simply by breathing. That she was often giggling like a schoolgirl, chattering away like a schoolgirl, and flirting like a . . . well, flirting like only a woman with her looks is able to flirt—this didn't help matters much.

That she was so conspicuous posed a problem only because Jennifer Dial was following Peter Williams wherever he went. She seemed to have gotten it into her head that the "hot story" was located wherever he was, and now Peter could hardly go to the men's room without her following him in and offering to lend a hand. *TeenVibe*'s young reporter found this attention flattering at first, but it had long since started to wear on his nerves. He was, after all, trying to shadow Hector Elizondo, and if there was one thing that could cramp his style, it was the highly conspicuous Jennifer Dial making him all the more conspicuous by association. Peter now found it necessary to shake his own stalker before he could stalk successfully himself, and at this delicate task he managed to be effective only about half the time. The night in Boston was not one of those times.

Peter was leaning up against a column outside the Hynes Convention Center when Jennifer Dial approached. The young reporter had been eyeing Hector from about two hundred yards away, trying to discern what Campman's valet was up to on this most important of evenings. Turns out, he was not up to very much. With the second and final debate scheduled to begin inside the convention center in less than an hour, Hector was hanging about the black Town Car, looking not unlike most of the other drivers from the two motorcades parked on this closed-off section of Boylston Street.

The only difference was his eyes, and it was a subtle difference. The other drivers seemed guarded, calm but cautious. This was a major, high-security event, both presidential candidates in the same location, and everyone was hoping to avoid trouble. Their eyes glanced up and down the block, looking for any sign that things were not going exactly according to plan.

Hector's eyes also darted about, but for a different reason. Hector Elizondo wasn't afraid—at least not of any outside disturbance. He was eager. He was searching for an opportunity, searching for trouble. Hector was *dying* for some trouble. Peter could see it in his eyes.

"What are you doing out here?"

It was Jennifer Dial.

"I'm expecting a call."

"What kind of call?"

"Cell phone."

"From who?"

"Top secret."

To Peter's chagrin, this answer had the unfortunate effect of increasing rather than diminishing Jennifer Dial's interest.

"Really? That sounds exciting."

She was being too loud, and as usual, she was drawing attention. Hector was sure to notice him before long.

"Yes, well," Peter said, checking the time on his cell phone, "it seems I won't be getting that call in time for the debate. I guess I should go back in."

As if on cue, his cell phone rang.

Jennifer Dial seemed more excited than he was.

"Oooh! Looks like they're calling just in time."

And with that, Jennifer Dial stayed absolutely put, waiting and watching as Peter answered his phone.

It was Mary.

"Hi, Peter."

"Hey. What's the story?"

He was trying to sound top secret.

"Okay," she said breathlessly. "So I'm sorry I've been acting so weird lately. I think it's because I just really need to know how you feel about me"—her voice quavered with emotions she was trying hard to control—"because I—I know I'm not supposed to be telling you this, but I think I really, really love you, more than I've ever loved anyone before—not that I ever *have* loved anyone before—except I guess my parents and my sister, which doesn't count—but what I'm trying to say is that I have very strong feelings—of love—for you—and I think I've been upset because you're so far away all the time, and I just don't know how you feel. And I can't believe I'm so emotional, I know I must sound stupid now. . . ."

"No, no," said Peter.

"And you don't have to say you feel the same way if that's not how you feel, but I just—I need to know honestly what your feelings are about me."

"Over the phone?" he asked. "It's just not a secure line. I'm here at the debate; everything's crazy now."

"I'm sorry. I'm sorry. I know this probably isn't a good time, but you can just tell me quickly. Do you still like me? Do you love me? I just need to know."

"Oh, wow. Um. I'm not alone at the moment."

"Oh, Peter! Are you ashamed to say how you feel?"

Peter Williams suddenly realized there were tears in his eyes. He couldn't for the life of him figure out why. He wasn't sad. He'd taken his allergy medication. He hadn't been teargassed, at least so far as he knew. Why were there tears in his eyes?

Was this love? His initial thought was no, it was not love. He would concede that he was feeling emotional. He would even admit to feeling sad for his girlfriend. No, not sad. Something else. But was it love?

Quickly, ever so quickly, Peter weighed the evidence for and against, and then the arguments for his response, pro and con. There was no time for proper analysis. But then an impulse swept over him, a jolt he could actually physically feel rushing from his toes to the top of his forehead.

"I have to get back to the debate now. I love you. Bye."

He pressed the end button and the call was over.

Silence.

He'd said it.

It was quick and off the cuff, but he had definitely said it.

But had he meant it?

Shoot. *He still wasn't sure.*

This wasn't the way this sort of thing was supposed to go. It was supposed to be a romantic occasion, the two of them together, everything carefully planned out in advance. And he was supposed to be sure, unmistakably sure, irrevocably sure, beyond-a-shadow-of-a-doubt sure.

But it had happened. He had definitely said it, and lots of big things had definitely changed.

He tried to imagine Mary back in Bethesda, fresh off the phone. She was probably happy—after all, he'd told her what she'd wanted to hear. But then, he wasn't very convincing, was he? It was an off-handed "I love you," a "by the way, I love you," an "I love you" served up as a side dish, not the main course. Peter realized this probably wasn't the sort of "I love you" she had undoubtedly dreamed of.

But he had said it. And she knew he wasn't prone to speaking flippantly. She had to be excited.

Yes, he'd definitely said it, hadn't he? But had he meant it? Did it matter? Of course it did! But *why* did it matter? He hadn't lied, had he? No, not really. But then he hadn't quite told the truth, either. What was it called when one did such a thing?

Peter started to wonder about the implications of his proclamation of love. And he wondered how Mary would act when next they met. And he wondered about that great unmentionable (yet overly mentioned) physical act to which the gates had suddenly been flung open. Dare he enter those gates under false pretenses? What about a pretense that was neither false nor true?

Yes, you could say that Peter Williams's young brain was hard at work on this whole "love" business, and it would continue to be until the evening's events took a most surprising and historic turn.

But in the immediate aftermath of the call, he had to deal with Jennifer Dial. The busty reporter wore a curious smile as Peter flipped his phone shut.

"Was that your *girlfriend?*" she asked, her tone spiraling gleefully upward on the last word.

Peter did not respond, and it turned out he didn't need to. Ms. Dial could tell from his red cheeks that she'd hit the nail on the head. This caused her grin to expand exponentially, and she let out a wistful sigh.

"Oh, that's beautiful. She must be a very lucky girl."

"We need to get back inside," said Peter. "The debate's going to start soon."

FLAME FANNING

This was the night they would take the lead. There was simply no other option. It was October 19, and the election was two weeks away. Tonight's debate was the last major public forum of the campaign. It was their last opportunity for redemption, their final chance to make an impression on the American people. Yes, it had to be tonight.

Their man was ready. He'd been scandal-tested. He'd walked through the fire without getting burned. Not only had he not been burned, but he'd also acquired a healthy tan in the process. He'd even swallowed a bit of that fire for good measure and had learned to release it at will, breathing it out at his opponent through highly charged rhetoric. Where he was once tentative, he was now fierce.

He just needed that final push, and Thomas Campman had an ace up his sleeve. It was the video clip of the president, giving his opinion on Melissa's newly released pictures. Campman had gone to great lengths to keep Ben in the dark about the president's comments, from tampering with his morning paper to enlisting the cooperation of Charlie, Kiley, Mayweather, and Sorn. It had worked so far. Ben knew about the public reaction to the pictures but had no idea what the president himself had said.

"Okay, Senator, it's time to get to the stage."

Ben looked at Melissa, and she smiled back warmly. There was that old smile! She was teaching the next morning but had flown into Boston for just a few hours. She wouldn't dream of missing the debate.

Ben looked over his advisors one by one.

"Okay, gentlemen. Now, it's time."

It *was* time, thought Campman. It was time for one final push. One tiny match to help light Ben's fire.

"Remember you're a new man," said Campman (Melissa shrugged at this), "and remember what this bastard said yesterday. I mean, don't let a little sound bite make you crazy or anything, but don't forget what kind of guy you're talking to tonight."

At this, Ben stopped.

"What are you talking about? What did he say? What sound bite?"

"Kiley, you didn't play him the clip?"

This was Derek Kiley's cue. Once again, he had the thankless job.

"No, I forgot. But I figure he must've seen it on the news. You saw it, right?"

Ben was upset.

"What? No! I haven't seen anything. Look, it's time already. Is this something I need to know about? Can you just tell me quickly?"

"Well, the clip's cued up," said Kiley, "we were watching it before."

"Oh, good! You have to see this," said Campman.

"Can you just tell me, for God's sake?" asked Ben. "I don't have time for this nonsense."

"This'll just take a second," said Campman as Kiley pressed PLAY on the dressing room VCR.

Melissa didn't like what was going on.

"What is this? Is this about what the president said? Ben, this doesn't matter."

"Shhh!"

"Tom."

"Just watch."

The president's figure filled the small TV screen.

"Look, sex sells, doesn't it? Throughout history there have always been those people . . . men . . . women . . . who use 'sexual' titillation' to advance their cause. And if Senator Phillips or his lovely wife think that sort of thing is 'appropriate' in a presidential race, well that's their decision, isn't it? I'm not going to comment. It's for the 'American people' to decide what they think of that."

There was something about seeing it on video, something about hearing that prideful southern accent, seeing that subtle smirk on his face, and observing that unmistakable wink when he spoke of a woman—wink, wink—who used "sexual titillation" to advance her cause.

Ben's face did not move. The intense scornful gaze he'd initially directed toward the TV had stayed there and remained fixed even after the clip had finished playing. Campman tried to get a read on his candidate but couldn't.

Necks were craned, eyebrows lifted, eardrums set to their most sensitive calibrations. Everyone wanted to hear Ben Phillips's reaction. When he did eventually speak, he said only three words and he said them evenly, bereft of any obvious inflection:

"Play it again."

"Come on, Ben," said Shelly, "it's time to go on."

"Play it again."

As the clip rolled a second time, Campman could see gears shifting within the senator's brain. Things were heating up. Ben's expression gradually melted into one of disbelief, but still he stood there unmoved, watching the clip with a killer's intensity. He looked like he was about to explode.

"He's calling her a whore," he said when it was over. "He's calling my wife a whore."

Bingo! Campman tried to suppress a grin. Here's our angry hero!

he thought. This was just the Ben Phillips he wanted. Not the meticulous patrician of the spring, but the passionate everyman of the fall. He was revved up and ready to do battle. For honor! For family! For love! For—

"Senator, you've got to get to the stage!"

"Ben, don't worry about what he said," began Melissa, "you just have a good debate. And remember . . ."

"That son of a bitch," Ben muttered under his breath.

He turned and started walking to the stage. The entourage followed, keeping pace with him every step of the way.

"Remember to smile," said Greenblatt. "Don't let him get you riled up. Remember, you are the one in control this time."

"Don't forget what an asshole he is," echoed Campman, more for Greenblatt's benefit than the candidate's.

"Keep your head," said Greenblatt. "Just be the better man."

Campman smiled now. He sensed the battle about to ensue, and he smelled victory. Ben seemed unstoppable, more driven than ever before—never mind that he was the smarter debater and had the issues on his side. This is going to be beautiful, thought Campman, and for a moment, he wondered whether tonight might represent the culmination of the Almighty's original prophecy. He wondered if tonight would be the night it all came together.

Greenblatt and Melissa were more concerned. They'd been at Ben's side long enough to know his every mood, and this was not one they'd seen before. As the senator waited for his cue to walk onstage, Greenblatt confronted him.

"Ben. Ben, look at me. Ben, are you okay?"

"I'm fine, Shelly. I'm going to be fine."

"Ben, remember what this is all about," said Melissa. "I don't care who called who what. I just want you to remember why we started all this."

Ben Phillips turned to look at his wife and smiled.

Melissa waited for a reply, but Ben said nothing. Then he kissed her. It was a fierce passionate joining of lips, and it took her by surprise. She tried to be an eager participant, but somehow the kiss felt awkward, forced. When it was over, they heard Ben's name announced over the loudspeaker.

He said, "I love you," and marched out into the light.

Across the country, millions of Americans watched as Oklahoma Senator Ben Phillips and President Greg Struck walked on from opposite ends of the stage to meet in the middle. Struck was grinning from ear to ear. Phillips, surprisingly, was not. His face was neutral, impassive, and his posture, uncharacteristically relaxed. When the two men met in the middle of the stage, the president extended his hand. Senator Phillips paused for a moment, raised his right hand, and slapped the president across the face.

BRAVE

Ben Phillips saw combat for three seconds in Vietnam. It was just enough time to spot a Vietcong sniper, feel a bullet pass through his leg, and shoot back. There was no buildup, no warning, and no time to think. It was finished before it had even started. When it was over, Ben was happy to have survived but also disappointed his one brush with action had been so unceremonious, so brief, so lacking in the sort of drama he had grown up with on the silver screen, where brave American soldiers crouched in trenches and steeled themselves for the battle ahead. He did not march off to risk his life for God, glory, and the United States. His story had no prologue. In fact, his story barely had a story. It was his first night in the jungle, and then suddenly, unexpectedly, it was his last. All in the course of three seconds.

While Ben was not foolish enough to have wished for more time in Vietnam, he felt he had gotten off easy. Superiors would later praise him for having the strength to shoot back at his aggressor after he'd been injured, to have killed the sniper before the man could hurt anyone else, but Ben knew that was all bullshit. It wasn't courage or bravery. It was reflex. The man raises his gun, you jump to the side, you raise your gun, he shoots, you shoot back. Bang. There it is. Game over. No time for thought. No time for choices.

Choice is the key. Being thrust into a life-threatening situation doesn't make you brave, thought Ben. Bravery is when you put yourself in such a situation by choice, when you charge into enemy fire, when you storm a beach, when you jump from an airplane. Choice is what matters.

Ben Phillips never had a choice. And so he left Vietnam untested, without ever knowing the true limits of his bravery.

BEN WOULD NEVER publicly claim that slapping the president of the United States on live television was a brave thing to do. In the years to come, when the event would be brought up during interviews, he would concede it was, in fact, quite foolish. But at the time, it was oddly satisfying.

Something had snapped in Ben when he saw the video clip of the president. His most sensitive of buttons had been pushed. It was injustice, and injustice—of all things—drove Ben crazy.

He knew he deserved whatever came his way. He had compromised his principles and would have to pay the price. All the suffering and humiliation that had befallen him in the last two months was therefore acceptable because it was deserved. It was his cross to bear.

But Melissa . . . she was blameless. She hadn't wanted to go along with Campman's crazy plan in the first place. She'd been the voice of reason, the voice of morality, the voice of conscience. She had not wavered. Under the worst of pressure she'd remained a supportive wife, a principled critic, and a shrewd politician. Of all people, she was not worthy of further punishment.

And certainly not from him, from anyone but that smug good old boy president. As loudly as the voices in Ben's head cried, "Anyone but Melissa! Anyone is worthy of retribution *except* Melissa! Not her!" other voices were crying, "Anyone but Struck! Anyone can hurt me, but not him!"

That Struck could attack *Melissa, that* was injustice.

Ben's mind seethed with anger, anger at himself, anger at Campman, anger at his advisors, anger at God, anger at Sharon Balis, anger at Vietnam, anger at Luke Travis, anger at Randy Denholme, anger at high school, anger at the Republican Party, anger at the media, anger at his own ambition, and, above all, anger—venomous anger—at President Gregory Xavier Struck.

Yes, with all the blame and all the names that popped about inside his head, Ben kept coming back to Struck. He kept circling and returning to the one man who had done the most wrong, the one man who was the biggest fraud, the biggest danger, the most shameless bully in the world.

Ben recognized himself as being in a heightened state, no longer participating in the world like a normal human being. He was suspended in that slowly billowing ether several feet off the ground, in that place where you know your every move dances in time with the pen that writes the story of your life. And here in that heightened state, burning with self-righteousness, Ben saw something before him with great clarity: a choice.

Without hesitation, he made it. And his decision was to go to battle. He didn't know quite what that meant at the time; he had no idea, in fact, what he was going to do, but in that moment he surrendered his actions to instinct, he let anger drive him, and he trusted God and the angels of justice to make everything come out all right. He kissed his wife and walked out to greet his enemy with a thousand thoughts newly banished from his head. He walked forward, uncertain of what the next moments would hold, uncertain if he had the ability to make it to the podium, uncertain he even had the ability to speak, uncertain of almost everything, thinking of nothing, and yet, at the same time, very certain of one thing and one thing only: *he felt brave.*

THE SLAP

It was the slap heard round the world. The one moment, itself so indefinable, that somehow came to define the campaign. In the months and years to follow, it would be the source of inspiration for countless books, essays, plays, and films, a moment burned so indelibly into the American consciousness as to leave a mark far greater than its actual historical importance.

And there would always be those 170 seconds of video, playing back the same way again and again. For decades to come the two men would always approach each other, one smiling, the other not. Every single time, the smiling man would extend his hand, and every time, he would be slapped in the face. He would reel backward, shocked, and look about him, as if hoping to find his next course of action written on a cue card somewhere. Finding no answer, he would hurry to the podium and grab the microphone:

"This man's a lunatic and I will not debate him."

Every time the video played, the president would stalk off, leaving his attacker alone on the stage, and every time, his attacker would turn to the cameras with a sorrowful look, like a father who's just been forced to discipline his child in public. And then, in accordance with the script, that man, the senator, would fearlessly approach the podium and say his lines:

"I'm sorry you all had to witness that. In the course of political struggle, there are many things a man must be expected to tolerate. For me there are two things I have never and will never tolerate. One is an attack on my country and the other is an attack on my family. So . . . I demand an apology from the president for his unkind words about my wife—words I learned about only moments ago. If he's willing to apologize, then I'll apologize for my impulsive response, and then hopefully we can begin this very important debate and talk about the real issues our great country is facing."

The senator would pause for a moment, and then finish:

"Mr. President . . . *I am here, and I'm ready when you are.*"

And then there would always be that wonderful silence as the senator waited on a half-empty stage for an opponent who would not return.

The camera would cut to the shocked face of Taz McDonald, who looked like he'd just swallowed an albatross. He would speak haltingly.

"Uh, we need to take a short break. We'll be back in a b-boh-ment from, buh, Boston."

Those 170 seconds of video would live on, Zapruder-like, in the American consciousness for the remaining years of the democracy, every frame as familiar as the one-dollar bill. In 2032, a NewsNet poll would rank it as the fourth most universally recognizable political event of the last century.

In the moment immediately following the actual slap, there was an audible gasp from the audience, a woman's voice screamed, and two male voices could be heard shouting, one of them clearly saying, "Oh, my God!"

Backstage, Shelly Greenblatt turned purple, launched into a coughing fit of epic proportions, and then passed out on the floor for a solid minute. The moment of the slap, Ralph Sorn dropped his Mountain Dew on the floor, soaking the bottom of Ozzie Mayweather's trousers.

Mayweather did not notice. The assistants Wyatt and Charlie turned to each other in disbelief, as if to confirm that neither was hallucinating. Derek Kiley froze with his mouth open wide, while Melissa Phillips froze with her eyes closed. Both were jolted back into action when Greenblatt hit the floor.

On the other side of the stage, Daisy Struck swallowed her butterscotch candy and shouted a hoarse, "Greg!"

Dennis Fazo muttered, "Holy fucking shit!"

At the foot of the stage, Elayne Cohen-Campman saw the slap through the lens of her Canon ProDigi 3000 and kept clicking away, despite her sudden inexplicable urge to go to the bathroom.

XLGNN's Jennifer Dial grabbed a clump of Peter Williams's hair and pulled it tightly, whispering, "Oh, wow. Oh, wow. Oh, wow." Peter was so transfixed by the sudden turn of events, his eyes darting furiously about the room, trying to take it all in, that he never even wondered why he was having so much trouble moving his head.

Back in Bethesda, Mary Templeton leaped toward the TV set, hoping to see a picture of her boyfriend in the audience.

In West Memphis, Arkansas, Sharon Balis nearly choked on her popcorn, while in Los Angeles, California, Tina James watched in quiet amazement, thinking, I kissed that man.

Eddie Dulces, who was watching with his wife, Sophie, grabbed the phone and called his *Nightly Shocker* coproducer Lonny Volls, saying, "Are you watching this fucking thing?!"

In the Hynes Convention Center, the six Secret Service men closest to the podium hesitated, waiting for an order. The president didn't seem to be in danger. Neither did the senator. Their instincts told them to do something. But what? There was no protocol for this sort of situation. The order came through their headsets a moment later: "Hold steady."

As Struck stormed offstage, one of them asked him, "Mr. President, would you like to press assault charges?"

"*What do I look like?! A pansy?!*" Struck barked back and stomped toward his dressing room.

Fazo chased after him, pale as a ghost. "Mr. President, we should arrest him—"

"Dennis, what the hell was that?!"

"I—I don't know. . . ."

"What the hell was that?!"

"We should arrest him, Mr. President, get him in handcuffs."

"*I will not give him the pleasure!* What *the hell* was that?"

On the other side of the stage, Thomas Campman did not move a muscle. Even when Shelly Greenblatt hit the floor beside him, Campman remained still as a statue, gazing in astonishment at this strange new beast he'd created. The only parts of him to move were his lips, although no sound came from them. He just mouthed:

"Oh, Lord my God, Jesus, and all spirits inhabiting this world and others . . ."

He didn't know what else to say.

He just repeated the motion slowly with his lips.

"Oh, Lord my God, Jesus, and all spirits inhabiting this world and others . . ."

And then again.

"Oh, Lord my God, Jesus, and all spirits . . ."

His brain could process no more. He continued to watch in wonder.

When moderator Taz McDonald announced it was time to cut to a commercial, network news and cable programmers alike commenced one of the more infamous panic sessions in Western television history. The debate had been scheduled to run commercial free for ninety minutes, and in the shock of the moment, Taz McDonald had forgotten this altogether. His instinct was to cut away, and some of the networks followed his cue. ANC, the most watched of these channels, famously cut to a Super Duck Toilet Bowl cleanser spot (a thirty-second commercial that would live on in the public memory much longer than it deserved to). Other channels kept their cameras running as McDonald waited for his cue to continue.

All the while, Senator Phillips stood dutifully at his microphone, eagerly awaiting the questions he felt would surely come. After a few moments, Wendy Relsh took the stage to try and end things officially.

"Look, this debate is over. I think we all need to go home."

She didn't speak to anyone in particular. She just spoke. And although she was aware how ridiculous she sounded, she had no idea what else to say.

Senator Phillips spoke.

"I came here to debate, and I'm ready to answer questions."

No one had any authority. No one was in charge. But the senator spoke with confidence, and Wendy Relsh did not. So she backed off the stage, repeating herself but with less conviction.

"The president is not debating this man. The debate is over. The debate is over."

But, of course, the debate was not over.

Moments later, the lights (which had dimmed slightly at the announcement of a commercial break) were turned up again, and the show was back on. Except that now, there was only one candidate.

"I'm ready to answer any questions you may have," said Ben Phillips, "absolutely anything."

The questions came. Tentatively at first. About health care. Then about foreign policy. Then education.

And Ben answered. He spoke eloquently. And the people listened.

Some would later criticize the media and the debate commission for not pulling the plug on the Boston event immediately following the infamous slap. For their part, network executives felt they had little choice in the matter. They had no alternate programming planned and no reason not to show what they showed. If the *Titanic* had been sinking, would you have turned the cameras off? Besides, the president could have come back to the podium if he'd wanted to do so.

Eventually, he did. But he was hard to convince.

"Mister President, the debate's still happening."

"What the hell do you mean, '*The debate's still happening*'?" Struck roared.

"Just that. Phillips is still there. He's answering questions."

"Well, stop it! Tell them the show's over!"

"Can we arrest him? We really should—"

"I think I answered that question! Do you want us looking like the secret police? You want him being a martyr? No! Just—just—*Will someone tell me why the hell we can't just stop this thing? I am the fucking president!* I don't understand how the hell this thing is still going on!"

"Well, we have no authority over the program, really. Unless you want to make an arrest or use some specific—what sort of executive privilege would we invoke here?"

"Oh, holy shit."

"Look, Mr. President"—it was Fazo speaking now—"I think you need to go back out there. He's getting a free ride right now, and you need to challenge him."

"No way. Dennis, you heard me say I was not going to debate that man. Do you want me to go back on my word—what I said only minutes ago!—right now in front of the American people? I do NOT go back on myself! You know that!"

"I understand, but . . . it doesn't look good if you don't go back and challenge him."

It took a good deal of convincing, but eventually Struck agreed. He would go back on.

It was a dramatic reentry. There were great cheers as the president strode back across the stage to his podium. Struck grinned and nodded, the hero returning to the battle, attempting as much swagger as he could believably muster.

But there was fear in his eyes now. He was a bully who'd been bested, a wiseass whose confidence had been shaken, a chief executive whose bravado was now transparent.

"Someone told me I was missing out on all the fun," he said.

This met with laughter and applause.

"Mr. President."

Struck flinched at the mention of his title.

"Mr. President, I'd be more than willing to apologize for striking you, if you'd be willing to apologize for the comments you made about my wife."

It was a direct challenge, something the prelitigated debate rules did not permit. But then, those rules seemed somewhat out-of-date in the wake of Ben's unrehearsed act of violence.

The president looked uncomfortable. Then after a moment, he managed a smile.

"Look, Senator, if I've said anything to *offend* you, then I'm sorry, that was not my *intention*. But I do not believe anything I've said warrants the sort of reckless, irresponsible behavior you have displayed tonight in front of the American people."

It was an apology of sorts, but it was hardly apologetic.

America and Struck waited breathlessly for Phillips's response. They did not have to wait long. To everyone's relief, Ben let the president off the hook.

"You're probably right about that," he said. "But what's done is done and it cannot be undone. Mr. President, I accept your apology, and I offer you my own. I humbly apologize for my actions. And I will cede the next question to you."

Suddenly, the debate was on as if nothing had even happened.

Except everything had changed. The power dynamic had completely reversed itself. Ben Phillips was now the boss. He was setting the rules, and Struck was doing his best to play by them.

The president seemed off his game, nervous, unsettled. Like a superhero going to battle without the use of his superpowers, Struck was naked. His usual arsenal of wit and condescension had been stripped away the moment he was slapped. Without them, his inferior debating skills were more readily apparent, and it became clear to everyone watching that, after Phillips's command solo performance only moments before, Struck's reentry into the debate had noticeably lowered the level of discourse.

In the end, both sides would spin the story to their advantage. Naturally, there were many people (Republicans *and* Democrats) who were outraged that the president had been slapped on national TV, and the right wing tried to fuel that outrage as best they could. They called Phillips unstable and sang a chorus of, "Would you trust this man with his fingers on the nuclear trigger?" Most left-wingers, on the other hand, downplayed the slap, drawing attention to the debate itself, where Ben Phillips delivered a clearly superior performance.

As for the mainstream pundits, they were consistent. They declared the historic evening to be a Phillips victory, and their reasoning was simple: Ben Phillips looked strong, and Greg Struck looked weak. Few people could argue with that.

AFTERMATH

He was a winner. He was cool. He was the man.

Ben Phillips knew it wasn't right to feel as good as he felt, not after what had just happened, but he couldn't help it. He'd defended his wife's honor, he'd spoken eloquently to an eager public, and he'd succeeded in wiping the smug grin off the face of the world's most powerful man. It may have been wrong, but Ben felt like a million bucks.

"You are one crazy son of a bitch," said Campman, when he got offstage. "But I think I love you."

"Thanks, Tom. Where's Melissa?"

"Dammit! I can't believe what you did!"

"Can anyone tell me where my wife is?"

Amid the swarm of advisors and backstage folk, Ben spotted his wife. She was wearing a polite smile, but he could tell she was upset. She was the one sad face in the stunned-but-enthusiastic bunch.

He kissed her, and to be polite she kissed him back, but she was cold as ice.

THE FIRST CALL he received was from the general, and the old war-horse was characteristically brief. "I know you've got a lot of people to talk to," he said, "but you should know I've been wanting to smack that asshole for the last four years. You beat me to it, you bastard! Congratulations!"

"DAD, WHAT THE hell happened?"

It was Stacy. She was less pleased.

"I lost my head, honey. I don't know. Did you hear what he said about your mother?"

"Yes, but don't you think what you did was a little drastic?"

"You're right. What if I promise not to do it again?"

"Daddy, please don't."

"Don't worry, honey, I won't."

LAST BUT NOT least was Jim. It was the easiest of the three calls to receive.

"Dad, you are my personal hero," he gushed.

"I shouldn't have done it," said Ben Phillips, "but thank you, son."

THE POSTDEBATE RECEPTION had cooled down, the spin room had cleared out, and Ben found himself back in the green room with several others from his inner circle.

"I thought you were appearing on Jack Sternhom," he said to Shelly Greenblatt.

"No." Shelly sighed. "Tom's taking that one. Or *took* that one by now, probably. I was interviewed by the *Miami Minstrel*, which I didn't know existed until tonight. Do you think that means he's put me on the bench?"

Ben chuckled.

"Our spin is working, Senator," said Ralph Sorn, hanging up his cell phone. "Preliminary Internet polling is very positive."

"Our spin, nothing!" said Derek Kiley, who was staring at his laptop. "They're doing it for us! I'm at New York Tribune dot com. Harry Maxwell writes, 'The president slunk offstage with his tail between his legs and stayed there for some time, presumably sulking and nursing his wounded ego.'"

"Did any of you see the printout of the Chip Rogers piece?" asked Greenblatt.

"Got it right here," said Kiley. "Listen to this: 'Even in his impulsive rage, the Oklahoma senator seemed more presidential and (if it's possible) more in control of himself than his incumbent rival.'"

"Incumbent rival!" cried Sorn gleefully. "I like the sound of that."

"This could work," said Greenblatt in disbelief. "This could actually work."

Several feet away, Ben Phillips smiled. He'd just shaken his three thousandth hand of the evening, but he looked like he was just getting started.

Elayne Cohen-Campman snapped a picture.

"Did you get my good side?" he asked.

Elayne smiled, and started to speak.

"Senator Phillips . . ."

"I know. I know. We gotta do that photo session, Elayne. I'm not getting any younger."

It had become something of a joke between them. Elayne had reminded the senator about his promise for a private photo session so many times, he'd begun to anticipate the question and now brought it up at random whenever they were together. "That photo session" became synonymous with that thing that you really want to do but never have time for, like "one day, I'm gonna write that novel" or "one day, I'm gonna learn to play the piano." "One day, Elayne, we're gonna have that photo session," Ben had said to her countless times, each time meaning it in earnest, each time actually looking forward to the thing.

"Just say the word, Senator."

"Okay. The word," Ben said, calling her bluff. "Let's do it. I feel terrible stringing you along like this. Let's do it tonight or tomorrow . . . sometime in the next day or two. I don't care what I have scheduled. Let's make some time."

He was too good for words. Elayne marveled that a man with such monumental worries could still find space in his brain to care about her own personal artistic project. And to bring it up tonight, of all nights, after what had just happened onstage . . . Her admiration knew no limits. In light of the ruckus caused by the release of Melissa's photo session, Elayne knew the senator could have easily weaseled his way out of his promise. She was impressed that he chose not to do so.

"Ben, perhaps it's best not to worry about more pictures now," said Thomas Campman, entering the room.

Elayne felt instantly betrayed by her husband, but the senator put her at ease again.

"A promise is a promise, Tom," he said. "When do you want to do this thing, Elayne?"

"What? Oh, anytime. You're the one with the busy schedule."

"Who? Me? Busy?" he joked. "I've got nothing but free time. I'll give you a call when I get back to the hotel, and we'll figure this out."

Ben was in a good mood. Time to take advantage of the moment, thought Derek Kiley.

"Senator?"

"Yes, Derek."

"I have those revisions you wanted for your speech in Fort Lauderdale," he said. "I know you liked the introduction, but I actually changed it to go with the new ending. I think it's more focused now; I think you'll like it."

"I'll take a look at it later this evening, Derek. Thank you."

"What time are we visiting that school tomorrow?" he asked Campman.

"Ten A.M."

"Ten A.M.? That's late. Hell, we could sleep in if we wanted to."

The room laughed.

"Of course, in light of current events," said Campman, "I think we should meet in headquarters at nine so you can schmooze with the rest of the Boston staff, and we can see how things shook down in the press overnight—get our message straight."

"Beautiful."

Then a new voice.

"Excuse me, Missus Phillips? Your car is ready. You need to leave now if you're gonna make your flight."

It seemed everyone had forgotten that Melissa Phillips was in the room at all. While she'd been her usual outgoing self during the reception, playing the role of soon-to-be first lady with typical panache, she'd broken character and become quiet since stepping out of the limelight. She'd hardly said a word to anyone.

The senator looked over at his wife, and he could tell he was in hot water. He knew it was time for damage control but secretly wondered why that had to be. Why couldn't Melissa just put aside her judgments and share in the good mood with everyone else? Why did she have to be so uptight? Ben sighed.

"Okay, could you all clear out for a minute?" he said. "I want to have a moment alone with my wife before she jets back home. I mean, seriously, what are you clowns doing here anyway? Don't you still have TV airways to pollute?"

One by one they started to leave, and soon the room was empty, save for the senator and his wife.

Ben Phillips smiled at Melissa, hoping to elicit a smile in return, but his charm did not work now.

Melissa's eyes were swollen. She seemed to be steeling herself for a breakdown. Worse than he expected.

"God, what's wrong, Mel?" he asked.

She stared at him in disbelief, saying nothing, her silence unbearable. When she finally spoke, the words came haltingly to her lips.

"What did you do, Ben?"

He felt ashamed.

"I know. I know," he said, "I shouldn't have slapped him. It—"

"How could you do that? Who are you? *Do I know you?*"

"Mel, I . . . I know. I shouldn't have done it. I know. You're right. It was stupid. It was impulsive. . . . I was just . . . I was so *mad* for you."

"Oh, no. No, no, no. Don't make me a part of this. I don't need some chivalrous cowboy, Ben, okay? . . . killing for me? . . . I never wanted that. That's not me. This is not *us*. It's not *you*."

"Honey . . ."

"Are you a Republican, suddenly?" She grasped his shoulder fiercely. "Are you Greg Struck? I don't understand it, Ben. You've lowered yourself to their level. You're no better than them. You're a bully."

Ben knew the words were intended to hurt, but somehow they didn't. He didn't buy himself as a bully. However far he may have slipped, Ben knew he was still fundamentally the same good and decent man he'd always been. So while his wife's words saddened him, they did not wound him.

But still she continued, growing more impassioned:

"What happened to our high road?" she asked. "There is none. I mean, what have we been running on? What have we been fighting for? What's the whole point here?"

"Mel. Mel, come on," he said. "You know what we're fighting for. And you know we need to get elected in order to do it."

"And the '*How?*' Does the 'How' even *matter* to you anymore? Or does anything go?"

"Look, if we can win this thing—"

"Then what? Then you're gonna be the perfect president? This'll all be forgotten? You'll be the 'thinking man's president,' the guy who got elected by slapping the other guy in the face?"

"I'm not saying it was the right thing to do."

"Good! Fine! Okay!" she said suddenly. "I need to go. And we can't have this discussion right now—because I'm gonna be late and you're not listening and I'm not gonna get upset and go out there all emotional and have everyone tell stories about me. I know my role and I know how I'm expected to behave."

"Let's talk later, okay?"

"Good-bye, Ben."

BACK IN THE hotel, Ben Phillips phoned his wife. She was curt and said they'd speak the next day. He hung up the phone feeling frustrated but also—he had to admit—mildly euphoric.

Strange.

Concerned though he was about his wife, the buzz from earlier in the evening had not entirely dissipated.

He wanted to feel happy. He wanted permission to savor the moment. He wanted confirmation that everything was okay in his campaign and his world. He wanted to know that none of the bad stuff really mattered. Melissa wouldn't give him that kind of reassurance.

He desperately wanted his wife to like "the new Ben Phillips," but she did not. It wasn't that he wanted her to endorse his moral compromises. He didn't like those, either. He knew he shouldn't have agreed to Campman's scandal plan, and he knew he shouldn't have slapped the president.

But were those compromises really essential elements of the new Ben Phillips? Couldn't he separate the two? Couldn't he govern honestly but keep his newfound persona? The new Ben Phillips wasn't about lying. He was about attitude, about style, about confidence. The new Ben Phillips was loved by women and envied by men. He had a spring in his step and passion in his voice. And he was popular. People identified with him. They wanted to invite him over for dinner. They liked him. They loved him. They *listened* to him. The new Ben Phillips was cool. What was wrong with that?

It troubled Ben that Melissa couldn't see past his compromises and enjoy the benefits they had wrought. Everyone else could. How could she dislike the new Ben Phillips when everyone else liked him so much better than the old one?

And why was she making him feel so guilty about the whole thing? Didn't he have enough guilt on his own? If he could rationalize his actions, why couldn't she? What was done was done. Why couldn't she accept it and move on? Why was she spoiling his fun?

This line of thinking was getting him nowhere. Besides, he only partly bought his own argument. Ben's logical side kicked in. He was wasting time on an issue he could not solve. At least not tonight. He should go to sleep. He should put all these worries to bed and pick them up with a clear head in the morning.

But he was too wired.

He reached for the phone.

SURPRISE ME

Isn't it weird to be doing this at night? I mean, in terms of the lighting. It's not a particularly inspiring setting."

"I think that's sort of the point, isn't it? Don't worry, Ben, I won't make you look bad."

"But you'll make me look sexy, right? Just like my wife?"

"Is that what you'd like?"

"Well, I think it's best if I kept my nipples to myself. I'll be upfront about that right now."

Elayne smiled. "If you think that's best."

And now Ben laughed. It felt good to flirt a little. It felt liberating.

"So how does this thing work?" he asked. "I just mope around my hotel room and you take pictures?"

"You're not far off," said Elayne, and she began her spiel: "As you've probably figured out, I'm not a fashion photographer. I don't believe in posing. I just want you to . . . exist. Just exist in the space of your hotel suite, and that is what I will capture."

She was smiling at him. He smiled back.

Ben wondered about her age. She was definitely younger than her husband, but by how much, he couldn't tell. She was in her fifties; the lines on her face gave that away. But she had a youthful energy. As she squatted to rifle through her camera bag, Ben took inventory of her physique. She was slender and strong. Breasts of average size, but perfectly proportioned. Like most women in her fifties (those who have not been cosmetically enhanced), Elayne had skin that was not always taut, but it didn't sag, either. And the way she moved . . . She actually bounced, her joints elastic, like a child's. It was as if her enthusiasm could not be contained by her body.

In his mind, Ben turned back the clock on Elayne Cohen-Campman, and it was not a difficult thing to do. He saw her as an expectant mother with long flowing hair and a ripe center ready to burst, as a bride with a white cinched waist and floral crown, as a young woman sitting against a tree with bell-bottom jeans extending out from under an open sketch pad. She was in college. She was in high school. She was a knockout. Ben realized happily that this was exactly the sort of girl he never would have had a chance with as a teenager. And now she was taking his picture. Now she was flirting with him.

She photographed Ben sitting at a small desk in the corner of the living room. He was reading Kiley's speech, making notes. They restaged these reading and writing pictures in a leather armchair and then with Ben lying on his bed.

"How am I doing?" asked Ben.

"Oh, these are great," she said, but seemed hesitant.

"But . . ."

"But nothing. They're great. They're a little conventional, that's all. They don't really tell me anything about . . ."

For a moment, Elayne wanted to spill the beans completely. She wanted to tell Ben that he fascinated her, that she wanted to get to the bottom of him, to take him apart and put him back together again, that she longed to figure out the true Ben Phillips, to capture him and own him and print him and view him and explore him a million times over and over again. But she stopped herself. She said instead,

"The pictures show a part of you I already know. You work hard. But what else do you do?"

Ben eyed her curiously.

"I brush my teeth. Do you want me to do that?"

She smiled. "It's a start."

The Oklahoma senator brushed his teeth. The campaign manager's wife photographed it.

"Oh, no! You took a picture of me spitting? That's blackmail material there! I'm gonna need to destroy the negative."

"Okay, okay," she said, giggling. "I'll delete that one."

"What do you mean? That's not digital, is it?" he asked, pointing to the ProDigi 3000.

Elayne nodded.

"It looks just like a regular camera."

"Well, it's top-shelf."

"Okay then."

They held each other's gaze for a moment.

"We can take pictures of anything," said Elayne, "and if you don't like it, we delete it on the spot."

"SO, THIS IS Ben Phillips getting ready to turn in for the night?"

"Yes, but I'm not showing my nipples."

He smiled.

"That's just fine," she said, smiling back.

Ben's top shirt was unbuttoned, and his white undershirt was visible beneath it. He lay on the bed, reading a copy of *Weekly Turn* magazine.

"If you could just scoot a little bit closer to the night table."

He did.

"Oh, that's amazing. You are *amazing*."

Elayne worked her way around the bed until the night table's lamplight hit Ben's face from the side and reflected off a picture frame to provide both backlight and key light. He looked relaxed, like a tired king, but with the light bouncing off his head like a halo, he looked energized, enlightened. All focus was drawn upward to the glow, which seemed to emanate from his brain. Oh, to be inside the mind of this man! Elayne's hands were sweating as she gripped the camera.

"Are you getting my good side?"

"Every side . . . oh, just look over there . . . Great! . . . Every side is perfect . . . and every side . . . just lower your eyes . . . yes . . . every side is so . . . different . . . it's just . . . amazing."

Ben basked in Elayne's adulation. She was so warm, so attentive, so effortlessly affectionate—and without any ulterior motive that he could discern. She just seemed to like him for who he was. Her gaze was without judgment. And it was genuine. Ben missed genuine. He allowed himself a deep exhalation and relaxed as he hadn't in a long time.

Ben Phillips had been beaten up so much in the last year that he'd almost forgotten what it was like to let his guard down, to open himself up and trust that the person he was with was going to adore him unconditionally. Of course, he knew Melissa would always love him, but that was different. Things with Melissa had gotten so complicated recently, so labored. He knew it wasn't fair to compare Melissa to Elayne, but he couldn't help himself. Elayne was effortless. Melissa was difficult. *Now why did that have to be?* Despite himself, Ben couldn't help but feel frustrated with his wife. You'd think he actually cheated on her, the way she treated him. Maybe he should have. Maybe that would have made things simpler. Ben longed for simplicity now more than anything else. He longed to clear his head. He took another deep breath and, with it, allowed himself to focus on the situation at hand.

Elayne was close to him now. Very close. And she was completely focused on him. There was something thrilling about her attention. Ben felt a surge of adrenaline.

"Could you stand up?" she asked.

"Yes."

Elayne backed away from him until she could see his whole body. He stood facing her, somewhat awkwardly.

"If you're not sick of me yet," she said, "I'd love to do some more stuff just for fun."

"Okay."

"But I can't tell you what that is, of course. I don't want to impose my ideas on you. So surprise me."

Ben couldn't help but grin. *Why was that?*

"Surprise you?"

"Mmm hmm."

"And if I don't like it, we can delete it?"

"Of course. Surprise me."

He paused for a moment, creating the necessary suspense. He got a wicked look in his eye. Then Ben Phillips lifted up his undershirt and exposed his left nipple.

He giggled as he did it, hoping Elayne would appreciate the joke.

But Elayne didn't laugh. She just looked at him. Ben suddenly became very conscious of the hairiness of his chest, of the contours of his nipple, set as it was on a pectoral made more of muscle than fat. He'd forgotten what these parts of his looked like, but he could see them now in Elayne's eyes.

She drew closer to him, her camera poised but not firing, not yet. She stopped two feet from his chest and took a picture, a close-up of his left nipple. Then, she took a picture of his face.

"Take off your shirt," she said quietly.

The smile had faded completely from Ben's face. But he obeyed. *Why the hell not?* The buttoned shirt fell to the floor, and the undershirt was lifted over his head.

Elayne stepped back and started taking shots.

"Oh, God," she said. "You don't even know how sexy you are. It's unbelievable."

No more doubt now. The breathtaking Elayne Cohen-Campman found him sexy. She'd said it. Ben's pulse raced, and he was taken aback by how powerless he was to control his body's reaction. His system was suddenly on overdrive. It was as if his body had already decided on a course of action before his mind had a chance to weigh in. The sensation was not dissimilar to what he'd felt earlier in the evening after watching the video clip of the president. At that time, his feelings were of anger. Now, they were euphoric, lustful.

He flexed a bicep. Was he joking now? Was he being sexy? He wasn't sure, but again, she smiled in response. He was in uncharted waters here, he was acting foolish, but it still seemed he could do no wrong in Elayne's eyes. He wondered how far this game would go, but just like earlier in the evening, he was surprisingly free from worry. He trusted himself to act properly in the moment—and what's more: he trusted her. He trusted her completely.

"Take off your belt. Get on the bed."

He unbuttoned the belt and whipped it off, like an amateur stripper.

They both laughed.

He jumped on the bed, posing with the belt wrapped around his shoulder.

"Ooh," she moaned, firing away.

She felt as if she were touching him. But she wasn't. She just circled round, taking one shot after another as Ben undressed.

Suddenly he was reclining on the bed in only his boxer shorts.

Elayne continued to circle the bed, taking pictures from different angles. Several times she leaned on the mattress, and Ben felt the vibration travel down his spine. For the second time that day, he felt himself in a heightened state, participating in an event that he was also observing, a scene that was both hyperreal and imaginary.

He was surprised by the thrill he got from following Elayne's simple commands. She was so easy to please, and he was reminded of the ancient pleasures he once derived in adolescence from successfully executing a concrete task, back in those days when a girl like Elayne Cohen-Campman would have rocked his world.

She didn't have to tell him to take the boxers off. She just looked in his eyes, and he looked back.

He trembled ever so slightly as he reached down to unpack himself, like a teenager exposing his body for the first time as a nude object. He tossed aside the last remaining fabric and lay before his photographer with a vacant expression. He felt the cool of the air-conditioned room against his bare skin.

Elayne bit her lip and held her breath as she looked through the viewfinder of her Canon ProDigi 3000. Her heart was racing. Before her was the body of a large, physically fit, sexually aroused, fifty-three-year-old man, and the face of a seventeen-year-old boy.

BIG T

Elayne Cohen-Campman's obsession with the Democratic presidential candidate ended rather swiftly on the night they had sex. After twenty minutes of decidedly pedestrian intercourse, the formerly godlike senator had become a normal man, and Elayne was no longer interested.

It wasn't that Ben Phillips didn't have his charms. He did. There was something about the unusual way he sucked on her earlobe, for example, that she found mildly thrilling. She was also fond of the way his fingers dug into the back of her thigh as they rocked back and forth, as if he were holding on for dear life. The senator was in good shape. His body was firm, muscular, and not too hairy. He was more than adequately endowed. And while he certainly set no endurance records in their twenty minutes of lovemaking, Ben was not too quick on the draw, either. As a lover, he had some skills.

All that being said, it was still mediocre sex. There was no way around it. After a most intriguing foreplay, the main course was mechanical and ordinary by comparison. It was awkward, too, both parties trying to play their respective roles by folding their parts into the expected positions, but each one having practiced their motions with different teachers, each partner schooled in a series of incompatible moves, specialties all too quickly jettisoned in the frantic search for a universal, one-size-fits-all erotic experience, one bound to neither thrill nor disappoint.

When it was over, Ben became upset. Like a typical man, his guilt had kicked in about two seconds after ejaculation—she could see it in his eyes—but, like a politician, he'd waited for a sufficiently polite interval of time before freaking out. Once that time had passed, he started apologizing profusely and talking about his wife, saying she had been right, saying how foolish he'd been, saying how much he loved her, all that remorseful husband stuff. He spoke more than once about what a strange time it was for him, how he'd been confused, unsure of who he was, etc. He spoke altogether too much, and she felt every word like raindrops, further eroding his remaining sense of mystery until the once formidable mountain of intrigue had been reduced to no more than a hapless pile of stones.

Elayne returned to her husband that night, pleased to be finally released from the senator's spell. She would still respect and admire Ben Phillips, but she would no longer revere him. It was healthier that way. On the whole, Elayne had no guilt or regrets about her actions that evening. She didn't view her fling with the senator as true infidelity, mainly because it wasn't about sex, at least not for her. It was a life experience, an opportunity to get to the bottom of a great mystery, a once-in-a-century chance she would have surely regretted had she let it pass her by. And it wasn't about Tom, either. If anything, she felt closer to her husband, now that she'd had the chance to experiment with another.

And wasn't that all it was in the end? An experiment gone wrong?

In the wake of their sexual congress, all necessary precautions were taken. Clothing was rearranged, stories were coordinated with regard to the length of the photo session, and, most important, incriminating pictures were deleted.

It was a shame, too. The photos were brilliant. To say they captured a side of Ben Phillips the public had never seen before would be an obvious and painful understatement. Some were crap, to be sure, clichéd soft-core images to rival the Internet's shoddiest wares, but others were downright beautiful. They were honest in a way Elayne's other pictures of Ben had not been, suffering as they did from a bit too much reverence. In these new images, the photographer's perspective had changed, but so too had the subject. He was open. He was honest. He was real. He was a man, not a monument.

And Elayne got it. She finally got it.

It was that first picture, when all his clothes were off. Ben was reclining on the bed. His toes were closest to the camera, and they possessed the sort of momentary relaxation possible only when book-ended by moments of extreme tension. It was as if the toes were gasping for breath. The senator's fully erect penis was craning Pisa-like to the left, as if working in conjunction with his shoulders, which possessed a similarly disjointed angular relationship to each other. His chin balanced itself on the bulk of his neck, which provided a cushion between the head and the left shoulder, and his arms lay at his sides, the fingers passive and fidgety at the same time.

His facial expression put it all into context. But what context was that? How can one describe an expression that is neither happy nor sad, neither tired nor energetic, neither old nor young? Because no generic descriptor could be properly applied to this expression, did that mean it was vacant? No. It wasn't vacant, nor was it full. It was not something, but it was also not nothing. It resisted all commentary and defied all descriptions except for one: *It was Ben.*

At long last, Elayne had managed to capture a Big T photograph of Ben Phillips, and she absolutely could not erase it. She wasn't sure what she would do with the photograph, but she knew she couldn't part with it—at least not yet. The second after snapping the picture, she'd copied the file to another folder so that it would not fall victim to any postcoital deleting session.

She would take all the necessary precautions, to be sure. She would show no one (she could *never* show anyone), and she would hide the photo in the middle of the main folder on the camera's memory card, rearranging its position among the files so that it would be one of the last pictures anyone would see, in the unlikely event that anyone other than her was flipping through those closely guarded pictures. The next time she was alone with her laptop, she would download the picture to her hard drive, hide the file where no one could find it, and delete the original from the photo memory card. Throughout the years she would look at the secret picture occasionally, and it would give her chills each time. She decided that if, at some point in the future, the photo failed to give her chills or if she feared it might somehow fall into the wrong hands, she would delete it at once, and the thing would be gone forever. Until then, it would be her private indulgence, the lingering digital memory of her once living obsession.

That night Elayne reorganized and deleted her photo files accordingly, fixed her clothing, and crept back into her bedroom, where Tom had only recently fallen asleep. Her obsession was over, and there were still two weeks left in the campaign.

HUMAN

I started like any other day might start, assuming that day was the day after your candidate slapped the president of the United States on national TV. The plan was to assemble at Phillips's Boston campaign headquarters on Commonwealth Avenue at 9:00 A.M. to mingle, have breakfast, and talk strategy before the day's big events. At Campman's request, Greenblatt, Mayweather, Kiley, and Sorn arrived forty-five minutes early.

They were greeted by Hazel Shapley, the Massachusetts chief of operations, whom Campman had met twice before. She was a tall woman in her forties with fierce green eyes who liked to hug her co-workers and did so with great energy and very little warmth. After offering coffee, doughnuts, and bagels to the entourage, which also included Elayne Cohen-Campman and a few early-rising journalists, Hazel took the advisors on a brief tour of the office.

For its limited purposes, the office was deceptively large, taking up all four floors of the Back Bay brownstone ("Although three and four are just for storage," Hazel said). Breakfast was in the second-floor conference room. The five chief advisors grabbed food and walked next door into Hazel's office, where they could discuss things in private.

The men quickly realized they had little to discuss, as most of the news from the last eight hours was good. It appeared their spin was working. While the campaign had been inundated with calls and e-mails overnight, the majority of them criticizing the senator for his brash behavior, the discontented Americans behind those calls and e-mails seemed to be in the minority, at least according to preliminary polling. Internet surveys and online blogs all suggested Americans were responding favorably to the senator's debate performance, and there was hope his overall poll numbers might rise as a result.

"Unbelievable," said Sorn. "Un-fucking-believable."

"We're lucky he's not in jail," said Greenblatt.

"But he's not in jail, is he?" reminded Campman.

"And did you see what they're doing now with the clip of the president?" asked Mayweather.

They all had.

News channels were replaying the clip of the president's "women who use sexual titillation" quote and showing it in conjunction with the clip of the debate slap. The effect was magical. Audiences got to see the president making an arrogant remark about a woman, and then getting his clock cleaned by the offended woman's husband. It was a story of chivalrous revenge, the tale of a bully being humbled, and it played like pure Hollywood gold. The average American might argue that the senator overreacted, but at the same time, he or she couldn't help but cheer once Ben got his revenge. It was an automatic response, programmed by years of film and TV in which the nice guy kicks some well-deserved ass at the end of the story. With the media showing both clips, Ben Phillips came off as the ass-kicking nice guy and Struck, the arrogant blowhard.

"I think I'm gonna frame this," said Derek Kiley.

He was holding the front page of the *New York Tribune*, which was graced by a half-page color picture of the now infamous slap.

"That's nothing, Kiley. Did you see the *D.C. Daily Herald*?"

"That's a bigger picture, but the angle's not as good."

"Let me see," said Campman, grabbing the second paper.

"Is there any way we can use this image, boys?" he asked jokingly and then changed his mind, "No, not this one. The one after it. That's what I want to see. None of these show it."

"What?"

"I want to see the moment after the slap. The look on Struck's face. *That* was the real prizewinner—not the slap itself. It was that look of absolute shock on his face. It was just so damn beautiful— *someone* must have a picture of it."

"Have you asked your wife?" prodded Greenblatt.

Campman laughed.

"Why isn't Elayne in here?" he said, "Are we really discussing any government secrets now? Where the hell is she? Kiley, go find her."

Kiley, go find her.

That was it. That was the last straw, thought Kiley.

"Tom . . . gentlemen," he would begin, "I'm sorry, but I've had enough. I was hired by this campaign to be a speechwriter. That is what I have been paid to do. . . ."

The words were on the tip of his tongue. He had only to deliver them. Kiley paused for a moment and swallowed, finally ready to launch into his speech.

"What are you doing? Please, Kiley! Find my wife!"

Damn. It was a tough call. Campman's request was moderately charming, self-effacing, humorous . . . oh, hell, who was he kidding? It wasn't mean enough. After all the abuse he'd taken, Kiley needed a bigger fuse to ignite his rant of explosive self-righteousness, lest he look like a crybaby. And, besides, the chance had passed. *Another stupid chance had passed!* Derek Kiley wasn't sure if he was more annoyed with the way his superiors treated him or with his own inability to take a stand against it. Once again, his moment of justice would have to wait. Kiley gritted his teeth, as he had so often these last few months, and did exactly what he was asked to do.

SHE ENTERED THE room like a force of nature, with a camera bag on her shoulder and a devilish twinkle in her eye. It was an entrance all the advisors had grown to appreciate and even look forward to after almost three months on the campaign trail.

"How are the Boy Scouts doing?" she asked.

"Elayne, honey, I want to see your pictures of the slap. Didn't you say you got good ones?"

Thomas Campman reached for his wife's camera bag, but she casually turned it away from him. She smiled and removed the Canon ProDigi 3000.

"Oh, I've got great stuff," she said.

Campman chuckled gleefully and reached for the camera.

"Are they on here?" he asked, taking possession of the device and turning it on.

This is all too close for comfort, thought Elayne. Even though she had prepared for just such a far-out situation, even though the one incriminating picture was nowhere near the top of the digital pile (and at least a hundred pictures away from the debate shots), even though she knew she would probably be in the clear, it was still all too unnerving, watching her husband handle the camera.

"Yes. Here, let me find it," she said, grabbing it back from him. "I have over three hundred pictures on this memory card, and it'll take you forever to get the right ones."

She breathed a sigh of relief. That was *way* too close for comfort.

Elayne would cue up the memory card to the proper photos, knowing that Tom couldn't find the Big T picture unless he was actively searching for it; and even then, it would take him a while. She also knew Tom was aware how much she disliked sharing her work on the tiny digital screen. He would respect that, she was sure.

Still, the close call of the previous moment—which wasn't a "close call" really, but rather a "miles-and-miles-away-but-still-closer-than-she'd-like-it-to-be call"—had made Elayne question the wisdom of not deleting her precious photo when she had the chance. She should have downloaded it onto her hard drive while Tom was in the shower that morning. Why hadn't she? She'd been asleep, that's why. Shoot.

Never mind regret. Elayne determined that she needed to get the photo off the memory card as soon as possible, and that was that.

Tom was sitting on Hazel Shapley's desk, and Elayne made herself comfortable next to him. She would hold the camera, and he would look over her shoulder.

"Here you go," she said.

Thomas Campman looked at the two-inch digital screen on the back of the Canon ProDigi 3000, and a smile came to his face.

"Now that's something," he said.

It was yet another picture of that infamous slap, but the angle was different from those he'd seen before. Elayne had been sitting away from the press photographers, stationed to the side of the podiums, up close and low to the ground, and, as a result, even on the two-inch screen, her photograph possessed an energy the others lacked.

"I want to see his face. How do I zoom in?"

Elayne let him hold the camera while she operated the zoom button for him.

"It's a great picture, but . . . hmm. How many did you take?"

"I think there are about twelve or thirteen of the slap and the immediate aftermath."

Elayne advanced the camera to the next photo.

"No, not that one, either," said Campman, "It was a look he had. . . ."

He didn't say any more.

As Ralph Sorn munched on his doughnut and Derek Kiley stewed quietly in his seat, as Ozzie Mayweather and Shelly Greenblatt read their respective newspapers, Thomas Campman went through each and every one of the thirteen debate slap pictures with his wife, looking for a facial expression that was nowhere to be found. Every now and then, one of the men would peek over Campman's shoulder to get a glimpse of the private photo-sharing session, but this hobby proved more trouble than it was worth, as Campman futzed with each tiny picture, traveling across the pixels, zooming in and out obsessively.

"I think we should joke about the slap—make light of it," said Kiley, backtracking to a prior discussion.

"Not now," said Mayweather. "Too soon."

"Not a lot now, but a little. As more time elapses, we joke more."

"We've got to be careful," said Greenblatt. "We'll sound arrogant and weird if we make a big deal about it."

"Of course, but in the next couple days when he's asked questions about it, he needs some funny responses. Now, I wrote up a few things last night—"

"Dammit!"

All eyes shifted back to Campman.

He'd shuffled through all thirteen debate slap pictures and now found himself looking at a picture from the postdebate meeting.

"Don't you have any more?" he asked.

Campman had begun flipping through the pictures, pressing the next button over and over again. Elayne knew it was time to retake ownership of her camera.

"Sorry, babe, that's all I have," she said, reaching over for the camera.

He pulled away from her, still clicking the next button and watching the screen, zombielike.

"You must have more of the rest of the debate," he protested.

"I stopped taking after a certain point. Okay, gimme. Sharing time is over."

Tom knew she didn't like sharing her pictures while they were still on the camera.

"No, I'm not looking at the pictures," he said, "I'm just trying to find that expression—maybe it got mixed up in the order."

It was an emergency. She knew it would still take a while for Tom to find the one photo he absolutely could not see, but she needed to stop this thing and stop it now. She put her hands on the camera.

"Nothing's mixed up, I promise. Now that's it. I've shown you too much already."

Campman's grip wrestled playfully with that of his wife's while he pressed the NEXT button with his free finger.

"I'm just looking at the pictures." He laughed.

"No! I refuse! . . . Tom . . . I'm warning you now. . . ."

She was trying to keep things light so as not to arouse suspicion, but she'd gone too far. She realized it right away. In trying to joke around, Elayne had done the worst thing imaginable: *She'd made it into a game.*

Anyone who knows Tom Campman knows that Tom Campman loves games, and more than that: Where there is a game, Tom Campman MUST win.

Now the game was keep-away, and Tom had turned from husband to taunting older brother. He clicked the next button feverishly with a wicked grin on his face, flipping past two-inch pictures as fast as the camera's computer would let him.

Elayne knew she couldn't protest anymore. It would give her away completely. She needed to change strategy by 180 degrees and quickly. She did just that.

Elayne stopped reaching for the camera and feigned disinterest.

"You know what? Fine," she said, "if you want to look through all three hundred pictures, be my guest. But I have something much juicier on the other memory card."

It was a bluff, but it worked. Tom looked up, and then stopped clicking.

"Really?" was all he said.

Elayne nodded.

"If you just give me the damn thing."

Tom smiled.

Then he looked down.

Then his expression changed.

IT FELT LIKE a minute, but really it was only a second—or if we're being completely accurate, perhaps ten seconds. Regardless, it was enough time to rock Thomas Campman's world. It was enough time to thrill him, devastate him, and crush him completely, to turn his universe upside down and back again, and to break his heart.

It started with a two-inch image of a naked man with a hard-on. No, not just any naked man. It was Ben Phillips, the Democratic candidate for the presidency of the United States, the man to whom Campman had devoted the last year of his life. Ben Phillips was lying on a bed, two inches tall, with a hard-on. It was, to say the least, a most shocking sight.

But wait. The longer Campman gazed at the two-inch screen, the more he realized this wasn't just any old dirty picture. There was a power to it, something Campman couldn't quite put his finger on but something strong, something undeniable. The picture entranced him, and when he zoomed in on the pixels of Ben's face, he suddenly felt dizzy.

It was Ben Phillips in his truest form—Ben Phillips as plainly as he'd ever seen him. Suddenly, the man Thomas Campman had followed across the country for months seemed like a cardboard cutout, an imposter by comparison to the man on the two-inch screen. *This* was the real Ben Phillips. This was the real man. And that's exactly what he was: a real man. He was real. He was genuine. He was human.

Campman felt something within him drop.

He was human.

Tom Campman's brain raced to reconstruct events. What exactly had happened? What exactly did it mean? Clearly Elayne had been unfaithful to him, and clearly Ben had been unfaithful to his wife as well. How did this happen? Scenarios started to bounce about his head, scenarios he didn't want to imagine, scenarios that made him sick, but he stopped them before they could get too far. There'd be time for that agony later. Now a more pressing connection was being formed in his brain. He knew the connection had been made instantly because he felt it hit him in the gut when he first saw the picture, but now he needed his conscious mind to catch up: Ben Phillips had been unfaithful to his wife, and this picture was the evidence—or the cause, or the by-product . . . or the result.

Could it be?

"Sin . . . Will . . . Make . . . Him . . . Human!"

Those were the heavenly words Campman had received almost three months ago. Now he finally knew what they meant. He didn't have all the pieces of the puzzle, but it was enough to get the picture. The senator had committed a sin—and not a fake sin or an accidental sin, but a real honest-to-goodness sin, a sin with a capital *S*—and that sin had, in some strange way, made him human.

Campman now realized his divine message had nothing to do with the presidential race. It was not a suggestion at all. It was a prophecy, a very personal prophecy, a prophecy that had now come true.

There were still questions. There were a thousand questions. So much was still unclear, but Campman's insides, his guts, his instincts were unequivocal in their verdict. They knew the divine mystery had been solved, and so did he. Campman exhaled a tired breath, and as if to sanctify his discovery with a punctuation mark, he uttered two words: "Holy shit."

Only fifteen seconds had passed since he first saw the picture, and his mind was still on overdrive. What were the ramifications of this prophecy? What did it mean that he had orchestrated a campaign of fake scandals based on a misinterpreted divine message? How did this affect his relationship with the Almighty? What about the candidate?

What about his wife? And through all these questions, he kept return-ing to the most simple, the most obvious of them all: *What now? What the hell happens now?*

Elayne was looking at him. Her face was white. She knew he knew. She knew he'd found it.

Tom looked into her eyes as a husband now, and the weight of his discovery knocked him upside the head. He felt pain but couldn't name its origin. He felt sad and angry.

But how to proceed?

Campman set into motion his muscle fibers and vocal cords, an automatic task that seemed suddenly deliberate and challenging. He put on a face that could not be hurt, set his vocal attack to a high-pitched tone and then modulated downward as he started to speak.

"Gentlemen, I was wondering if you might indulge me for a mo-ment," he said. "I'm sure your coffee cups have run dry by now, and I'd really appreciate just a minute or two alone with my wife. There's a brief but very important matter we need to discuss."

It was an unusual request, particularly from Campman, who never got touchy-feely or familial around his colleagues. Perhaps that's why no one argued.

"Are you insinuating that we're being less than productive, look-ing at pictures and reading the newspaper?" asked a smiling Shelly Greenblatt, rising from his chair.

The others laughed. It was true there seemed to be little business that couldn't wait until the candidate arrived.

"I hope they still have that chocolate glazed number," said Sorn. "I had my eye on that one."

One by one, the men shuffled out of Hazel Shapley's office and back into the conference room next door.

Tom and Elayne just stared at each other.

When they were alone, Tom spoke.

"Are you trying to destroy me?"

The words echoed in his wife's ears.

"I'd like an opportunity to explain," she said.

"No!" said Tom, "Let *me* explain!"

And he was off. He wasn't quite sure what to say, as his emotions had not yet organized themselves into a clear strategy. He didn't know how he wanted this conversation to play out. So he made it up as he went along.

He didn't talk about cheating. He didn't mention the fact that his wife had just had sex with Ben Phillips. He didn't ask how long it had been going on or how she felt about Ben or how she felt about him. He didn't ask why his wife had betrayed him and didn't inquire as to whether she ever planned on telling him. These were topics he couldn't broach. They hurt too much.

Instead, he talked about the picture. And when he wasn't talking, he yelled.

"*What on earth were you thinking?*" he cried. He ejected the photo memory card and waved it in the air. "*Do you REALIZE this thing could bring down the entire campaign?! This little thing can change the course of history—of human history—and you're just carrying it around with you? Do you have any idea how IRRESPONSIBLE that is?! All that we've worked for . . .*"

He continued. After he'd gone on for a while, he slammed down the memory card on the edge of the desk, right in front of where Elayne stood, and she was forced to look at it, forced to ponder the potential consequences of her actions. The flat silvery cartridge seemed alive to her now, like Tolkien's magical ring or the amulet from that Indiana Jones movie, a tiny object of enormous power.

Elayne tasted tears and realized they were streaming down her face.

Tom continued:

"I would have thought you, of all people, would've had the sense not to put us in danger like this! What if you were mugged? What if someone stole the camera? What then?"

He couldn't talk about the affair. He just kept on about the camera.

Elayne realized she wasn't crying for herself, but rather for her

husband. She'd hurt him more deeply than he'd ever been hurt before. That she had the power to do this frightened her. That she'd
actually done it crushed her. So she cried for him, for the angry man
who couldn't cry himself.

His speech could only go on so long. There was no time for a family crisis now, and they both knew it. The day had to move forward.
But how would they move with it?

"This is disappointing, Elayne," Tom finally managed. "This is
very, very disappointing."

It was one of the worst things Elayne Cohen-Campman had ever
heard.

There was a moment of silence and then a knock on the door.

"Eeeeehboss! Boss!"

It was Hector.

Elayne turned and walked to the windows, dabbing at her eyes.
She was not ready for anyone to see her. Not yet.

"Yah?"

Hector entered the room nervously. He seemed short of breath.

"Eeeeehboss . . . phone call-eh-for you . . . number three . . . very
eeeemportant!"

Campman looked confused and turned his attention to the phone
on the desk.

"Line three?"

He was filled with a terrible sense of foreboding and realized he
was beginning to dislike phones. Imagine that: Thomas Campman,
master of the prank phone call, turning on his favorite invention.
Suddenly all his anxiety, all his fury, and all his rage were directed
toward the phone. And not just this phone—*all* phones! Yes! Phones!
They were the problem! It was now perfectly clear: *He hated phones.*

Line one was lit, but line three was not. He tried it anyway. There
was just a dial tone. He looked up to question Hector, but his valet
had already gone.

"Are you sure it's line three?!" he yelled after him, and then muttered, "Oh, what the hell."

He tried line one, but got a beeping noise. Dammit. Now he'd have to find out what was going on.

Did this mean their conversation was over? He looked at his wife, who had turned, teary-eyed, to face him.

"I'm sorry," she said, and thus broke his heart a second time.

He couldn't manage a response. He just nodded to let her know he'd heard.

Campman let his eyes fall from hers and they wandered back to Hazel Shapley's desk. It was a suspiciously neat desk, no loose papers, no yellow sticky notes, not even so much as an errant tape dispenser. There was just a clean smooth oak finish, uninterrupted by office-grown clutter or debris of any sort.

Campman's blood ran cold.

The memory card!

NOSRAPO

Hector Elizondo had always been fascinated by sharp corners. To him, whenever two pieces of plywood possessed a ninety-degree relationship to each other, it was a sign of luxury, and he was inevitably drawn to the forever diminishing hypotenuse between them. A corner was the place where a building was most a building, and that was where Hector liked to be.

His family's first home on San Gomez was little more than a hut with a roof of palm leaves. It was vaguely rectangular in shape, but the corners were rounded and the walls consisted of upright poles covered with lime and clay. Although Elian Ramon Elizondo made a healthy living from his fishing boat, it took many years for him to pay off the price of the boat itself, and they did not move from that first house until Hector was eleven years old.

The Elizondos' second home was a tremendous step up. The house contained four rooms and walls made of red brick, and, sure enough, these bricks formed corners of ninety degrees—not sharp corners like those Hector would come to know in the United States, but corners nonetheless, linear crossroads, places of structural security.

Hector's cot was stationed in one such corner, and it immediately became his favorite place in the entire world. If he was having trouble sleeping he would run his right hand up the crack between the two walls and feel the red clay as it scraped off into his fingernails. For whatever reason, this comforted him.

ON THE MORNING after the now infamous debate slap, Hector Elizondo entered the conference room of the Ben Phillips campaign headquarters on Commwealth Avenue in Boston. He grabbed a doughnut and coffee, and naturally gravitated to the seat in the back corner of the room.

Hector was depressed. The previous evening, he'd missed out on the single biggest event of the campaign. He'd been outside the Hynes Convention Center babysitting the black Town Car while Ben Phillips was inside making political history. To Hector this was indicative of his greatest frustration as a spy: access. As close as he could get to the major players, Hector was never close enough and never at the right time. Now the campaign was almost over and he had yet to make a really big score. He'd been looking for opportunities left and right, sneaking about like nobody's business, but this had yielded nothing more than a few minor conversations (of which he made a few minor recordings and was paid a minor price). Now he felt helpless and pressured. There were only two weeks left. What could he hope to get in that time?

Feeling the need for comfort, Hector pushed his chair back into the place where the back wall met the window and rested his head in the angle. The back wall was one of those modern paneled numbers, segments of solid wall lined with frosted glass panes of the sort that allowed light and color to pass through from room to room, but not discernible shapes. Hector's head now rested between such a glass pane and a normal windowpane that looked out on the alley behind the building. The glass was cold against his scalp. He felt a slight draft breezing through his dark hair, and to his surprise, he heard laughing.

What was this?

Hector pushed his head back farther, and suddenly the laughter became louder. It was as if he were listening to a group of people inside a seashell. There was an echo but also a sharpness to the sound. He quickly determined the noise was coming from the adjoining office, and the voices he heard were those of the top advisors.

He looked now through the frosted windowpane and saw blurry objects in motion. This matched what he was hearing: The room was clearing out. Now, as he examined the frosted panes, he noticed a crack. It was not the pane at head level but rather the one below it. He scrunched down farther in his chair—anyone watching must have thought him the very picture of the sloth—and from his new position he noticed the crack was actually quite wide—about one inch. He could see through it.

Now this is real spying! he thought to himself.

He could see Campman and his wife, and he could hear them, too, although they weren't saying much.

About this time, the other advisors entered the conference room: the fat one, the young one, the old one, and the black one. He had learned all of their names by now, but Hector was still partial to his own nicknames: Fat, Young, Old, Black. They were stuffing their faces now with doughnuts and bagels. No one seemed to pay him much mind. This was typical. He imagined that to everyone else he probably looked like he was zoning out, reclining as he was back in the corner with his head against the wall.

Back in the adjoining office, it didn't take long before Campman was talking, and he talked quite a bit. He was yelling actually, yelling and waving a tiny silvery object in the air. It looked like a miniature computer disk of some sort.

Hector slowly started to put the pieces together. While he would never know the full story of what he was witnessing, he would grasp enough to understand the stakes involved, and by the time he heard Campman yell, *"Do you REALIZE this thing could bring down the entire campaign?!"* Hector knew what he had to do.

He had been waiting for an opportunity. Now here it was. And sure enough, it was a do-or-die proposition. He could steal the disk and make a run for it or he could ignore the opportunity and stay in the boss's good graces. He knew it wasn't possible to have it both ways.

Hector suddenly thought of his father's advice to him: "Sometimes, a man needs to take chances to give his family a better life."

It was advice that had always served him well. How could he not heed it at a time like this?

He would do it. He would take the chance.

Once Hector saw the boss place the silvery object on the wood desk, he got up from his chair in the corner and walked casually past the other campaign folk who were congregated around the food table. He walked out into the hallway as if he were going to the bathroom but stopped short in front of the door to Hazel Shapley's office. Here he waited until the conversation seemed to quiet down. Then he made his move.

What struck him was how easy it all was. The boss seemed distracted when Hector first entered the room. He looked at his wife, who had turned to the windows, and this allowed Hector the opportunity to zero in on his prize, still located at the edge of the desk. He knew where it was. Now he only needed a moment to grab it.

"Phone call-eh-for you . . . number three . . . very eeeemportant!"

His voice had quavered a bit, but the boss believed him, and the older man turned his attention to the phone. Suddenly, Hector's moment had arrived.

He pictured it like an American film with everything moving in slow motion, but it wasn't like that at all. It was quick. Just like his days on San Gomez, just like his days as Nosrapo, performing for the children, his agile hands flitted out and then back. He didn't pause, he didn't hesitate, and if you weren't watching carefully you'd have missed it. Out and then back. And then he had it in his hands. And then he left. And then he was gone. And then there was no turning back.

REACTION TIME

*T*he memory card!"

Elayne whirled around, eyes ablaze.

"What?"

"Holy shit, he took it!"

Every second mattered. There was no time for discussion or even thought.

Campman bolted from the office and toward the conference room.

"Derek!" he shouted.

Inside the conference room.

"Have you seen Hector?!"

Only blank faces.

"Derek, follow me!"

It was a forceful order, and Derek Kiley knew enough to obey. Campman was already halfway down the stairs. Kiley caught up with him amid a sea of reporters.

"Has anyone seen a short Mexican in a suit?!" Campman cried.

More blank stares. So much for the watchful eye of the press, he thought.

A few people pointed out the front door.

No shit—he's out the front door! Big fucking surprise!

Campman worked his way through the reporters, several of whom attempted questions. He ignored them and made his way out the building into the Boston air.

He looked left and then he looked right. All at once, he spotted him! One block away, a black Town Car turned the corner.

Campman ran a few steps but then stopped.

It was no use. He turned and clutched Derek Kiley.

"Kiley! Follow him! FOLLOW HIM!"

And for young Derek Kiley that was about all he could take. He'd heard his cue.

"Tom, I'm sorry," Kiley began, "but I've had enough. I was hired by this campaign to be a *speechwriter*. That is what I have been paid to do—"

"What the fuck are you saying?! Get a car—let's GO! He's GETTING AWAY!"

Suddenly, there was applause.

Campman took in his surroundings. Indeed, there was a small crowd of well-informed supporters who had gathered outside Phillips's headquarters to catch a glimpse of the candidate as he made his way inside. But why were they applauding? Of course! From the east, the candidate's motorcade was approaching.

"Oh, shit."

Thomas Campman now saw everything he'd missed when he first bolted out the front door. There were policemen everywhere, reporters and Secret Service men, too. He was standing in an area that had been blocked off from the public, looking toward the southwest, where Hector's car had disappeared. In between him and that empty stretch of street were police barricades, and people. Lots of people.

And the candidate was approaching. They were trapped. It would take at least a couple of minutes to get any of the official vehicles out of this mess of densely choreographed campaign movement. Campman wondered for a brief moment how Hector had managed to escape so smoothly only seconds before. But then, Hector had always been the master of such things.

I've been had, thought Campman. It was hitting him for the first time. He looked around and saw only coconspirators. Every face in the crowd seemed to be purposely ignoring him and yet closing in on him at the same time. Those bastards. The magnitude and inevitability of his impending doom began to stir his innards. Hector was gone—he was long gone—and there'd be no way of catching him. Campman felt like he'd fallen off a tightrope. He felt helpless. He felt like he was going to die.

And then, from a few feet behind where Campman was standing, a new voice chimed in:

"I know where he's going."

Campman whirled around. He found himself looking straight into the bright blue eyes of a young man who could not have been more than sixteen or seventeen years old. For a moment, Campman did not recognize him.

"Who the hell are you?" he snapped.

"Peter Williams, sir. *TeenVibe* magazine."

Campman eyed Peter curiously.

"Well, where did he go?"

The young reporter did not blink.

"Take me with you, and I'll tell you."

FOLLOWING HIM

"How quickly can you get us to Logan Airport?"

The car shifted into a higher gear, and the three men fell back against their seats.

"How quickly do you need?" asked the female cabby in a thick Boston accent.

"Better than your best. The faster we get there, the larger your tip," said Campman, "and I can be a *real* big tipper."

With that, the cab took a hard right on Arlington, and they were on their way.

There might still be time, thought Campman. This lady was fast, whoever she was, and she had home court advantage in this little race, even if Hector did have a head start.

"Could you tell me what the hell's going on?" asked Kiley.

Campman looked over at Kiley, which meant he looked at Peter Williams, too; the young reporter was sandwiched between them. The aging campaign manager eyed them both, these two rookies beside him, and thought: So, this is the future. These are the men who will replace me when my number's up—whenever that is.

He'd always thought he had a few more years in him, another decade perhaps, and then he'd ease into a slow retirement, maybe write a book, make occasional television appearances. . . . That was a good plan.

But maybe it was no longer up to him to decide. Maybe his career was going to end today. Maybe his marriage, too. Maybe his life. Who could tell?

Peter Williams and Derek Kiley stared at him with eager eyes.

"Hector's a spy," Campman finally said. "He's stolen some sensitive information and we need to get it back. It's on a small silver memory card, about this big."

"Holy shit."

"Exactly."

He turned his eyes to Peter Williams.

"Now, how do you know he's going to the airport?"

BOOM!

The cab flew over a large bump.

"Because that's what he does," Peter replied, not losing a beat. "I've seen him do it in L.A., in Portland, and in Phoenix. I think he did it in Madison, too, but I didn't catch him there."

"Wait—you've been following him?" Kiley asked, clearly impressed.

Peter smiled slightly but avoided the question.

"Usually it's at night. He goes to the American Airlines arrival gate of the closest major airport and he meets up with this guy who's always in a blue car—an expensive blue car—and he follows him to someplace out of the way—some random place—and they make an exchange of some sort."

"Oh, my God," said Campman, under his breath.

"So, he's been doing this for months?" said Kiley.

"At least a month. That's when I first found out."

"Holy shit."

Campman's mind was on instant replay now, cycling back through the moments he'd spent in Hector's company, reviewing every car ride, every conversation, every second they'd spent together, but seeing them now from a frighteningly different perspective. He wondered: Had the Yucatecan valet been a plant from the very beginning or had his loyalty been bought somewhere along the line? *And what about the very beginning . . . ?*

Campman thought back to that snowy night in February when they first met, the night Hector helped him steal the Lannahan files from Warren Muddville's office, the night that set in motion a blackmail operation that would cause a man to take his own life.

Did Hector have dirt on him? You bet your ass he did.

Suddenly, the mysterious phone calls made perfect sense. Hector had spilled the beans to the Republicans, and Dennis Fazo was probably just waiting for the right moment to release the damning evidence. It could come any day now. Any second! And to think, he'd been taunting him the whole time!

"I know about Muddville . . ."

That was *so* Fazo! Dennis loved to rub it in.

And now . . . now Dennis Fazo and his Republican mudslingers were about to receive an equally volatile little nugget in the form of the senator's centerfold shot. Campman could just see it, staring back at him from every newspaper page, from every website, from countless television sets across the country, those honest Oklahoma eyes and that awkwardly beautiful naked form, the candidate's naughty bits front and center in their blacked-out, grayed-out, smudged-out glory!

It was all coming tumbling down, and Campman realized every bit of it was his own fault. *He* was the one who'd blackmailed Muddville. *He* was the one who'd hired Hector. *He* was the one whose wife had taken the nude photo. *He* was the one who started the whole fake-scandal snowball in the first place: Tina James, Sharon Balis, alcoholism, the debate slap, every single damn thing could be traced directly back to him!

Him. And not the heavens.

Even the heartbreaking revelation of his wife's infidelity. Campman realized that even this could—if he was honest with himself—be linked to his actions. Had he really been the best husband he could be? Had he driven her away? Had he ignored vital signs? Had he screwed it up? These were complicated questions to which he had no easy answers, and they ate away at him.

There was quiet inside the taxicab as it rocketed through the entrance of the Callahan Tunnel.

They were underground now, and Campman appreciated that it would be the perfect time to mumble a prayer, to reach out for some divine assistance in this most trying of times.

But he said nothing.

What could he say? How could he know his prayers would be heard? What could he realistically expect in return? And if his prayers were heard, even if they were somehow *answered*, would that answer be one he could understand?

Campman hadn't lost faith, not exactly, at least not in the heavens. How could he lose faith in the heavens when he'd been spoken to by the Almighty Him/Her/It/Them-Selves? He had lost confidence, however, in his ability to communicate, in his ability to send and receive divine conversation.

"Sin . . . Will . . . Make . . . Him . . . Human!"

He'd heard the words plain as day. But he'd gotten them wrong. And look what he'd done as a result! He'd heard not what the Almighty actually said, but rather what he *wanted* Him/Her/It/Them to say!

How maddeningly typical, he thought. I'm no better than the Crusaders or the terrorists, just another ass who's misinterpreted his verse and is making the whole world pay for his faulty comprehension.

"Shit."

I've gotten myself into this mess, he thought, and then followed that idea to its logical conclusion. He knew what he had to do.

"Is this as fast as you can go?!" he barked at the driver.

The stakes were just too high. He had to find Hector.

He had to. He had to. He had to.

KENNEDY AT LOGAN

N ow?"

"Very-Eeeemportant! Bosseeee knows! Eeeeeeeh-BeegBeegBeeg! Verybeegthing! Ehs-pensive! Very-Eeeemportant!"

"Okay, okay. But it's gonna take me twenty-five minutes to get there."

Hector grimaced. He knew he'd get to the airport first. He would have to wait there for Kennedy like a nervous wreck. There was no way around it.

Eight minutes later, when Hector entered the Callahan Tunnel, he checked his rearview mirror for the two-hundredth time. Still nothing. He expected sirens, police cars, the National Guard perhaps, but there was nothing. At least not yet.

Perhaps they were waiting for him on the other side of the tunnel. Hector didn't like tunnels. They made him claustrophobic. He always worried the two open ends would close up, trapping him inside, underground forever. It hadn't happened yet, but who was to say today wouldn't be the first time? It was a long tunnel. Too long.

When he finally emerged into the air of East Boston, Hector

breathed easier. He was almost there. He felt a wave of exhilaration pass through his body. Could it really have been that easy?

But no. Things weren't easy. He reminded himself that he was now a criminal. He'd committed a crime.

Or had he? Was there any proof? Had anyone seen him? So long as he disposed of the evidence, it would be their word against his. All he had to do was get rid of the disk.

He needed a hefty sum for it. There were no two ways about that. The disk had cost him his job, and it would take a lot of money to make it worth his while. How much should he ask for? Fifty thousand? A hundred thousand? A million? How much could he get?

Rearview mirror. Still nothing.

Hector had taken a few twists and turns on his way to the tunnel. He was pretty certain no one was following him. But had the boss called the police? If the police were looking for his car, it wouldn't matter where he went. They could find him. Eventually. Advantage: police.

But, of course, Hector did not need to stay out of sight indefinitely. He just needed to steer clear of the authorities until he had the chance to give the silver card to Kennedy. Then he could drive right back to campaign headquarters and pretend nothing out of the ordinary had happened. They could fire him if they wanted to, but he would deny any wrongdoing. And what would they be able to prove? They could search the car. No problem. All he had to do was keep out of trouble until Kennedy arrived, and he was home free. Advantage: Hector.

"WHERE THE HELL is he?" asked Campman.

Peter Williams looked puzzled.

"He usually waits in his car until the guy comes. Or the guy is already waiting when he gets there."

"Do you see the guy now?"

"I don't . . . I don't think so. There are no blue cars here, I don't think."

The men scanned the arrival gate from inside the taxi.

"Could we have beaten him?" asked Kiley.

"It's possible."

They waited silently.

"Is it possible he's already made the handoff?" asked Campman. "Is it possible we missed it?"

"So, who is this guy you're looking for anyway?" asked the cab-driver.

Campman handed her another twenty-dollar bill.

"Here's for no questions, okay?"

The woman pantomimed zipping her lips and nodded graciously.

"Oh, my God, he's coming," cried Peter. "Get down!"

Peter was used to crouching out of sight. The other men weren't, but they ducked down immediately at the force of Peter's suggestion.

The black Town Car drove past them and pulled up to the curb sixty feet in front.

"Let's go!" said Campman.

"No wait!" said Kiley, "don't go now or he'll just pull away. Wait a second."

Campman frowned, but obeyed.

"What if we blocked him in?" he asked.

"That'll take just a sec," said the driver, but Campman looked to his left and realized the cab itself was blocked in by a large van.

"No, no, wait—look," Kiley said, pointing to a station wagon moving forward on their left side. "That guy will trap him in just a moment . . . assuming   he   slows . . . wait . . . wait . . . wait . . . NOW! Let's go!"

The two men exited from opposite ends of the cab, and Peter ran after them.

"CRAP," SAID HECTOR.

It was the boss and the young one! In the rearview mirror! Running his way! Where had they come from? He hadn't seen, but suddenly, they were here, at the airport, approaching fast!

Hector revved the engine and looked to his left.

"Crap!"

He was blocked in. He couldn't drive away. He had no choice but to leave the car. Hector opened the driver's-side door and leapt out. He walked briskly toward the doors of the American Airlines terminal.

Was he running? No, of course not. Why would he possibly be running? He had nothing to hide. He just happened to be in the airport, going for a stroll, just happened to be . . . he just happened to be . . . he was just . . .

No story was believable, no excuse sufficient, and they were right on his tail. Hector entered the airport doors and broke into a run. He thought of Brinita and the girls. He thought of what might happen if he was caught. And he ran. He ran as fast as his legs would carry him.

THE AIRPORT CHASE AT THE END
OF THE MOVIE

Hector bolted into the terminal, and the three men followed him. He arced his way around the check-in line and headed straight for the counter. He jumped past a large mahogany suitcase and onto the conveyor belt behind it.

Shit, thought Kiley, this guy's not fooling around. He knew Hector was running for his life, and this caused Kiley to reassess his own personal stakes in the matter. He swallowed hard and kept running. *This had gotten intense.*

Campman was yelling, "Catch this man! He's a thief! Catch him!"

Kiley leapt over the counter followed by Campman and then Peter Williams. One by one they ducked through the hole in the wall as Hector had, following the luggage to its final destination, that grand unknown beneath the airport's skin.

Young Peter Williams's adrenaline pumped like a highway truck stop at lunchtime. He was fully aware of the trouble he was getting into—he was breaking a million different rules—but he had no choice. This was his moment, the one he'd been waiting for, for the last sixteen and three-quarter years. This was his story and he wasn't about to lose it.

"Hey! Stop it!"

The airport worker tried to block Peter's entrance, but he wasn't fast enough. Suddenly the young reporter was standing with Campman and Kiley on the other side of the wall. Large men were piling suitcases onto a cargo truck.

"Where did he go?" shouted Campman.

There was no sign of Hector anywhere.

Campman met the gaze of one of the baggage handlers, who tilted his rather large head to the left. Campman's eyes followed in the direction of the head tilt until he found himself looking at a door.

"This way," he said, opening the door.

On the other side was a hallway, which the three men raced down.

"Check those doors, check those doors!" Campman shouted.

He was referring to the doors on the sides of the hallway, which Peter Williams and Derek Kiley dutifully pushed open as they passed. Closet. Restroom. Restroom. No Hector.

Campman burst out the door at the end of the hallway and found himself back in the main terminal.

"Okay, sir, you're gonna have to come with me now."

It was a police officer.

About eighty feet away, Campman could see Hector running back toward the entrance of the airport.

Dammit, he thought, he's doubling back!

"You don't understand—I'm with the Phillips campaign," Campman said, still in motion, flashing some sort of card from his wallet— probably a driver's license. "That man's a spy! He's stolen something!"

"Whoa!" said the officer. "Hold it. *That* man?"

IF ONLY HE could get back to the car . . .

If only Kennedy was waiting for him . . .

Hector realized if Kennedy had arrived, they could both be long gone in minutes. He would leap into the blue car and tell Kennedy to step on the gas. They'd be uncatchable.

Hector was almost at the door.

He stopped short. There were policemen outside. They were looking at his car. And where was Kennedy? Hector didn't see him.

"STOP THAT MAN!"

Now he was trapped. The police were coming from inside the terminal. They were behind him and in front of him.

He kept going. He headed outside. Outside was closer to freedom. He just had to get into a cab. But now, the policemen by the black Town Car had noticed the chase and they were focusing their eyes on him.

This wasn't going to work.

He had to get rid of the evidence. *He had to get rid of the memory card.*

Hector reached his white gloved hand into his jacket pocket and grabbed the tiny item. He cocked his wrist and let it fly.

A few moments later, he blacked out.

THE TINY SILVERY memory card was small enough that no one saw it leave his hands. No one saw as it sailed upward and hit a concrete beam, and no one saw it ricochet onto the roof of a Green Sparrow bus, where it remained for a few moments before sliding down the long windshield, finally coming to rest on the vehicle's wiper blades.

Hector had blacked out when the first policeman tackled him, and now, as he was brought to his feet, he showed only minimal signs of consciousness.

"Where's the card?" yelled Campman. "The memory card! *Where is it?!*"

"Calm down," said the officer in charge, whose name tag read JOSH NELSON. "If he's got it, we'll find it."

Hector blinked lazily as his hands were cuffed to a neighboring signpost. The two remaining officers searched his pockets.

"What are you looking for again?" asked one of the men.

"It's a small silver/gray disk, a photo card like you might find in a digital camera."

"Nope. Let's try the back pockets."

As the men continued to search the semiconscious Hector, Campman's mind went again to damage control. He surveyed the immediate area and was surprised to find that no crowd had really formed. There were a few rubbernecked tourists, but most people seemed intent on catching their planes and did not have the time or desire to gawk at a minor arrest.

Just then, something caught his eye.

"No way," he said in disbelief.

He took several steps forward, trying to see if his eyes were indeed playing tricks on him. They weren't.

"Oh, Lord almighty."

There, directly at eye level, perched upright on the windshield of a Green Sparrow bus, was a small silvery rectangular object. If the sunlight hadn't hit it at just the right angle, Campman would have missed it entirely.

"It's on the bus," Campman said breathlessly. "It's on the damn bus!"

The policemen turned their heads. Peter Williams did not.

"He's right there!" yelled the young reporter.

"It's right there!" yelled Campman.

"No, him!" said Peter, "the man in the blue car. He's right there!"

Even Hector raised his eyes at this.

No more than twenty feet from where the bus was idling sat a blue Mercedes sedan. Inside was a man in a Red Sox cap and sunglasses with a pointy chin.

The man known as Kennedy felt their gaze and saw he was being watched. He noticed Hector and immediately diagnosed the situation as being exactly what it was. The car pulled out instantly.

"We've got to stop that man!" cried Kiley.

"We've got to stop the bus!" cried Campman.

The bus had also pulled out and was heading their way. Suddenly both targets were in motion, and everyone panicked.

The Mercedes peeled out, and Derek Kiley ran directly into its path. The car swerved without slowing down and Kiley leaped to the side at the last second, thereby spraining his ankle and forfeiting one of the most unevenly stacked games of chicken in recent Logan Airport history. Peter and one of the officers ran after the car in his stead.

"Get the license plate number!" yelled the officer.

Meanwhile, Campman had made a dash of his own. He ran in front of the bus, which—unlike the Mercedes—screeched to a halt in front of him.

When the bus stopped short, the silver memory card rocketed off the windshield and landed edge first on the hard pavement, where it bounced like a pebble in a straight line toward the end of the drop-off area. Campman chased after it with one of the officers, a pursuit that ended abruptly when the small silver object bounced its way into a sewer grate and disappeared.

"Wait!" he cried.

Thomas Campman collapsed onto the cold cement and peered through the sewer grate into the blackness below. He was aware of the dirt on his hands, aware of his fine fabrics rubbing up against the gravel floor, aware of a pain in his hamstring, of the cold metal grate on his cheeks, and the tears welling up in his eyes. He was lower than low, he was one with the ground, and for the moment, it was exactly where he needed to be.

"I'm sorry," he whispered, and then repeated the phrase. *"I'm sorry."*

"Do you see it down there?" asked one of the officers.

Campman didn't answer. He lay motionless on the cement.

HECTOR WAS GONE. No one had seen him leave, but when the dust settled in the wake of the blue Mercedes, the Green Sparrow bus, and the flying silver memory card, the short bearded Mexican was nowhere to be found.

"I don't understand it," said Officer Josh Nelson. "I fastened the cuffs myself. The keys were on my person the whole time . . . at least I think they were. It's just the damnedest thing."

"Do you think it had something to do with those gloves he was wearing?" asked the officer named Will McCauley. "Do you think maybe . . ."

"Why would it matter if he was wearing gloves? I put the cuffs on, and somehow he got out of them. I mean, the cuffs themselves are still on the pole, aren't they? Why isn't he?"

"Are you sure you tightened—"

"They were damn tight!"

"Well, if you're sure—"

"Of course, I'm sure."

"He probably slipped out in a taxi while we were distracted."

"*I'm sure he did* slip out in a taxi, but how did he slip out of *the cuffs* is what I want to know! Is he some kind of magician?"

"I don't know. . . . I just don't know. . . . You said you tightened them."

"They were tight as all hell. I'm telling you!"

"Okay then."

"Now what did you say his name was?"

"I didn't say," said Campman.

"Well, what is it then? We're gonna find this son of a bitch."

Kiley responded, "It's Hect—"

"No," interrupted Campman. "No, I don't think we need to pursue this matter any further. We found what was stolen, gentlemen. I feel no need to press charges."

Officer Nelson eyed him suspiciously.

"That's all well and good for you, sir."

"The name's Campman. Thomas Campman. I run the presidential campaign of Democrat Benjamin Phillips."

"All right, Mr. Campman. As I said, that's all well and good for you, but we have a suspect resisting arrest, and that is a serious offense."

"But why were you arresting him?"

"I'm sorry, sir?"

"Why were you arresting him in the first place? Because I said so? We never actually saw the stolen goods on his person. You took my word for it and then stopped a man without any evidence. A Hispanic man. Interesting."

"I don't understand. You said he was a thief—"

"And I thought he was. I assumed he was. So did you. But was he?"

Officers Nelson and McCauley seemed displeased. They had not expected to be under scrutiny themselves.

"Look, boys," Campman said, "I don't think any of us have been at our best today, and I think we should just forget the whole thing. As far as I'm concerned, we thought we had a thief on our hands, but when we apprehended the suspect, it turned out to be a mistake. If your superiors have any questions at all, they should feel free to contact me."

With that, Campman handed them his business card, and the matter was closed.

"You'll need to do something with that black car," said Officer Nelson. "That zone's for loading and unloading only."

"Not a problem. Thanks so much, officers."

With that, they parted ways. Then, as Kiley waited in the black Town Car, Campman went back into the terminal and purchased ten large cups of Mountain Dew, which he proceeded to pour down the sewer grate.

"Just to make sure," he said.

Once the final drop of sugary liquid had fallen to the sewer below, presumably dousing any still-viable zeros and ones and dooming any digital survivors to a short life of corrosion and malfunction, Thomas Campman and Peter Williams joined Kiley in the abandoned black Town Car and headed back to Boston proper. As the car pulled out of the terminal, Campman turned to the young reporter and said, "Well, kid, if nothing else, it looks like you've got yourself a good little story."

"Yes, I think so," Peter responded, trying to suppress a smile. "There are just a few things I still don't quite understand."

"Fire away," said Campman. "I'd hate to leave any questions unanswered."

EPILOGUE

The first billboard to feature a likeness of newly elected President Ben Phillips was hung high above Sunset Boulevard in Hollywood, and every time Tina James drove past it, she had to laugh. It was an advertisement for her new TV talk show, *Wednesdays with Tina,* which was two weeks away from airing its first episode. The billboard featured a thirty-foot-tall photo of Tina holding an empty fishing rod. To her right, a cartoon fish with the face of Ben Phillips swims off, dressed in a highly presidential suit. The caption reads: SOMETIMES THE ONE THAT GOT AWAY IS A REAL CATCH!

There it was: her ridiculous life in a nutshell, blown up for all to see, smack in the middle of the Sunset Strip. Tina could either laugh or cry. She chose to laugh.

In the days to come, similar billboards would pop up in major cities across the country, heralding the debut of her new show about women's health, sexuality, and "life issues" set to air on the Estrogen Network. The show had been the brainchild of TV producer Eddie Dulces—wonderful old Eddie!—who'd been Tina's guardian angel and savior ever since she moved back to California. Eddie had always believed in Tina more than anyone else in her life, and the moment she got into town, he had her meeting with producers, publishers, and agents galore. Tina knew she owed him more than she could ever possibly repay.

While Eddie helped set up *Wednesdays with Tina,* he'd taken great pains to be anonymous in his participation. He knew if word got out that "Dangerous" Eddie Dulces was producing something for the Estrogen Network, the damage to his reputation could be incalculable. So, typical Eddie, he was discreet. He focused most of his public energy on his other new project, a reality TV show called *Who Wants to Be My Mistress?* Loosely inspired by the scandals of Ben Phillips, the show featured a real-life married man who wanted to have an extramarital affair, and the twenty women who competed to be his mistress. Lucinda Fox was the host. To Tina and his wife, Eddie would privately brag that he had cornered the market on the president's fake mistresses.

Tina used the advance from her recent book deal to put a down payment on a two-bedroom condo in West Hollywood, and Eddie, in a climactic act of generosity, bought her an Audi convertible to replace her ancient blue Oldsmobile. She now drove the convertible every day to the television studio, passing underneath the billboard of her new show each morning with the California sun shining in her face.

For the first time in a long time, Tina James was happy, and it surprised her. She'd almost forgotten what happy felt like.

ON NOVEMBER 2, Oklahoma Senator Ben Phillips won the presidential election by fifty-two electoral votes, in the greatest political comeback since Harry Truman's upset victory over Thomas Dewey in 1948. Most pundits would speak of the strong boost the senator received in the wake of the now legendary "debate slap," a show of temper many felt should have cost him the election but actually wound up hurting his opponent, Greg Struck, instead. The public found it easy to forgive Phillips's outburst, particularly after his stirring and sincere apology, but they found it much harder to forget the image of a cowardly president who had shrunk from the stage with his tail between his legs after he'd been hit. It was the picture of a strong vivacious challenger against a weak flabbergasted president that the public remembered.

Lingering suspicions of Republican foul play were also said to have contributed to the Phillips victory. By November 2, the accusations of Sharon Balis and the ladies of W.A.L.L.O.P. had been all but completely discredited, leaving many to wonder whether they had been secretly working for some anti-Phillips organization all along, perhaps one tied to the president himself.

Then there was the Peter Williams article. Eleven days before the election, Peter broke the story of a mole within the Phillips campaign, a man named Hector Elizondo, who had been selling top secret information to an outside source, possibly within the Republican Party. While the only direct link ever proposed between the Republicans and Hector was an August meeting at NRA headquarters in Washington that may or may not have actually occurred (depending on who you believe), the stories of Hector's duplicity were confirmed by the campaign itself and in several subsequent investigations conducted by rival news teams. Once the word was out that a spy had been working against the Democrats, the wild conspiracy theories about Dennis Fazo and the National Republican Association seemed suddenly a little less wild.

The Republicans did their best to repudiate these claims in the final week of the campaign, but they were fighting a losing battle. Ben Phillips had momentum, and by the time voting began on the morning of November 2, there wasn't a pundit in his right mind who wasn't predicting a Phillips victory.

ON THE MORNING of November 3, Ben Phillips felt relief more than anything else. He was happy to put the ugliness of the campaign behind him and happy to go back to serving the public full-time, his real passion. That he'd be serving the public as president now—no longer just as a senator—well, that only sweetened the deal.

Ben was tired of traveling, tired of airplanes, tired of hotels, and tired of being stretched to the point of breaking. More important, he was tired of the lies he'd had to tell and tired of the "New Ben Phillips" who was telling them.

It wasn't until after he'd made love to Elayne Cohen-Campman that Ben realized the full extent of the changes that had overtaken him in the last few months. He had let his ambition and insecurity drive his actions, and they'd led him to commit an act he'd always considered unimaginable. That he could cheat on his wife—never mind that this occurred on the same evening he struck a sitting president on national TV—that he could stretch his moral fiber to such an extreme . . . it frightened him. He was, to put it bluntly, ashamed. And he knew for certain that the New Ben Phillips would have to go.

But who would replace him? Certainly not the Old Ben Phillips. No, there was no going back. The Old Ben Phillips was as dead as his successor, and Ben knew it. What would remain was the only thing that could remain, the only thing Ben could logically become: a *New* New Ben Phillips. This incarnation would invariably be a mix of old and new. He'd try to retain the spirit, the confidence, and the sheen that the New Ben Phillips had acquired in the last months of the campaign, but ground those with the values and priorities that the Old Ben Phillips had always held dear. The *New* New Ben Phillips would no longer allow himself to be compromised for the sake of popularity, and he would govern with his conscience, not his ego. At least that was the plan.

Once the campaign was over, determined to break the chain of lies he'd felt strangling him for the last two and a half months, Ben came clean to his wife about his one-time real affair with Elayne Cohen-Campman. Melissa was not as surprised as he thought she'd be, but she was devastated all the same and didn't talk to him for a full week, speaking only as public appearances demanded. The affair proved to be the straw that broke the wife's back, and Melissa's back proved to be the damnedest thing to fix.

Eventually, politics, the very thing that had torn them apart, would help to heal their wounds. After moving into the White House, Ben and Melissa found themselves once again fighting the good fight for causes they believed in, and, once again, *her* best interests and *his* seemed inextricably bound. There was simply not enough time in the day to be spiteful, and neither of them could afford to lose their favorite allies: each other. So they worked as a team, as they always had, and in their roles as president and first lady, their relationship thrived.

But as man and wife . . .

Well, as Ben himself once remarked, a couple doesn't rebuild trust overnight. For Ben and Melissa Phillips, it would take nearly a decade, but they would get there.

MARY TEMPLETON HAD read that it was rare for a woman to achieve orgasm the first time she has sex, so it didn't bother her that Peter Williams finished first. Once he realized his girlfriend had not climaxed, Peter tried to apologize, but Mary wouldn't let him. She explained that most men tend to think sex is all about the orgasm, when in fact, that's just not true. Peter said he'd read that as well.

As they continued to talk, Mary reached her hand between Peter's legs and held him—much to his utter delight and surprise.

Lying there, not moving, slowly growing inside his girlfriend's fingers, it finally hit him. It didn't hit him in a "ton of bricks" sort of way, but rather slowly and gently. It was a warm feeling, a feeling he'd been waiting his whole life to experience.

"I love you," he said.

And he did. And he meant it. For the first time.

"I know," she said and kissed him on the lips.

He thought how funny it was: Mary couldn't have sex until she knew he loved her. For him, he didn't really know he loved her until after the sex. He wondered whether having *more* sex with Mary might cause him to love her even more than he did at that moment. Was it possible to love her more? Well, he thought, it couldn't hurt to try. And on the subject of more sex, both boyfriend and girlfriend were in agreement.

"They say practice makes perfect," she said. "So we really should practice this as much as possible."

Peter thought this was a very good idea.

IN THE MONTHS following the election, Ben Phillips assembled his cabinet. His longtime advisor Shelly Greenblatt would be offered the post of deputy chief of staff, which he would refuse, preferring instead to remain a private political consultant to the president. After so many years in politics, Shelly knew his place, and that place was not in a government job. But he'd stick around. As much as Shelly Greenblatt may have wanted to ease into retirement, he couldn't bear the thought of leaving the game completely, particularly now that his main man, Ben, was running the show.

Others in the campaign brain trust were offered positions, and most would accept. Ralph Sorn would land a job in the office of policy development, Ozzie Mayweather would become the White House press secretary, and young Derek Kiley would assume the role of head speechwriter.

Kiley, in particular, was thrilled with his new assignment. It was every speechwriter's dream to work for a president, and the fact that he was no longer answering directly to either Sorn or Campman made him savor the promotion all the more. Kiley even scored a success his first time at bat, drawing raves for the inaugural speech he cowrote with Ben Phillips in which the new president offered his vision for "a more responsible America."

One key player from the Phillips campaign who would not make the transition to the White House was Thomas Campman. This was a mutual decision. Ben was uncomfortable with Campman's working methods and privately blamed him for creating the lies that had so plagued him during the campaign, lies he was certain would continue to plague him until the day he died (acknowledging at the same time that it was probably these very lies that got him elected in the first place).

For Campman, he knew he simply couldn't keep working (at least not directly) for the man who'd slept with his wife. Ever since the morning he saw Elayne's Big T photograph of Ben Phillips, Campman could not so much as look at the candidate without picturing him naked and aroused, and it was not an image he wished to be reminded of.

To show there were no hard feelings (and perhaps due to some lingering guilt over having bedded the man's wife), President Phillips did offer Campman a job in his new administration, but he made sure it was something Campman would refuse, and refuse it he did.

Campman would have other offers. While the presidential campaign may have left him personally exhausted and disillusioned, it had done wonders for his reputation. He was now the brilliant political guru who had turned around Ben Phillips's sinking campaign. He was the mastermind who had orchestrated an image makeover in the midst of multiple political scandals. He was a hot property. In the months to come, Campman would receive calls from several Democrats in Congress requesting his services, and not knowing what else to do with himself, Campman would say yes to more than one.

HECTOR ELIZONDO CAUGHT a train back to Washington, D.C., on October 20. He stayed at the home of his friend Fernando's cousin for two days, until Sabrina Elizondo could get reassurance from the Maryland police that her husband was not wanted for a crime in any of the fifty states.

When Hector returned home on the morning of the twenty-second he was surprised to find the house swarming with reporters, eager to ask him questions about some article that had just been published. Concerned this publicity might have something to do with the incident in Boston, Hector ignored the reporters and went inside, where he remained for two solid weeks without once leaving the house or even answering the phone. Brinita's friend Carmen had a brother who was a lawyer, and he advised Hector not to talk to anyone in the press about anything. If he'd committed a crime, it was best not to give his potential prosecutors ammunition.

Two days before the presidential election, Hector received an envelope in the mail with no return address. In the envelope was four thousand dollars in cash and a note with three Spanish words: *Para su silencio.*

For your silence.

Hector could only assume it was the Republicans who had sent the letter. They were obviously concerned he would spill the beans about Kennedy and the transactions that had gone on between them. Perhaps it was Kennedy himself who'd sent the letter. In the end, Hector decided it didn't really matter. He was not planning on talking. If they wanted to pay him to not do what he wasn't going to do anyway, he wouldn't object.

With the four thousand dollars from the envelope and the money he'd received for his recordings, Hector had made a healthy profit. It was equivalent to a year's salary of normal work, before taxes. Not bad. The money had already paid for a brand-new washing machine and dryer, orthodontic work for his youngest daughter, Josie, and Hector's own personal indulgence: a wide-screen TV and DVD player. And now, this same money was financing his two-week indoor vacation.

At the end of two leisurely-if-claustrophobic weeks at home, when the last of the stubborn reporters had vanished from the Elizondos' sidewalk, Hector decided it was time to reemerge and start looking for work. He made the trek into Washington to see his old boss, the proprietor of Speedy Taxi, who, having lost several of his drivers in recent months to a curious spate of health problems, was more than happy to welcome Hector back into employment.

In the next few days, he was approached by several reporters who had been waiting for him to leave his house before making their move, but once they realized Hector was not about to answer their questions or even acknowledge their presence, even the hardiest of these journalists gave up. They could snap pictures, but he would give them nothing to write about.

SNOW FELL ON December 10, a little over a month before the inauguration, and Washington, D.C., was caught unprepared. Of course it wasn't as if snow was a newcomer to the capital city. In its more than two-hundred-year history, the District had averaged fifteen inches of the white stuff annually. But there was always something about the first big snow of the season that caught everyone off guard.

Government buildings closed early that day, and the streets were soon packed with the odd and dangerous mix of children, politicians, and wintry precipitation. The air was electric, the roads slushy, and the traffic unbearable. Hector loved it.

He'd never seen snow before moving to Washington, and he continued to be fascinated by it, even after two years. He became a quick expert in the art of snowman creation, snowball throwing, and downhill sledding (using lunch trays from the local high school cafeteria— a particularly challenging venture that required the collaboration of his teenage neighbors). Snow brought out the mischievous side of Hector Elizondo, and perhaps that was why, more than anything else, he loved to drive in it. The other employees of Speedy Taxi cursed the snow: *It was dangerous, it was uncontrollable, it was messy.* Hector loved it for these same reasons. Snow thrilled him, and he prided himself on his ability to drive in the stuff, a skill that would have surely been the envy of the heartiest Alaskan car owner.

That afternoon, Hector had a pickup at Dirksen, one of the Senate office buildings. He would be driving a Mr. Warren, who knew enough to wait outside once the Speedy Taxi dispatchers informed him of Hector's imminent arrival. Due to new security precautions, cars were not allowed to stop in front of the building, but a taxi could usually pause in the street to pick up a passenger so long as the embarkation was swift. This Mr. Warren seemed to know the drill. He wore a long gray overcoat, and as he made his way toward Hector's decelerating cab, he shielded his face from the wind with a heavy red scarf.

"You-eh-MisterWarren?"

The man nodded and got in the cab.

"Eeeeh-Airport, yes?"

From the backseat, Hector heard a familiar voice.

"No, I'm sure my flight's been canceled. *Why don't you take me to 2427 Kalorama Road?*"

Hector's hair stood on end.

"Don't worry, Hector. I'm not mad at you."

Thomas Campman smiled.

"Well, perhaps I was a bit piqued before, but that's understandable, don't you think? After all, you really tried to screw me."

In the rearview mirror, Hector's eyes met those of his former boss.

"I respect you for it in a way. Isn't *that* weird?"

Campman chuckled to himself, then changed his tone. He sat forward in his seat and put his head as close to Hector's as he could manage, clutching the passenger-side headrest with his right hand.

"You got the second envelope, right?" he whispered. "The money?"

Hector nodded his head. He had, in fact, received a second anonymous envelope in the mail only three days before. This one contained two thousand dollars in cash. Like its predecessor, Hector assumed it had come from the Republicans. He knew now he'd been wrong.

"I'll give you two years," said Campman, "*Dinero por dos años!*— that's more than fair. Hell, it's more generous than you deserve. But that's it! *Es todo!* After two years: no money. And you stay quiet for good. *Cállate. Por siempre.* Not a word about anything. Not now. Not in two years. *Nada.* Never. Understand?"

Hector nodded. He *did* understand. And it wasn't just because the boss had peppered his speech with Spanish. In fact, hearing the Spanish words only confirmed for Hector that he'd properly translated the English ones. And this sparked a new realization: Despite himself, Hector Elizondo's English comprehension had improved. It hadn't improved a lot, just a little, but it was an improvement nonetheless. Hector was surprised how much this pleased him.

"Let me hear you say it," said Campman gruffly.

"TwoYears—eh, moneee for-eh-TwoYears."

"Yes, and after two years?"

"*Nada*—eh—nothing."

"That's right. And you?"

"I-ehhhh-NoTalk."

Campman seemed to relax at this. "That's right," he said.

But of course, this was the part Hector did not understand. Yes, he would be paid for two years to be quiet, but what exactly was he supposed to be quiet about? This he didn't understand. Still, if Campman wanted to pay him to say nothing and do nothing, Hector was not about to object. It sounded to him like the best gig in the world.

"I'm paying you so they don't have to," Campman said. "Now, I'm not happy about it, but you've got me in a rough place, and I'm gonna do what's necessary to make sure we're cool. . . . So . . . are we cool?"

It took a moment, but Hector answered.

"*Sí.*"

Campman took a deep breath and sat back in his seat,

"Shame, too. You're a damn fine driver."

Nothing more was said.

Thomas Campman leaned his head back against the taxi's imitation leather upholstery and tried to enjoy what he knew would be his last Zen-like car ride under the steady hands and feet of Hector Elizondo. He allowed his mind to wander, as it often did when Hector

drove him home, and he reflected on the irony that he was now paying blackmail money to his former driver in order to keep his mouth
shut about the night they stole files from Warren Muddville's office,
files they intended to use for blackmail.

That's justice for you, thought Campman. He thought of the old
"what goes around comes around" platitude and rubbed his scalp.

At the time of the Muddville situation, Campman had assumed
Hector to be unaware of the significance of his actions, unaware a
major breach of campaign ethics was being committed. But then,
he'd always underestimated Hector, hadn't he? Why? Was it an eth-
nic thing? A comprehension thing? Had he been prejudiced toward
this short bearded Mexican with the language problem? Perhaps he
was an elitist. For whatever combination of politically incorrect reasons, he'd never thought Hector to be all that sharp. Once again,
Campman's failings (this time in the form of an unconscious preju-
dice) had come back to bite him in the ass.

His mind now drifted to the theft of the Lannahan papers, to
learning of Muddville's suicide, and finally to thoughts of the mysterious phone calls he'd received in the last months of the election:

"I know about Muddville . . . and I know what you're doing now!"

Once again, he wondered: Who had made the calls? Who had ordered the calls to be placed? The questions continued to drive him
crazy.

As many times as he racked his brain (and he racked it quite a bit),
Campman could only come up with one suspect who made any
sense: Dennis Fazo. He knew it certainly sounded like the sort of
message Fazo would have sent. But had he? And if he had done it,
what was the reason? And more important, *what had he known?* If
Dennis Fazo actually knew the full story of the Muddville blackmail
attempt, why did he keep it a secret, particularly in those last weeks
of the campaign when his candidate fell behind in the polls? Campman wondered: Had Hector told Fazo a portion of the story but not
the whole thing? Had Fazo known the truth but lacked the proof necessary to do anything about it? There was no way of knowing.

It turns out that Campman guessed at just about every scenario but the real one. No, in fact, Dennis Fazo had zero knowledge of the Muddville blackmail attempt. *However,* he *did* order the calls to be placed. Now why did he place the calls when he had no proof of any wrongdoing? Let's just say he had a hunch. Fazo correctly diagnosed the Muddville suicide as both tremendously fishy and tremendously beneficial to Ben Phillips. And Fazo knew if something fishy *just happened* to benefit the man Tom Campman was working for . . . odds were good that Tom Campman had *something* to do with it.

So he ordered the calls to be placed. As a bluff. To tease his former partner. To taunt. To provoke. Fazo didn't know exactly what Campman had done, but he could bet it wasn't completely kosher and he wanted to make him sweat. At the very least, that's just what the calls would do. The best-case scenario, of course, would be that the calls would somehow cause Campman to slip up, to make a mistake, to show his hand. And much like Fazo's more elaborate strategy, the W.A.L.L.O.P. attack, it almost worked.

But Thomas Campman would never know any of this for sure. And the nagging questions would puzzle him for the rest of his life.

As Hector's cab navigated the arc of DuPont circle, Campman's mind shifted again, this time back to his wife, who was waiting for him at home, hopefully with steaming hot Chinese food. Elayne and he agreed that delivery fare always tasted twice as sweet during a snowstorm, and she'd probably ordered within the hour.

Ah, Elayne.

Things had been good recently, and he was surprised to admit it. The revelation of his wife's fling had been a frightening moment for them both, but they had survived. Elayne had been upfront about the whole thing once the infamous picture had been discovered. She told Tom all about her obsession with Ben Phillips. She tried to explain the nature of the thing, that it was both asexual and sexual at the same time (but never romantic), that it was something that existed independent of her feelings for him, and that it was something which ended abruptly the moment the candidate entered her.

Once Elayne had made her full confession, none of it really seemed that bad to him. Campman believed his wife was sorry for what she'd done, and while he was upset by Ben Phillips's actions, he didn't feel threatened by the man. Campman had been hurt, but he would heal; and he knew that when Elayne claimed she felt closer to him now that she'd strayed, even though it sounded like a crazy thing to say . . . he believed her.

As he replayed Elayne's words in his mind, Campman started to recall something she had said early on in her confession, perhaps within the first twenty-four hours. For whatever reason, he hadn't thought much of it at the time—he was undoubtedly too absorbed in his own self-pity to ascribe an objective analysis to her words—but now as he considered them, he found himself in a state of disbelief, mystified at how the significance of her comments could have escaped him when they were first uttered.

She'd been talking about the act of making love to Ben Phillips.

"I can't quite describe the change that occurred," she told him. "It was like I'd built Ben up to be this god of sorts. But then the moment we started—really, the moment he was—the moment we were officially . . . in sin, I guess you could say—well, he just became—he was suddenly . . . just a man like any other man."

Campman shook his head.

How could he have missed it! Elayne had practically echoed his heavenly message word for word:

"Sin . . . Will . . . Make . . . Him . . . Human!"

As he looped Elayne's words alongside those he'd received from the Almighty nearly five months ago while sitting on the toilet, a new troubling and outrageous thought suddenly presented itself: *what if the heavenly message I received was actually meant for my wife?*

The more Campman thought about it, the more it made sense. As much as he'd recognized the prophecy as having been fulfilled the moment he saw Ben naked in that photograph, he had been at a loss to explain the exact nature of that fulfillment. Every time he'd tried to deconstruct his heavenly message and apply it to the situation at hand, he'd found the message to be a reasonably good fit, but never a perfect one.

It fit flawlessly for Elayne. Far better than it did for him. Ben Phillips had become human to Elayne after he sinned *with* Elayne! Sin had *indeed* made him human! It had been a prophecy perfectly tailored to Campman's wife in every way imaginable.

And yet *he* had been the one to receive it!

Was it possible, Campman wondered, *was it even conceivable* that this heavenly message had simply struck the wrong person? That it had made a wrong turn upon entering the house and headed toward the bathroom instead of the living room? That it had entered the brain of the wrong Campman?

And what of the implications? Could it be possible that all that had transpired as a result of Campman's supposed "heavenly inspiration"—the scandals, the debate slap, the whole damned presidential election!—could it all have been nothing more than a big cosmic mistake?

"Eeeee-HereWeGo."

The car stopped in front of 2427 Kalorama Road.

Campman's body was frozen.

Did any of it matter? If the right man was in office, was there really any harm in what he'd done? Campman's brain was in rationalization mode, but it was sputtering; his most comfortable gear was not working. He felt unsteady.

He took a moment to reenter the present, to come back to the cab that was parked in front of his house, to reengage those muscles that existed in the real world and acted with real-world consequences.

It took a moment. Then he moved his head.

Campman looked up at the meter and, upon reading it, shoved his right hand into his jacket pocket. He whipped out his wallet and then two large bills from inside and handed them to Hector.

"You have a good evening."

"Eh-Goodnighty boss," Hector answered, and for the first time allowed a small smile to creep across his face.

Of course he's smiling, thought Campman. He's just been paid.

He's getting rich off me. And his mind is not troubled by these volatile questions of heavenly consequence.

But then, perhaps Campman was underestimating Hector again.

What a damned fool I am, he thought.

He stepped out of the cab, and his foot crunched into the snow. He stepped forward, closed the door, and looked back at his former valet.

"Good night, Hector."

The two men held each other's gaze for a moment longer, then the car shifted into gear and pulled away, leaving Thomas Campman alone in the snow with his terrible thoughts.

Acknowledgments

It's nearly impossible to get anywhere as a writer if you don't have people who, for some crazy reason, believe in you. I was blessed with an incredible group of such folks at the start and have been lucky enough to pick up a few more along the way.

The biggest thank-you goes to my parents, to whom this book is dedicated, for their inexhaustible love and support over the years, and for only once asking, "You just finished two and a half years of film school so you could write *a novel?*" Your belief in me is pathological— it's almost enough to make a person suspicious—and I'm forever grateful. Thanks to the rest of my family and friends, particularly Trish and Dave for your silliness.

Thanks to my teachers, from the authors of the books that line my shelves to the brave souls who teach at Brandeis and Boston University and the Easton, CT, public school system—particularly those who taught me about storytelling, and those who pushed me to work harder than I might have on my own.

Thanks to Liza Folman, Rina Zelen Souppá, and Jason Taylor for being brilliant, reading my early drafts, and letting me know when I was good and when I was rotten. Thanks to Samrat Chakrabarti for your help and brainstorming powers. Thanks to Matt Chapuran for listening to my pitch four and a half years ago and saying, "It would be real funny if you made the reporter a teenager." Thanks to Mark Hannah for being my campaign trail reality check. Thanks to Susan Kusel and family for always making me feel so welcome in D.C., and to Dan Wodiska for the world-class tour. Thanks to Bruce Schwartz for your advice and encouragement and for helping me tighten up the opening chapters.

Thanks to my angels, Jill Kneerim and Cara Krenn, and everyone at Kneerim and Williams. To Cara, thanks for taking my book from the slush pile, falling in love with it, and forcing everyone else to read it. To Jill, thanks for your passion, your warmth, your insight, and your savvy, and for being one of the most delightful human beings I have had the privilege to know.

Thanks to everyone at William Morrow for your support of this book, particularly my editor, David Highfill. David has been a fierce advocate and a sharp editor, and also he wears glasses, which I personally believe has contributed greatly to his success. Thank you for everything, David!

Finally, thanks to Carin for your constant love and sometimes brutal honesty. You make me a better writer and a better human being. And, yes, I'll say it in print, you are almost always right.